THE
PORTRAIT
OF
ELOISE
LECLAIR

THE PORTRAIT OF ELOISE LECLAIR

a novel

ERIK RICHTER

cakebar
PUBLISHING

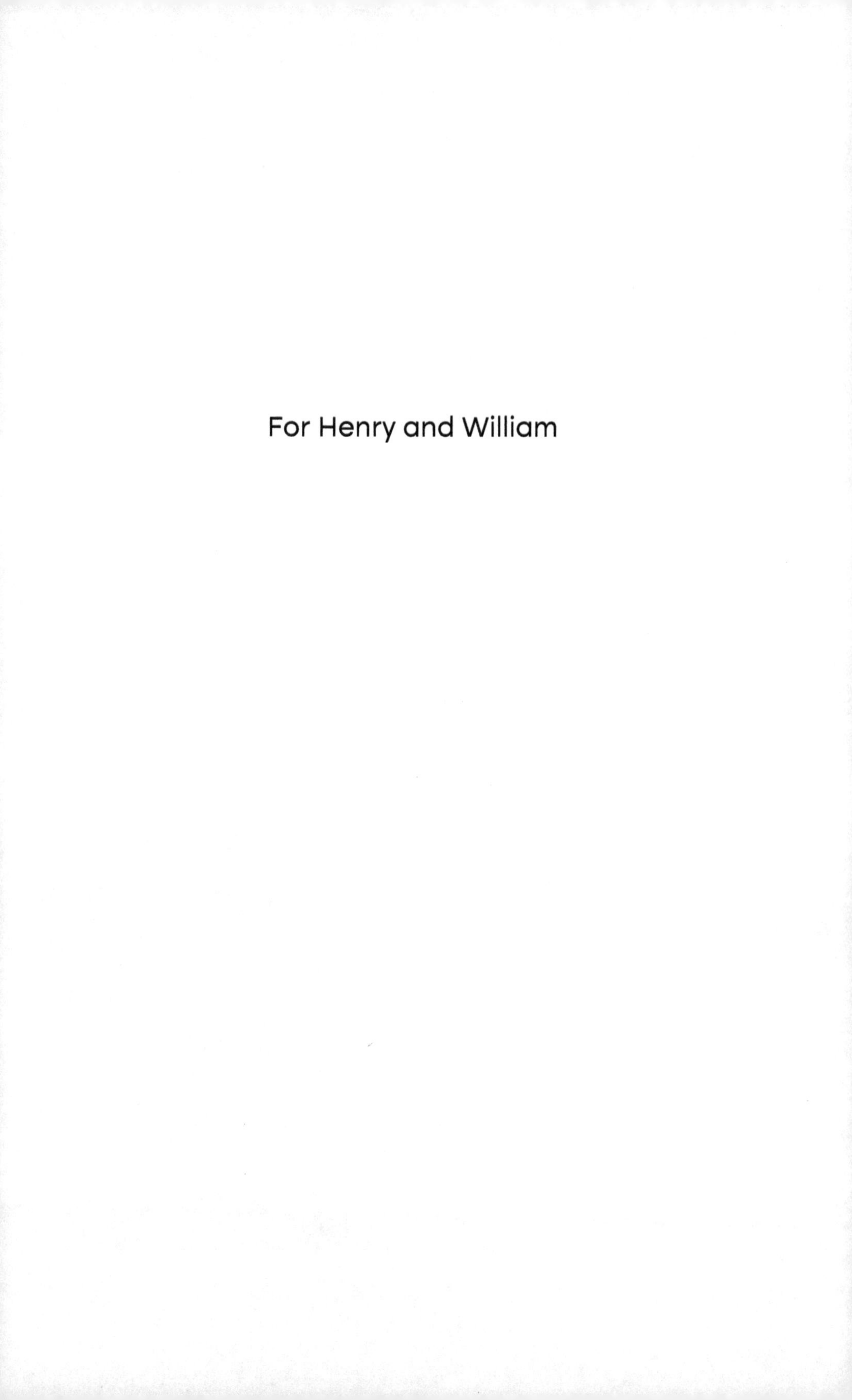

For Henry and William

*What's hidden is not lost.
It's simply waiting to be found.*

Inspired by true events

Prologue

The knocking grew louder. What began as a firm rap on the door quickly escalated into steady, angry pounds. Inside the dim apartment, a man frantically rifled through his study drawers, hands shaking as he shuffled through papers and trinkets. He wasn't entirely sure what he was looking for, but surely would be if he found it. Time was running out, but years of careful preparation gave him a small sense of security.

Could I have been more careful? he wondered.

There wasn't much in the office, just a few drawers and a desk. The closet was already empty except for a rolled-up carpet and a few bundled stacks of "Le Monde" newspapers that no longer served their original purpose. He rarely worked in here anymore and, aside from the occasional visit to open the window, had little reason to enter. Thankfully, the walls couldn't speak.

Satisfied that everything appeared in order, he made his way to the bedroom, limping on a leg that never quite healed right. Outside, the pounding grew more urgent, as if the door might give way under the force.

"Une seconde!" he shouted. All his neighbors would've heard the commotion, yet none would dare investigate its source. *The door will hold,* he told himself, trying to summon confidence. Though a darker voice inside him whispered back, *I hope it will hold.*

He fumbled through the top drawer of his dresser, ignoring the few hundred francs tucked inside. *A good decoy,* he thought. After all he had been through, losing this would be the least of his concerns. Maybe it would even spare him further distress. His gaze briefly fell on the Bible next to his bed—another misdirect, hopefully to steer suspicion elsewhere.

As he hobbled back through the narrow hallway toward the main door, his mind churned with dread. Had he delayed too long? *Would they be forgiving to a man who struggled to move quickly on a broken leg? ...probably not.*

Reaching for the door, he opened it fully, knowing that if he opened it just a crack, they would simply kick it in and knock him over.

"Oui? Comment je peux vous aider? How may I help you?" he asked. But despite the veneer of curiosity, he knew exactly why they were here. This is the moment he had been expecting. It was the reason his life had changed so much in the last few years. It was the reason for the cast on his leg. It was the reason he was in the flat alone. And now it was the reason three men in dark uniforms were standing in his doorway, each staring at him with a cold and predatory fierceness. Despite his fear, the man tried to appear casual.

"Sorry I couldn't get to the door quicker," he said, glancing down at his leg. "My leg is... well, it's in rough shape."

They didn't care.

"Monsieur Bourget?" the first man said. It was more of a statement than a question.

"Oui?" he replied, barely finishing before the officer thrust a piece of paper in his face.

"By authority of The Führer, we are hereby ordered to seize any and all illegal items you have in your home."

His family name was still most definitely on their list. Though the bulk of their wealth had largely dissipated, at one point, they had a collection of Renaissance, Baroque, and Impressionist paintings. The Nazis had long been "confiscating" such treasures under the guise of seizing "illegal contraband." But those paintings were gone now.

"I've already submitted the declaration. I have nothing illegal," the man said, trying to explain. But his words were meaningless. He knew they would be, but he played along anyway, pretending that trust still held value. The soldiers weren't here to believe him—they were here to intimidate, to take. The lead officer pushed him aside, allowing the other two to step past, their boots heavy against the wooden floor as they began their search.

"If you have any contraband in here, we will find it," the officer said flatly. "And then you will be arrested."

The man didn't respond, standing silently as the soldiers moved through his apartment. He knew how this would go. They would rummage through every drawer, overturn every piece of furniture, and if they found nothing, they would try again. There was no point in resisting. As far as he knew, they would find nothing here.

He had moved into this space a few years ago, after everything had happened, and lived a purposefully meager life. Money and valuables were no longer of any interest to him. While he had them, it was nice. But he soon realized there are some things money cannot buy, and with that realization came a true distrust in its false sense of security.

The soldiers split up, two heading for the bedroom and study, while the third stayed back, keeping a close watch on him. From where the man stood, he could hear drawers crashing and papers rustling in each room. It pained him to think about what he would find when he went back in there… *If I ever go back in there*, he thought.

Minutes stretched into what felt like hours. When the two soldiers finally returned to the main room, their expressions were dark with frustration. They were accustomed to finding what they sought, to wielding the power such discoveries afforded them. But this time, they had almost nothing. The man's eyes caught the edge of the francs from his study, now visible in one soldier's side pocket. *I'm glad they found "something."* Yet as their search of the living room continued to yield nothing, their irritation only grew.

"Where are these?" the first officer barked, firmly thrusting a list at the man.

"I told you," he said simply. "I don't have those paintings anymore."

And he didn't. It was true none of his family's paintings on the list were inside his flat, or at their ancestral estate just outside of Paris that the Nazis had looted many times since the occupation started. What little he had now was of no interest to them—old photographs, letters, fragments of a life that held value only to him. Most of these things could not have a price put on them. Most of them would be worthless to the men searching his home.

Most of them.

He had no items they *declared* contraband in his possession. He had no secrets to hide—except one. And with all that was going on, he knew this secret was one he needed to protect. It wasn't contraband, not officially, but he knew that if the Nazis found it, they would seize it without hesitation. But no matter how much money he had or needed, he would never give it up. It was worth more to him than its value, which was extremely high.

And it was here, right now, in the room with all of them, hidden in a place they would never think to look. As the soldiers finished their search, frustrated to not find anything that met their expectations, they departed, leaving the apartment in shambles.

But the man remained, standing in the center of the wreckage, his heart pounding as a small, fierce triumph warmed his chest. Once he was certain they were gone, he let out a knowing chuckle, his gaze drifting to a small object tucked in the corner of the room. They had come, searched, and left, never realizing how close they had been to uncovering what was just within their reach.

Part I

Echoes of the Past

Chapter 1

The old oak door off Rue du Bac arduously opened under its own weight to the brisk autumn breeze of an early Paris October. Splintered on every edge and weathered to a point where its original color could only be imagined, the door had seen centuries of use and, deceptively, looked like it could fall apart with an ambitious close. In truth, it was verifiably solid and would most likely withstand centuries more of repeated use.

Pivoting on a trio of equally aged black iron hinges, the door effortlessly collided with an unequal match in a tiny bell suspended above by a steel coil, producing a quick succession of three diminished rings. The delicate chimes blended harmoniously with soft strains of classical music playing in the distance, echoing through a winding maze of walls and filling the back room of the space with an enchanting symphony of old meeting new.

In this dimly lit, climate-controlled room, Amelia Beckett immersed herself in a world of colors, textures, and time-worn canvases. With a magnifying visor perched on her forehead and fine brushes in hand, her auburn hair was pulled back into a loose bun, revealing the faint splatter of paint on her cheek—a remnant of the day's work.

Her blue eyes, deep and expressive, squinted as they adjusted to focus on the minuscule details of the painting before her. The canvas depicted a Parisian streetscape, its vibrant hues dulled by age. Time had taken its toll on the artwork, with tiny cracks forming a spiderweb of patterns across the surface.

The room smelled of linseed oil, old paper, and a myriad of chemicals—each with a specific purpose in the restoration process. Complementing the soft background melody, the rhythmic hum of specialized equipment monitoring the room's temperature and humidity added to its tranquil ambiance, creating a soothing backdrop for Amelia's focused work.

Her fingers danced deftly over the canvas. Her touch was gentle yet firm—a dance between reverence for the original artist and the desire to restore the painting to its former glory. Every stroke, every blend, was a testament to her years of training and innate talent.

Her surrounding workspace showed creative organization. Neatly lined up jars of pigments, solvents, and varnishes contrasted the reference books and color charts which lay scattered across her desk. Beside her, on an easel, was a black-and-white photograph of the painting taken decades ago, a point of reference to guide her restoration.

Even in such intense concentration, there was a grace to Amelia—a passion evident in the curve of her lips as they pursed in thought, or the gentle furrowing of her brow. For those who saw her in this element, it was clear: she was not just restoring a painting; she was breathing life back into history.

A soft *"Bonjour?"* resonated behind the chime of the bell, its delicate tone weaving through the harmonious blend of music and the rhythmic cadence of brushstrokes. This subtle intrusion gently coaxed Amelia away from the cocoon of concentration that surrounded her in her canvas-filled sanctuary. She let out a soft, contemplative sigh and set down her brush, its bristles still glistening with a rich blend of ochre and sienna.

With careful, reverent movements, she removed her magnifying visor and placed it beside the painting. Rising gracefully from her stool, she paused, letting the momentary light-headedness pass, then smoothed her apron, adorned with vibrant flecks—each a testament to her journey through art's vast tapestry.

Navigating the maze of her studio, Amelia emerged into the front room where the afternoon sun of Paris cast a welcoming glow. The transition was palpable: from the dense, aroma-filled air of her working space to the brighter, fresher atmosphere of the front room. Here, the walls were a gallery of her craft, displaying an array of framed artworks—some bearing the final touches of completion, others still hinting at their stories, awaiting her restorative touch.

There, standing in the doorway with the poise of a figure stepped out from a classic French novel, was Madame Geneviève Laurent. Over the years, Geneviève, a woman whose age contradicted her graceful bearing, had become a regular. Her eyes, sharp and discerning, had witnessed decades of Parisian evolution, yet they always held an appreciation for the arts. Her perfectly coiffed silver hair shimmered under the afternoon sun, and her blend of classic elegance and modern attire spoke of her impeccable taste.

"Madame Laurent!" Amelia greeted, her voice a blend of professional warmth and genuine fondness. "It's always a pleasure to see you."

Geneviève's lips curved into a smile, one that had graced countless social gatherings and hinted at stories she had yet to tell. "Amelia, my dear, I do hope I'm not interrupting. But I simply couldn't wait to show you my latest find!"

"Not at all!" Amelia said warmly, gesturing her inside and guiding her toward the small consultation area.

As Geneviève walked, she filled the room with the fragrance of her perfume—a hint of lavender and something unmistakably vintage. It was the scent of old Paris, of stories nestled in the corners of small shops and the pathways of the covered markets in the Third. In her hands she carried a large package, wrapped with the care and anticipation of someone presenting a treasure.

She placed the brown-paper-wrapped package gently on the table, her eyes gleaming with excitement. "I found something special this time, something I think you'll appreciate!"

As Geneviève slowly unwrapped the object, a beautifully ornate frame appeared—its once attractive gold leaf, now faded and chipped, showed many dignified scars of time. However, the frame's intricate craftsmanship stood out undiminished, a testament to whatever skilled hands had created it centuries ago. A faded painting, nestled within the frame, revealed details lost to time, but still showed a charm that spoke of a long-forgotten era.

Amelia's eyes lit up with recognition and admiration as she leaned closer, her gaze shifting between the frame and the ghostly image it held. "This is beautiful, Geneviève! Late Baroque, isn't it?" she said softly, her voice mixed with professional appraisal and genuine awe.

Geneviève watched Amelia's admiration with a growing smile. "Exactly!" she responded, her excitement matching Amelia's recognition of the frame's era. "I thought you would appreciate it. It's not every day that one stumbles upon something with such history and... elegance."

Like the misshapen pearl it was named for—*barroco* in Portuguese—Baroque art refused to play by the rules. It burst into 17th-century Europe with a rebellious spirit, thumbing its nose at ordinary beauty. Unlike the balanced and harmonious designs typically found in Renaissance art, Baroque embraced the grand and dramatic—its complex style mirroring the turbulent period it came from. It was an era where art became a sensory feast, almost theatrical in its expression, designed to awe and engage.

Amelia's eyes traced the frame's wild beauty. Every inch told a story of excess, particularly in two striking patterns that kept appearing. Bold, swirling acanthus leaves held tight at each corner, which was a Baroque staple symbolizing immortality and enduring life. Additionally, detailed scrollwork featuring motifs of shells and floral designs all added to its texture, and highlighted scientific advancements and new discoveries of the time.

The frame's inner border, with its more understated carvings, offered a contrast to the bolder elements of the outer design and drew the eye towards the faded painting within. Yet, for Amelia, it was the frame itself that stood out as the true masterpiece.

After giving Amelia a moment to fully take in the piece, Geneviève gestured towards the frame with affectionate reverence. "Pieces like this... they carry with them so many untold stories just waiting to be revealed by the right hands. That's where your talent shines, Amelia."

Standing before it, the frame seemed to pull Amelia in, refusing to be merely observed. Like all things Baroque, it demanded complete immersion. This piece was not just seen. It was experienced.

She acknowledged Geneviève's comment with a nod while her fingers gently traced the contours of the frame. She let her touch follow every ridge and groove of the detailed carvings, exploring the intricate patterns and noting where the gold leaf had chipped away, exposing the bare wood beneath. Her eyes, trained with the precision of an art restorer, took in every detail. She observed the way the light played on the raised swirls, the deep shadows found inside the crevices, and the faint signs of its former splendor, now softened by time. "It feels like it has seen more than we can imagine," she said. "The care that went into every detail... it's incredible."

Geneviève's gaze flickered, as if recalling something. "Yes... it makes you wonder, doesn't it? Where it's been, who has touched it, and how it ended up here."

Amelia looked up, intrigued by Geneviève's choice of words, but before she could comment, Geneviève smiled warmly and rose from her chair. "I won't keep you from your work any longer. I just had to bring this to you as soon as I found it." Her eyes sparkled with a mixture of excitement and relief, knowing she had placed the frame in the right hands.

Amelia stepped back for a moment, taking in the frame as a whole. In her mind's eye, she envisioned the restoration process: the careful cleaning, the repair of the damaged areas, and the nuanced task of bringing back its lost luster without diminishing its historical integrity.

"It will be a pleasure to work on this!" Amelia said, filled with genuine enthusiasm. This was more than just a job; it was a journey into the past and a chance to breathe new life into a piece of art that had witnessed centuries of change. The frame wasn't just a border for a painting; it was a story in itself, waiting to be told and Amelia had every intention of telling this story to anyone who would hear it. "I'll take good care of it, I promise."

Geneviève smiled again, this time more lightly. "I know you will, my dear. Whenever you get around to it. There's no one else I trust with something like this."

With a brief, graceful nod, Geneviève made her way to the door, leaving the scent of lavender and aged parchment in her wake. The door's gentle chime echoed behind her, returning the studio to its familiar, quiet rhythm.

Amelia ran her fingers over the delicate swirls once more, then stepped back, already excited about the challenge of restoration ahead. "It *will* be a pleasure to work on this," she murmured to herself again, filled with determination.

With a soft exhale, she returned to the back room, the lingering scent of history and possibility trailing behind her.

Chapter 2

A few days had passed since Madame Geneviève Laurent's visit, and in that time, Amelia Beckett had spent hours preparing for the delicate restoration ahead. In the mellow light of her studio, with the autumn sun coming in through the windows, she stood before the ornate frame that had consumed her thoughts. Today, she would finally begin breathing new life into it.

The Baroque period had always fascinated Amelia, its pieces embodying a sense of fearlessness and defiance. A far cry from the restraint of the Renaissance before it, Baroque art surged with movement and energy, drawing viewers into its complex layers of emotion and narrative.

As she prepared her tools—brushes, pigments, and solvents—she wondered about the frame's history. Most-likely crafted in the late 1600s, it would have been a product of stormy times. In the wake of the Protestant Reformation, the Catholic Church turned to art, wielding it like a weapon to reclaim its power and speak to the hearts of its followers.

While Amelia respected the history, she was drawn not by the Church's influence but by the raw artistry that had emerged from it. It was a testament to human creativity and how artists could push beyond the limits of the time. Everything about this piece let the world know it was designed for full impact.

However, as Amelia began cleaning the surface, she noticed an unusual material peeking through areas where some of the gold had flaked away. Even this material was unique for such a unique piece. It was not the typical gesso or bole usually found in frames of this period, but something else. Something rarer.

With a magnifying glass, she examined the material and found a faint glint of iridescence beneath the layers of dust and decay. It was mother-of-pearl, the smooth, lustrous inner layer of certain mollusk shells, celebrated for its shimmering play of colors. Hints of whites, pinks, and soft blues danced subtly across its surface, delicately inlaid into the frame with remarkable precision, adding a subtle yet mesmerizing radiance.

Among all the bold, golden excess typical of Baroque frames, this delicate mother-of-pearl detail stood apart. Its rarity and fragility during the period made it a prized material, a minor detail that elevated the frame from beautiful to extraordinary.

Curious and intrigued, Amelia realized that such a restoration would require not just skill but also the right materials, faithful to its original craftsmanship.

Finding the right mother-of-pearl would be tricky. The type used centuries ago had a unique character to them, a wild, natural beauty that modern harvesting had somehow tamed away. And the craftsmanship of the Baroque period was precise. Without these period-accurate materials, the restoration could lose its authenticity and betray the integrity of the original frame's design.

Resolved to find the perfect match, Amelia's mind turned to the one place she knew could possibly offer the rare materials she needed: the Marché aux Puces, an antique flea market located just outside the heart of Paris.

The market twisted and turned like a living thing, its cobblestone paths weaving drunkenly between countless eclectic stalls. Corrugated metal doors, often rusted from years of use, slid open to reveal treasures hidden behind them—everything from antique furniture to forgotten trinkets.

Stacks of old wooden crates and weathered boxes lined the paths, spilling over with vintage fabrics, aged books, and odd curiosities curling with time. Steeped in history and mystery, the market seemed to stretch endlessly in all directions, and each narrow turn offered a new discovery to those who knew where to look.

She also knew her decision to visit the sprawling flea market was more than a practical necessity; it was steeped in personal relevance.

As a child, shortly after her family expatriated to Paris from Boston, the Marché had become a place of wonder and excitement. A place where she and her father would spend entire weekends wandering through the maze of vendors just to see what interesting things they could find.

For young Amelia, the market was an endless trove of forgotten relics, with every turn revealing something new—a worn tapestry, a tarnished silver locket, or a mysterious artifact that seemed to echo the past.

Her father, an art history professor at the Sorbonne in Paris, would tell her, "Amelia, every piece here has a story waiting to be told… waiting for the right person to uncover it."

Together, they played games of hide and seek among the towering stacks of furniture and bins filled with old postcards and photographs. Amelia would squeeze herself between dusty armoires or under tables laden with vintage lamps and books, her giggles muffled by piles of old fabrics.

During these visits, her father would encourage her to pick one item —any item that caught her eye. It didn't matter if it was a broken watch, a faded painting, or a chipped porcelain doll. The real find was in the stories they imagined for these objects. "Who might have owned this? What tales could this old watch tell us if it could speak?" her father would muse, sparking Amelia's imagination.

These early experiences at the Marché planted something in Amelia's heart—a hunger for history that grew with each treasure hunt, with each brush against the past.

Even as she grew up and her interests turned more towards art restoration, the flea market remained her go-to for inspiration and materials that were not just rare but full of history.

Now, as a professional restorer in search of Baroque-era mother-of-pearl, Amelia knew the Marché was her best chance. The market had grown since her youth, but its essence remained unchanged.

After not visiting for a few years, she felt a hint of excitement at the thought of returning, not just as a seeker of materials, but as an explorer, rekindling her childhood wonder.

She packed her essentials—magnifying glass, gloves, a notebook, and a sample of the material she needed—then set out, a thrill building as she approached the entrance. The chipped blue *Vernaison* market sign greeted her like an old friend, its porcelain white letters still brightly visible, just as she remembered.

As she crossed the threshold into the maze of stalls, the market was already alive with energy, its narrow, winding paths brimming with forgotten stories and hidden treasures. The vendors, a mix of weathered veterans and eager newcomers, arranged their wares under the dim morning light.

Surrounded by this activity, Amelia slowed, letting the familiar sights and sounds wash over her. She just stepped into another world—one where history lingered, the atmosphere itself drawing her deeper into the labyrinth.

A shiver ran through her, that sense of discovery from her early years returning.

Today, something was waiting.

Chapter 3

The grand halls of Château Bourget shimmered under the glow of crystal chandeliers, their light reflecting off polished marble floors and the golden frames of exquisite paintings. The air buzzed with a hum of admiration and whispered conversation, highlighted by the occasional clink of glasses. While the evening drew Parisian elite, art collectors, and artists to its doors, the Bourget family's hospitality ensured the château remained a welcoming haven for all who shared a love of culture and history. It was a night to celebrate art, and every corner of the château told a story of pride and creativity.

Arnaud Bourget stood in the heart of it all, a glass of champagne in hand, watching as guests floated through the gallery. At thirty-four, he had spent years honing his skills in the family merchant business, mastering the art of negotiation, and securing rare goods from far corners of Europe. Tonight's event, in a way, was a testament to his efforts—an exhibition that seamlessly blended contemporary and classical pieces, bringing together works from established masters and promising new artists. It should have filled him with pride. But as he stood beneath a towering portrait of his great-grandfather, Jules Bourget, the family patriarch and visionary collector, Arnaud felt only a restless, gnawing discontent.

He scanned the room, his eyes lingering on familiar faces—longtime patrons who had supported the Bourgets' efforts to nurture emerging artists, and new ones eager to be part of a legacy rooted in culture and creativity. The château, with its sprawling halls and curated art collection, was a symbol of everything his family had built over centuries. But to Arnaud, it also felt like a gilded cage. His heart wasn't in the family business deals that filled his days; it was in this—in the art—and in the vibrant energy of Montmartre, the heart of Parisian creativity, where ideas and inspiration flowed as freely as the wine in tonight's celebration.

From across the room, Lucien Bourget, Arnaud's father, approached with a broad, proud smile. Lucien's presence was commanding, his tailored suit hinting at both elegance and authority. He embodied a quiet duality, proudly declaring himself French first yet never losing sight of the Jewish heritage that shaped the Bourget family's values and resilience. This duality defined his life's work as well, where he spent decades balancing two worlds—business and art—ensuring that the wealth accumulated from the first could nurture the second.

As he drew closer, Arnaud watched his father's eyes soften as they fell upon a Surrealist painting by one of Paris's emerging talents, a young Spaniard named Dalí. It was a work that Arnaud had personally selected for the exhibition.

"Magnificent, isn't it?" Lucien said, nodding toward the painting. "I can see why you insisted on this one. There's something… raw about it. The kind of potential your great-grandfather would have spotted." His gaze shifted to Arnaud, his expression warm yet measured. "You've done well, son."

Arnaud's chest tightened. "Thank you, Father," he replied, though his voice was tinged with something less than gratitude. "I'm… glad you approve."

Lucien's smile held, but there was a knowing glint in his eyes. "I do. You've been a vital part of everything we've achieved this year. The new deals, these exhibitions—it's all because of your dedication." He paused, his tone shifting, becoming more pointed. "But soon, you'll need to focus more on the business. You're ready to take on more responsibility, to lead."

Arnaud stiffened, the words heavily settling over him. He had known this conversation was coming, but it didn't make it any easier to hear. "I've done everything you've asked of me, Father. I've expanded the business, secured new trade routes, and kept the accounts in order. But the art… that's where my heart is. It's what makes the Bourget name matter."

Lucien's eyes darkened, his smile fading slightly. "And it always will," he said, his voice low and firm. "But the art cannot survive without the business that supports it. Our family has built something remarkable, a blend of culture and commerce. That balance has kept us strong."

Arnaud clenched his jaw, as frustration flashed across his face. "Balance?" he repeated, his tone sharper than he intended. "What balance? I've spent my days negotiating contracts and calculating profits. That's not who I am. You know I belong out there," he said, gesturing toward the paintings, "finding new talent, bringing their work to life. That is the true Bourget legacy."

Lucien sighed, glancing around the room as if to draw strength from the opulent surroundings. "And who do you think made that possible?" he asked, his voice tinged with a hint of sadness. "Your grandfather built this family's fortune by understanding that art and industry could coexist. Without the business, we would have nothing. No gallery, no exhibitions, no legacy."

The argument between father and son seemed to echo through the gallery, even though they kept their voices low. To the guests, it was merely a private conversation between two men of the same bloodline, but to Arnaud, it felt like a battle for his soul. "I can't live a life chained to an office, Father," he said, his voice shaking with the force of suppressed emotion. "I want to immerse myself in the world of art, to be part of it. Not just fund it from afar."

Lucien's eyes hardened, the warmth that had been there moments ago cooling. "The family needs you to be more than a dreamer, Arnaud. We need you to lead."

Arnaud's heart pounded, frustration boiling over as he felt the walls closing in. He had always known his father's expectations, but the reality of them felt suffocating. "Maybe I don't want to lead," he said, the words slipping out before he could stop them. "Maybe... I just want to be free."

For a moment, there was silence between them, a chasm that neither seemed willing to bridge. Lucien's face was impassive, but Arnaud could see the hurt in his eyes, the sting of betrayal. Without another word, Arnaud turned sharply and walked away, his steps echoing through the gallery.

He didn't look back as he strode out of the château, past the glittering guests and the grand displays, past the paintings that had brought him so much joy. He knew he was leaving behind more than a room full of people—he was distancing himself from a life he no longer wanted to live, a legacy that now felt like a shackle around his heart.

Outside, the night was cool and crisp, and the lights of Paris twinkled in the distance. Arnaud found his driver, his breath visible in the chilly air as he leaned down to speak. There was only one place he wanted to go, one place that still felt like it belonged to him.

"Montmartre," he said, the word escaping his lips like a sigh of relief.

As the car pulled away, the grand silhouette of Château Bourget loomed behind him, an elegant, imposing reminder of everything he was trying to escape.

But as the city streets blurred past, Arnaud felt something awaken within him—a spark of excitement, a sense of freedom that was raw and untamed. What he had just done felt good. He was breaking the rules, stepping outside the lines, and for the first time in years, he didn't care. Tonight, he wasn't the Bourget heir, bound by tradition and duty. He was simply a man chasing the passion and freedom he craved.

The car sped toward Montmartre, its vibrant, chaotic energy pulling him in, calling him home.

Chapter 4

Wrapped in a light scarf against the crisp fall Parisian air, Amelia walked through the bustling lanes of the Marché aux Puces. The cobbled paths felt alive beneath her feet as she wound her way through its narrow, winding alleys. The market was in full swing, a living tapestry of old and new, and the air carried scents of dust, wood polish, and forgotten stories.

She passed booths brimming with mismatched chairs, piles of worn-out books, and vintage clocks that had long since lost their ability to mark the passage of time. But for Amelia, time itself seemed to slow as she immersed herself in the familiar chaos of history, her eyes scanning the maze of vendors with purpose.

Today, she was on a mission. Somewhere in this sprawling market was the piece she needed to restore the Baroque frame to its original glory. The thought of the mother-of-pearl hidden within its intricate design kept running through her mind. She would need to find a match for the material, and that would not be easy. It would need to be something rare, something that carried the same soul as the original craftsmanship.

As she walked, she pictured old masters at work on the frame, their careful hands layering crimson gesso under gold leaf, coaxing warmth from the frame until it seemed to glow from within, embracing its painting like a lover. With something called the Bolection profile, they further shaped each edge with endless patience, pulling the canvas forward, drawing viewers eyes inward.

She loved how they obsessed over every tiny detail. They weren't just making pretty things; they were crafting doorways into wonder. Every curve, every flourish, was deliberate, meant to evoke awe and wonder. And mother-of-pearl, inlaid within the intricate designs, was no different. It was a material that demanded patience and precision in order for its shimmering surface to lend an ethereal quality to the bold grandeur of

Baroque works. The thought of working with such rare materials thrilled her because she was connecting her hands with those of the craftspeople from centuries ago.

Booth after booth offered possibilities, but nothing seemed to match what she needed. Some frames were too new, others too damaged, and the pieces of mother-of-pearl she found were either too small or too modern in their iridescence. She frowned slightly, knowing this would not be easy, but she couldn't settle for anything less than perfection.

Her inner monologue shifted to her own artistic process as she searched. To her, restoration was never about making something look new again. It was about bringing it back to life—letting the item breathe with the history it held while gently revealing its original beauty. This frame deserved the same reverence as any masterpiece.

After what felt like hours, she turned a corner and saw something promising—a small booth tucked away near the end of an alley, almost hidden from view. The stall was cluttered with frames of all sizes and conditions. Some broken, some covered in grime, but something about this place felt right.

She stepped closer and her heart quickened with anticipation. Her eyes scanned the disarray, and there, among the clutter, she found a small, cracked frame with just the right amount of mother-of-pearl inlay. It was worn but still intact, and its age was evident by the fading of its color. The iridescence was perfect, and it caught the light in the exact way she had imagined.

Carefully, she lifted the frame, inspecting it more closely. It had clearly been discarded and forgotten—yet it held the piece she needed to complete her restoration.

Amelia smiled with a sense of accomplishment as she carefully examined the frame in her hands. This was it. The delicate mother-of-pearl glistened faintly in the dim light of the booth. Its faded elegance was a perfect match for the restoration she had in mind.

As she chatted with the vendor, a woman with silvery hair who had spent decades sourcing antiques, the vendor casually mentioned that the frame had once belonged to a château in the Loire Valley. The words struck a chord with Amelia—she had always been captivated by the rich history of the Loire, with its rolling vineyards and storied castles. Many of them held untold artistic treasures.

"Loire Valley?" Amelia repeated, her interest deepening. "Do you know anything more about it?"

The vendor scratched her head, thinking. "Not much more than that, I'm afraid. The frame came from an estate sale many years ago." She paused, her expression thoughtful. "If I remember correctly, I think this château had a collection of antiques from the Baroque period that were passed down through generations."

Amelia felt a wave of connection wash over her. The Loire Valley, with its long history of nobility and art, felt like the perfect origin for such a piece. She could picture it now—this small, ornate frame hanging in a grand château with the glint of candlelight catching on its iridescence. It seemed almost fated that the frame had ended up here, just waiting for her.

After negotiating a fair price with the vendor, Amelia bought the frame and felt a deep sense of satisfaction settle over her. It was more than just a transaction—she could feel the connection between the old frame in her hands and the one she was restoring—almost as though the two pieces were meant to find each other.

As she walked away with the frame tucked securely under her arm, she felt lighter, almost like the weight of her search had been lifted. Now, the journey ahead seemed even more exciting.

———

As she made her way toward the exit, something else caught her eye. It wasn't big—just a weathered, old toolbox sitting on a wooden crate—but its craftsmanship immediately stood out to her. She paused to look and found herself comforted by its presence.

The wood was darkened with age, its edges softened by time. The dovetail joints still held fast after all these years, a testament to the care that had been placed in its making. She knelt beside it, tracing the rich patina with her fingers, reading stories in every worn groove.

What truly caught her attention, though, was the small brass key still hanging from a thin, frayed string attached to the box. Most antique toolboxes of this kind were missing their keys, either lost to time or removed by sellers to be sold separately. That this one still had its key felt significant, as though the toolbox had somehow remained whole despite its age and use.

She gently turned the key, hearing the satisfying click of the lock as the lid opened. Inside, the compartments were perfectly sized for her restoration tools, almost as though the box had been waiting for her all along. She imagined her chisels, brushes, and pigments sitting snugly within the worn wooden dividers, an old vessel breathing new life into other old things—a perfect symbol of the work she did.

Amelia's fingers traced the dovetail joints again, each one meticulously cut and fit together seamlessly. To her, *this* was a mark of true craftsmanship. The box was simple but elegant, utilitarian yet beautiful, and she felt a connection to it, much like she had with the frame she just purchased.

She started to wonder about its story and wished her father were with her to experience the moment. It was more than just an old toolbox; it was a piece of history, something that had once been essential to someone's craft, and now, it could be essential to hers.

She didn't even try to haggle. The old vendor peered at her through his thick glasses, clearly surprised anyone would want the box, but happy enough to let it go. As she handed him the money, Amelia couldn't help but feel as though the box was meant to find her, much like the frame had been.

It was a small, silent reminder that history wasn't just something to restore—it was something to live with, something to cherish.

With the frame carefully tucked under one arm and the toolbox cradled in the other, Amelia left the market. The day's finds felt more profound than mere purchases. They were pieces of the past that would now become part of her present. Tools to restore. Tools to create. Tools to breathe life back into what time had worn away.

As she walked through the maze of graffiti-covered walls and narrow alleys, Amelia felt a renewed sense of purpose. Each item had its own history, and in her hands, it would be reborn.

Chapter 5

The streets of Montmartre bustled with a life and energy that was utterly unlike the refined, stately world of Château Bourget. Here, in this bohemian heart of Paris, the cobblestones seemed to pulse beneath Arnaud's feet, carrying the rhythm of artists and poets who made their way through the narrow alleys, lost in their own creations. A warm, golden light spilled from the windows of small cafés, mingling with the glow of street lamps, casting a soft, inviting haze that made everything feel alive and immediate.

As the car rolled to a stop, Arnaud stepped out, exhaling as a wave of relief washed over him. The suffocating expectations that had weighed on him at the château melted away, leaving behind a sense of freedom and the comforting rhythm of the quarter. He nodded to his driver before pausing to take in his surroundings. The scent of roasting chestnuts mingled with the faint tang of oil paints, and somewhere in the distance, the soft, melancholy notes of an accordion drifted through the air.

This was where he felt most at home—not among the suits and grandeur, but here, in the vibrant, untamed streets of Montmartre.

The night was crisp, with a hint of a chill that made him pull his coat tighter around his shoulders. But it wasn't uncomfortable—it was invigorating. He could hear the clatter of drink glasses and the low murmur of conversation spilled from nearby cafés, mingled with bits of laughter that echoed through the streets. On the corner, two free spirits, likely buoyed by too much wine, were belting out *La Marseillaise*, their voices unsteady but full of joy. It felt as though the entire district was alive, and he was a part of it again.

Arnaud wandered through the winding alleys, watching as artists worked on street corners, their easels lit by the lamplight. With bold strokes of color, they brought fleeting moments of life to their canvases—

lovers walking hand in hand, a dog curled up beneath a café table, the distant spire of Sacré-Cœur. Musicians played for passing crowds, their fingers moving quickly over strings, weaving melodies that rose and fell like a complement to the vibrant chaos of the streets.

He had spent many nights here before, slipping away from the formality of his family's estate to seek solace in the world of creativity and passion. But tonight felt different. More urgent. The argument with his father echoed in his mind, a reminder of everything he was trying to escape. As he walked, he found himself searching, though he wasn't entirely sure for what—something to fill the emptiness he felt, to soothe the restlessness that gnawed at him.

Arnaud's feet carried him to a small café he had visited many times before, an unassuming place with a faded green awning and narrow, fogged-up windows. Inside, the air was warm and filled with the smell of coffee, tobacco, and something sweet, like vanilla. The hum of conversation was a comforting backdrop, punctuated by the occasional burst of laughter. The walls were lined with canvases, some large and bold, others small and intimate, all works of local artists hoping to catch the eye of a someone passing by.

He stepped through the door, feeling the familiar creak of the floorboards beneath his feet, and let the warmth of the room wrap around him.

He made his way to the bar, where the café owner, a man in his prime with a kind smile and a twinkle in his eye, nodded in recognition.

"Bonsoir, monsieur," the man said, his voice gruff but warm. "Back for another look at our little gallery, eh?"

Arnaud smiled, but there was a heaviness to his expression. "Something like that," he said softly, his gaze drifting across the room to one of the side walls lined with frames. Each time he looked, something new seemed to emerge. But tonight, his eyes settled on something exquisite—a canvas near the top, partially obscured by shadow, holding him captive.

It was a narrative painted in deep, rich hues. A woman, her face framed by soft, dark curls, gazing out with eyes that seemed to hold a world of emotion within them—sorrow, resilience, and something undefinable, something that made it impossible to look away. The brushstrokes were raw yet delicate, capturing every nuance of her expression, the way her lips curved into the slightest hint of a smile, like she knew a secret no one else did.

Arnaud felt an intimate pull toward the painting, his mind momentarily stilling, and all the chaos muted by this one image.

The signature in the corner read "E. Leclair," scrawled with a fluid, almost careless grace. He had never heard of the artist, but the name was already etched into his mind. He turned to the café owner, catching his eye before nodding up to the painting. "Who painted that?"

The man followed Arnaud's gaze, his eyes crinkling with a knowing smile. "Ah, Eloise," he said warmly. "She's a regular around here. Always working, always painting. You'll find her at that table over there," he said, gesturing to a corner near the window.

Arnaud looked and saw her, sitting alone, sketching in a worn notebook, her fingers smudged with charcoal. She was nothing like the women he was accustomed to seeing at the château—the ones draped in silk and diamonds, every strand of hair perfectly in place. Eloise was different. Her hair was loosely pinned, strands falling around her face, and she wore a simple dress that spoke more of practicality than fashion. There was an understated confidence in the way she held herself, as though she didn't care who noticed her or what they thought.

For a moment, he hesitated, unsure of how to approach her. But then he took a breath and made his way to her table, his heart pounding with a mixture of nerves and anticipation. She was so immersed in her work that she didn't notice him at first, her pencil moving steadily across the page, sketching lines that seemed to flow from some place deep within her.

"Excuse me," Arnaud said, his voice gentle, almost hesitant. "I hope I'm not disturbing you."

Eloise looked up, her eyes meeting his, and for a moment, he felt as though he was standing on the edge of something important, yet didn't fully understand. She blinked, as if pulling herself back from wherever her mind had been, and gave him a polite, curious smile. "Not at all," she said, setting her pencil down. "What can I do for you?"

Arnaud gestured to the painting on the wall, trying to find the right words. "I was admiring your painting. The one of the woman... there's something about it, something..." He trailed off, realizing how inadequate his words sounded, how they failed to capture what he felt. "It's beautiful," he finished simply. "And haunting."

Eloise's expression softened, and she tilted her head slightly, studying him. *"Merci,"* she said. "Most people just say it's sad." There was no bitterness in her tone, just a simple acceptance, as though she was used to hearing it, used to being misunderstood.

"I don't think it's sad," Arnaud said, and he meant it. He turned to the painting and studied it some more. "There's sorrow, yes, but there's also strength. Like she's been through something, but she's still here, still standing." He realized he may have been speaking as much about himself as he was about the painting, but he didn't stop. "It's... real."

Eloise's eyes flickered with something, a hint of surprise, and for a moment, he thought she might laugh at him, but she didn't. Instead, she smiled, a small, genuine smile that seemed to light up her face. "You're not from around here, are you?" she said, her tone light, but her gaze sharp, like she was trying to figure him out.

Arnaud hesitated, surprised by the question. "No, not really," he said, choosing his words carefully. "But I wish I were."

Eloise's smile widened, and she leaned back in her chair, her posture relaxing. "Then what brings you to Montmartre, *Monsieur?*"

"I needed to get away," he said, and the words came out before he could stop them. He continued, a bit more guarded, "From my family, from everything. I needed... I needed to see something beautiful."

She studied him for a moment, her eyes searching his face, as if trying to decide whether to believe him. Then she nodded, as though she had come to a conclusion. "I'm Eloise," she said, holding out her hand.

"Arnaud," he said, taking it, feeling a jolt of warmth at the touch. "It's a pleasure to meet you, Eloise."

They talked for a while, about art, about Paris, about the things that inspired them. Eloise spoke passionately about her work, how she painted not for fame or money, but because it was what gave her life meaning. "It's like breathing," she said, her eyes shining. "I don't think about it, I just do it. I have to."

Arnaud listened, captivated by her honesty, by the way she spoke with such conviction. She seemed fearless, unafraid to follow her passion, to live by her own rules, and he found himself wishing he could be the same. "I envy you," he said quietly, and when she looked at him, he saw a glimpse of understanding in her eyes.

"What's stopping you?" she asked, her tone gentle but firm, as if she already knew the answer.

He opened his mouth to tell her, to explain everything, but before the words could form, the café door burst open. A group of rowdy men stumbled in, their laughter and boisterous voices jarring against the intimacy of the moment.

Eloise's gaze shifted toward them, her expression darkening as the smile faded from her lips. Arnaud watched her carefully, sensing the way her focus fractured. Her hand drifted to her pencil, almost instinctively, twirling it between her fingers as though grounding herself amidst the disruption. Her eyes flicked toward the noise, and the subtle tension in her posture—her stiffened shoulders, her fingers tense—told him everything. The fragile connection they had shared was unraveling.

For a moment, he thought about pushing through, about telling her the truth anyway, but he felt her guard was already going back up. It seemed as though she had retreated into a safer, reserved corner of herself. The timing was gone.

"Maybe I should go," he said, standing up, his chest heavy with unspoken words. He hesitated, meeting her eyes once more before adding, "But… I'd like to buy your painting."

Eloise blinked, surprised. "You would?"

"Yes," he said, smiling. "It's beautiful. And I'd like to have it."

She hesitated, then nodded, a small smile tugging at her lips. "Alright," she said. "But you have to promise you'll take good care of her."

"I will," he said. And he meant it.

As he left the café, the painting tucked under his arm wrapped in brown paper, Arnaud felt a strange mix of emotions—hope, uncertainty, and a calm determination. He had come to Montmartre searching for something, and he had found it, but he didn't know how to hold on to it.

As he stepped back out into the night, he knew one thing for certain: he would be back. He had to see her again, to find out what lay beyond that guarded smile, to bridge the gap between their worlds, no matter how wide it seemed.

Chapter 6

The elegance of St. Petersburg gleamed under crystal chandeliers as Nadia Vallois drifted effortlessly through the crowded gallery. Her gaze swept across the walls, pausing on each masterpiece, captivated by the stories they told. Tonight's collection had been curated with a reverence that evoked Paris's golden age of creativity. The soft strokes of Impressionism and the warm hues of a Parisian spring filled the room, evoking a world she adored.

Her father, Étienne Vallois, stood among a cluster of diplomats, his voice low and measured, his every word carefully chosen. Nadia watched him out of the corner of her eye. In his understated manner, Étienne possessed more influence than most realized at first, with his connections in Europe's highest offices. To him, culture was a tool of influence, a symbol of the nation's strength and pride to be protected, but never something he felt personally connected to.

Étienne valued art, but he would never passionately collect it. He financed its preservation, supported cultural initiatives, but always from a respectful distance.

As her father spoke with a Russian dignitary, Nadia drifted to the far side of the room, where a set of Impressionist paintings hung in a quiet alcove. The colors, vibrant yet restrained, captivated her, and her gaze settled on a piece by Sisley. Each brushstroke seemed alive with a rebellious spirit, reflecting the artist's desire to capture a moment, an impression, unfiltered and unrefined.

It was then she noticed a presence beside her. A man with an understated command over the space. His tall frame, with subtle streaks of gray peeking through his dark hair, hinted at his age and experience. He looked at the paintings with an intensity that spoke of reverence, his eyes tracing each line and color. He noticed Nadia's gaze and turned with a slight nod that was both polite and appraising.

"You appreciate Sisley," he observed, his voice warm with a thick Russian accent.

Nadia returned his gaze, intrigued by his presence. "Very much so," she replied. "His work is like a breath of air… he captures the intangible, makes you feel it. Like memories made visible."

The man smiled, his eyes bright with understanding. "The intangible—yes, precisely. The beauty in things that cannot be seen with the ordinary eye," he agreed. "It's what makes this art so dangerous."

She looked at him, curious. "Dangerous? Most people would say beautiful."

He turned back to the painting with a hint of defiance in his posture. "The Louvre refused them, you know. They were considered too radical, too unsettling. The Impressionists challenged the accepted, the understood. Their art invited people to look beyond what was expected. That is dangerous… in its own cunning way."

She looked at him anew, sensing that he, too, had experienced this art as more than mere beauty—as something transformative. "You speak as if you know it personally," she ventured.

The man inclined his head, his gaze steady. "Perhaps." He reached out his hand. "I am Sergei Shchukin. A collector, some would say. Though I see myself as more of a… steward."

Nadia's eyes widened with recognition. Sergei Shchukin, the man behind one of the most extraordinary private collections of French modern art, rivaling the most esteemed galleries in Paris. She offered her hand in return, a small nod of respect beneath her smile.

"I've heard of your collection, Mr. Shchukin," she replied, her admiration clear. "It's a privilege to meet you."

"And you are?"

"Nadia Vallois." She said with confidence, sensing there was little need to elaborate—he would recognize her family name. The Vallois had ties across Europe, their influence spreading beyond the limits of finance and diplomacy.

He regarded her with renewed interest. "Ah, Vallois," he murmured. "Your family is known for its dedication to preserving France's stature and strength… in different ways than art, it seems."

She smiled, acknowledging the nuance in his words. "My father sees culture as something that needs protection, but from a distance," she said in a measured tone. "I suppose I've inherited a different perspective."

They both turned back to the painting, and Sergei's voice softened. "Art has a strange power, Nadia. It is more than just an object to be admired. It carries with it a world of history, of emotion… of resistance. These paintings were created during times of significant change. They carry that unrest with them."

Nadia studied the canvas, his words reshaping her understanding of the work. Sergei's passion was unmistakable, a commitment to preserving something greater than himself. And yet, what struck her most was how his words echoed her own unspoken fears about Europe's uncertain future.

She chose her next words carefully, aware that such candor was rarely welcome in most circles. But Sergei didn't seem like most people, and she could sense he might appreciate her honesty.

"Europe feels… precarious," she said in a low voice. "There's a tension, a sense of something waiting to tip. I worry about what that means for art, for culture. For France—for all of us."

Sergei turned to her, his expression thoughtful. "Yes. There *is* a sense that something is coming, a darkness. But you should know, art can be a shield against that darkness, a reminder of who we are, of what we must preserve."

His words stirred something within her, a recognition of a shared purpose. She glanced at him, aware of her father's occasional gaze drifting toward them. Étienne was simply observing, not intruding. He valued his daughter's passion for art, though he had always framed it as an enhancement of their family's legacy, another avenue for influence.

As Nadia kept conversing with Sergei, she sensed it was more than an alliance-building moment; it was an understanding of a deeper, more profound connection to culture, to art, and even, possibly, to what it meant to be human.

The gallery's chatter dwindled as the evening drew to a close, and Sergei turned to her, his gaze assessing, almost weighing a decision.

"I would like to show you something… if you'll allow me, of course," he said finally. "My private collection in Moscow."

The offer startled her. Shchukin's collection was a legendary assemblage of Cézannes, Matisses, Picassos, and others. Many had seen it, of course; she had heard he opened his gallery to anyone with a love of art. But this felt different. This was not a public invitation, but a personal one —a gesture of trust.

She nodded, filled with gratitude. "I would be honored!"

Sergei's smile was gentle. "Come while you are in Russia… bring your father if you like. I think you will find it… enlightening."

They exchanged a few details and a polite nod before Sergei turned away, moving through the remaining guests, heads turning in his wake. As he disappeared into the evening, a growing sense of anticipation bloomed within her, a feeling both exhilarating and unnerving.

Her life had been a steady stream of gallery openings, diplomatic dinners, and exhibitions. But this encounter felt different. Different from the stuffy façades of art and society she was accustomed to. Sergei's invitation to view his private collection felt like more than a mere gesture. It felt like he was offering her a chance to see something more honest, more personal—art treated as more than just an asset or a status symbol.

Nadia glanced across the room at her father, who was deep in conversation with the Romanian Ambassador, likely advising more on the nonaggression treaty they were establishing with the Soviets. She could almost sense his silent approval of the meeting from afar. Étienne valued alliances with powerful figures like Sergei Shchukin, seeing them as another step in their family's long strategy to secure power and prestige.

And though her father might come along, Nadia doubted he would understand the depth of her own fascination with the visit. He valued the works they helped finance and restore, but he did not see the soul within them or the stories held within each brushstroke.

And yet, for all his cynicism, she understood his perspective. She'd been raised to see art as a form of currency, something that opened doors and shaped reputations. Sergei's comments hadn't overturned that perspective outright, but they nudged her to consider something else. Maybe art *could* stand on its own, something cherished for its meaning rather than its utility. A fragile reminder of who they were and what they valued, worth protecting for its own sake—not just because it impressed the right people.

As the last guests slipped into the night, anticipation stirred within Nadia. Soon, she would step into Sergei's private collection, not as a Vallois, but as someone who truly belonged in the world of art. Excitement swelled. This meeting felt like more than an opportunity. It felt like a turning point, one that might redefine not just her relationship with art, but her understanding of herself.

Chapter 7

Back in her studio, Amelia set the newly acquired frame from the Marché on her workbench beside Madame Laurent's Baroque piece. The two frames seemed to speak to each other in silent conversation with their shared history, linking them through time.

Her mind wandered to the artisans of centuries past who had labored over these rare materials, choosing to use mother-of-pearl for its artful elegance. She wondered about their inspirations—whether they sought to capture the divine, or evoke emotion, or simply create something enduring. What challenges had they faced in sourcing such materials and what stories had those hands told through the wood, the gold, and its iridescent shell?

Amelia was eager to start the delicate process of extracting the mother-of-pearl from the smaller frame and start breathing new life into Madame Laurent's piece. But her eyes slowly drifted to her other purchase resting next to her workstation. Its patina seemed to gleam under the soft studio light and provided just enough distraction to coax her thoughts away from the frame.

She was filled with satisfaction thinking about organizing her restoration tools within its worn, but beautifully crafted compartments. It called to her in a way she couldn't ignore. Now, the ritual of cleaning and organizing it felt almost necessary, as if preparing the toolbox for her work would ground her and provide a small act of respect for the past.

After all, the tools it would hold were the very instruments that would help her breathe new life back into centuries-old artifacts. It was symbolic, and for her, setting the stage was just as important as the restoration itself.

With a soft sigh, and a twinge of delight, she set the Laurent frame aside for just a little longer, knowing that tending to the toolbox would somehow prepare her for the intricate work ahead.

Amelia reached for the box and slowly moved it in front of her. She paused for a moment, then ran her fingers over the smooth, weathered wood, feeling where time had worn its outer shell. It was almost like she was acquainting herself with its history, hoping to absorb any secrets the box might yield. The small brass key still hung from its delicate string and, as she picked it up, its weight felt satisfying as it dangled from her hand.

She gently unlocked the lid and lifted it, the wood releasing a soft creak as it opened. Inside, the box exhaled the musty breath it had held for decades.

Amelia's fingers traced the smooth interior, darkened with age yet still showcasing the precision of its original craftsmanship. Each divider had been perfectly shaped for tools long forgotten and now seemed to wait patiently for a new purpose.

Amelia smiled softly and felt a sense of calm washing over her as she set to clean the interior. The compartments, though dusty, were solid and ready. She could already picture her fine brushes, chisels, and delicate tools nestled within, preparing to bring new life to the treasures of the past.

Satisfied, she shifted the box slightly to continue cleaning when, unexpectedly, a soft rattle echoed from within. The sound was so faint at first, she almost thought she'd imagined it. But after tilting it again, just as before, the same rattle cut through the silence of the studio.

Amelia paused, her brow furrowing.

The box had been empty when she bought it—she had checked it thoroughly at the market. And yet, there it was again: a distinct, muffled rattle.

Setting her cleaning cloth aside, she opened the lid wider and inspected the compartments more closely, looking for any loose hinges or forgotten screws. She checked the dividers, the joints, and the edges, but everything appeared solid and intact. The lock clicked smoothly when turned, and the wood, while aged, showed no sign of damage or weakness.

She tipped the box slightly, letting it tilt from side to side, the rattle continuing—a soft, hollow sound, like something loose moving back and forth inside. Each movement sent her heart pounding a little faster, and what was originally curiosity started turning into a creeping sense of unease.

What could be inside? The box was empty. So, where was the sound coming from?

Amelia leaned in closer, her breath shallow as she pressed her ear to the smooth wood. Her fingers lightly tapped on the bottom. A hollow thud echoed back. She paused.

The wood wasn't solid? It was hollow beneath the surface?

She knocked again, this time harder. The thud was clearer now, more pronounced, and with it came that same faint rattle. Her pulse quickened as her thoughts raced. It sounded like there was something beneath the bottom panel, hidden inside the box.

Amelia's mind spun. *A hidden compartment?*

It wasn't unheard of, especially in older pieces of furniture. Craft workers from centuries ago had often embedded secret compartments into boxes, desks, or drawers, meant to conceal valuables or letters.

She ran her hands over the maroon felt that lined the bottom of the box. What was once used to muffle rattling tools within continued its purpose after all these years.

Her eyes narrowed as she inspected the bottom panel closer. At first she saw nothing—from her view, it appeared solid. However, continuing, her trained gaze finally caught a slight detail—almost imperceptible to anyone else. The felt-covered bottom was just slightly higher than the edges of the exterior base. It was subtle, maybe a centimeter or two, but now that she saw it, the difference was undeniable. The plane was off. The interior bottom didn't quite rest where it should.

A thrill shot through her, her heartbeat pounding in her ears as the realization hit her.

A false bottom!

She ran her fingers along the edges of the felt, her movements slower and more deliberate now. Her hands tingled with a mixture of excitement and trepidation. What was hidden beneath? What could it be?

The air around her grew heavy with possibility, while the room narrowed down to just her and the box.

Feeling for any seams or gaps, her breaths grew shallow as she pushed on the felt, pressing along the edges, but it gave nothing away. Her instincts as a restorer urged her to proceed carefully, to not damage the box in any way. She couldn't just force it open—if there was something hidden, she had to find a way to release it without destroying the craftsmanship she so admired.

After what felt like an eternity of trying to nudge, press, and prod at the wood with her bare hands without success, Amelia knew she needed to change tactics. Grabbing a small flashlight from her workbench, she shined it along the edge of the felt, squinting to see if there was any sign of a seam.

And then she saw it—a barely visible line along one edge, hidden by the felt but unmistakable under the light. There was a gap, a sliver of space where the panel met the side of the box, almost too small to notice.

Her hands trembled slightly with anticipation as she grabbed one of her restoration tools—a tiny pallet knife that was thin and delicate enough for the job.

Carefully, she slid the blade into the gap, feeling the resistance as the panels clung to themselves after decades of disuse. She held her breath while applying the gentlest pressure, trying to coax the bottom panel to move. But nothing happened.

Frustration mounted as Amelia wiggled the knife, pushing just a bit harder. Still, the bottom held firm. A part of her wondered if she was wrong—if it really was just a trick of the wood, and there was no false bottom at all. But she knew the signs. The gap was there. The hollow thud. The rattle.

She tried again, this time pushing the blade deeper, feeling the resistance give ever so slightly. Her heart raced as she twisted the knife, prying gently. A frictional click echoed through the quiet studio—wood against wood, a sound from this box that hadn't been heard in decades. Amelia froze, her breath catching in her throat.

The bottom panel had shifted.

It was the tiniest movement, but enough to send a jolt of adrenaline through her. Her heart pounded in her ears, and each beat reminded her she was on the verge of discovering something long hidden.

Trembling with anticipation, she slid the blade back into the gap, the tool now feeling like an extension of her hand. She applied more pressure this time, cautiously twisting the knife as if the very act might disturb the delicate history concealed within.

Slowly, agonizingly slowly, the false bottom began to lift, the wood groaning as it released its grip after decades of silence. Her breath came in shallow gasps as she pried it upward, the panel moving just enough to slip her fingers underneath. The grain of the wood felt rough against her skin, its surface worn by time yet still holding onto its secrets.

Amelia's mind spun, a thousand possibilities flickering through her thoughts. *What could be hidden in here?* Her imagination raced as her hands shook, not just with excitement, but with the weight of the unknown. She could feel the decades, maybe even centuries, between her and the original owner, and in this moment, she crossed that distance, touching their secret.

Her fingers curled beneath the false bottom, and with a final effort, she pried the panel fully open. The wood gave way with a soft sigh, revealing a dark, concealed space below.

Time seemed to slow as Amelia peered into the once-hidden area. The dim lights of the studio barely reached inside and the small cavity was veiled in shadow. Her eyes struggled to adjust and make sense of what she was seeing.

For a moment, everything seemed to hold still—the air, the silence, even her breath. Then, as her vision sharpened, she caught sight of something.

Amelia gasped.

Chapter 8

After meeting Eloise, Arnaud's life divided into two: the dutiful son navigating Château Bourget's rigid expectations by day, and the man who came alive in Montmartre's vibrant streets by night. At the château, he reviewed ledgers, corresponded with suppliers, and entertained visiting patrons, all with the practiced ease of someone performing a role in a legacy not of his own choosing. Yet every moment spent among its silent corridors and priceless art collections reminded him of the freedom he craved but couldn't claim.

In Montmartre, he was *just* Arnaud. Among the laughter, music, and the scratch of charcoal on canvas, he found a version of himself he didn't have to hide—a version his father would see as a betrayal of everything the Bourget family represented. And it was there, in the lively cafes and winding alleys, that he saw Eloise again and again.

A little over a month had passed since he first asked to buy her painting. In that time, their conversations deepened. What began with idle talk about technique and style now ventured into the meaning of art, the purpose of creativity, and the courage it took to defy expectations. Arnaud found himself drawn back to that small café near the window, where Eloise often sat with her sketchbook, feeling a warm thrill each time he saw her welcoming smile.

Late one afternoon, he arrived as usual. The familiar scent of coffee and tobacco drifted through the café, and there she was, hair loosely pinned back, a few wayward strands framing her face and falling just to her shoulders. A fine gold chain caught the light at her collarbone, the tiny star charm resting gently against her skin. A smudge of charcoal graced her fingertips. She was working on a new sketch, something delicate. He approached with care, hesitating for a moment just to watch her.

She was beautiful, not in the polished way society celebrated, but in the effortless way she moved through the world, unaware of her own allure. His pulse quickened. It wasn't just the curve of her figure or the gentle fall of her hair—it was the way she inhabited her space fully, unapologetically herself. As he watched her bent over the lines of her new sketch, her focus unbroken, he couldn't help but think how stunning she looked, as if she belonged in a portrait herself.

"Arnaud," she said, noticing him. "You're here!" Her eyes brightened.

"I couldn't stay away," he replied lightly, slipping into the chair across from her. "How's the masterpiece coming along?"

Eloise laughed softly, glancing down at her sketch. "It's not a masterpiece, but it's coming along," she said. "I'm trying to capture the way the light hits the rooftops at dusk. It's tricky… it almost disappears if you're not paying attention."

Arnaud leaned in, studying the delicate interplay of light and shadow in her sketch, and the careful attention to detail that gave the drawing its depth. "You have an incredible eye," he said. "Not just for what's there, but for what others might choose to smooth over."

Eloise offered a small, knowing smile. "It's not about perfection. It's about seeing what others don't *want* to see—the flaws, the fractures, the stories that make it real."

Something in her words struck him. He swallowed hard. She wasn't just talking about art.

"Is that why you paint?" he asked. "To tell the stories no one else sees?"

Eloise hesitated. "I paint because it's the only way I know how to make sense of the world," she said finally. "It's like… when I'm painting, everything else disappears. The noise, the chaos, the expectations—it all fades away, and I'm left with something pure. Something true."

Arnaud listened, captivated. She spoke with fearless conviction—something he admired but had never embraced. He tried to focus on her words, but his gaze betrayed him, drawn to the curve of her lips, the way they shaped each thought with confidence. The urge to close the small distance between them was impossible to ignore.

He exhaled slowly, forcing himself back to her voice, to the meaning behind her words.

"I wish I could do that," he said. "I wish I could just… disappear into something."

She looked at him gently and tilted her head. "What's stopping you?"

He opened his mouth to answer, but the words refused to come. A thousand thoughts raced through his mind. He wanted her to see him for who he really was—his substance, not his status. But he remembered how Eloise had once confided her discomfort with wealth, how easily it could bury what was real and overshadow what truly mattered. Because of this, he dreaded telling her about his family, worried she'd see him as just another privileged heir, trapped in opulence.

As an artist, Eloise did okay financially—not poor, but far from rich—and she feared how wealth might stifle her creativity. Yet the privilege that shaped Arnaud's life was the very thing she rejected—an obstacle to authentic art and purpose. He feared the truth might drive her away. He had worked so carefully to keep Château Bourget separate from Montmartre, but now the two worlds were colliding. And for the first time, he wasn't sure how to stop it.

After a pause, Eloise leaned closer, her voice softer but insistent. "So… what's stopping you?"

Arnaud exhaled, his voice low. "There are… responsibilities I can't ignore. Things I have to do, whether I want to or not."

Disappointment flickered across her face. "People who hide behind duty often end up living someone else's life." She studied him for a moment, then said, "If you love something, you fight for it. You don't let anyone take it away."

He wanted to tell her he was fighting—that every moment with her was a rebellion. But how could he explain that without telling her everything?

They moved on to lighter subjects—the musicians tuning their instruments outside, the latest scandalous painting that had stirred up talk among the local artists. As evening approached and the café grew livelier, she packed up her sketchbook.

"Will you be here tomorrow?" he asked as they stood.

She nodded. "I think so. The light changes every day, and I've yet to do it justice."

Arnaud hesitated, searching for something else to say. Instead, he only nodded and turned toward the door.

Outside, the night had deepened, Montmartre alive with music and laughter. He stepped into the street, but the warmth of the café still clung to him.

His secret could not stay hidden forever.

Chapter 9

Paris, 1933

Arnaud hurried through the narrow, snow-covered streets of Montmartre, breath curling in the cold air as he made his way to their café—a tucked-away spot where time seemed to slow.

January had hushed the quarter, muffling footsteps and blurring the familiar outlines of rooftops and railings. The usual bustle had retreated indoors, leaving a stillness that felt strangely intimate.

Through the frosted window, he spotted Eloise at their usual table, a woolen scarf wrapped around her neck, her hands curled around a cup of tea.

The bell chimed as he stepped inside, shaking the snow from his coat. Eloise looked up, her breath catching for just a second.

"Arnaud!" she greeted warmly, but it came out softer, as if caught off guard.

His dark eyes met hers, pinning her in place. She had seen him countless times—admired the sharp cut of his jaw, the confidence in his posture. But today, something was different.

Maybe it was the damp strands of hair falling loose against his forehead, or the way the cold had sharpened the angles of his face. Or maybe it was something else entirely, something that had been building in her for weeks, too slow to notice. But now, it was undeniable. Something about him felt... closer. More certain.

Had he always looked this good?

The intensity of it unsettled her, made her pulse quicken despite herself.

She felt warmth rise to her cheeks, caught off-guard by how easily her composure unraveled. Lowering her gaze, she pretended to adjust her scarf, but even as she looked away, her awareness of him only deepened.

He slid into the seat across from her, his hands instinctively finding hers. Despite the cold outside, his touch was warm and comforting, a welcome contrast to her chilled fingers. The gesture felt so natural that neither felt the need to explain it.

"It's beautiful out there," he said, nodding toward the snowfall. Then, with a playful shiver, he added, "But freezing."

She laughed. "I think Paris is more beautiful in the winter. It feels like the city is eager, waiting for something to come alive again."

Arnaud felt something had shifted between them recently, a closeness more profound than before. Not just shared laughter or playful teasing, but a sense that their time together was forging something unbreakable. But as they talked, Eloise noticed something.

She sipped her tea, and reached for his hands again, tilting her head to read his mood. "You're quieter than usual. Everything all right?"

He paused, looking at their intertwined hands. "I'm just... thinking," he answered carefully. "About how things change, I suppose."

Eloise studied him for a moment, then offered a sympathetic smile. "I think change can be a friend," she said. "Sometimes we resist it because we fear what comes next. But if we never risk anything, we never discover what we're capable of."

He nodded, exhaling slowly. "You're right," he admitted. "And I think that's why I've been struggling. I feel like I'm living in two worlds. One here, where I'm truly myself. And another where I'm..." His voice trailed off. "Somebody else."

Eloise's eyes softened. She squeezed his hand gently. "Well," she said kindly, "at least you know who you are here." Her gaze held understanding, but she didn't press further, respecting the line he wasn't yet ready to cross.

When she finished her tea, Eloise stood, tugging him gently toward the door. "Come, I want to show you something," she said, mischief dancing in her eyes.

Outside, the snow crunched beneath their feet as she led him up the winding alleys of Montmartre. At the top of the hill, a small park stood hushed, the world softened by fresh snow.

"Wait here," she said, releasing his hand as she turned and moved a few steps ahead, her eyes bright with a playful glint.

Then, to his astonishment, she began to twirl, her arms lifting gracefully as she spun in the snow, her laughter drifting through the air like music.

She was beautiful, light and movement wrapped in the winter air, and he watched her with a mixture of wonder and awe. No expectation or regret could ever bind her.

Finally, she stopped and turned to him. "Do you know what I love about Montmartre, Arnaud?" she asked, still catching her breath from laughter.

He shook his head, captivated, with a perplexed grin.

"It's the freedom," she said, staring directly into his eyes. "Here, you can be whoever you want. You don't have to pretend."

His chest tightened. She had no idea how much those words meant.

In that moment, he knew he couldn't keep lying to her. She deserved the truth, deserved to know who he was and the world he came from. He hesitated, heart pounding, aware that his words might shatter this delicate, perfect thing they found. Still, he gathered his courage.

"Eloise," he began, his voice unsteady, "I… I want you to know that —"

But before he could continue, she gently pressed a finger against his lips, her eyes filled with compassion. It was like she sensed the struggle within him and understood he wasn't truly ready—that speaking now would be forced and painful.

"Don't," she whispered. "Not tonight." Her gesture wasn't rejection, it was understanding, an acknowledgment of the courage it took for him to try.

Relief washed over him, and without another word, he pulled her into an embrace, letting the snow wisp around them. She leaned into him without question.

One evening, they were sitting on the rooftop of her small apartment, Paris stretched out below them.

Eloise turned to him, her gaze searching. "Arnaud," she said gently, "what do you want?"

He hesitated. He could feel the heaviness of his secret, but tried to look past it. What did he want? To hold on to this feeling—the warmth of her presence, the spark of their connection—without the burden of explaining himself.

"I want…" he began, voice trailing off as he tried to pin down the thought.

Eloise's fingers grazed his. "You can tell me," she encouraged.

Arnaud's throat tightened. He wanted to say a thousand things, to put words to the pull between them, but the silence felt heavier than anything he could offer. The glow of the distant street lamps flickered in her eyes, and for a moment, he thought about holding back, about walking away before this became something he couldn't control. But control had slipped through his fingers the moment he met her.

He exhaled, slow and unsteady. "I want to feel this," he finally said, "Without regret or hesitation. Just this."

The space between them shrank, charged with something unspoken. She tilted her head slightly, her lips parting just enough for him to feel the warmth of her breath against his skin. The invitation was there, but the choice was his. "Then let's have that," she said.

Arnaud didn't think. He just moved—closing the space between them, his lips finding hers in a kiss neither of them could take back. She gasped softly against him, the sound barely lost in the night air before she responded, her hands tangling in his hair, pulling him closer. It was intoxicating, a kiss with no restraint, no hesitation—just the culmination of everything they had wanted but hadn't allowed themselves to take. Until now.

When they finally pulled apart, her cheeks were flushed, and her eyes shone with something raw and unguarded.

Arnaud pressed his forehead to hers, his heart pounding, breathing unsteadily.

He knew the weight of his family's expectations loomed just beyond this moment, waiting.

But for tonight, he let himself forget.

For tonight, there was only this.

Chapter 10

Arnaud pushed open the heavy door to his father's study, the weight of expectation settling over him like an unwelcome guest. Lucien sat behind the oak desk, hands steepled, his gaze sharp and unrelenting.

"You can't keep disappearing like this, Arnaud," Lucien began before his son could even sit. "This family cannot afford an heir who spends his days wandering Paris, chasing distractions."

Arnaud took the seat across from him, his fingers pressing into his knees. "I'm not aimless, Father," he said, keeping his tone steady. "I'm working—just not in the way you expect."

Lucien's expression hardened. "Is that what you tell yourself? That your little excursions are productive? You may think you're doing something meaningful, but you're just running away."

Anger flared in Arnaud, but he swallowed it. Lucien would see Eloise as nothing more than a distraction, something to be erased before it veered him further off course. And Eloise—she didn't even know yet. Until she did, there was no reason to bring her into this.

"I'm not running away," Arnaud said evenly. "I'm… finding something. Something that makes me feel alive."

Lucien leaned forward. "And what about your responsibilities? What about this family? The Bourget name is not just about art and culture, Arnaud. It's about our business. You can't chase a fantasy. I won't be here forever. As the only heir, it's time you took your role seriously."

The words stung, but Arnaud said nothing. He knew his father wouldn't understand—couldn't understand. Lucien had been raised in this world, groomed to lead, to command, to control. To him, the family business was everything, and there was no space for dreams that didn't serve the empire.

Lucien sighed, shifting tactics. "There's a gala next week. I need you to attend with me, and I want you to make it clear that you are committed to this family—to our business."

Arnaud's heart sank. He knew what this meant. "Do I have a choice?" he asked, though he already knew the answer.

Lucien didn't even pause. "No, you don't."

A beat of silence. Then Arnaud exhaled. "Fine. If that's what you want."

Lucien said, "It's not just what I want—it's what this family needs. And you will see, in time, that it's what you need too."

Arnaud left the study, the door's closing feeling oddly final. As he walked past the portraits that lined the hallways, the faces of his ancestors stared down at him, their expressions stern and unyielding. They had all played their part, fulfilling their roles with dignity and grace. But Arnaud didn't linger under their stares.

Gazing out from the terrace, he fought a wave of dread. The gala wasn't just an event—it was a sentence. A line drawn between the life he wanted and the one his father demanded.

Outside, an early spring dusk settled over the estate as Arnaud walked toward his waiting Bucciali— a gleaming symbol of everything he was meant to inherit, everything that tethered him to this life.

He slid into the back seat and shut the door with finality. Meeting the driver's gaze in the rearview mirror, he gave a single directive: "Montmartre."

The car jolted forward, and Arnaud leaned back as the wheels crunched over the gravel. The gala, the expectations, the legacy—it all loomed, but he felt something shift inside him. He was done living a lie, done being torn between two worlds. He was finally ready to confront the truth he had been hiding for so long, no matter the cost.

As they neared Anvers, at the base of Montmartre Hill, he told the driver to stop. Stepping out into the cool night, he inhaled the stillness. Ahead, the winding streets rose toward Eloise.

That ascent was more than a path to her door. It was a metaphor for everything he needed to overcome—the tangled expectations, the secrets he carried, and the courage he'd need to summon to finally tell her the truth.

He didn't know what he would say when he saw her or how she would react. Only that he couldn't keep lying.

Drawing a steadying breath, Arnaud began to climb.

Chapter 11

Paris, Modern Day

Amelia stood frozen as she stared down at the contents of the hidden compartment.

For a long moment, all she could do was gaze in awe at what lay before her, hardly able to believe what she was seeing. Her pulse quickened, sending a rush of excitement through her that left her covered in goosebumps.

She was no stranger to the mysteries of history—her work involved uncovering layers of time hidden beneath dust and dirt. But this was different. This was history, buried not in artifacts or paintings, but carefully concealed within the very box she now held.

That realization pressed down on her as she stood in the presence of something long forgotten, something once treasured.

Inside the false bottom lay a folded handkerchief, its edges slightly yellowed with age, yet still remarkably intact. Amelia's fingers trembled as she lifted it, feeling the slight coarseness that spoke of its long history. She could also feel the subtle weight of something tucked securely inside, adding to the growing anticipation.

Embroidered in one corner were the initials "EB," crafted in an elegant script. Though the light blue stitching had faded over time, the letters remained legible, carrying with them the burden of an untold story. Her father would have been giddy just to see this, and Amelia couldn't help but feel the same way.

Slowly, she unwrapped the contents of the handkerchief, the fabric stiff from disuse. Her heart fluttered at the sight of the small shape tucked securely within, and as the last flap slipped away, a wave of surprise washed over her.

For an instant, she simply stared, speechless.

There, nestled in the soft folds, was a beautiful antique diamond ring.

Amelia gasped softly as the diamond caught the light from her studio, its brilliance still visible despite the years it had lain hidden. It was quite large and its facets shimmered, appearing almost new.

Five delicate prongs held the stone, each one crafted to cradle the diamond in a way that highlighted its size and brilliance. The band was made of yellow gold and had an intricately engraved floral motif, which felt heavy with significance—almost like the love and history it symbolized had somehow seeped into the very metal over the years. She could tell it was a piece from another time, a ring that had once meant everything to someone.

Her eyes shifted back to the handkerchief and then to the box, where some folded pieces of paper still rested. The pages were worn, brittle, and stained with age. Amelia would have usually fetched her gloves, but in the thrill of discovery, she couldn't bear to distance herself from this. The moment felt too personal, too immediate. She knew how to handle old documents with care. As she lifted the papers to her nose, the distinct smell of time itself—old paper, dust, and the faint scent of ink—washed over her.

With great care, she unfolded them—eight pages in total—and her fingers moved as expertly as they would with any fragile artifact. The handwriting inside was elegant and slanted, and she could make out the date: 1934.

The letter was signed by someone named Arnaud, written to a woman named Eloise. Amelia's heart raced as she read the first few lines, her mind spinning with questions. This was a love letter, written nearly a century ago, full of tenderness and longing. Arnaud's words to her spoke of a deep, passionate love, one that was both poetic and raw. He wrote of their stolen moments together, the way he cherished every second with her, how her smile lingered in his thoughts long after she had left. The ink had slightly faded, but the sentiment remained as powerful as ever.

Amelia felt a pang in her chest, as if she had stumbled upon something far too intimate, far too personal to be found by a stranger. And yet, she couldn't stop reading, drawn in by the emotion that poured from Arnaud's words. This letter, carefully folded and hidden for all these years, was a testament to a love that had outlasted even time itself.

She then noticed the last item in the compartment—a black-and-white photograph, also yellowed at the edges, of a woman in 1930s attire standing in a rural setting. The woman in the photograph, posing with a soft, playful smile, exuded a certain charm. She was young, with dark, wavy hair pinned up neatly, her face framed by curls that fell just at her ears. Her eyes were wide and expressive, full of life and laughter, and her features were soft but striking. The backdrop—a modest field with trees swaying in the distance—was simple, but the woman herself seemed to bring the image to life. Her presence radiated from the photograph, like she had just stepped out of the past.

Amelia's pulse quickened as she studied the woman's face. There was something about her, something naggingly familiar, that Amelia couldn't quite place. She stared at the photograph, tracing the woman's features with her eyes—her high cheekbones, the small curve of her lips, the spontaneous elegance of her hair, and the light in her eyes. Her mind raced, trying to remember where or if she had seen that face before. But it was just out of reach, lingering at the edges of her memory like a dream half-remembered.

Why did this woman seem so familiar?

Amelia stood there, staring at the photograph, her hands still trembling with excitement. Each discovery—the ring, the love letter, the photograph—felt like a piece of a puzzle she had yet to solve. A story she had yet to find. She had uncovered history before, but this was different. This wasn't a layer of grime she could simply clean away to reveal a forgotten artifact; this was a life, a love story, hidden beneath the surface of this unassuming box.

The thrill coursing through her reminded her of the days spent with her father at the Marché, when they would hold random objects and spin stories about the lives they might have touched. But here, there was no need to invent a tale—this was real, personal, something that had profoundly mattered to someone. That realization settled over her. It was a sense that she had stumbled upon something far more intimate than she could have imagined.

She couldn't help but wonder: Who was this woman? And what story had Arnaud and Eloise shared that had led to these treasures being hidden away?

Chapter 12

Arnaud's heart pounded as he and Eloise reached the steps of the Sacré-Cœur, its white domes glowing softly against the deepening sky. He tightened his grip on her hand as he turned to face her. Tonight, he would finally tell her.

"Eloise..." he began, his voice soft but heavy.

She turned to him with curiosity in her eyes. "Yes?"

Earlier, he had appeared unannounced at her flat, asking her to join him for a walk. She had been charmed by the spontaneity but sensed the unease beneath it.

Now, as he faced her, fear coiled in his chest. He was afraid—of breaking what they had, of the words he had to say. But he couldn't hold them back any longer.

"I need to tell you something," he said. "Something I should have told you long ago."

Eloise's eyes softened, though he could see a trace of worry. "You can tell me anything, Arnaud."

He took a deep breath with the confession lodged in his throat. "Eloise... my name, my full name..." He paused, glancing toward the darkening skyline. "I'm Arnaud Bourget."

Her eyes stayed on him, steady and searching, as the name settled between them. He braced himself and watched the flicker of emotions cross her face—confusion at first, then a dawning recognition.

She repeated it, almost to herself, "Bourget?"

He nodded and sighed, feeling almost instant relief at the revelation regardless of the outcome. "Yes. The château, the art... the merchant empire... all of it."

Eloise's hand slipped from his. Her gaze held him in place, unreadable. He could see the shift in her expression—her mind turning over this revelation, piecing together everything she thought she knew about him.

Arnaud swallowed hard before continuing, filled with desperation. "I didn't mean to deceive you. I thought that if I told you, you'd see me differently. And I couldn't bear that, Eloise. I couldn't bear for you to think of me as just another man from that world."

For a moment, neither spoke. He waited, heart in his throat, braced for her to recoil or to pull away. He had mentally prepared himself for that possibility.

Finally, Eloise lifted her gaze to him, her expression unreadable but calm. "Arnaud," she began softly, her voice steady yet tinged with a sadness he hadn't heard before. "Why didn't you trust me with this sooner?"

He bowed his head, ashamed. "I was afraid," he admitted. "Afraid that you'd see me as part of that world. But when I'm with you, I feel free from it."

She took his hand again, her touch steady and kind. Her eyes were clear, as though reading every truth he'd tried to conceal.

"Arnaud," she said softly, "I don't admire wealth, or privilege, or the society tied to a name like Bourget. I don't love the expectations they place on people, or the way they keep people in chains. But I do love you. And the man I know, he's not defined by any of that."

The words pierced through him, filling him with a relief so deep it was almost painful. She understood. She saw him beyond the legacy he had always thought would overshadow him.

He closed his eyes, overcome. "Thank you, Eloise," he whispered. "I'm so sorry I waited this long. I feared you'd turn away."

She cupped his cheek, her thumb brushing softly against his skin. "What matters is that you told me now." she said softly. "You are more than your family's name. When we're together, I see the man you are… the man you want to be."

He exhaled, his breath unsteady as the weight of his secret finally lifted. But the thought of facing his father still loomed, a shadow he couldn't outrun. "I don't know what the future holds," he admitted. "My family won't understand this. They won't understand us. But I can't lose you."

She gazed at him, steady and sure. "Then don't."

Chapter 13

Arnaud paced the length of his father's study, heart hammering, rehearsing his words. He no longer had anything to hide. Eloise knew the truth. Now, it was time his father did too. There was no going back.

The heavy oak doors opened, and Lucien Bourget entered with measured authority. His eyes fell on Arnaud, taking in the tension that betrayed the importance of this conversation.

"Arnaud," Lucien said with a hint of caution. "I was told you needed to see me?"

"Father," he began, his voice steady. "I need to speak with you."

Lucien's forehead creased slightly. "Is something wrong? The business—"

"No," Arnaud interrupted firmly. "This isn't about business. It's about… Eloise Leclair."

An almost imperceptible shift crossed Lucien's face. Arnaud knew his father had noticed his frequent absences and late returns from Montmartre. Now, after nearly a year of carefully guarding this part of his life, he was ready to speak.

Lucien set a stack of letters aside. "And… Eloise… is that the reason you've been slipping away so often?"

"Yes," Arnaud said. "She's someone I've come to know over this past year."

He continued to speak about her—about how they met, about how she made him feel, and about the passions that drove her. He described her creativity and brilliance as an artist, recounting everything that needed to be said. Though his heart felt lighter with each word, his tone remained steady and resolute. When he finished, he straightened, meeting his father's gaze.

"I love her, Father," Arnaud finished, the words coming quicker than he'd planned. "And I intend to marry her."

The silence that followed was suffocating. Lucien studied his son for a long moment, but revealed nothing. Arnaud braced himself for the rebuke, but none came.

At last, when Lucien spoke, his tone was unexpectedly level. "You understand what that would mean, don't you, Arnaud?"

"I do," he replied, his voice unwavering. "But it's a life I want, Father. With Eloise."

Lucien exhaled slowly and turned, eyes drifting to the portrait above the fireplace. It was a painting of Arnaud's late mother, Colette, captured in gentle brushstrokes, her expression serene yet full of life.

"She had nothing when we met," he said, his voice softer than before. "You know that. Some in society thought me foolish for pursuing her. Her family worked vineyards in the south—they weren't the type to host galas or hold influence. But she had warmth, Arnaud. She saw beauty in the simplest things, and that reminded me of what actually mattered."

A wistful smile flickered across his lips. "So I fought for her. And I never regretted it."

The admission caught Arnaud off guard. He had never heard his father speak of his mother this way, with such raw honesty. When Lucien turned to him again, his eyes held an emotion Arnaud had rarely seen.

"Your mother," Lucien continued, "was my rock, my compass. Without her, none of this would matter. Our legacy, the estate… it's nothing without love." He paused, a faint sadness coloring his voice. "When she died, I poured my heart into the only love I had left. Our family's legacy." He briefly paused in thought, still staring at Colette, before continuing. "Maybe I took it too far… Maybe I've been too hard… on you."

Lucien looked back at Arnaud who was standing motionless, mouth wide, before him. The admission left him speechless and he didn't know what to say.

Lucien continued, almost playfully. "So that's why you've been slipping away to Montmartre," Lucien mused. "I assumed you were avoiding your responsibilities. But love... I didn't expect that."

They both chuckled, as relief surged through Arnaud, softening the tension that had gripped him since he'd entered the room. He hadn't expected this understanding, this openness from his father. At last, Arnaud felt as though Lucien was speaking to him as a son, not just as an heir or business associate.

Lucien continued. "I understand your heart, Arnaud. More than you realize. I know what it's like to face society's judgment. But I won't pretend it's easy. You, of all people, must know the weight the Bourget name carries."

His tone shifted, now gentler. "I also know that love matters. Wealth and status mean little if you can't share them with someone who truly gives life meaning. Your mother taught me that."

Arnaud swallowed, emotion tightening his throat. "So… does that mean you accept Eloise?"

Lucien's gaze sharpened, his posture straightening. "I accept that you care for her—desperately, it seems. But you must understand what this means. Marrying a struggling artist from Montmartre invites scrutiny, especially from those who guard their exclusivity. Society won't welcome her easily. Even those closest to us may hesitate. Are you prepared for that?"

Arnaud fought against frustration. "Why should that matter? Didn't you always say our family's strength came from within? You, of all people, should understand, Father. Eloise isn't some trifling fling. I love her. That should matter more than the opinions of bored aristocrats."

A hint of empathy crossed Lucien's face. "It does matter. Believe me, it does. The Bourget name is more than a title. Generations have built this legacy—artists funded, factories run, commerce established. If we handle this poorly, or if you lose sight of your responsibilities, we risk everything." He held Arnaud's gaze. "I won't forbid you from marrying her, but I will ask you to consider the cost."

He paused again, as though weighing his next words carefully. "Perhaps," he said slowly, "it would be wise to start with a private ceremony. Something intimate. The world doesn't need to know everything at once —this way, you and Eloise can have your privacy, have your time to adjust before facing the inevitable scrutiny. The paperwork can come later, when the time feels right."

Arnaud's shoulders sagged, a mix of relief and apprehension settling over him. "You may be right," he said, his tone thoughtful. "I don't want her overshadowed by our name, nor do I want her scorned just because she doesn't come from money. That's not what she deserves."

Lucien moved closer, resting a hand on Arnaud's shoulder, gentler than he'd been moments ago. "Your mother walked that path. Yet she persevered. She gave me a reason to become a better man. I see that same strength in you and, if what you say of Eloise is true, I see it in her too." He let out a soft sigh. "If you're willing to fight for her—truly fight—then you have my blessing. But if you do this, you do it with full acceptance of the burdens that may come with it."

Arnaud felt tears threaten to rise, a mix of gratitude and apprehension. "Thank you, Father. I promise I won't let you down."

"Then," Lucien said, his voice softer now, "I give you my blessing."

With a turn, he walked to a tall cabinet by the window and retrieved a small, velvet-lined box, and extended his arm to his son.

Arnaud took it hesitantly, his heart pounding as he lifted the lid. Inside, nestled in deep blue velvet, was a ring—an heirloom gleaming in the dim light. The diamond, flawless, had been passed down through generations of Bourgets, its facets catching and fracturing the light into a thousand tiny stars.

"This belonged to your mother," Lucien said, with reverence. "And before her, my mother, and her mother before that. It has always been a symbol of commitment and loyalty."

His gaze moved to the band. "The leaves engraved here," he continued, "represent the growth of our family tree, each one marking a new chapter in our lineage. If you marry Eloise, she will become part of that legacy." He met Arnaud's eyes. "Give this to her as a sign of that."

Arnaud swallowed hard, overcome with emotion. "Thank you, Father. I promise I will honor it—and her."

Lucien nodded, the slightest hint of a smile on his lips. "Just as I once promised your mother," he said. "Go, then."

Arnaud closed the box carefully, gripping it tight as he turned for the door. His father had given him his blessing—but more than that, he had given him something unexpected. Understanding.

When Arnaud left the study, determination burned within him. He would ask Eloise to be his wife. It might not be easy, but with her, he would face it all.

And for the first time, he felt free.

Chapter 14

The shtiebel was hidden, tucked away in a secluded corner of the Marais. Unlike grand synagogues, shtiebels were intimate and humble where small groups gathered in a close community. Inside, soft candlelight flickered against ancient stone walls, casting a warm glow on the tall vaulted ceilings.

Arnaud stood at the front, his heart pounding as he adjusted his tie. He chose an understated suit for the occasion—deep charcoal and finely tailored, but free of the opulence that marked his life at Château Bourget. This day wasn't about the Bourget name or legacy. It was about Eloise and the promises they were about to make.

He glanced at Lucien, who stood to one side, his gaze steady, offering quiet support. His father's presence was both a comfort and a reminder of the line Arnaud was crossing—one that separated duty from desire, legacy from love.

The soft creak of the door drew Arnaud's attention, and as he turned, a smile spread across his face. There, Eloise entered with her parents, Bethany and Claude, close behind. She wore a simple white dress that brushed softly against her ankles, unadorned except for a thin blue ribbon at her waist. The dress suited her in every way—graceful, unpretentious, yet somehow radiant, as though she carried her own light. Her dark hair, usually pinned back or loosely falling around her shoulders, was swept into a gentle twist, a few stray curls framing her face. She was beautiful.

As she approached, Arnaud reached for her hand, feeling the warmth of her skin against his. At that moment, the world outside faded. This was their world now, hidden away from judgments of society, a sanctuary just for them.

The rabbi began the ceremony. Eloise's parents stood beside Lucien, their expressions thoughtful and sincere. Arnaud sensed that, while Bethany and Claude had their doubts about the life Eloise was about to enter, they had given their cautious acceptance. Lucien's face remained composed, but in his eyes, Arnaud caught something unexpected—a hint of contentment, perhaps even respect.

When the rabbi finished, Arnaud turned to Eloise, still holding her hand. He took a deep breath, steadying himself before starting his vows. The words were simple and honest, spoken only for her.

"Eloise," he said softly. "Today, I give you everything that I am. Not the name, not the legacy, but the man who stands before you. I vow to be your protector, your confidante, and your partner in all things. Together, we will build a life in the spaces where the world cannot touch us. And whatever may come, I swear to stand by you through it all."

Eloise's eyes glistened, and a soft smile formed on her lips as she held his hands tighter. She responded with the same confident strength Arnaud had always loved in her.

"Arnaud, I love you not for your name or status, but for your kindness, your passion, and the life we create together. I love you for *you!* Today, I vow to be your anchor and your shelter. Together, we will create a world of our own. No matter what comes, my love will be your shield, as your love has been mine."

As the rabbi signaled for the exchange of rings, Lucien stepped forward, offering the small velvet box that contained the Bourget heirloom.

Arnaud opened it, lifting the antique, floral-engraved band nestled within. With care, he slipped it onto Eloise's finger. She gazed down at the ring, a sense of wonder in her expression as the diamond caught the light, reflecting softly in her eyes. In that moment, Arnaud felt something change—the ring was no longer just his family's past, but the future they were building together.

The rabbi pronounced them husband and wife, and Arnaud's heart swelled. He lifted Eloise's hand and pressed a soft kiss to her fingers, the scent of lavender lingering in a memory he knew he would cherish forever. They were each other's now, united by the love and promises they had chosen to share.

The rabbi closed his book and stepped back, giving them a moment just for themselves. For these few precious seconds, the world fell away, leaving only the hush of the dimly lit room and the strength of their vows. Eloise closed her eyes and rested her head against her husband's chest, comforted by the gentle rhythm of his heartbeat.

Just as Arnaud was about to speak, a distant bell tolled, its sound echoing through the stone walls—a reminder that life beyond this moment continued. Beyond these walls, Europe was changing. But here, in the candlelight, there was only them.

Eloise must have felt it too. She looked up at him, her expression thoughtful, as if savoring the quiet before the unknown. Without a word, she placed a hand against his cheek, grounding them in the present. Arnaud pulled her closer, grateful for her warmth, her certainty.

"Whatever comes, we'll face it together," he promised.

Eloise nodded, content to be held by the man she loved, trusting the strength they found in each other.

They left the shtiebel and stepped into the soft morning light of the narrow street. Waiting nearby were Lucien and Eloise's parents, their presence reserved but supportive.

Lucien approached, meeting Arnaud's gaze with an understanding. He reached out and placed a hand on his son's shoulder. "The world won't make this easy. But you have her love."

Arnaud nodded with gratitude swelling in his chest. This was a moment of acceptance—no grand speeches, just a gentle acknowledgment of what mattered most.

Bethany held her daughter close, whispering heartfelt blessings and hopes for the future. Claude respectfully nodded his head to Arnaud, his eyes steady while acknowledging this new chapter.

And then, with nothing left to say, Eloise's parents and Lucien departed, leaving the newlyweds alone on the building's steps.

This was their beginning. From here, they could build anything.

Arnaud turned to Eloise, the morning illuminating her face. Joy sparkled in her eyes, and he couldn't help but smile as he tilted his head slightly. "Shall we go home... Madame Bourget?"

Eloise's lips curved into a playful grin. "But of course, Monsieur Bourget."

They walked side by side into an uncertain future. But together, they *were* certain.

Chapter 15

Paris, Modern Day

Several years earlier...

The smell of linseed oil and solvents filled the air as Amelia sat hunched over her workbench, deep in concentration. The hum of the graduate studio surrounded her, the steady rhythm of brushes against canvas mingling with the indistinct murmur of students discussing their projects. But for Amelia, the world beyond her workspace faded into the background. She was absorbed in the challenging restoration that lay before her—a painting, nearly lost to time, depicting a lively Parisian salon scene.

The painting was signed "Henri Vallin," though little else was known about the artist or the work's provenance—the documented history of ownership that traced each painting's journey. Donated anonymously to the Museum of Jewish Art and History in the 1950s, the canvas had suffered severe water damage over the years, the vibrant life once captured on its surface now dulled and faded. The painting had arrived in the studio without a frame, a sign that it must have been stored separately, the canvas left to bear the brunt of the water that had marred its beauty.

The scene itself, despite the damage, was striking. At over two meters tall, the canvas featured an elegantly dressed woman lounging in a Parisian salon. Her posture was relaxed, like she had been candidly captured mid-conversation with figures just beyond the edge of the frame—giving the illusion she was speaking directly to the viewer. Tall windows out of sight flooded the room with warm sunlight, catching the gold accents on the furniture and the soft sheen of her silk dress. The brushstrokes were loose and confident, suggesting a fleeting moment caught in time, yet there was care in the details—the intricate embroidery of the fabric, the delicate gesture of her hands, the subtle play of light on skin.

Vallin's skill in weaving all these elements into the canvas showcased his mastery as an artist.

But the colors had faded, and the once-vivid hues of gold, emerald, and deep sapphire were now muted and washed out. Where the water had seeped into the canvas, streaks of damage ran like ghostly veins through the image, distorting the once-clear lines. Features had blurred, especially in the lower half of the painting where the water had pooled. The furniture had become shapeless, the floor warped. What should have been crisp and defined was now a pale imitation, just like the painting had slipped into a dream.

Amelia studied the woman in the scene, her eyes drawn to her immediately. She was seated on a plush velvet chaise with an elegant yet relaxed posture, and appeared to be listening intently to the conversation around her. Dark, wavy hair framed her face, complementing her wide, expressive eyes and a slight smile that gave her undeniable charm. The dress she wore was a rich emerald green. It had suffered the worst of the water damage, and the fabric now appeared mottled and dull. But her face, though faded, still held a certain life and managed to escape the worst of the painting's decay.

Amelia spent countless hours painstakingly working to restore the painting, determined to breathe life back into the faded image. The restoration process was slow and methodical. Every step needed to be a precise balance between preservation and revival, with no room for error. As she once read in a famous quote by Leonardo da Vinci, "Art is never finished, only abandoned." For Amelia, the goal was to rescue this painting from abandonment and to ensure that its story could be told once more.

The first stage was surface cleaning. Using ultra-fine brushes and cotton swabs dipped in a custom solution, she gently removed layers of dirt and grime that had accumulated over the years. Each movement was deliberate, her touch as light as possible to avoid damaging the fragile paint layer beneath. This process was like peeling away layers of time— gradually, the original vibrancy of the painting began to peek through.

Once the surface was clean, Amelia turned to the most critical part of the restoration: stabilizing the paint. The water damage had caused the pigments to lift from the canvas, creating delicate cracks and blisters where the paint had flaked. To fix this, Amelia used a tiny syringe to inject an adhesive behind the loose areas. She was careful to apply just the right amount, ensuring that the adhesive would bind the pigments without seeping through and discoloring the image. After each injection, she pressed lightly with a spatula, flattening the paint back into place and smoothing it out like a surgeon repairing delicate skin.

Amelia also had to deal with areas where the paint had entirely eroded. Here, she employed a technique called "inpainting." This involved carefully matching the missing colors to the original palette. Using pigments specially mixed to match the painting's original tones, she rebuilt these areas stroke by stroke, layering thin washes of color, gradually restoring the depth and texture lost to age. It was essential that her brushstrokes followed the artist's original direction and energy, ensuring that the restoration remained faithful to the painter's intent.

One particularly challenging part was the water-stained section near the bottom, where the image had become distorted and blurred. She had little to guide her—no reference materials, no sketches, no history on Henri Vallin or his subjects. Everything she needed to restore the painting had to come from what was left on the canvas. For this, Amelia meticulously mixed pigments to match the faded colors, applying them in thin, translucent layers, gradually rebuilding the lost areas. Her brushstrokes mimicked those of the original artist, small and precise, following the direction and texture of Vallin's hand. Each stroke was careful, with the goal of making the restored areas almost invisible to the untrained eye—a hallmark of good restoration. As one of her mentors had once said, "The best restoration is the one you never notice."

It was tedious work, but for Amelia, it was the perfect blend of art and science—a process that required both technical skill and artistic intuition. This blend ran in her blood. Her father, William, had been a wellliked art history professor at the Sorbonne, and her mother, Maggie, a renowned infectious disease biologist. The three of them had moved from Boston after Maggie received a prestigious grant to study and isolate the effects of HIV at the Institut Pasteur in Paris. Perseverance and patience were second nature to Amelia. So, as hours melted into days working on the painting, she welcomed the meticulousness, knowing that every small change brought the painting one step closer to its original state.

For weeks, she worked on the woman's portrait, reconstructing the soft curve of her lips, the shadows around her high cheekbones, the light glinting in her wide eyes. Amelia had grown intimately familiar with her, so much so that she could almost see her even when she wasn't at the studio. She had restored dozens of paintings by then, but something about this woman—the elegance of her posture, the delicate strength in her gaze—had lingered with Amelia. Day after day, the woman's face became more vivid in her memory, until it was ingrained in her mind as if she had known her.

As Amelia brushed the final touches onto the painting, she stepped back to admire her work. The room of the scene, once faded and forgotten, now seemed alive again. The woman in the emerald dress appeared in her spontaneous Degas-like pose with light filtering in through the tall windows, drawing warm shadows across her. She was now restored to her full vibrancy, sitting at the heart of it all, her presence commanding yet understated, as though she held the room in her gentle gaze.

As the painting was carefully packed for transport back to the Jewish Museum, Amelia had no idea, standing there in her graduate studio, that this would not be their last encounter.

Chapter 16

And then it hit her.

The flashback jolted through Amelia's mind, pulling her back to the grad school studio—the scent of linseed oil, the hum of students at work, the canvas spread before her. The painting she had painstakingly restored.

The woman in the emerald dress.

Amelia inhaled sharply, her pulse quickening. She stared at the photograph from the toolbox, her heart hammering. The resemblance was undeniable—the high cheekbones, the expressive eyes, the delicate curve of her smile.

It was her.

The painting had been one of her first major projects, arriving at the studio with no frame, no clear provenance, its history obscured by time and circumstance. The painter, *Henri Vallin*, was an unknown name—possibly an up-and-coming artist, *very* skilled, but one who had never quite made it into the annals of art history. The museum had hinted at Nazi looting, but nothing had ever been confirmed, and no one had been able to trace it to its rightful owner.

And now, here she was.

If this woman had been immortalized in such a lavish painting, she had mattered. She had belonged to a world of elegance, wealth—perhaps even power. But why had someone hidden her away? Who had tucked her into a forgotten toolbox, wrapped in cloth, sealed in time?

She stared down at the ring, the love letter, and the photograph, her mind desperately trying to piece together the connections. They weren't just artifacts. They were deliberate. Pieces of a life someone had tried to preserve—or erase.

A shiver ran down Amelia's spine. Why had the painting been separated from its frame? Why had the photo been hidden away? And what secrets did the woman in it hold?

She had spent weeks bringing the woman's image back to life, stroke by careful stroke, never realizing she was restoring more than a painting —she was uncovering a story. A story someone had tried to bury.

She gripped the edge of the table, steadying herself.

This wasn't just a coincidence.

It was a message.

The puzzle was still incomplete, but the pieces were falling into place. She didn't know where it would lead, only that she had to see it through.

There was no turning back now.

Chapter 17

Nadia stepped out of the car into the crisp morning air, the scent of birch and frost sharp against her senses. Before her stood Sergei Shchukin's estate, its pale blue façade standing stark against the gray winter sky. The overnight train from St. Petersburg had offered her a rare escape from her father's presence, and as she approached her thirtieth birthday, she embraced the independence of traveling alone. Moscow, with its grandeur and heavy history, felt like another adventure waiting to unfold.

The estate's baroque splendor was both imposing and inviting. Pilasters framed tall, narrow windows capped with floral and shell motifs—remnants of an era steeped in opulence. Wrought-iron balconies clung to the structure like aged jewelry, their scrollwork softened by time. The palace exuded grandeur, but Nadia wasn't here for its architecture.

She was here for the art. For the collection that had created a legend.

A housekeeper greeted her at the entrance and led her through a maze of rooms, each one offering a glimpse into Sergei's world. Paintings filled every single wall; there wasn't a bare space to be found. In the morning glow peering through the windows, the canvases seemed alive with light and color. In one room, a large Matisse hung over a doorway, its dancers exuding joy as if celebrating the collection itself. Yet, despite the sheer number of works housed here, each painting seemed to hold its own, each telling its own story of a time when art was simply art, not weighed down by politics or power.

The housekeeper guided Nadia into a larger sitting room, and there he was: Sergei Shchukin, seated by the window overlooking the frost-covered garden. He rose to greet her, his smile warm and surprisingly kind.

"Nadia," he said warmly. "I'm so pleased you could come."

She returned his smile, unsure what to expect. "Thank you, Sergei. It's… remarkable, really, to be surrounded by so many masterpieces in one place."

He chuckled, his gaze drifting toward a Degas on the far wall. "They're pieces of history, you know. I've tried to keep them safe from the world that would see them as mere assets. But now…" He exhaled, his expression darkening. "Now, I wonder how much longer I can protect them."

Nadia picked up on the fear in his tone. "Why? The collection is safe here, isn't it? With your resources—"

He raised a hand, stopping her gently. "Resources mean little when entire ideologies are at stake. In my homeland, art is no longer something to be celebrated—it's something to be controlled." His voice dropped lower. "It's a tragedy in the making."

They took their seats, and Sergei spoke of the relentless efforts of the Bolsheviks to suppress individual expression, and how famine and fear had tightened their grip under Stalin. His words shook her. He spoke of friends and family lost to the regime—artists and thinkers whose only crime had been to love something more than the state. "Art used to connect us," he said, his voice edged with anger. "Now, it's either a weapon or a threat. It challenges order, invites people to think beyond what they're given. That makes it dangerous. And so, they strip it of its power, mold it into something uniform and safe."

Nadia's curiosity grew as she listened to his words. His reverence for these paintings went beyond admiration—it was personal. "You speak of art as if it's more than a possession," she ventured, feeling her way through her thoughts. "Most collectors see their pieces as symbols of wealth or legacy, but this… it sounds like something else. Almost like a form of rebellion."

A glimmer of something appeared in Sergei's eyes—understanding, perhaps, or even relief. "That's because it is!" he replied. "Art is one of the last places where individuality still exists, untouched by power. It's something they haven't fully taken yet, something that still breathes life into a world that's rapidly suffocating." He glanced toward a Monet, the fading Parisian light captured in delicate strokes. "I don't just collect them to preserve them, Nadia," he said slowly. "I collect them to resist. To hold on to art is to hold on to the memory of something pure—something they can't corrupt."

His words struck her like a realization she had always felt but never voiced. He wasn't just a collector. He was a guardian of something essential, something fragile. His collection wasn't just a tribute to beauty—it was an act of defiance.

"Then your collection… lives, in a way," she said, leaning closer, captivated by his vision. "Not just in these rooms, but beyond them."

Sergei nodded. "These paintings aren't just beautiful," he said. "They are proof that something beautiful once existed. That something still matters." His voice lowered. "I'm not their owner, Nadia. I'm their custodian—their steward. I protect them for those who will come after us, for those who might forget if no one fights to preserve them."

A shiver passed over her. He wasn't speaking about paintings—he was speaking about history itself. She leaned in slightly, drawn to his conviction.

"And what happens if we lose that memory?" she asked. "If we can't hold on to it?"

Sergei's eyes darkened. "Then we lose more than paintings," he said simply. "We lose a part of ourselves."

For a long moment they fell silent, letting his words settle. Nadia realized that in Sergei, she had found someone who saw the world as she had never dared to. Art wasn't just something to be admired—it was something to be defended. Something that, if lost, would leave them all diminished. It wasn't a luxury. It was hope.

She raised her head and met his gaze with a hint of admiration. "I wish I could say I understood," she admitted. "I've never had to fight for the things I love. Art has always felt safe, like a refuge. But listening to you… perhaps it's time I see it as more."

Sergei's gaze softened, and he leaned forward. "Nadia, *most* people haven't had to consider such things. But I see in you a certain strength—a curiosity—that could withstand such tests." He paused, studying her carefully. "Have you ever been in a situation where the very things that make you who you are were called into question, forced into silence?"

A memory stirred within her, one she hadn't voiced in years. The diplomat—her mother's favored candidate, handpicked for his status, his connections, and his polished reputation. It had been a match of strategy, not affection, created to solidify the Vallois family's political standing.

Her mother had been relentless in her meddling, and Nadia could only watch, trapped beneath expectation, as arrangements took shape.

The courtship was hollow—a performance where she was meant to smile, nod, and eventually yield.

Her father, Étienne, had played the role of an amused spectator, never pushing, never demanding—just offering observations when they were alone. *"If you can't love him, ma chérie, then don't marry him. Your mother will wail, declare it a tragedy, and likely spend a week mourning in bed. But she'll survive."*

Nadia had hesitated—until the moment she didn't. She had refused, voice steady, gaze unflinching. In front of her mother, in front of the diplomat, in front of all those who assumed she would be an obedient daughter.

The fallout had been immediate. Her mother was horrified, launching into a tirade about wasted opportunities and a future Nadia would regret. The Vallois name carried weight—how could she be so reckless? But her father had simply leaned back in his chair, watching with silent approval, as though he had known all along that his daughter would never be anything less than herself.

That was the day her family saw her as something more than a pawn to be positioned for advantage. They saw her as a woman who would stand up for herself.

"Yes," she said in a low voice. "I have," as she proceeded to describe it briefly, not dwelling on details.

Sergei's eyes softened with understanding as he listened, and Nadia felt truly seen in a way she never had before. She continued, the words rushing out before she could second-guess them.

"I felt like an artifact myself—like I was owned—like something to be polished and displayed, to be moved as one sees fit. But I refused. I rebelled." She looked away, heat rising to her cheeks. "My mother was furious."

"And your father?" Sergei asked, his tone careful.

A small, wry smile touched her lips. "Later, when we were alone, he just looked at me for a long moment, then he chuckled and said, *'That's my girl.'* Like he'd been expecting it all along."

Sergei's expression shifted, with admiration in his eyes. "And that was the day you became more than their daughter. You chose your own path, stood up for yourself—not for duty, not for expectation, but because you knew what you wanted. And that," he said, with certainty, "is freedom."

Over the following weeks, Nadia found herself returning to Sergei's estate from St. Petersburg again and again, drawn by something she couldn't yet name. Though he had lived slightly more years than she, their minds moved in tandem, their conversations spanning art, politics, and the delicate balance between preservation and rebellion. The years between them felt irrelevant in the face of their shared curiosity.

As time passed, their connection settled into something meaningful and undeniable. Nadia found herself drawn to Sergei's resilience, to the way he spoke of history's fragility with a reverence she'd never encountered. Here was a man who had lost so much and yet still clung to something pure, something unbreakable. A man who refused to let beauty vanish, even as the world conspired to erase it.

They sat together one chilly evening, bathed in the warm light from the fireplace, the space between them charged. Nadia noticed the slight lines of strain around his eyes, but also the gentleness in his hands resting on his knee, close enough to brush against her own. She dared to ask a question that had lingered on her mind for some time.

"Sergei, how do you find the strength to keep going? To keep fighting for these things when it would be so easy to give up?"

He glanced at her, holding her eyes for a moment before he spoke. "Because I must. The world is intent on taking and taking, Nadia. It's up to people like us to preserve what we can, to protect the memories that keep us whole." His gaze grew distant, like he was looking beyond the walls of his home, beyond the reaches of time. "This regime might strip me of everything, but they cannot erase the spirit of what I've preserved. And in that small defiance, there is hope."

For the first time, Nadia felt the beginnings of a fierce desire stir within her—a desire to be part of something greater, to fight for something beyond her father's world of diplomacy and influence. Each visit to his estate felt like an entry into a world of secrets and memories, a place where they could talk freely without the weight of expectation and duty pressing down upon them.

———

After Nadia returned to Paris, they began exchanging letters, their words filled with thoughts of art and freedom, stories of resistance, and musings on the future. In ink and paper, their bond deepened—not just an exchange of ideas, but a promise. A promise to fight, to resist, and to protect the legacy of those who came before.

One evening, Nadia sat with one of Sergei's letters in her hands, tracing the familiar strokes of his script. She had met no one like him—someone who had lost so much yet still fought to preserve what mattered. And yet, there was something more. He was slightly older, yes, but somehow the years between them felt inconsequential—an afterthought overshadowed by the connection they shared. In his words, she found a kind of courage her father's ambitions had never inspired. It wasn't about grand transformations or sudden revelations, but about seeing things a bit differently and valuing what lay beyond politics and power.

The thought of this new purpose filled her with a sensation that she could not explain. Sergei had shown her that to truly protect something, one had to be willing to risk everything for it. Could she do the same?

That night, as she lay in bed, he lingered in her mind—the certainty behind his words, the defiance in his eyes. A restlessness stirred within her. The covers felt stifling, and she pushed them away, letting the cool night air slip over her skin.

She thought of his hands—strong, expressive, always in motion when he spoke, as if shaping his ideas in the air. His mind had captivated her first, but it wasn't just that anymore. It was the way he leaned in when he spoke, the way his voice softened when he was deep in thought. It was the way he looked at her like she mattered.

She liked him.

And with that realization, something settled deep inside her. Not just admiration. Not just attraction. *Something more.* Warmth stirred beneath her ribs, revealing something raw and unshaken.

Purpose.

She exhaled, steadying herself.

She would help him.

Somehow.

Chapter 18

Amelia sat in her studio with thoughts of her discovery churning. The woman in the *Vallin* she'd restored in grad school had somehow found her way back into her life, bringing an avalanche of questions. Who was she? How had she been immortalized in a lavish painting and then reduced to an image tucked away in a forgotten toolbox?

Her eyes flickered to the antique ring resting on the handkerchief. The diamond gleamed, untouched by time, yet now, knowing its connection to the woman, it seemed even more perplexing. Why had it been hidden away?

Determined to uncover more, Amelia knew she needed an expert. The size of the diamond, its intricate floral engraving, and its surprising presence in such a hidden compartment all pointed to something valuable. But how valuable? And why conceal it?

A quick call to Jacques, a trusted Parisian jeweler whom Amelia had worked with on several previous restoration projects, set the plan in motion. Jacques wasn't just any jeweler—he was a master of his craft, a wealth of knowledge who could trace a piece's origins with a glance. If anyone could unlock the ring's secrets, it was him.

———

The bell above the jeweler's door chimed as Amelia stepped inside, bringing with her the scent of cigarette smoke from the bustling Left Bank. The shop, tucked away off Rue Boneparte, felt like a time capsule. Its vintage décor, with worn wooden counters and brass accents, matched the old-world charm of the surrounding neighborhood. Outside, the murmur of conversation from a nearby café mixed with the occasional honk of scooters, but inside, the atmosphere was quiet and intimate.

Rows of velvet-lined cases displayed glittering rings, necklaces, and brooches, all illuminated by soft golden light that reflected off the polished glass. The shop carried a faint, musty scent of aged velvet and wood, with a hint of earthiness that spoke of its age.

Behind the counter stood Jacques, a tall, gray-haired man with a magnifying loupe clipped to his glasses. His eyes lit up as he recognized Amelia, the years spent unraveling the mysteries of precious objects evident in his hunched posture.

"Ah, mademoiselle Amelia," he greeted her warmly. "It has been too long. What mystery do you bring me today?"

Amelia managed a smile, though her mounting curiosity tempered her excitement. "It's good to see you, Jacques. I have something… unusual."

She reached into her bag and carefully pulled out the ring, still cradled in the folds of the handkerchief. Placing it on the counter, she said, "I need to know more about this diamond ring. Its age, its value, anything you can tell me."

Jacques picked up the ring with care, turning it over in his hand as he examined the intricate floral engraving on the band. "Beautiful," he murmured. "You don't see work like this often anymore. Let's have a closer look."

He slipped the loupe over his eye and held the ring closer to the light, his gaze narrowing with an intensity that made everything around them seem to stand still. Amelia watched, her heartbeat quickening with every passing second. As the silence stretched on, it amplified her anticipation. She studied his face, searching for clues in the minute shifts in his expression, but Jacques gave nothing away. The ring spun slowly in his fingers, catching glimmers of light that danced across the walls—but still he said nothing.

The tension in Amelia's chest tightened as the seconds ticked by. Finally, Jacques straightened, the loupe moving up from his eye as he set the ring down with care. His forehead remained creased and his expression was darkened by something Amelia hadn't expected.

"I'm afraid this is not what you think," Jacques said, his voice low with a note of disappointment.

Amelia's stomach dropped. "What do you mean?" she asked, leaning forward.

Jacques hesitated. "The craftsmanship is exquisite—early 20th century, by my estimation… perhaps older. The engraving on the band is authentic and quite rare. But… the diamond… it's not real."

Amelia blinked, for a second thinking she had misheard him. "What?"

Jacques nodded somberly. "It's glass paste."

His words lingered as Amelia stared at the ring, struggling to process what he said. The shimmering stone that had seemed so real, so valuable, was nothing but a carefully crafted imitation?

"Glass paste?" Amelia echoed with confusion. "What does that mean?"

Jacques folded his hands, his face taking on a look of expertise. "Glass paste, or '*pâte de verre*…' it's a form of imitation diamond. They commonly used it as a diamond simulant in the 18th and 19th centuries. But we still see it in the mid-20th century as well. It's created by melting glass with lead oxide to increase the brilliance and refractive index. This allows the gem to mimic the sparkle of a genuine diamond. Some pieces were used for costume jewelry, but others—like this—were carefully crafted to look authentic."

He turned the ring under the light. "The quality is remarkable. Someone went to great lengths to make it look this good. But at the end of the day, it's still glass."

Amelia had a perplexed look on her face as she leaned in, her mind racing. *Then why hide it?*

Jacques didn't know about the false-bottomed toolbox or any of the other treasures. He didn't know that someone had taken deliberate steps to conceal this ring, treating it as though it was something of immeasurable value—something worth protecting. Why would someone go to such lengths to hide a counterfeit diamond? It didn't make sense.

"Do… people usually treat glass paste with much care?" she asked carefully.

Jacques shrugged gently, his eyes thoughtful. "It depends? Glass paste is not valuable in the traditional sense, but sometimes, the value of an item is not in its materials but in what it represents. This ring could have sentimental meaning—something beyond what it is." He studied her, sensing her unease. "There are many secrets hidden in a piece like this."

Amelia nodded, but her mind had already drifted. To Jacques, she seemed frozen, her gaze fixed somewhere beyond the walls of the shop, lost in thought. She was partially there, but mostly somewhere else— caught up in the problem that was unfolding in her mind.

"Amelia?" Jacques' voice broke through her trance, his tone laced with concern.

The sound pulled her back, her eyes refocusing on the present. She blinked, forcing herself to shake off the haze. "Sorry," she murmured. "I was just... thinking."

Carefully, she wrapped the ring back in the handkerchief and thanked Jacques with a warm but distracted smile. Reaching into her bag, she pulled out a 50 euro note.

"Oh! Mademoiselle, please!" Jacques protested, raising his hands. "This is unnecessary. We go back many years—"

She held up a hand, cutting him off. "I insist, Jacques. It's been too long, and I appreciate your help. Merci."

Jacques hesitated, then smiled gently, his eyes softening. "As you wish. *Merci.* You know where to find me if you need anything else!"

The bell chimed again as she stepped onto the street. The air smelled of fresh bread and coffee from a nearby café, but her appetite was gone. She tightly clenched the ring inside the small handkerchief, lost in thought as she wandered the narrow, ivy-lined streets of the Left Bank.

Jacques' words replayed in her mind. *"There are many secrets hidden in a piece like this."*

The late afternoon sun stretched across the quaint Parisian buildings, bathing them in a warm, golden hue. The city hummed around her, but Amelia felt as though she were walking through a different Paris—a Paris of the past, where a woman in an emerald dress had once been painted, remembered, and then forgotten.

A counterfeit diamond, carefully concealed. A hidden photograph. A love letter. Fragments of a larger mystery, just out of reach.

She paused outside a café, tempted by the scent of fresh espresso, but the thought of sitting still was unbearable. Instead, she reached for her phone, hesitating as she considered her next move. She could return to the studio, lay everything out, look for something she had missed. But even then, she felt like this was only the beginning.

A pang of longing hit her. *If only dad were here.* He'd know exactly what to do. He always had the instinct, the knack for peeling back layers others would miss, a talent she'd admired since she was a child. They had spent countless hours solving puzzles, tackling challenges that seemed impossible, asking each other *"what's next?"* and *"but what about…?"* More than ever, she wished she could hear his voice now, steady and certain, urging her forward.

She could almost feel him beside her, nudging her to keep going, reassuring her that every mystery has a key if you're willing to look closely enough.

That thought was enough.

Amelia tucked the ring and phone back into her bag as her persistence hardened. She needed to dig deeper. Who was this woman? How had her life become entangled in these relics of the past? And what truth had someone tried so hard to bury?

There was more to this story—something just out of reach, waiting to be uncovered. And whatever it was, Amelia was determined to find it.

Chapter 19

Nadia stood in the soft light of the Matisse Room, her eyes tracing the flowing lines of *La Danse*, a piece Sergei had commissioned from Matisse in 1909. Its bold strokes and vibrant colors hinted at a sunset somewhere far away, where people danced freely, in a world untouched by fear. Their movements were fluid, alive, uninhibited, and profoundly human.

She felt Sergei's presence beside her, his gaze resting on her. Not in a demanding way, but warm, peaceful, as if he were admiring her transformation over the past year.

By now, these visits to his home were a familiar routine, and something that had become essential to her. And as evening settled over Moscow, a hushed snow blanketed the grounds, muffling the world in a stillness that heightened the intimacy within.

She turned, catching his eye, and for a moment they simply looked at each other. A surge of heat stirred in her chest, sending her pulse racing. The painting seemed to mirror something between them: a shared intensity simmering beneath the surface, passion restrained but undeniable. Nadia shifted her weight slightly, as though to steady herself, but her breath quickened all the same.

A strange, almost surreal realization washed over her. Here, in Sergei's home, she was not the diplomat's daughter or the cultured socialite. She was just herself. And Sergei, the enigmatic Russian collector, was no longer an untouchable figure, but someone as vulnerable and as real as she was. Their differences fell away, leaving them as two people bound by the connection and purpose they now shared.

"Nadia," he said softly, breaking the silence. His voice was calm. "There are times I look at these walls, these paintings, and wonder how long any of it will survive."

His words made her heart tighten. She knew what he meant. Everything he had worked to protect stood on fragile ground. "It's terrifying, isn't it?" she said. "To realize that everything we love, everything we are… it could just vanish."

He nodded, his gaze holding hers. "And yet, it's that very fragility that makes it worth preserving, worth fighting for. Individuality, friendship… love—these are the things that make life worth living, Nadia. Without them, what do we have left?"

Sergei reached for her hand, his grip warm despite the cold pressing at the windows.

"To fight for something you love, to refuse to let it be taken… it's not easy. But it's necessary." His gaze swept the room before returning to hers.

Nadia swallowed, caught between admiration and something deeper. She had come here for art, but Sergei had given her something she never expected: purpose.

"You've shown me something I never understood before," she said. "Art isn't just meant to be admired. It's meant to be defended."

He reached up and cradled her cheek—a fleeting touch, but one that sent warmth spiraling through her. In that moment, everything else —her heritage, her family's expectations—all seemed to dissolve.

"Nadia," he said warmly. "I've lived through revolutions, seen the world tear itself apart. But I've never met someone who makes me believe it's still worth fighting for."

Her pulse quickened. She knew he wasn't speaking of art anymore.

His hand moved back to hers, his thumb tracing the ridge of her knuckles. It wasn't just art and politics that bound them. It was trust. Respect. And something deeper that had been building, layer by layer, until now.

He shifted closer, the firelight casting gentle shadows across his face, softening his sharp features. His eyes searched hers with an intensity that made it impossible to look away.

"Marry me, Nadia," he whispered, so softly she almost doubted her ears. "Let us build something together, something that even this world cannot destroy."

The words landed softly, but their weight sent her heart into a freefall.

And for a moment, time seemed to stop.

She saw the future stretched before her—uncharted, filled with both beauty and loss, joy and heartbreak. She knew this was more than a marriage. It was a partnership. A shared mission. Together, they would stand against forces that sought to erase and control. Together, they would protect something precious.

But doubt crept in.

He was older—was it too much? His world was so different from hers: the distance between their cultures, their heritages, their lives up until now, felt vast. Could they bridge that gap? Could love and purpose truly be enough to overcome everything that stood between them?

This was her moment—to break free from the expectations that had bound her, to step into a life of meaning. A life she chose. The future might test them, but here, in Sergei's steady gaze, she felt strength.

Nadia took a breath, her heart pounding, knowing her answer would change everything.

Chapter 20

The Artisan's Lodge was cloaked in ivy and surrounded by wild gardens, a retreat nestled at the edge of Château Bourget's grounds. Though near the opulent château, the lodge was a world apart—a home where Arnaud and Eloise had built a life uniquely their own. Inside, the scent of oil paints mingled with the warmth of the brick fireplace, crackling as a low fire fought back the damp chill of the day. It was cozy.

Canvases leaned against the walls, a collection of unfinished sketches, Parisian landscapes, and familiar faces bringing the space to life. It was a place where Eloise could create freely, away from the grandeur she had never sought. Arnaud had gifted her the lodge when they married, understanding that while Château Bourget was his birthright, it could never truly feel like home to Eloise. Just like the heirloom diamond ring she couldn't wear, opting instead for a simple gold band, opulence was never where Eloise felt comfortable.

Shortly after their wedding, she made "Leclair" her middle name—not as a rejection of her new life, but as a declaration of who she was and where she came from. Though legally "Eloise Bourget," she refused to let her identity be consumed entirely by the Bourget name. She was a Leclair, born into a family of modest means, shaped by the vibrant streets of Montmartre and the raw, unpolished beauty of its artistic community. It wasn't an act of defiance, but one of pride—an unwavering statement that her roots, her artistry, and her past were integral to the woman she had become.

Arnaud admired this deeply. Her pride in her heritage, her ability to balance the weight of her past and present, only deepened his love for her. Together, they made the lodge their refuge, a place where Eloise could paint and Arnaud could escape the burdens of his family legacy.

No grand halls or glittering parties here—just the gentle hush of two people seeking peace amid an increasingly uncertain world.

In those quiet moments at the lodge, however, an unspoken sorrow lingered between them—a shared grief they rarely voiced but carried within them daily. They had both dreamed of children, of little feet pattering across the floor, and of a future where their love would live on through another generation. Yet, as the years passed and their hopes faded, the absence grew like a shadow over their lives, silent yet pervasive. They had tried to fill this hollow space with art, love, and each other, but there were times, particularly in the lodge's stillness, when the ache felt too deep to ignore. Eloise would often paint portraits of children, perfectly capturing their faces tender with life's promise. Arnaud would catch her gaze lingering on them a little too long, her smile softened by a bittersweet acceptance he, too, was understanding.

Though they had built something beautiful here, within these walls, even this place seemed fragile as the storm brewing beyond their gates drew closer each day.

Arnaud sat at his desk with newspapers and letters sprawled around him. His gaze was dark and unfocused, and his face was marked with lines of worry. Headlines screamed from the pages, words like *invasion* and *occupation* displayed alongside maps that showed Germany's grip tightening on Europe. France held its breath, waiting for the inevitable. Arnaud gripped the edge of the desk, his knuckles white. Five years of marriage had brought him and Eloise a haven. But it felt now as though the events raging beyond the estate would soon invade even their sacred space… *everyone's* sacred space.

A familiar rustle pulled him from his thoughts, and he looked up to see Eloise entering the room, a smile gracing her lips as she approached him. She wore her usual attire—a plain blouse with sleeves rolled up, a soft smudge of charcoal near her wrist from her latest sketch. Her presence softened the tension in his chest, but even in her eyes, he could see the same unease that had settled over all of France.

"You've been at that desk for hours," she said gently, her voice healing his troubled thoughts. "Step away with me for a moment."

After Lucien gave his blessing to their marriage and welcomed Eloise into the family, Arnaud had felt a renewed sense of responsibility to honor that support. He had thrown himself into the family business—

expanding it, protecting it, and preparing it for the uncertain times ahead.

Arnaud managed a smile and reached out for her hand. "I'm afraid I've been... lost in these," he admitted, gesturing to the papers. "Every report seems to bring darker news. Lucien insists we prepare for the worst, and... he's right."

She sat beside him, her voice calm. "Your father has always been a man of caution. But remember, no matter what, Château Bourget has endured for generations. It will survive this as well."

He sighed, his hand finding hers and holding it tightly. "It's more than the estate, Eloise. It's the businesses, the factories, and the workers—he's desperate to protect it all, and for good reason. The Nazis have begun targeting families like ours, confiscating private holdings, raiding businesses under the guise of 'requisitioning' for the war effort." He met her gaze and paused at the heaviness of his thoughts. "If they take these, they erase more than property—they erase everything the Bourget name has stood for."

Eloise's eyes softened, and she leaned closer. "Arnaud, your family's legacy is more than just the businesses and land. It's the countless artists you have sponsored, the beauty you've protected. It's in people's minds and hearts—it's in ours." She paused, searching his face. "We can't allow fear to make us forget who we are."

Arnaud took in her words, feeling their truth. The Bourget family was a foundation upon which artists had been able to rise, voices that might have been lost to poverty finding their way onto gallery walls, stages, pages, and museums. Artists who had struggled to find space in an elitist world had found in the Bourgets an unexpected ally. Together, he and Eloise had funded studios, paid for exhibitions, and supported galleries that dared to showcase unconventional work. This became a lifeline for those with raw talent but no resources, a way to elevate art and ideas that might have been discarded or overlooked.

Above all, Eloise's words reminded him that the heart of the Bourget legacy was in lifting others.

He closed his eyes and leaned into her touch, her presence steadying him like it always did. Eloise had a way of calming his doubts, reminding him of his strength when he couldn't see it himself. But that same grounding presence came from her own resilience—a strength that had only grown as the threat of war loomed over France. Her art, once a personal sanctuary, had transformed into something more. It had become a deliberate act of defiance, a way to protect and celebrate the culture she was intent to hold on to.

But her involvement went deeper than her canvases. He knew of her secret gatherings, the hushed meetings held behind closed doors of Parisian cafés, where writers, artists, and intellectuals came together to discuss the growing Nazi influence. She never talked about the meetings, but he recognized the way they weighed on her.

Late one evening, Arnaud was sitting by the fire when she returned. His eyes glanced over her, taking in the tension in her frame, the way her fingers tightened around the strap of her satchel, the urgency she tried, and failed, to mask.

"Eloise," he began softly, "you've been at those meetings again, haven't you?"

She looked away for a moment before meeting his gaze with a confident strength. "Yes," she admitted firmly. "They're becoming more organized. There's talk of what we can do to protect our culture from Nazi influence, to make sure that even if they occupy France, they cannot erase what makes us who we are."

Arnaud swallowed hard, fear tightening his chest. He admired her courage—no, he loved her for it. But the thought of her venturing into those dangerous circles, risking her safety for something so intangible, terrified him.

"Eloise," he said, struggling to keep his voice steady, "it's dangerous. The Gestapo... they're watching. They're already cracking down on people who speak out."

Her eyes softened, and she reached out, her hand cupping his cheek. "Arnaud, I know the risks. But I can't sit idly by while everything we love, everything we believe in, is threatened. Art isn't just a pastime. It's the soul of our country. If we lose it, if we allow them to take it... what's left of us?"

He closed his eyes, leaning into her touch, and felt the strength that radiated from her. She was right, of course. She always was. But that didn't make it any easier.

"I know," he said softly. "But the thought of something happening to you... I couldn't bear it, Eloise."

She pressed a gentle kiss to his forehead and lingered for a moment. "And I couldn't bear to leave you, Arnaud. But this—this is something I have to do. For us, for everything we've built together."

The fire crackled between them, its warmth a sharp contrast to the cold settling in Arnaud's chest. He knew he couldn't change her mind. She was as fierce as she was kind, and it was that very strength that terrified him now.

In the weeks that followed, the atmosphere in France grew more uneasy as rumors spread that the Nazis would soon march into Paris. Arnaud spent hours in his study, poring over accounts and logistics alongside Lucien. Together, they worked to secure the family's assets, determined to protect what they could. The family businesses, the industrial holdings—these were more than just a source of income. Their operations provided livelihoods for hundreds of workers across Europe and their families. Losing them would mean losing not just the family legacy, but a vital part of their identity.

And yet, every evening, when he returned to the lodge, the worries would fade, if only for a little while. Eloise would be waiting, her hands still stained with paint, her eyes filled with a warmth that anchored him and gave him strength. They continued to share their fears, their dreams, and their hopes for a future that felt increasingly uncertain. Despite the darkness pressing in around them, their love had grown deeper and was the steady light that guided them both through the unknown.

One night, as they sat by the fire, Arnaud reached into his pocket and pulled out a small envelope.

"This from my father," he said grimly. "He... he wants us to prepare. To make arrangements to protect ourselves, the estate—everything. He's asked me to consider hiding some of the pieces, to keep them out of Nazi hands if they come."

Eloise's shoulders sagged as she read the letter. "It's come to that, then," she murmured with resignation.

Arnaud nodded. "If it comes to war, we may need to make sacrifices. We may need to leave this place behind. But... I won't leave you. Whatever happens, Eloise, I'm by your side."

She looked up, her eyes glistening with unshed tears as her gaze searched his face. Then, with a smile, she leaned forward and pressed a gentle kiss to his lips, sealing that promise.

But even as he held her close, she knew she couldn't tell him every-thing. The paths *she* had chosen carried risks she couldn't share—not yet.

For now, she would hold onto this moment.

And the fragile hope that they still had time.

Chapter 21

The fire crackled softly in the Artisan's Lodge, sending a gentle warmth through the small living space. Arnaud sat in his armchair, a thick woolen blanket draped over his knees as he read by the light of the fire. Eloise sat beside him, fingers weaving absently through his, her gaze distant.

For a moment, they could pretend the world outside did not exist. But beyond these walls, Europe teetered on the edge, and all of Paris felt the strain.

Eloise exhaled slowly. "Arnaud," she said, "there's something I need to tell you."

She turned to him, firelight reflecting in her eyes.

"The people I've been meeting with… they're… *we're* not just trying to save paintings. We're protecting books, ideas, memories—everything that makes up our culture. It's *all* art, Arnaud, and we're fighting to preserve it before it's erased, piece by piece."

He set his book aside and looked at her closely. He'd always known Eloise was dedicated, but now he saw a deeper persistence. Her work, her passion for protecting France's cultural heritage, had drawn her into a world he had only glimpsed from the edges. She was more than an artist; she had become a protector of France's spirit, and he could see that this fight meant as much to her as their life together.

"You're brave, Eloise," he said with admiration. "But this… this is different from anything we've faced before. The Nazis—"

"Are relentless," she finished for him. "I know. But we can't just sit here and watch it all fall to pieces. Our collection, yes, it's important—but it's just one thread in a tapestry they're unraveling. I've seen people risk everything to smuggle out literature, paintings, manuscripts—entire histories that the Reich wants to erase."

Arnaud swallowed hard. For years, his focus had been on protecting the Bourget legacy, securing what was his. But Eloise's battle was bigger. While he had fought for his family, she was fighting for everyone—for France itself. It made him question whether he had been too narrow in his perspective.

"You've always seen things differently than I have," he admitted. "While you fight for something bigger, I've been content on protecting what's ours. And maybe that's enough for me. My family, our legacy— that's where I stand."

Eloise's hand found his cheek, her eyes gentle. "Your family's legacy is more than just the objects you own, Arnaud. It's in the countless artists you've supported, the beauty you've preserved—not just on canvas, but in the spirit of creativity. What you've done matters. But if we only protect what's *ours*, then we lose sight of what makes it all worth saving."

She leaned in, voice soft but urgent.

"This isn't just about paintings on walls, Arnaud. The Nazis want to erase our voices. Our stories. Who we are. Every book burned, every painting seized, every idea silenced—it's another piece of us gone. This isn't just about beauty. It's about defiance. It's about freedom."

Her fingers traced a line on his cheek.

"They want us to forget. To wake up in a world where our history has been rewritten, where our dreams have been crushed under their boots. But we can't let them. We have to fight for more than *just* the Bourget name. We have to fight for the heart of our country."

She paused, exhaling.

"And if we don't stand up now, if we don't resist, then one day, we'll look around and there will be nothing left of us. Nothing of what we loved, nothing of what made us who we are. This is our fight, Arnaud. Not just for us, but for everyone who believes in a world where beauty, truth, and freedom still exist."

Arnaud felt a warmth flood his chest. Eloise was right; they couldn't let fear narrow their vision. This fight was about more than just art. It was about protecting everything that defined them as a people.

But the moment of resolve was fleeting.

Just days later, their fragile peace shattered.

————————

A mist clung to the streets as Eloise hurried through Montmartre, her heart hammering with every step. The meeting had run late, but she couldn't shake the unease pressing against her chest.

As the meeting concluded, a fellow resistant from her group pulled her aside his expression grim.

"Be careful," he warned. "Word from a contact in Vichy… the Nazis… they know of Château Bourget."

Eloise's eyes widened and her pulse quickened. "What do you mean?"

"They've started seizing private collections," he said. "And the Bourget collection is known across Europe. They will come for it."

A cold fear settled in her chest. She had known the danger was mounting, that their world was becoming more fragile with each passing day, but hearing the warning spoken aloud made it feel all too real.

Without another word, she turned and ran.

Through streets that felt smaller than they once had. Past cafés that no longer hummed with music. Everything about Paris felt darker, heavier, waiting under threat of the Gestapo's reach.

By the time she reached the lodge, her heart was racing, her cheeks flushed. She burst through the door and Arnaud looked up from his desk, alarmed.

"Eloise, what's wrong?" he asked, standing to meet her with worry in his eyes as she rushed across the room.

She caught her breath, forcing the words out. "The Nazis… they know about Château Bourget. They'll come for it, Arnaud. If they do, they'll take everything."

The color drained from his face. He had always known this could happen, but hearing it from Eloise made the threat feel immediate, inescapable.

"We've prepared as best we can," he said carefully, trying to keep his voice steady.

"But what if it's not enough?" Eloise pressed, her voice rising. "They're relentless, Arnaud. They'll find out. They're targeting everything—art, books, ideas. It's not just about the collection anymore. It's about erasing everything that makes us… us."

Arnaud placed his hands on her shoulders, steadying her, though his own pulse was racing. "I know, Eloise. I know. And that's why we can't give up now. We have to fight back any way we can."

Eloise looked up at him, her eyes searching his face. She saw determination. But she also saw the toll this burden was taking on him—the sleepless nights, the desperation hidden behind his every decision. She realized he was not only trying to protect his family's legacy, but also protect her and the world they both held dear. The burden was heavy, but she made a simple decision.

"Then let's do it together," she said, firm and confident. She placed her hand gently on his cheek. "We'll do whatever it takes."

Arnaud nodded with relief, softening his expression. They had always been stronger as a team, and he knew this bond would guide them through what lay ahead.

Outside, the wind howled, a warning of what awaited them. But inside, their hands entwined, their breaths mingling, and the world faded away.

Tonight was a rebellion of its own.

Their touch deepened, fueled by primal needs and a hunger to feel alive in the face of so much uncertainty. Anchored by raw desire, passion, and the love they shared, they didn't just defy the shadows clawing at their door—they mocked them.

This was their battlefield too, fought skin against skin, heartbeat against heartbeat, each moan and gasp a rallying cry that said:

We are here.

We will not yield.

We will not cower.

In that intimate blaze of hunger and devotion, they claimed victory —not over an enemy, but over fear itself. No war, no threat, could steal their flame.

Tomorrow, they would act.

But tonight, they lived.

Chapter 22

The Marais was a place where history didn't just linger—it was lived.

Nestled in the heart of Paris' 3rd arrondissement, its narrow cobblestone streets wound through a maze of medieval buildings, chic boutiques, and hidden courtyards. Once the center of aristocratic life in Paris, the neighborhood now held a vibrant mix of the old and the new, with Renaissance-era mansions standing side by side trendy cafés and art galleries.

Known for its rich Jewish heritage, the Marais was home to synagogues and bakeries that have been in operation for generations. The area brimmed with life, from the lively shops along Rue des Rosiers to the hidden corners where time seemed to have slowed.

Amelia had always loved this part of Paris. But today, as she moved through its streets, her usual admiration was drowned by the urgency in her chest.

The woman in the painting.

Her footsteps quickened as she neared the Museum of Jewish Art and History, housed in the historic Hôtel de Saint-Aignan. The museum's courtyard was a masterpiece of illusion—its symmetrical design a clever deception by 17th-century architect Pierre Le Muet. Where space had been too tight for a full left wing, he had crafted a façade of false windows and pilasters to create the impression of perfect balance. It was so well executed that most visitors never realized they were looking at a farce, the symmetry disguising something hidden in plain sight. It made her wonder, *"How much of what we see is a trick of perception?"*

Inside, the museum was hushed, its stillness amplifying the sound of Amelia's heels against the parquet floors. She barely noticed the security guard nodding in recognition as she passed. Her focus was singular.

"Unknown" by Henri Vallin.

She rounded the corner into the gallery with excitement, her breath catching as her eyes locked onto the piece that had once consumed weeks of her life.

A Parisian salon scene, bathed in warm afternoon light. An elegant woman in emerald silk, her dark curls framing her face, her lips curved in a soft, knowing smile.

The same smile from the photograph.

"Hello, my dear," Amelia whispered as she approached, holding her breath as she took in the scene once again. It was unmistakable—this *was* the woman. Amelia's heart raced with the certainty of it.

She leaned in, her eyes scanning the details she had painstakingly restored. This thing looked good! The soft light filtering in, the shimmering fabric, the golden glow spilling across the chaise—it was all coming back to her. But then, something sparked her attention.

Amelia's gaze moved down to the woman's hand, resting delicately on the arm of the chaise. There, she wore a striking ring, its band both delicate and ornate. It featured an intricate floral engraving that spiraled around the gold. At the center, a large round-cut diamond gleamed in pure, Titanium White, its brilliance cutting through the muted light of the gallery. Amelia's mouth widened in shock.

It was *the* ring.

The band, the petals, the diamond—it was unmistakably the same one she had found hidden in the toolbox!

But as she stared, trying to process what she was seeing, a chill ran down her spine. Something was wrong.

The ring in the painting sparkled in the sunlight, the stone catching the light just so—just like the one she had found. But there was a subtle, almost imperceptible difference.

The setting.

She counted the prongs around the gem in the painting—one, two, three, four. Four prongs held the diamond in place.

Amelia's mind raced. The ring she had found, the one sitting in her studio, had five prongs. She was certain of it.

Why would the artist—someone who seemingly paid such close attention to every intricate detail, from the embroidery on the dress to the delicate features of the woman's face—miss such a glaring difference?

Her thoughts tumbled over each other in confusion. She stared at the painting, the unease in her chest deepening. The connection between the photograph, the ring, and this painting was undeniable. But now this discrepancy only raised more questions.

Amelia's eyes flicked to the signature at the bottom left of the painting: *Henri Vallin*. It had always struck her as odd that she could find no other works by this artist, no history of who he was or where he came from. The provenance of the painting was vague at best, and no further records of Vallin or his work existed. Who was he? Why had he painted this woman, only to have his identity, and hers, lost to time?

The problem gnawed at her, each detail deepening the sense that something larger—something hidden—was at play. Amelia couldn't let this go. There was more to the story, and she was going to uncover it.

A counterfeit diamond, hidden away.

An artist who didn't exist.

A ring with two versions of itself.

A puzzle with missing pieces.

Her mind raced as she stepped back, scanning the painting as if it might suddenly offer an explanation. But there were no answers—only more questions, growing heavier with each passing second.

Amelia exhaled sharply as her thoughts swirled with newfound urgency. She needed to see the ring again. *Now*. Something about it, something she hadn't seen before, was waiting to be uncovered.

Turning swiftly, she made her way out of the gallery, heading for the museum's exit. The urgency in her movements barely left room for the unease creeping up her spine—the feeling that she was being watched.

She glanced over her shoulder. *Nothing*.

And yet, as she pushed through the museum's heavy doors and stepped into the cold Parisian afternoon, the sensation lingered, pressing at the edges of her awareness.

Amelia quickened her pace, the streets of the Marais stretching ahead of her.

This mystery wasn't finished.

It was only beginning.

Chapter 23

Amelia shut the door of her studio behind her, her thoughts spinning as she crossed the room to her workbench. The ring sat there by the tool-box, nestled innocently in the folds of the handkerchief, but after the revelation at the museum, it felt anything but ordinary. The discrepancy in the prongs didn't sit right with her—a seemingly minor detail that could hold the key to unlocking a deeper secret.

She approached the bench, her fingers hovering over the ring for a moment before she picked it up. Holding it between her thumb and forefinger, she turned it over slowly, inspecting the floral engraving along the band and the stone's gleaming surface. One, two, three, four, *five*. Yes, there *were* five prongs on this ring, just as she remembered.

But now, staring at it with fresher eyes, something about the fifth prong caught her eye—something she hadn't noticed before. While all the prongs were the same size at the top, the fifth was thicker at the base, noticeably more solid than the other four.

Amelia frowned, her curiosity piqued. She had handled countless pieces of antique jewelry—and while slight variations in craftsmanship weren't uncommon, this difference felt intentional, as if someone crafted it that way on purpose.

Her heart beat faster as she carried the ring over to her microscope, one of many tools she frequently used for restoration work but now needed for this investigation. She gently placed the ring beneath the lens, positioning the fifth prong in view.

Peering through the eyepiece, she scanned the prong carefully, her eye tracing the metal from its delicate tip down to the thicker base. The texture was smooth and polished, but, other than its size, no obvious differences revealed themselves.

She adjusted the focus, zooming in tighter, trying to see any lines or grooves that might explain the prong's unusual design. But there was nothing. She switched the angle, tilting the ring slightly to catch the light, but still, the prong remained elusive.

Frustrated, she moved the focus away from the prong and onto the diamond itself—or rather, the glass paste. Its facets caught the light and cast small glimmers across her view. Even though it was an imitation, the gem was magnificent—both expertly cut and polished. But as she continued studying the stone under magnification, something caught her eye. A faint reflection. A glint of light bouncing back from the base of the thicker prong—something she hadn't noticed before.

Amelia's breath caught in her throat as she adjusted the lens, zooming in on the area where the prong met the stone.

There it was again, something small and barely perceptible, but definitely there—something hidden within the base of the prong, or, rather, *on* it, just beyond the surface of the paste stone. The thicker structure was concealing something, and now that glint was giving it away.

Her heart raced, the thrill of discovery surging through her. There's something here, she thought. *I just can't quite see it.*

Her fingers trembled slightly as she turned away from the microscope. She grabbed a pair of tools—a small set of pliers and a delicate nylon pick—and her loupe, intent to investigate further. She had to dismantle the ring, but she couldn't afford to damage anything, not if this prong was hiding something important.

With precision, Amelia began to work. She carefully wedged the pick between the prongs and the paste diamond, applying gentle pressure to loosen the stone. She did't want to bend the prongs—just move them enough to dislodge the glass paste. Her hands were steady, but her mind burst with excitement and tension.

Slowly, the gem gave way, the prongs releasing their grip just enough for her to wiggle the stone free. Her breath came in shallow gasps as she pried the stone off the band, now revealing the inner base of the fifth prong. She brought the ring closer to her eyes, nervously fidgeting it to focus on the spot through her loupe until it was clear.

Amelia froze.

There, hidden beneath where the stone had sat, was an engraving—tiny, almost imperceptible to the naked eye, but clear as day through the lens.

Her eyes widened, a mix of shock and awe washing over her as the realization of what was now before her settled in.

Chapter 24

Moscow, 1933

"Yes!" Nadia said with joy. "Yes, Sergei! I *will* marry you!"

A smile spread across his face, filled with relief and gratitude. He brushed a stray strand of hair from her face, his touch gentle and respectful. Nadia closed her eyes, savoring the warmth of his hand against her skin, the soft brush of his breath as he leaned in, sealing their promise with a kiss that was as much a vow as it was an embrace.

When she opened her eyes, the room seemed brighter, the colors of the surrounding paintings more vivid, as though acknowledging this new bond between them. She felt a peace settle over her, an unshakable strength that she knew would carry her through whatever lay ahead.

They sat together in silence for a moment, bound by this promise that tied them not just to each other, but to a purpose. Whatever lay ahead, they would face it as partners.

Paris, 1933

In a private ceremony at the Vallois mansion on Rue de Rivoli, Nadia and Sergei were married. There was no grand display, no lavish reception —just a simple gathering that stripped away the usual pomp. It felt honest, even a bit defiant, a stark contrast to the expectations that had always weighed on her.

Standing before both a Russian Orthodox priest and a Jewish rabbi, with Sergei's hand in hers, Nadia felt like she was casting off the roles her family and society had dictated. This was *her* decision, *her* choice. And as the words of both officiants rang out, pronouncing them husband and wife, she embraced a name she felt her heart calling: Nadejda.

It wasn't just a name—it was a choice to honor Sergei's heritage and to adopt a part of herself she hadn't fully known existed. By becoming Nadejda, the Russian form of "Nadia," she wasn't simply calling herself something new; she was symbolically stepping into a role with Sergei, committing not just to a man but to the ideals they both held so dear.

And with that, she felt herself grow into the woman she was meant to be—one who stood unyielding before the forces that sought to control and suppress.

Nadejda glanced at Sergei, his eyes softening with admiration as she repeated her new name. To him, she wasn't a foreigner adopting another culture's name; she was someone willing to join the struggle he had fought alone for so long. Art, individuality, love—these were not separate ideas, but threads woven into a single tapestry they would protect at all costs.

———

Their union marked the beginning of a life shared between two cities, with moments of joy and discovery.

In Paris, they moved through bustling streets and galleries, with Sergei showing Nadejda hidden corners of the city she'd never noticed, places that breathed with history and art. In Moscow, they would sit for hours by the grand windows overlooking the frost-touched grounds, sharing stories, ideas, and the simple comfort of each other's company.

Together, these places formed a rhythm that felt new yet right, as if they'd always belonged there side by side.

But neither city was free from the world's troubles.

In the cold of Moscow, Nadejda noticed Sergei's health slipping, small signs that worried her. He seemed more tired than before, his breathing sometimes strained. With each passing day, his attachment to art seemed to intensify, like he found strength in the collection when his own was fading. Their marriage had become a partnership supporting each other through this new uncertainty.

Paris, too, had its shadows hidden beneath the city's vibrance and sophistication.

The city remained free, but murmurs of unrest and political tension filtered through the salons and cafes they frequented. There was a growing unease, a sense that the city's cultural heart was under threat, as authoritarian regimes swept across Europe, casting long shadows even over French soil. For Sergei and Nadejda, their evenings in Paris often carried these fears—discussions of threatened freedoms and the uncertain future of art and individuality.

It was during one of these evenings, as they sat by lamplight in their Paris residence, that Sergei's voice took on a more urgent tone. He and Nadejda had been poring over news clippings and pondering the fate of creativity under rising oppression. Finally, he set his cup of tea aside and spoke.

"Oppressive regimes have always sought to crush the spirit of their people, to erase culture and rewrite history. But art... art has always been a weapon for those who resist. It holds truth, even when buried beneath silence."

Nadejda met his passion, understanding that art wasn't just an investment or a family legacy—it was a lifeline, a reminder of what truly mattered.

In Paris, as they hosted gatherings in the Vallois mansion, she found herself drawn to discussions about art's role in times of war and unrest. To some, these works were commodities, investments with rising value in a volatile world. But to her, and to Sergei, they were symbols of human freedom, each brushstroke an act of defiance.

Slowly, her purpose became clearer. She and Sergei began to talk about how they might best protect the more vulnerable pieces, how to move them if danger approached, where they might hide them.

As Nadejda embraced her new identity and her new life, she also embraced the responsibility that came with it. No longer was she just the daughter of a powerful family or the wife of a renowned collector. She was part of something bigger—a shared mission to keep the light of art alive, no matter how dark the world became.

And their mission had begun.

Chapter 25

Months passed for Sergei and Nadejda, their lives moving between the elegance of Paris and the shadowed beauty of Moscow. Yet each return to Russia seemed to steal more of Sergei's strength as the political climate worsened.

One clear winter morning, he asked her to come to his study, where letters lay scattered across the desk—many bearing names of collectors and acquaintances who had once been part of his inner circle. He gestured to them, his hand trembling slightly.

"These are letters from friends," he began, heavy with worry. "Some have been interrogated. Others—" he paused, looking away—"I've heard rumors that the government is taking an interest in private collections. Some have hinted that they know of my . . . *our* collection . . . and that it may be next."

Nadejda felt a shiver run through her. The veiled threats, the letters from colleagues whose loyalties could shift under pressure—it was the clearest warning they had received yet. Her mind raced, considering the implications. Moving the collection would be risky, attracting unwanted attention. But keeping it in one place was equally dangerous. They were caught in a trap with no easy way out.

Sergei gripped the edge of his desk, his knuckles pale. "I've been thinking, Nadejda. It's time to start hiding the pieces—moving them to places the regime can't reach."

She understood the need for this decision. Sergei was no longer just a collector or a husband; he was a man staring down the loss of everything he had fought to protect.

"Sergei," she said softly, her voice filled with hesitation, "we need to be very careful. If we rush this, if we trust the wrong people, or even move in the wrong moment…" Her gaze dropped to the desk. "We could lose everything. Your collection… our lives… I'm not sure we're ready."

He nodded, but the determination in his eyes didn't waver. "I know, Nadejda. But if we do nothing, they'll come for it all. They'll strip this place bare."

Silence stretched between them, the enormity of the choice looming. Nadejda reached for his hand, their fingers intertwining. His skin was cool, his grasp weaker than she remembered, and in that moment, she realized much of this responsibility might soon fall on her. Sergei's health was deteriorating faster than either of them had acknowledged. If he couldn't lead this effort, how could she manage it by herself?

"We'd need allies," she said at last. "People we can trust who understand what this means. And we'd need to plan carefully—go slowly if we must. I'll speak to my father, see if he can help." Her voice grew quieter. "I just… I don't know how much we *can* do in such a climate."

Sergei's hand tightened around hers, his gaze filled with gratitude. "I trust you, Nadejda. I trust that you'll know what to do when the time comes. I don't think I have… much time left. But if we can protect even a part of this collection… maybe that will be enough."

His words scared her. Between his failing health and the political turmoil, this felt impossibly risky. But at least she could talk to her father, gather information, and bide her time. Perhaps circumstances would improve—maybe the worst wouldn't come so soon.

The months ahead would test her nerves and judgment like never before. She would have to navigate the treacherous waters of Moscow's underground circles, secure safe havens, and orchestrate moves that would keep their collection out of the regime's grasp. But a part of her already questioned whether she could act swiftly enough, or if Sergei's condition—and her own fear—would slow her down.

She would have to become more than Nadejda Shchukin, the Frenchwoman who married a Russian. She would have to embody the resilience and defiance Sergei's art represented. A guardian, a steward—one prepared to make decisions that could cost them everything.

Sergei's voice shattered her anxious thoughts. "We may not have the luxury of time, Nadejda. But we still have the ability to resist. And that, my love, is our greatest weapon."

She nodded, though her heart felt heavy and uncertain. She told herself she would act when the moment was right—but she couldn't banish the doubt in her mind. For now, she simply held Sergei's hand, letting that unity be enough. Even if one day she would have to shoulder this burden alone, she hoped she'd be able to do what needed to be done.

Chapter 26

Paris, Modern Day

Amelia's hands trembled slightly as she held the ring in front of her loupe, mouth agape in silent disbelief as she stared at the newly discovered engraving. There, etched with meticulous precision into the base of the prong, were what appeared to be two tiny letters.

The form was odd: an amalgamation of an "F" and an "O"? Or perhaps the "O" was a rounded rectangle, vertically aligned underneath the "F"? Either way, the clean lines and lack of ornamentation made it seem out of place on something as ornate as this ring—especially on an antique that had been carefully concealed for decades.

Amelia's mind raced. As an art restorer, she knew that even the smallest details could hold immense historical significance. Years ago, she had learned this lesson firsthand with a 16th-century woodcut of unknown origin.

Initially, she had noted an odd scratch on the piece—a mark she had assumed to be nothing more than a flaw, something she planned to cover up in the restoration process. But something about it nagged at her, urging her to look closer. After hours of careful examination and research, she realized that the "scratch" was actually part of a signature, barely visible but unmistakable upon closer inspection. That mark, hidden in plain sight, was the key to identifying the work as a missing piece by Albrecht Dürer.

The experience had changed her perspective forever. Since then, she approached every restoration with heightened sensitivity, knowing that every mark, every chip, and every imperfection could be a clue—a whisper from the past waiting to be understood by those who knew how to look.

Now, as she examined the ring's engraving, she felt that same thrill of discovery, knowing it meant *something*. Whoever had etched the "F" and "O" went to great lengths to hide it.

Was it a jeweler's mark? That was her first thought—yet a jeweler's mark would more likely be on the inside of the band, not tucked away beneath a prong. Or did it have a deeper connection to the woman in the photograph, the painting?

Why on *this* prong?

The fifth prong, which was absent from the painting, had been added with precision, and now this strange mark lay hidden beneath it, as if someone had taken great care to bury its meaning. Her heart raced as she stared at the tiny engraving, trying to make sense of it. What story was it waiting to tell?

Amelia's thoughts spiraled. The engraving felt like something bigger, something she had only just begun to unravel. But its meaning remained just out of reach, teasing her from the shadows of history. What was this ring really hiding? And why had it been buried in that toolbox for so long?

She leaned back, her breath shallow as Jacques's words echoed in her mind: *There are many secrets hidden in a piece like this.*

Yes there are!

More questions pressed on. Why was the fifth prong made thicker, reinforced to hide something so small yet significant? And what if this ring—this imitation—wasn't meant to deceive in the way she thought? What if its real value had nothing to do with the stone at all, but with the symbol now staring back at her?

Suddenly, a chilling realization gripped her—this ring was no accident. It had been deliberately hidden, concealed with purpose, and someone, somewhere, knew this. Someone who understood the significance of the engraving. The truth was undeniable now: the ring wasn't merely an artifact—it was a clue. And whoever had hidden it might not be the only one who knew its secret. Someone could already be looking for it.

Amelia pulled her loupe up, her thoughts racing. This engraving wasn't just a minor inconsistency; it was a tangible lead in the mystery that had consumed her ever since she discovered the box. But the engraving didn't look familiar—she needed to dig deeper, to find out what it really meant.

Amelia crossed the room to her bookshelf, where rows of worn books lined the shelves. As an art restorer, her library was a random collection of knowledge spanning centuries of art, history, techniques, and iconography—each book a trusted companion in her meticulous work.

On the top shelf was an entire section dedicated to historical markings and insignias, and among them, one of her favorites was *Signatures* by Frédéric Castaing.

This was a unique compilation of thousands of handwritten signatures and initials of historical figures. It included marks from kings, queens, scientists, writers, and artists who had shaped history and culture. This book had always fascinated her—not just for the famous names it held, like Rimbaud, Freud, Mozart, and Van Gogh, but for the personal connection it provided through the handwritten marks of those long gone. It was a way of touching history itself.

She grabbed *Signatures* along with a few other books and settled down at her workbench, flipping through the delicate pages. While *Signatures* contained nothing resembling the engraving, it reminded her again of the importance of insignificant details—marks that could easily be overlooked but held the key to unraveling the past. These markings left by craftspeople, artisans, and even jewelers were essential to restoring and verifying the authenticity of a piece.

French jewelry markings, she knew, were notoriously difficult to track. Over the centuries, countless artisans had used unique symbols and letters to leave their mark on their work—everything from makers' initials to guild emblems and family crests. Jewelry, especially antique pieces, often carried stories within their marks, just like paintings and sculptures bore the touch of their creators. She had seen these marks not only on jewelry but also on frames, decorative objects, and sculptures she had restored over the years.

Flipping through an old reference guide on French jewelry, Amelia scanned the pages, searching for anything resembling the strange combination of "F" and the rounded rectangle. The delicate lines of the mark under her loupe still nagged at her. Yet, as she pored over the books, the mark remained elusive. It was like a ghost—there, but impossible to pin down.

She sighed, running a hand through her hair. Jewelry marks were often cryptic, especially on older pieces, where they could represent anything from a jeweler's signature to a place of origin or even a patron's initials. This mark could date back centuries, or it could be something more recent, made to look old. The possibilities were endless, and with no immediate leads, she knew it wouldn't be a straightforward search.

Reaching for her phone, Amelia decided it was time to call in some help. While she had her own expertise in art restoration, jewelry markings were a specialized field, and she knew several colleagues who might shed light on the strange symbol. She opened her contacts, scrolling past names of fellow restorers, curators, and historians she had met over the years—people whose knowledge spanned centuries of art, culture, and craftsmanship.

Her first call was to Laure, a seasoned jeweler she had worked with during a project involving the restoration of a Renaissance-era painting. She had encyclopedic knowledge of antique French jewelry, but even she couldn't place the mark.

Amelia then reached out to Luc, a historian specializing in French decorative arts, who promised to consult his colleagues but came up empty.

One by one, Amelia contacted her network—experts from the Musée d'Orsay, the Louvre, and private collections she had restored—describing the engraving and sharing a high-resolution image. Despite their curiosity, no one recognized the mark. It wasn't listed in any reference materials or tied to any known maker's mark, crest, or insignia from French history. Each response brought the same disappointing conclusion: a dead end.

Amelia sank back in her chair, staring at the image on her phone. The mark kept evading her each time she thought she was making progress, as if it had been designed to be untraceable. She was certain the engraving was important, but without more context, uncovering its meaning felt like searching for a needle in a haystack. She needed a new angle.

Her eyes drifted back to the items from the box—the ring, the letter, the photograph—all now laid out on her workbench in the soft light of her studio. She admired the delicate folds of the handkerchief while her fingers gently traced the faded blue initials embroidered on its corner. *E.B.*—they seemed to speak to her, teasing at some hidden truth. So simple, yet filled with so many unknowns.

She paused for a moment and lingered on them. *E.B.? Could the "E" stand for Eloise?* she wondered. The name was familiar now, tied irrevocably to the letter she had found, written by a man named Arnaud, filled with longing and affection. But beyond that single emotional connection and the year 1934, there was nothing else—no surnames, no cities or addresses, no clear sign of who Eloise had been.

Amelia picked up the letter once more, carefully unfolding the fragile papers, her eyes scanning the elegant, slanted handwriting. The words were tender, almost poetic, but they offered no concrete details about Eloise's life. Arnaud spoke of their stolen moments, their love, but beyond the emotions, there were only vague references to places and times Amelia couldn't place. It was maddening. The letter had survived all these years, tucked away with these other relics, but it provided her with so little to go on.

She looked again at the items from the box. The photograph of the woman with the knowing smile, posing in the French countryside. The ornate glass paste ring. And the handkerchief, its embroidery faded but still distinct: "EB." Could this small piece of cloth have belonged to Eloise herself? Was she the woman in the photograph? In the painting? And if so, who *was* she?

Amelia spent hours poring over online archives, scouring the Jewish Museum's databases, and even combing through old newspaper clippings and genealogy websites.

She checked birth and marriage certificates, hoping for a link between "Eloise" and anyone tied to the era or the painting's vague provenance. The *name* "Eloise" appeared here and there, scattered across incomplete or poorly digitized local records, but none of the women listed seemed to match the mysterious figure from the love letter or the woman in the painting. And without knowing more details, Amelia had no way to narrow down the region or parish she should focus on.

Frustration mounted as she tried every variation of the name she could think of—Eloïse, Élisabeth, even initials matching the "EB" embroidered on the handkerchief—but every lead fizzled out. The more she searched, the more Eloise seemed to slip through her fingers. It was as though this figure had been erased from the historical record, her existence reduced to a love letter and a single photograph, tucked away in a forgotten toolbox.

Amelia leaned back in her chair, staring at the glowing screen before her, the disappointment blanketing her. How could someone so deeply loved, as Arnaud's letter had made clear, have disappeared from history? Vanished without a trace?

She picked up the letter again, its emotional undertones undeniable. Eloise and Arnaud had shared something deeply personal—but what? The question tightened its grip on her, and she knew that whatever the next step was, it lay in uncovering who Eloise really was—where she came from.

As the evening shadows crept into her studio, Amelia couldn't shake the feeling she was so close to *some* sort of breakthrough. Yet, the deeper she dug, the more questions surfaced. The mark on the ring, Eloise's identity, and the hidden life she had uncovered were all pieces of the same puzzle—but more pieces had to be out there, waiting to be found.

Then a thought struck her. When assembling a puzzle, you always start with the edges, working from the boundaries inward.

The painting at the Jewish Museum—the *whole* painting—was *more* than just the inner canvas she had painstakingly restored. There was also the frame, the outer *edges* she hadn't examined. Frames could hold secrets of their own, with marks or stamps left by previous collectors. Perhaps this overlooked part of the Vallin painting held some answers she was searching for.

The more she considered it, the more certain she became. Every detail counted, and every hidden mark could reveal a piece of the story. To complete this puzzle, she couldn't leave any piece unexplored.

She needed to begin with the edges. And to do that, she would have to return to the source. To the Vallin painting. To Eloise.

Chapter 27

Paris, 1934

The morning sun filtered through the heavy curtains of Nadejda and Sergei's new Parisian apartment while Sergei sat near the window, staring blankly at the letter clenched in his hands. His knuckles were white, and his face, usually calm, showed a pain Nadejda had never seen before. She approached him, her heart pounding, wondering what news could hurt him so deeply.

She read the letter over his shoulder, and a chill shot through her.

It was a curt, official notice from Soviet authorities. Their entire collection had been "reclaimed" by the state. The words were cold, stripped of any compassion or understanding for what they were taking. They reduced decades of devotion, countless hours spent acquiring and preserving art, into a sterile declaration of government control.

For Sergei, it was more than a loss of paintings; it was the erasure of his very identity. His breath came in shallow gasps, his hands shaking, and in that moment, Nadejda saw something in him break.

"Gone… they've taken it all," Sergei exhaled, his voice hollow.

Nadejda reached out instinctively, wanting to console him or say something that would ease his pain, but her own guilt gnawed at her, rooting her in place. She'd known how real the threat was, had heard Sergei's worries many times, but she had hesitated. They had been safe here, in Paris, surrounded by the protection of her family's name. Now she realized that their distance from Moscow had allowed her to push aside the urgency of his fears, allowed her to imagine that the danger remained far away.

"Sergei," she said softly. "I should have—"

He cut her off gently, looking up with sad understanding. "We both believed… or hoped… that distance would protect us," he murmured.

"But we were wrong. They see no boundaries, no barriers. They'll reach across oceans, across walls, to claim what they think is theirs."

Over the following days, Sergei was restless, unable to sit still, consumed by a desperate need to reclaim some part of what had been taken from him. Despite his failing health, he insisted on returning to Russia, desperate to find anything they might still recover.

Nadejda stayed behind in Paris, her heart aching. Each day that passed without a word from him felt like a knife twisting in her chest. She imagined him alone in a place that had once been home, now turned hostile. The silence weighed on her, filled with fear and shame. Her days stretched into weeks, each one a torment as she waited for his return.

When he finally returned in early 1935, Sergei was a shadow of the man Nadejda had married. He moved slowly, his gaze distant, and his once-vibrant spirit seemed extinguished, replaced by a deep, unyielding sorrow. The loss had changed him. His voice was softer, his spirit dimmed. The confiscation wasn't just theft; it had drained him of the fire that once kept him going. Nadejda tried to care for him, but the damage was done. It was as though the stolen art had taken his soul with it.

She struggled with regret, wishing she had acted sooner or differently, wondering if there was anything she could have done to save him and their legacy. Sergei had once believed in her strength, but now she questioned whether that strength had ever truly existed. She had been raised to be steady, to stand firm, yet here she was, feeling helpless and uncertain.

One evening, as Sergei lay weak and tired, he called her to his bedside. His voice was frail, his hand cool in hers. He no longer spoke of retrieving what was lost. Instead, he seemed resigned, though something was still present in his gaze.

"The world will try to erase everything," he strained, his voice barely audible. "Not just the art, but what it stands for—the freedom to be, to think, to create. You mustn't let them."

His words pierced her doubts, giving her a purpose she couldn't ignore. It was as if Sergei were passing the torch, trusting her to carry on a fight he could no longer wage. But she couldn't shake the feeling that she had already failed him, that if he left her alone, she might not be strong enough to continue.

But Sergei's faith in her remained unwavering. "There will come a time," he said softly, pausing for breath, "when they will need you... to protect more than just the art... but the spirit behind it. Don't forget that."

Tears blurred her vision as she nodded, understanding what he was asking, yet gripped by doubt. How could she truly fight for what Sergei had cherished, when she hadn't been able to shield him from the very loss that had broken him?

His breaths grew shallow, and his grip on her hand loosened. But she held onto his last words, trying to draw strength from the belief he had placed in her. That one day, her resolve would be tested again, and that she would rise to the challenge. She could only hope he was right.

As his eyes closed for the last time, her world turned colder and emptier than she had ever known.

In the days that followed Sergei's passing, Nadejda drifted through Paris in a fog, the pain of his absence pressing down on her. Beyond their walls, tensions in Germany cast a growing shadow over Europe, deepening the sense of uncertainty that loomed over everything.

Yet in those quiet, lonely nights, she remembered Sergei's last words, turning them over and over in her mind. She would wait. She would watch. And when the time came, she would act, protecting the memory, the art, and the ideals Sergei had held dear. Without him, her path felt harder, but she would not let his legacy fade.

Chapter 28

Paris, Modern Day

The crisp autumn air of Paris wrapped around Amelia as she walked through the narrow streets of the Marais again, her mind spinning with questions she couldn't yet answer.

The cobblestones beneath her feet felt oddly familiar, and under other circumstances, she would have stopped for conversation. But today, as she approached the Jewish Museum of Art and History, there was an urgency in her steps, a feeling she couldn't shake. The ring and the painting—there was a connection there, she was sure of it. And now she needed answers.

As she crossed the threshold into the lobby, the familiar scent of aged wood and parchment greeted her again. It was a place she had frequented many times during her years as a restorer, but today she was wearing new shoes. Today, she wasn't just a restorer revisiting her work—she was a seeker of something hidden, something buried within the history of a painting she had once brought back to life.

Amelia approached the front desk. Though her heart raced beneath the surface, partially from nerves, partially from the brisk walk, her voice was steady. "I'm here to see Monsieur Duval," she said, her words holding the weight of her professional authority.

The receptionist nodded, recognizing Amelia from her earlier work with the museum, and promptly picked up the phone. "Of course, Mademoiselle. I'll let him know you're here."

A few moments later, the curator, Monsieur Aloïs Duval, one specializing in Nazi-era provenance, appeared. A tall man with sharp features and silvering hair, he greeted her with a warm smile. "Ah, Mademoiselle Beckett. What brings you back to us today?"

Amelia held her breath for a second, gathering her thoughts before approaching. "Monsieur Duval, it's nice to see you again!" she greeted him with a warm smile as they exchanged *la bise*, the customary kiss on each cheek. "I've come across something that may relate to the painting I restored here a few years ago—the Henri Vallin."

Duval's brow raised slightly, intrigued by the mention of the painting. "The 'Unknown,' correct? The one with the elegant woman in the salon?"

Amelia nodded. "Yes. There's a connection I've uncovered, but I'd like to confirm something. It's about the provenance of the painting. Some new information has come up that I think might help trace its origins more accurately. I was wondering if I could take a look at it again?"

Duval's eyes lit up with curiosity. "Of course! Though I'm very interested to know what makes you think it holds more information than what you already found," he said with a slight smile.

Amelia hesitated, choosing her words carefully. "Well... I'd like to look at the frame," she said. "When I restored it, I focused solely on the canvas. But I know frames from this period often carry collection marks or stamps, especially on pieces that passed through many owners. I didn't have a chance to inspect the frame during my initial restoration, but I'm beginning to think it might contain clues about its ownership history."

Monsieur Duval considered her words, a spark of excitement creeping into his expression.

"We did examine the frame shortly after it arrived at the museum," he said. "And... if I remember correctly, there was indeed a faded stamp, but we couldn't make much of it. At the time, we didn't have the technology—or, frankly, the resources—to trace it back to any specific collection. We hit a dead end."

Amelia's pulse quickened, though her voice remained measured. "I think, with a closer look, we might be able to uncover more? Perhaps new methods could help bring the stamp to light or reveal something we missed before? If you allow me to inspect it again, I believe I might be able to help us find a new lead."

Duval studied her for a moment, his gaze thoughtful. Amelia had earned a strong reputation as a restorer over the years, and her meticulous attention to detail had gained her respect within the museum community. But more than that, he could sense her determination—the sense that something significant lay beneath the surface of this request.

"We've always valued your expertise, Amelia. If you believe there's more to be uncovered, I'm open to having you take another look at the frame," he said, his tone encouraging. "After all, the museum has a vested interest in uncovering as much as possible about the provenance of its pieces. If this stamp can lead us to new information, it's worth the effort."

Amelia breathed a sigh of relief, gratitude swelling within her. "Thank you, Monsieur Duval. I believe we may be on the verge of discovering something important."

Duval nodded and motioned for her to follow him through the gallery. The halls of the museum felt heavier now, as though the paintings themselves held their breath, waiting for a revelation. They made their way to the room where the Vallin painting hung, the elegant woman in emerald silk gazing serenely from her place in the Parisian salon.

Amelia stopped in front of the painting, her eyes tracing the familiar contours of the scene. It had been a few days since she'd last seen it, but the emotions it stirred were the same. The woman, with her dark curls and knowing smile, seemed to watch her, holding the answers to every question Amelia sought to unravel.

"This is the one," Duval said, standing beside her. "The frame hasn't been touched since it was mounted. But I must caution you—what remains of the stamp will most likely be hardly visible."

Amelia nodded. "I understand. That's why I'd like to use a few techniques to examine it more closely—infrared scanning, perhaps? I'll need to see it under different light conditions."

Duval's expression softened with understanding. "Very well. I'll arrange for the frame to be removed so you can inspect it thoroughly. Give us a day or two. But I must insist on supervision, of course."

"Of course," Amelia agreed, without hesitation. "I'll need to document everything we find, but I believe this could help us trace the painting's origins—and perhaps lead us to more."

As they stood together in the quiet of the gallery, Amelia felt her first actual sense of hope. She would solve this puzzle, starting from the edges and working inward. The painting, the frame, the ring—it was all connected. She was sure of it. But unraveling the mystery would take patience and precision, just as her restoration work had done years ago.

Duval excused himself to make the necessary arrangements, leaving Amelia alone with the painting for a few minutes. She stepped closer, her gaze lingering on Eloise's face. There was something haunting about her expression, something that had always tugged at Amelia's subconscious.

What secrets do you hold? she wondered silently.

As the afternoon light filtered through the museum windows, casting long shadows across the room, Amelia knew the past was calling to her, and she was ready to answer.

As Mr. Duval returned and confirmed the painting would be ready for closer analysis tomorrow, Amelia should have felt a rush of excitement. Instead, she was distracted by a prickling sensation at the back of her neck.

Something was off.

Her attention drifted from his words, and her gaze flicked beyond the curator's shoulders to the doorway behind him. There, standing in the dim light of the corridor, was a man—tall, shadowed, and completely still.

He wasn't a casual observer, nor someone idly passing by; he stared, fixed on her with an intensity that sent a chill down her spine. His eyes seemed to study her, unblinking, as though he was searching for something only he could see. Her pulse quickened, a slow wave of unease building as their gazes met.

By now, Duval had stopped talking, sensing Amelia's distraction, and turned to see what she was looking at.

Then, as if realizing he'd been caught, he turned sharply and disappeared into the hall without a word.

Amelia's breath was rapid, and her pulse raced. *Who was that?* she thought. *And why was he watching her?*

Chapter 29

Paris, March 1941

Paris was unrecognizable. The vibrant city of light had dimmed under the occupation, its streets muffled by a silence heavy with fear. Hushed murmurs replaced lively conversation, and hurried footsteps dissolved into the shadows of grand monuments now dwarfed by the looming presence of the Third Reich.

For Arnaud and Eloise, the Artisan's Lodge had become both a sanctuary and a prison. The walls held memories of happier days, but now they closed in on them, a reminder of the freedoms they had lost.

Arnaud often found himself staring out of the small, mullioned windows, his gaze wandering to the vineyards and gardens beyond. The Bourget estate, once their refuge from the pressures of high society, felt exposed and fragile.

Inside, the fire flickered, drawing long shadows across the walls adorned with Eloise's paintings. Arnaud watched as she moved across the room, her hands slipping into the sleeves of her coat, fingers fastening each button with practiced ease. She was preparing to leave for another meeting in Montmartre, an act that had become almost ritualistic in recent months. Arnaud sat by the fire, watching her every movement, his heart gripped by a dread that only grew with each trip she took.

"You're going again," he said softly, with barely concealed worry. He tried to keep the sadness from seeping through, but it was impossible to ignore the nerves in his chest.

Eloise turned to face him, her expression calm but resolute. "I have to, Arnaud. They're counting on me. This meeting is… important. The Gestapo is targeting everything, and we're coordinating final efforts to get this important piece out."

Arnaud's jaw tightened, and he looked away, staring into the fire. "Every time you leave, Eloise, I feel as though… as though I'm losing you a little more." He turned his gaze back to her, his expression a mixture of fear and frustration. "They're tightening their grip—they know what's happening. They're watching, waiting. If they catch you…"

Eloise's face softened, and she moved closer to him, kneeling beside his chair. She reached for his hand, taking it between her own and clasping it.

"Arnaud, if I don't do this… if I just sit by and let them strip away everything we stand for, then we've already lost. Remember? We need to fight back. Not just for us, but also for the soul of France." Her voice was low, but her eyes held an unbreakable determination. "We can't let them erase who we are."

He tightened his grip on her hands, as if trying to anchor her in place, keeping her safe within these walls. "But is it worth the risk, Eloise? You're risking everything—our life, our future—for a few pieces of art."

Eloise blinked, taken aback. She hadn't expected those words from him, not after everything they had done to protect what they held dear. Though the thought that he valued her life more than any legacy warmed her, even as it pained her to see him so afraid.

She exhaled softly, a sad smile on her lips. "Arnaud, what's the point of all of this—of protecting our legacy, our family—if we let them take everything else? If we stand by and do nothing, then we're complicit. I'd rather risk my life knowing I tried than hide here, watching as they destroy everything we love."

Her conviction settled into him like a slow-burning fire, fueling his own worries and hopes. He could see how deeply this fight had become a part of her, how she had dedicated herself to a purpose so much larger than either of them. And yet, he couldn't shake the fear of losing her.

"Then let me go with you," he murmured, his voice filled with emotion. "Let's do this together."

"Arnaud," she said gently, "they know who you are. If they see you, it's over before we even start. You're the one protecting what we have here. If you're caught—if they use you to get to us—everything falls apart."

Her voice broke for a moment before she steadied herself, meeting his eyes. "I can move unnoticed. I've done it my whole life. You are too well-known, too... visible. That's why it has to be me."

Her words sank into him, heavy but undeniable. In truth, he probably would have been fine. But while he had been so focused on shielding her, she was already a step ahead—doubling back to protect him in ways he hadn't even realized. It was a game of resolve, and Eloise was winning.

He leaned forward, pressing his forehead to hers, breathing her in, memorizing her warmth and the shape of her face. But as she drew back, a bitter sense of inevitability washed over him. Unlike her other meetings, tonight, somehow, felt different.

"Promise me," he said softly. "Promise me you'll be careful."

She nodded with a smile curving her lips. "I promise."

But the words felt fragile, hollow. Deep down, he knew that all the promises in the world couldn't protect her from the darkness lurking in every corner of Paris.

Moments later, Eloise took off her ring and pulled on her gloves, ready to leave. Arnaud followed her to the door, his heart heavy with fears. Just as she reached for the handle, she turned and met his gaze.

"Arnaud," she began, "if anything happens to me… promise me that you'll continue what we've started. That you'll protect everything we've fought for." Her gaze held his, unwavering. "Promise me that our work, our legacy, won't be in vain."

He swallowed hard and his throat was too tight to speak. He simply nodded as his fingers clutched her hands with desperate strength. He knew, in his heart, that if anything happened to her, he would do everything in his power to honor her wishes. But the thought of a world without her was more than he could bear.

Eloise reached up, placing a soft, lingering kiss to his lips—a kiss filled with all of her love, a fragile moment of peace before she stepped away into the unknown. She looked at him for a long moment, almost trying to memorize every detail, then pulled away, her hand slipping from his grasp.

The door opened, and a cold gust of night air swept into the lodge, carrying with it the faint sounds of the city beyond. Arnaud stood still and watched as she stepped into the darkness, her silhouette blending into the dim light of the gravel path. She turned back with a teasing smile.

"I'll be back soon," she called lightly, as if she were simply running out for milk or bread.

But when the door closed behind her, sealing him inside the silence of the lodge, Arnaud felt an unmistakable finality settle over him. He moved to the window, watching as she disappeared into the night. He stayed there, his breath fogging the glass and his heart pounding with a mixture of love and fear.

"Protect everything we've fought for," her words echoed in his mind. They clung to him, heavy and binding, a promise he couldn't ignore as she drifted further from his reach.

Arnaud sank into his armchair, staring into the dying embers of the fire, the warmth barely reaching him. The lodge felt emptier now, more desolate than it ever had, but somewhere in the silence, he clung to the hope that she would return, just as she promised.

Chapter 30

The streets of Montmartre, once the heartbeat of Parisian art and spirit, now lay under an uneasy silence. Cafés where laughter and debates used to echo through the nights had become subdued, marked by secrecy and fear.

The bohemian paradise Eloise had cherished, the place where she grew up and where her soul had thrived, was now a shadowed trap. Each cobblestone and darkened window was a reminder of how tightly the Gestapo had woven their net around the city.

Montmartre's spirit fought on, but with each patrol and every cautious glance, it seemed to gasp for air.

Eloise pulled her coat tighter and slipped through the back entrance of a modest café on a side street. To anyone passing by, the building might look deserted, but inside, it pulsed with the quiet urgency of the resistance. Artists, writers, and intellectuals gathered here under the guise of conversation, but their eyes told the truth. This was no ordinary gathering; it was a covert fight against forces with a relentless desire to erase everything they held dear.

Eloise scanned the dimly lit room, her eyes meeting familiar faces. At the back table, Raoul, an amateur photographer with a shock of thick silvery hair and one of the group's key organizers, waved her over. Usually spirited, he now appeared grim and worn, the strain of their work visible in the creases of his forehead.

He and his wife, Marthe, both clerks at Le Printemps, had taken unimaginable risks, using the department store's darkroom to develop photographs of the Occupation—images the Nazis had expressly forbidden anyone from taking. Raoul had managed to capture everyday life in Paris under German rule, often with pointed, ironic captions that exposed the cruelty and absurdity of the regime. Those pictures, along with other art and manuscripts stored here in a hidden room, were evidence of their defiance.

Around him sat men and women she trusted, kindred spirits who had once gathered to discuss art but now met to save it from annihilation.

"*Bonsoir*, Eloise," Raoul greeted her, his voice low and concise.

Eloise gave him a brief nod, sliding into a chair. She took in the room—a handful of her most trusted comrades sat beside her, their faces weary but set with determination.

Raoul cleared his throat. "We have only a brief window of time," he began, unfolding a map across the table. "We move the piece tonight." He traced his finger along a narrow line on the map, showing a passage through the city that would eventually take them toward the Basque Region of Spain. "We've arranged for transport to Bayonne. From there, it'll be taken to the caves of the Basque Mountains. It's risky, but it's our best option. If it stays here, it's as good as lost."

Eloise listened, her heart racing. Raoul's words offered a glimmer of hope, but the risk weighed heavily. Moving the art would require precision, timing, and luck—all scarce commodities under the Gestapo's watchful eye.

Raoul lowered his voice, leaning in. "There's something else," he said. "We've heard the Gestapo might've been tipped off. Not about who or exactly what, but they could suspect something's going down soon. If that's the case, they'll probably start tightening checkpoints, maybe even poke around more. Every step, every choice matters now."

A hush fell over the group, and Eloise felt a chill slip down her spine. She scanned the faces around her, catching their shared fear, the dread-filled understanding of what lay ahead. After a moment, she leaned forward and spoke firmly. "If that's the case, we can't wait. This might be our only shot. We knew the risks when we started—we knew this could happen. We move now. We can't back down."

Without an objection from any others around the table, Raoul nodded, his gaze solemn. "Then it's settled. We go forward as planned, but with extra caution."

They spent the next several minutes reviewing the details, their voices hushed but hurried. Eloise could feel the tension rising within her as they finalized the last steps of their plan. It was fragile, teetering on the edge of success and disaster—but it was their best chance. It *had* to work.

Suddenly, the café door creaked open.

Eloise's whole body tensed and she instinctively drew her coat around her. A figure stepped inside, silhouetted against the dim light from the street. The man's face was familiar—a courier they had used before —but tonight he was pale, eyes wide with terror. He approached the table swiftly and whispered frantically to Raoul.

The color drained from Raoul's face, his hand going instinctively to his coat pocket, where Eloise knew he kept a small revolver. "The Gestapo is coming!" he hissed. "They know about the plan! They're on their way here!"

Panic rippled through the group, and Raoul shot a warning glance at everyone, his voice sharp and urgent. "Scatter!"

Eloise's heart pounded as she stood, her eyes darting to the back door. The café, their trusted haven, now felt like a death trap.

She reached for her coat, slipping it on with shaking hands, and moved towards her escape. By now, she could hear the rumble of footsteps on the cobblestones outside, the heavy thud of boots growing louder, closer.

The Gestapo were here.

Eloise ducked behind a table as the officers flooded in, barking orders and brandishing guns. Resistance members scattered, but some were cornered before they could reach the exits.

She pressed herself against the wall, her heart pounding so loudly it drowned out the surrounding chaos. She could feel the importance of her decision, knowing if she made one wrong move, it would all be over.

A scuffle broke out nearby. One of her group members, desperate to push past an officer, lunged forward. Four shots rang out, sharp and deafening. Eloise watched in horror as he fell, his hat tumbling across the floor, coming to a stop near her hiding spot. His body crumpled, his act of defiance silenced in an instant.

Panic surged through her, but she forced it down. She couldn't falter. She had to escape. She had to get back to Arnaud. She had to make sure their mission didn't die here.

With the Gestapo momentarily distracted, Eloise seized her chance.

She bolted toward the back door, her breath coming in quick, panicked bursts. Behind her, she could hear the frantic shouts of her comrades and the sharp staccato of more gunfire, but she forced herself to keep running… forced herself to ignore her fear.

She burst into the alleyway and the night air bit against her skin. Her chest heaved as she drew in sharp, ragged breaths that fogged in the cold, pausing just for a moment to steady herself. She had made it. She was out. The chaos of the café, the shouts, and the gunfire were all behind her now.

She glanced up at the dark sky and closed her eyes just for a second, welcoming the silence.

Once composed, she hurried down the cobblestone path, each step taking her closer to Arnaud. The thought of him waiting for her, unaware of the danger she had just left behind, pushed her forward.

But as she ran, she realized hers were not the only footsteps she heard. Another set of boots followed her, out of rhythm with her own. She wasn't alone.

At the next cross street, she slowed and turned. Her gaze locked onto the shadowed figure emerging from the darkness—a Gestapo officer.

Eloise gasped in fear.

Every instinct screamed at her to run, to put as much distance between herself and the figure as possible. She spun on her heel and bolted down the narrow alley, her feet pounding against the cobblestones.

Her breath came in heaving bursts, like she couldn't get enough air. The buildings seemed to close in around her, and she felt the desperate, clawing need to escape, to get free.

But the officer was gaining. She could feel his presence bearing down on her. Each sharp turn seemed to offer hope, but the narrow alleys twisted endlessly, leading her deeper into a maze of darkened passageways. Her only thought was to keep moving, to get away.

Before she could reach the end of the alley, a sharp voice rang out behind her, harsh and commanding. "Halt!" The officer's tone cut through the silence like a blade, full of authority. She froze, realizing how close he was.

Slowly, Eloise raised her hands as she turned to face him. Her chest heaved with exhaustion, but it was fear that made her limbs tremble.

For a brief second, their gazes locked, and she saw only emptiness in his eyes. At that moment, a chilling inevitability settled over her.

A thousand thoughts raced through her mind, memories flashing like lightning: her parents, Montmartre, her wedding day, meeting Arnaud for the first time in the café. She thought of the life they had built together, their quiet moments of love, and their shared dreams. She thought of daisies and summer mornings, of laughter and warmth, and the buttery aroma of croissants from the bakery two doors down from her old flat. She could almost taste them now.

In that final moment, she thought of Arnaud's face, the way he would look at her with such love and intensity, as though she were the very air he breathed.

She held onto that image, letting it anchor her, even as she heard the officer's grip tighten, his finger on the trigger.

The gunshot rang out, sharp and deafening. Eloise staggered, her hand going to her side, feeling the hot, sticky warmth of blood seeping through her coat.

Her knees buckled, and she sank to the ground, the cobblestones rough beneath her.

The world around her blurred, the sounds of the city fading into a distant hum. Her breath came in shallow gasps, each one more painful than the last. She felt the weight of her body pulling her down, the darkness caving in, but she forced herself to hold on, to cling to the last remnants of consciousness.

She reached for the locket around her neck, the one with the small picture of Arnaud tucked inside. Her fingers closed around it, the cool metal a comfort against her skin.

She thought of him waiting for her, his face illuminated by the firelight, his eyes filled with the love they had shared. She clutched the locket, saying his name, a faint murmur that barely escaped her lips.

Her vision darkened, the pain dulling into a distant ache. She felt herself slipping, her grip on the locket loosening as the world around her faded.

In her last moments, she thought of Arnaud, of their promise, of the legacy they had fought to protect.

"Arnaud," she whispered, her voice lost to the night.

With a final, shuddering exhale, she let go, the darkness claiming her.

The cobblestones beneath her grew cold, the city still once more as Montmartre held its breath, a silent witness to her final sacrifice.

Chapter 31

Amelia stood in the sterile, high-tech studio of the Jewish Museum with Mr. Duval by her side. The steady hum of climate control systems blended with the bright, focused lights overhead, creating an atmosphere of care. The room was small but designed for efficiency, every detail serving a purpose.

Before them lay the painting she logged countless hours restoring in graduate school, carefully mounted on a worktable with its frame and canvas ready for closer inspection. She was about to log some more, hopeful yet cautiously optimistic that somewhere within this piece, new answers about its provenance and perhaps even the toolbox—lay hidden, waiting to be uncovered.

Duval glanced at the painting, then back at Amelia with a slight smile playing on his lips. "It's been quite some time since anyone's taken such a close look at this piece." He paused and his gaze settled thoughtfully on the frame. "If there's something hidden here… I'd bet on you to find it."

Amelia felt a warm flush creep up her cheeks and smiled back, humbled. "Thank you, Aloïs. I'll do my best."

The collection stamp Duval referenced lay hidden between the frame and the canvas, and was inaccessible until the two were separated.

After conducting a quick initial assessment of the frame and canvas together, and not seeing anything of note, Amelia moved to the first step: removing the canvas from the frame—a delicate process requiring meticulous precision.

Amelia used a specialized tool resembling a thin spatula to gently lift the small tacks securing the canvas to the frame. This stage was usually a challenge, since older nails and adhesives often clung to the canvas, putting the work at risk of tearing. Even though they had been separated once before during her restoration, she still worked slowly, her hands steady, carefully easing the canvas away from the wood.

Once the canvas was free, she placed it gently onto a clean support table, leaving the frame alone for the first time in many years, and glanced back at Duval.

"Don't mind me," he said while stepping back a bit. "I'm just here to watch."

She peered through a magnifying lens and scanned the faded stamp on the inside edge of the frame. As Duval had warned, it was little more than a few blurred lines, almost entirely erased by the water damage it had endured. From exposure, the ink had bled over time and dispersed into the wood's fibers, settling deep within its crevices. Still, Amelia had hoped to reveal more, to unlock a clue that had been overlooked.

She ran her ultraviolet light over the surface, hoping the reactive light might illuminate something invisible to the naked eye, but nothing emerged.

Undeterred, she moved on to infrared reflectography, a tool often used to reveal hidden underdrawings and past alterations. She adjusted the wavelengths and ran it slowly over the area, watching as each layer of the frame responded differently to the light. Still, the stamp remained stubbornly obscured.

Finally, she tried a technique called raking light by positioning a bright light source at a shallow angle to cast shadows over the frame's sur-face—similar to the way car dent removers detect hidden dents. This method could sometimes highlight shallow engravings or other texture changes, revealing details even in undefinable markings. But as she scanned the area, hoping for a breakthrough, the stamp remained frustratingly incomplete.

After trying all her methods, Amelia took a step back and sighed deeply, exhaling through pursed lips. The tools and techniques at her disposal could reveal hidden details—but only if there was something left to find. Aside from the faded stamp, the frame had no additional marks on it. Frustration tugged at her as she cycled through other options—but determination kept her going.

She took a few photos of what remained of the stamp and set the frame aside, preparing to reassemble the canvas. Just as she was about to reset the canvas, a small flicker on the edge of its framing tape caught her eye.

Her pulse quickened as she leaned in closer, her breath growing shallow. There, beneath the new canvas tape she had applied during the restoration, was something subtle—a ghostly mark bleeding through from the canvas side. Amelia's heart raced. It was in the exact same spot, when assembled together, as the faded marks on the frame.

She gently peeled back the tape, her fingers trembling with excitement. Beneath the smooth surface of the adhesive on the canvas, a faint imprint had emerged. Small, barely perceptible, but unmistakably… a stamp!

Amelia blinked hard, then squinted, trying to convince herself that what she was seeing was real. Sure enough… there it was!

The solvents she had used during the restoration process decades ago—possibly the ethanol or mild alkaline cleaner—must have interacted with the residue of the original ink or pigment, which had absorbed into the fibers of the canvas from the frame over the years before restoration.

She blinked again, realization dawning. The mark could have been made with something like iron gall, a common ink historically used for official documents and stamps because of its durability. But over time, and with environmental exposure and the pH of the canvas itself, the ink could fade to near-invisibility. The chemical composition of the cleaning solvents she had used may have slowly reactivated the stamp, causing the faded lines to seep back into view, bleeding through the new framing tape. It was like the mark had been hidden in a time capsule, waiting for the right conditions to reveal itself once more.

Amelia gently ran her gloved fingers over the faint outline, her mind spinning with possibilities. Duval stood beside her, his eyes following her every movement. This revelation was new for him also and his excitement mimicked hers.

Using a magnifying glass, she examined the mark further. It was intricate yet simple—a skeleton key intertwined with what appeared to be a paintbrush. The filbert brush bristles formed the head of the key, while the key's unmistakable post and bit formed the key tip on the other end. A strange hybrid. Yet, somehow meaningful.

There was a brief pause. Then Amelia gasped, her thoughts suddenly locking into place. In a flash of clarity, she saw it.

The shape. The interplay between the skeleton key and the paintbrush. The lines. *The mark on the ring!*

Her heart raced. The realization hit her like a wave. The engraving on the ring from the toolbox—a simplified "F" and rounded rectangle—wasn't an isolated symbol. It was a distilled version of this more elaborate mark on this painting!

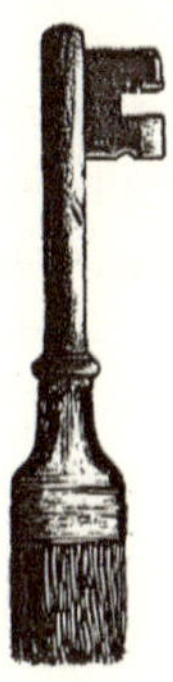

Amelia turned sharply to Mr. Duval, who was watching her with an excitement that mirrored her own. "This mark," she said, her voice laced with urgency as she pointed to the outline. "Do you know anything about it?"

Duval adjusted his glasses and quickly leaned in, feeling a thrill he hadn't experienced since he was a boy. It was the first time he, and possibly anyone at the museum, had seen this, and his hands hovered over the painting, trembling slightly, as if he'd stumbled upon a long-buried treasure.

"It's remarkable!" he breathed, his excitement spilling over. "It's not uncommon for families to use symbols like this to mark their possessions, especially during the Nazi occupation," he said looking at her, his words rushing out. "Many families went to great lengths to ensure their belongings could be identified later... should they ever be allowed to reclaim them." His eyes darted back to the mark, as though he were committing it to memory. "But to see this here, on this painting... it's something extraordinary!"

Amelia listened intently as Duval continued, his voice lower. "We've always suspected this painting might have belonged to an aristocratic family, but without documentation or a matching family crest, we couldn't trace it. The collection stamp was too faded to be of much help.… Until now!"

Amelia's mind raced as she processed his words. If this painting belonged to a prominent family, then the symbol on the frame—and the ring—could be a key to unlocking the painting's provenance. Duval's words tugged at her thoughts, suggesting pathways she hadn't yet explored.

He added thoughtfully, "Aristocratic families often kept extensive records and left lengthy paper trails with the state, many now hidden away in the French National Archives. If you're looking for answers, you might start there—in Pierrefitte-sur-Seine. Records from the WWII era might hold the key to identifying the family behind this mark."

Amelia nodded, this new information settling over her as she reassembled the painting. The stamp on the canvas, the ring, Eloise—they were all pieces of a larger puzzle, one that spanned generations, possibly buried beneath layers of history, hidden for decades. Starting with the edges had worked! The next step was clear.

She would have to dive deeper into the archives, into the forgotten records of France's historic families. Somewhere within those pages, the answers may lay waiting.

But as she turned to leave, a chill ran down her spine. The image of the man watching her from the doorway earlier flashed in her mind, a shadow that hadn't yet disappeared.

She wasn't the only one looking.

Chapter 32

A heavy mist lay over the Montmartre Cemetery, draping it in a somber veil as Nadejda stood alone by the maroon granite marker. The air was cool, heavy with the scent of damp stone and freshly turned earth. A pair of gravediggers finished their work nearby, their hushed voices and the soft thud of the final shovelfuls of soil marking the end of Sergei's journey. She hardly noticed them, all her attention on the patch of ground that now held the man she loved.

The sight of it was almost unbearable, the finality of the grave a stark contrast to the life he had led—a life filled with beauty, resilience, and a fierce devotion to the ideals he cherished.

Now, all of that seemed so far away.

Nadejda gripped a lace handkerchief in her hand, something that had belonged to Sergei, and clung to the small comfort it offered. A handful of mourners who had attended the brief service had already departed, leaving her alone with her grief. She was grateful for it, and didn't think she could bear anyone else's pity or comfort.

This moment, this grief, was hers alone.

She stared at the freshly covered grave, feeling hollow. Each grain of earth seemed to weigh on her heart, each settling speck a reminder of how much had been lost.

The maroon granite marker, with its simple greyed engraving, felt almost mocking. It was all that was left of the man who had once been so much more than a collector of art; he had been a fierce defender of human spirit, a guardian of the fragile spark that made people free.

Nadejda's heart ached, knowing the world wouldn't see Sergei as she had. They wouldn't understand that he had believed in art not as a luxury, but as a kind of silent rebellion—a reminder that human beings could think and feel beyond what any regime allowed.

Standing there, she felt as though she were burying not only her husband but the very ideals that had given her life purpose—a way to protect humanity's right to dissent, to resist, to dream.

Her doubt grew. She wondered if she had failed him, if she could have done more before his collection was seized, before his spirit had been so badly wounded. She had hesitated when he'd asked for help, had hidden behind her own fears, her doubts. If she had acted sooner, if she'd been braver… perhaps it wouldn't have come to this. Perhaps she would be standing beside him now, instead of mourning the man he had once been.

But it was too late for regrets. This was the reality she faced, alone by the grave.

Yet as she stood there, a thought surfaced. This *wasn't* the end. Sergei's fight wasn't over, because it had never been just his. She had been with him, beside him, every step of the way. His mission had woven itself into her.

But as quickly as that understanding came, so too did the doubt.

How could she possibly carry on? Sergei had always been the one with the vision, the plan, the strength to push forward. Without him, she felt adrift, overwhelmed by the tremendous task he had left her. Nadejda had supported Sergei, yes, but she had always followed his lead. Now, with him gone, the responsibility felt enormous.

Her gaze drifted to the gravestone as she recalled his final words— *the world will try to erase everything, but you mustn't let it.* She understood what he had meant, and she knew this moment had changed her. Still, the question loomed: how could she keep it alive when she hadn't protected him or his legacy when he'd needed her most?

The gravediggers placed the last stone over the grave, a weighty slab of granite that sealed Sergei's resting place. They nodded briefly in respect before retreating, leaving her fully alone in the stillness.

As the afternoon faded into evening, Nadejda remained by the grave, letting the silence settle over her. The cemetery grew darker, and the mist thickened until the world around her felt like a ghostly, forgotten realm. Her grief pressed down on her, but somewhere inside, a steady resolve formed.

After what felt like hours, she stepped back, glancing once more at the marker. This was an ending, yes, but perhaps also the start of a new chapter she couldn't yet imagine. Sergei's legacy, his memories, the art and ideals he had cherished—they would not be forgotten. Even if fear and doubt shadowed her path, even if she had to stand alone, she would carry on.

The cemetery's stillness intensified, and she glanced around once more, making sure she was completely alone.

Slowly, Nadejda reached into her bag and withdrew two small objects. Their cold weight settled into her palms, grounding her, as though affirming her next move. She closed her fingers around the solid metal and looked down at the grave with a sense of clarity that had eluded her for weeks.

In the fading light, she knelt. And clutching the objects with confidence, she reached out toward the stone.

Part II

The Art of Defiance

Chapter 33

Arnaud had moved out of the Artisan's Lodge. He couldn't bear another day surrounded by the lingering memories of Eloise—the ghost of her laughter, the warmth she'd infused into every corner. Even the château, also once alive with music, art, and conversation, had grown silent. He drifted through its halls like a stranger, each step reminding him of what he'd lost.

In the weeks since Eloise's death, each day passed without meaning. The artworks that remained on the walls had lost their warmth, becoming somber reminders of a happier time. The estate, once a vibrant sanctuary, felt more like a tomb.

The pain of Eloise's absence cut deeper than he thought possible, but in the silence, a memory surfaced—a promise she'd made him swear to uphold: *"If anything happens to me, continue what we've started."* Her words haunted him, stirring something within that went beyond grief.

Eloise had taught him the Bourget collection wasn't merely *his* family's history; it was a piece of France's soul. And with that realization came a daunting truth: he couldn't stop at protecting his own treasures. He had to continue her work and protect the art of other families as well, to shield the spirit of a nation under siege. Protecting one or two paintings at a time, as Eloise's group had done, wasn't enough. He needed to think bigger. France's entire cultural heritage was in danger, and it needed defending.

But how? Under Nazi occupation, this task was far too large for him alone. The sheer scale of what needed safeguarding, even just the Bourget collection, required resources beyond his reach. He would need allies —a network of people with influence, discretion, and the ability to operate in secrecy.

Eloise had been careful about not sharing the names of her resistance counterparts. Apart from a courier named Philippe, that door was likely closed, leaving Arnaud without a ready-made network. If he wanted to move forward, he would have to build his own—individuals who understood the stakes and could move undetected through occupied France.

His mind drifted through a list of possible names, but one stood out above the rest: the Vallois family.

Their influence stretched across Europe, synonymous not only with immense wealth but with deep political connections—a power honed not for show but for survival and careful intervention. Arnaud remembered his father once speaking of Étienne Vallois' talent for discreetly supporting ventures in morally gray areas, keeping vital projects alive through challenging times.

The Vallois family had the resources to back such an endeavor, and, just as crucially, the discretion and deception to operate unseen. More than that, they owned a significant art collection themselves, one that would surely be at risk. If anyone would understand the urgency of protecting art, it would be them.

Of course, reaching out to them was risky, but he saw no other way. To defend France's cultural soul—to continue Eloise's legacy—he had to go beyond his own grief and ally with those who could help.

After speaking with his father, Lucien, Arnaud wrote a letter to Étienne Vallois, calling upon the shared history between their two families. He kept his words careful, only hinting at the details, but his purpose was clear: France's cultural heritage was at risk. They needed discretion and a united front against the Nazi threat. A few days later, a response arrived. Étienne agreed to meet.

On the day of the meeting, Arnaud stood in his private study in Château Bourget, nerves on edge, as his guests entered. Étienne's reputation alone had made him vital to Arnaud's plan, but he hadn't expected Étienne's daughter to attend as well.

As Nadejda entered the room with her father, her presence caught Arnaud's attention immediately. She carried herself with a calm strength that suggested she, too, understood what it meant to lose something precious. Arnaud had heard of her past—her years linked to Sergei Shchukin, the famed Russian art collector whose life's work had been confiscated by the Soviets before his untimely death. He knew the bitterness of *both* losses must have burned deeply in Nadejda. If anyone could understand what was at stake here, it was her, a woman whose past mirrored his own struggle.

As her gaze met Arnaud's, he felt a glimmer of hope. Perhaps her influence over Étienne would be the force that turned the Vallois family's resources toward their cause.

After polite introductions, Arnaud laid out the situation. He explained the growing Nazi threat, the looting of private collections, and his fears that the Bourget estate—and other French families—would be stripped. His voice held a quiver of emotion as he spoke of Eloise's final plea, and the silent vow he had made to her memory.

"We need more than locked doors and hidden alcoves," Arnaud said, his tone resolute. "We need a network—a way to ensure that our cultural heritage stays out of their reach, whether in France or beyond its borders."

Étienne listened while Arnaud spoke, his face unreadable. Nadejda, however, was more direct. She asked about logistics, risks, the resources he would need, and how far he was willing to go. Each question honed the plan into something sharper, more purposeful.

When Arnaud finished, the room settled into silence. Finally, Étienne spoke:

"The Vallois family has always valued France's spirit, Monsieur Bourget," he said. "But we are also realists. This endeavor will come with substantial risks."

Arnaud held his breath as Étienne turned to Nadejda. "What do you think, Nady?" he said. The decision, it seemed, would rest with her.

Nadejda's eyes met Arnaud's with an intensity in her gaze. "This fight isn't just about protecting wealth or art," she said, her voice firm. "It's about resisting an ideology that seeks to erase our identity, our history." She paused, her expression softening as though she understood his grief.

"We'll help."

Chapter 34

I sit at the table, listening as Arnaud Bourget lays out his plan, his voice firm. The weight of his words sinks into the room, filling the space with an urgency I haven't felt in years. He speaks of the Nazis' pillaging of Europe's art, of their systematic erasure of culture and identity, and I find myself holding my breath, memories stirring like unsettled dust.

Next to me, my father, Étienne, sits with his usual steadfast calm, his hands folded neatly on the table, his gaze as neutral as ever. I know his mind is working, assessing the risks, weighing the potential gains and losses. For him, this meeting is another matter of calculated stakes, a decision grounded in practicalities, not in passion. But for me, there's something else here—a reminder of a different loss, a different moment when inaction cost me dearly. This time, I can't afford to stand by and let the tide of war steal everything we hold dear.

Arnaud's voice is unwavering, but I can sense the strain behind it, a note of desperation he's trying to suppress. His eyes flicker as he speaks, like a flame that refuses to go out, even when it's nearly snuffed by grief. I had heard about his wife—about Eloise. I can see his pain being masked by the will to do what is right. I feel it too, that raw edge, and it takes me back to the days after Sergei's death, to the dark silence that descended when the Soviets seized his collection. I can still see it—even five years later—Sergei's anguish as he watched everything he had cherished, everything he had given his life to protect, vanish under the banner of an iron-fisted regime. And I... I did nothing.

A heavy, familiar regret presses down on me. I told myself then that there was time, that maybe the winds of change would pass us, that it was better to lie low, to wait. But I was wrong, and Sergei paid the price. Now, listening to Arnaud describe the Reich's grip tightening around France, I see a reflection of that past—a dark, hungry force poised to swallow everything in its path. And I feel Sergei's voice at the edge of my mind, a faint whisper urging me not to make the same mistake twice. *The world will try to erase everything… you mustn't let them.*

Arnaud outlines the plan in meticulous detail, his eyes sparking with the conviction of a man who has nothing left to lose. He describes the need for a network, for resources and people who can navigate occupied France undetected, who can arrange safe passage for priceless pieces of art. He talks of bribing officials, of forging documents, of secret routes across borders—all measures necessary to keep these treasures out of Nazi hands. His voice grows bolder as he speaks, as though the very act of describing the mission strengthens his intent.

I glance at my father, trying to gauge his reaction, but his face remains unreadable, his silence speaking of calculations rather than convictions. He'll support the plan if it makes sense on paper, if it's "worth the risk," as he would put it. But for me, this goes far beyond practicality. This is personal. The Nazis don't just take art; they take people, lives, and futures. And if they're allowed to take France's culture, the very essence of our identity, then what remains? I can't let Sergei's fate repeat itself. Not again.

As Arnaud's words settle, I feel the decision closing in on me, the responsibility coiling around my chest. He looks at me, his expression open, waiting. It's as though he senses the turmoil within me also, the battle between duty and memory. This time, though, my choice is clear. I may not know how this will end, but I know I can't sit idle and watch history repeat itself. Now is *finally* my chance.

My father's voice is steady as Arnaud awaits our answer. "The Vallois family has always valued France's culture, Monsieur Bourget," he said. "But we are also realists. This endeavor will come with substantial risks."

I feel my father's gaze shift toward me, but I don't look at him. "What do you think, Nady," he says. I don't need his approval—not for this. The decision I'm about to make is mine alone—and I know it's the right one. A calm determination settles over me, the certainty filling my voice with a strength I hadn't expected.

"We'll help."

As the room falls silent, I realize we are on the brink of something momentous. This alliance we're about to form will be dangerous, yes, but it will also be a lifeline—a chance to stand up, to resist, to protect what the Nazis aim to destroy. And as I meet Arnaud's gaze, I feel a spark of something I thought I had lost—a purposefulness, a fire that tells me I'm no longer a passive observer.

The fight begins now.

Chapter 35

Paris, Modern Day

Amelia walked into the French National Archives at Pierrefitte-sur-Seine, her footsteps softened by the vastness of the vaulted hall. The space was modern, but imposing with clean lines and towering shelves that created a sense of reverence. Rows upon rows of meticulously organized files, books, and documents stretched out in every direction, reaching up toward the high ceilings. Each shelf held fragments of France's past—lost legacies, hidden treasures, and forgotten lives.

These archives were far more than mere storage; they were a labyrinth of history, carefully cataloged and preserved. Here lay an extensive collection of documents related to the French state: notarial records, legal proceedings, land ownership files, and estate inventories—all awaiting discovery.

Researchers and historians sat at wide wooden tables beneath the soft glow of reading lamps, surrounded by stacks of records. Some were bent intently over old manuscripts, their white gloves handling the fragile pages with extreme care. Others scrolled through digital records on sleek computer monitors, piecing together stories from pixels instead of paper. History was tangible in the air here—it felt almost sacred.

As she approached the research desk, Amelia felt the familiar tingle of anticipation, a thrill she'd chased throughout her career. Today, however, she was not just a restorer or an observer. Today, she was chasing a ghost.

Armed with Mr. Duval's vague suggestion about art collection stamps and old family crests, Amelia decided to delve into the labyrinth of notarial records, family histories, and legal documents, hoping to trace the mark from the painting and the ring back to a specific family. The archives were a daunting place, but her years of art restoration, and her father before that, had trained her to be patient and look for the small details that others might miss. Things hidden in plain sight. She was used to following invisible threads, even when the trail was vague and hard to follow.

Sitting down at one of the long wooden tables, she spread out some chosen files before her, taking in the soft scratch of paper against paper as she turned the brittle pages. Duval's mention of aristocratic families had given her a direction to start, but it was her own intuition that pushed her to focus on families with ties to the art world. The brush and key symbol from the engraving and frame *had* to mean something, and it made sense that it might point toward a family deeply entrenched in the artistic community.

As she sifted through the records, Amelia paid special attention to any families with surnames starting with "B"—the embroidery on the handkerchief still fresh in her mind. The task was daunting, the archives offering more questions than answers with every page she turned. Still, she pressed on, jotting down anything that hinted at connections to art or patronage.

Hours passed, the muted sounds of footsteps and distant murmurs in the archives blending into the rhythm of her search. Amelia's focus sharpened and waned in turns, the steady effort occasionally broken by a sip of coffee or a moment to stretch her neck. The records before her seemed endless, their faded text blurring as she flipped through one brittle page after another.

By late afternoon, sunlight slanted through the tall windows, casting warm light over the documents. One name stood out among the others: Bourget.

Amelia paused, her finger tracing the inked name on an old document from the 19th century. The Bourget family, renowned for their patronage of the arts, had deep ties to the Parisian art world. They had sponsored exhibitions, funded artists, and amassed an impressive art collection over the centuries. But as she read more about their influence, Amelia's pulse quickened. During the Nazi occupation, most of the Bourget family's art collection had been seized—confiscated by the regime, a fate that befell so many families of their background.

The pieces were starting to fit together.

The painting. The family's art collection. The ring hidden away in a toolbox, as if someone had been trying to protect it. Could the painting in the Jewish Museum be a Bourget family heirloom, lost or stolen during the war? Did that need protecting also? The idea took root in her mind.

Amelia dove deeper into the archives, searching through legal proceedings, estate inventories, and wartime records.

The Bourget family had clearly been active during the 19th and 20th centuries, and their art collection had been vast. She uncovered references to Lucien and Julien Bourget, two patriarchs whose influence had shaped the Parisian art scene across generations. But there were gaps in the records—documents missing, or vague mentions of items "lost" during the war. It was frustrating, but not unusual. So many families had suffered similar fates during the Nazi occupation. Their possessions had been scattered, hidden, or stolen. A few had reclaimed their heritage, but many treasures were lost forever.

Yet Amelia maintained the feeling she was on the right track. The Bourget family's ties to the art world seemed too significant to ignore. And then, as she turned the brittle pages of an old estate inventory, she found something that made her heart stop. In the margin, faint and faded, was a name:

Eloise Bourget.

Amelia stared at the name in shock as she inhaled sharply. *Eloise. EB.* The woman from the photograph and the letter hidden in the toolbox. The woman from the painting. The woman who she could find *nothing* about. Until now, it had only been her speculation that this was someone real, someone who had lived, breathed, and left traces of herself behind. But here it was, finally—tangible proof Eloise wasn't just a mysterious face on a canvas. Eloise was a *real* person. A *Bourget.* And her name was right there, inked onto the brittle page in front of her!

And if *she* was a Bourget, did that mean Arnaud was also?

The realization felt electric. This was her first real breakthrough. She had finally uncovered the one thing she had been searching for: confirmation that this elusive woman was someone who had existed, someone tied to a family with a name, a history, and a legacy. Eloise Bourget—a woman with a life that had been waiting in silence all this time to be unearthed.

But who was Eloise? The record was brief, almost like an afterthought in the larger tax-related estate inventory from 1935—one year after the date on the love letter. Scribbled next to her name were the letters "PA," hurried and added with little care. Yet, flipping through the remaining pages, there were no further details—no birth date, no marriage records, no mention of her life. Just a name left to fade into obscurity—a forgotten figure in a family whose legacy had been overshadowed by war and loss.

Amelia leaned back in her chair, her mind racing. The Bourget family's art collection, Eloise's portrait, the ring with its hidden engraving—everything was connected. But there was still one piece that didn't fit.

Her fingers absently traced the collection stamp as she studied the records. The symbol didn't just reference the Bourgets. Their family crest definitely featured a paintbrush, a nod to their patronage in the arts and, possibly, part of this mystery. But the key didn't belong—it hinted at something more, something hidden. Amelia frowned as her mind turned over the possibilities… until something hit her. What if the mark combined elements from *two* crests? An amalgamation—two families brought together through marriage, alliance, or some other connection? What if the stamp was more than a simple emblem? What if this was a layered message?

The idea sparked her curiosity. Had the Bourgets joined forces with another family, merging their symbols as a sign of shared interests or even mutual protection of their heritage? A brush for art, and a key for something else? Security? Trust? Ownership?

Renewed determination surged through her. If this were true, then there were more secrets buried in this story than she had initially thought. She needed more proof, but now she knew where to look. The archives held the answers, buried deep within layers of forgotten documents.

Eloise Bourget's story, long concealed, had revealed the faintest crack in its surface. But who was this possible other family? And what role had they played in this tangled web of art, loss, and secrets?

Chapter 36

Paris, Modern Day

I see her again. The woman from the museum.

She's sitting at a table in the archives, the same one where I've spent countless hours buried in documents. From my vantage point behind the shelves, I'm watching her, careful to remain out of sight. She's methodical, her fingers skimming over old pages with a familiarity that tells me she's been here before. *Too comfortable.* I wonder if she even knows what she's looking for, or if she's just stumbling through the past, hoping for answers.

I don't approach her. Not yet. But something about her search... it's unnerving. It's too close. She's asking for documents, names that brush against the same history I've been chasing. The Bourgets. *Does she know about the Vallois? About their Alliance?*

I can't decide if she's a rival or just a coincidence, drawn into this by chance. But the more I watch her, the more I'm certain—she's not just another restorer. She's looking for something, and whatever it is, it's valuable. I'll have to keep my distance, for now. But I won't let her out of my sight.

Chapter 37

Paris, Modern Day

The ticking of an old clock echoed somewhere in the archives, but time had lost meaning. Each day blurred into the next as Amelia combed through brittle pages, chasing the past.

Buried in notarial records and legal documents, she followed faint threads linking the Bourgets to France's art world and the shadows of wartime Europe. But one element remained stubbornly unclear: the skeleton key in the stamp. Unlike the paintbrush, which fit naturally with the Bourget family's artistic legacy, the key was an anomaly.

What did it signify? Why was it included in the mark? And more importantly, who else could be involved?

Her thoughts drifted to the Nazi occupation, to the partnerships formed out of necessity in the chaos of war. Families, communities, entire nations didn't survive those years by chance; they collaborated, joining forces to preserve what they could from the destructive reach of the regime.

But who would the Bourgets have collaborated with?

By the fourth day, her search expanded beyond the art world to families with political influence—those who might have had the means to protect not only their own interests but those of others as well. Perhaps the Bourgets' partners needed to bring something to the table the Bourgets couldn't.

She combed through more documents, following vague connections until a name emerged, recurring just often enough to draw her focus: the Vallois family.

One of France's most influential political and financial dynasties, the Vallois had shaped French and European policy throughout the 19th and early 20th centuries. But it wasn't just their power that caught Amelia's attention—it was the mention of a business partnership.

A faded contract from the early 1940s referenced a "mutual arrangement" between Lucien Bourget and Étienne Vallois. The language was vague, referencing financial support for an art exhibition. But Amelia's experience told her that art could often mask other motives, especially in turbulent times.

Why would a powerful political family like the Vallois involve themselves in something as trivial as an art exhibition?

Her mind raced as she considered the implications. Could the connection between the families have been more? Could it have been a merger to use the Bourgets' cultural influence with the Vallois' political reach? And if that was true, could their collaboration have extended beyond business?

As she pieced together the possibilities, Amelia's pulse quickened when her eyes drifted to the Vallois family crest printed on the top of the document. There, crowning the family name, was the unmistakable image of a skeleton key.

She leaned closer, comparing the crest with the collection stamp. The connection was unmistakable. Could it be a deliberate blending of two family symbols, an emblematic union between art and power? A mark of shared efforts to fulfill a specific goal? A mark of an alliance?

Amelia sat back. Could this really be the answer? Two families working together to achieve *something*. Something significant enough to require secrecy? The brush and key may have been their way of subtly marking their shared efforts, recognizable only to those who understood its meaning.

But why would these two families have an interest in the painting of Eloise? And the ring?

It clawed at her thoughts, and Amelia dug deeper into the stacks in search of more records connecting the Bourgets and the Vallois.

Frustrated after days of combing through estate documents, financial ledgers, and legal filings, she let her mind wander. She recalled a university lecture about wartime censorship. During World War II, the French Vichy government—operating under Nazi influence—routinely intercepted personal letters from those suspected of aiding the Resistance or hiding assets. After the war, the Fourth French Republic attempted to return these intercepted items to their rightful owners. Anything that couldn't be returned was archived as a state record and catalogued in the wartime censorship department of the archives.

Could there be intercepted correspondence between the Bourgets and the Vallois? If their actions had been deemed suspicious, it was worth a shot.

Determined, she approached the reference desk where an older archivist was meticulously organizing a stack of documents.

"Excuse me," Amelia began softly. "I'm researching two families and their connections during the 1940s. Is there any chance confiscated letters from that period are accessible?"

The archivist looked up, his eyes brightening with interest. "Ah, the wartime censorship records. Not many venture into that collection," he said. "But we do have those here. They're organized by date and recipient. Do you have specific years?"

Relief washed over her. "Yes! 1939 to 1943."

He nodded. "Follow me."

He led her to a more secluded section of the archives, where rows of boxes were neatly labeled with years and alphabetized by surname of the recipient.

"These are the files from that period," he explained. "It's quite extensive, but with names and dates, you might find what you're looking for."

"Thank you so much!" Amelia replied, her excitement renewed as he returned to his desk.

She began methodically working through the boxes labeled '1939 - B.' The musty scent of aged paper filled the air as she carefully sifted through envelopes, each bearing the marks of censorship—opened seals, official stamps, redacted lines.

But nothing.

———

Time seemed to blur as she worked her way through the stack. She moved to '1939 - V,' and then to '1940 - B,' '1940 - V,' and '1941 - B'—all with no results. With each box, her heart sank further. It was starting to feel like another dead end.

Then, in '1941 - V,' she gasped.

Her fingers froze on an envelope. The slanted, elegant script was addressed to Étienne Vallois. The return address: Château Bourget. Her heart pounded. Slowly, she turned it over and opened the flap.

Inside was a letter.

Amelia lifted the delicate paper and scanned the faded ink. Dated May 1941, it was written to Étienne from… Arnaud Bourget. She froze, mouth wide, as her eyes locked onto the name. *Arnaud Bourget*—likely Eloise's husband—had finally emerged from the shadows of her research!

Her hands trembled slightly as she read on. The letter's tone was vague and filled with the unease of the era. It spoke of wartime fears, of the looming threat of art seizures, and an urgent need to protect their most valued items.

But then, a line made her heart stop:

"Étienne, the key and the brush will guide us. In these times, we must remember to mark what we safeguard. The ledger will hold the rest."

Amelia's grip tightened on the paper. *The key and brush!* This was it! It *wasn't* just a collection stamp! It was a mark of protection! A symbol used to identify items they intended to safeguard and possibly hide!

And the ledger?

Her pulse quickened as she considered the word. *What was this ledger?* Could it be a record of all the Bourget and Vallois family treasures hidden during the Nazi occupation? A carefully kept list of items meant to survive the war, protected by their united front?

But then a startling thought struck her. *Why would Arnaud send such sensitive information in a letter, knowing it might be intercepted?* He must have been aware that wartime correspondence was closely monitored. Was it a calculated risk, vague enough to evade suspicion yet clear to Étienne? Or had desperation outweighed caution?

Amelia's mind spun as the implications set in. This whole secret might not be just about a single painting or a single ring. It might be about an entire cache, hidden away—items of personal, historical, or cultural significance, preserved against a common threat!

And if the ledger still existed, it might hold the key to uncovering all that had been lost, waiting to be returned to its rightful place!

The painting, the ring, even the engraving on the prong—they were all fragments of a much larger story, a legacy of resilience and preservation. But where was this ledger now? And why had it been buried in secrecy for so long?

The thought exhilarated her, but as she returned the letter to its protective sheath, an uneasy awareness settled over her. She wasn't alone in this search. Someone else had to know about the key and the brush, the ledger, and perhaps even the hidden items. It might even be the same person who had been watching her.

The idea brought attention to her surroundings.

Her eyes flicked up, catching a shadow at the edge of her vision. She squinted. Down the aisle, barely visible through the shelves, stood a man —dark, motionless, watching her.

Her heart pounded in her chest as recognition set in. It was the same man from the museum.

Without thinking, Amelia jumped to her feet, the chair clattering behind her as she bolted through the rows of documents, her eyes fixed on the figure. But before she could close the distance, he turned and slipped through the door.

She raced after him, her footsteps echoing loudly in the stillness of the archives. When she reached the hallway, her breath came in shallow bursts as she scanned the corridor. But it was empty. The man—whoever he was—had vanished.

Her heart hammered in her chest as she stood frozen in the empty hallway, the reality sinking in. She'd been followed. Watched. Someone else was after the same answers she sought.

But why?

And more importantly—who?

Chapter 38

Paris, Modern Day

I watch her from the shadows, her silhouette framed by the dim light of the archives as she steps out into the fading afternoon. She doesn't see me, doesn't know I'm standing here. But wherever she goes, I follow. It's not stalking—I tell myself that—but the lie is thin, barely holding.

She's digging too deep into a world far more dangerous than I think she realizes. I've quickly learned the art world isn't just about restoration and provenance. It's full of traffickers, thieves, men who would kill for a hint of what's been lost. And if she keeps searching, keeps tugging at these threads, she might find herself in crosshairs sooner than she thinks.

Maybe I should warn her. Maybe I should stay away. But I can't. Not now. There's too much at stake. She's too close to something valuable, something I need. Whether she knows it or not, her search is leading her straight to it. The question is, do I protect her or let her lead me there?

She has no idea who I am. And for now, I prefer it that way.

Chapter 39

The room was dim, the tension palpable as Arnaud surveyed the faces gathered around the table. Each person here was not just a participant, but an essential pillar holding up a shared mission. France's cultural heritage hung in the balance, and the stakes had never been higher.

"My contacts within the French Resistance have already agreed to help us set up safe houses," Arnaud began, his voice steady but brimming with urgency. "We'll need more than a few of these to create an effective network. The works can't stay in one place for too long. The Reich has become relentless in their searches and seizures."

Lucien sat across from him, his fingers pressed tightly together as he listened. "The Resistance can be relied upon for safe houses, yes," he replied, "but what about movement across borders? We can't count on keeping these pieces hidden forever, especially with the Gestapo's unpredictable raids."

A sign of agreement passed through the group. Nadejda looked to her father, Étienne, who sat silent and thoughtful, a man of imposing calm even amid such deliberation. She could sense he was letting her take the lead.

"My father and I," she said, looking back at the group, "can arrange for certain... paperwork to be overlooked." She leaned forward. "We'll need to bribe officials and forge documents. It will require a network of bureaucrats we can trust or control."

Étienne finally spoke, his tone matter-of-fact. "Discretion is everything. If the Nazis suspect even a trace of what we're doing, it will be over before it's begun. I can provide the necessary funds and connections to secure a discreet passage for our... 'shipments.' But each movement must be handled with absolute precision." His eyes shifted to Arnaud. "Tell us, Arnaud, how will we decide which pieces to prioritize?"

Arnaud straightened, his grief over Eloise lending strength to his voice. "Using our resources in the art world, my father and I have been compiling a list—pieces that hold irreplaceable cultural value. They are more than just paintings; they are symbols of what it means to be French. These works, I believe, carry a message of our resilience, of our identity. We cannot risk losing them."

He paused, letting that sink in. The selection process had been careful and ongoing. It began with the well-known masterworks and treasures from major collections, but it didn't end there. They knew they needed to protect others—farmers' families with a cherished portrait passed down through generations, small-town churches with centuries-old pieces, modest households that had saved for years to commission one genuine painting. Arnaud had insisted that their protection efforts not favor only the rich or famous. A humble watercolor hanging in a shoemaker's home could be just as important to that family's legacy as a Monet was to the nation's cultural identity. No matter their origin, these artworks told stories that transcended wealth or status.

Ultimately, if a family, gallery, or museum wanted an artwork protected, the group would do their best to ensure it was.

A silence followed as everyone absorbed Arnaud's words. Nadejda felt a stirring resolve within herself, recognizing the delicate balance between national heritage and individual memories. She glanced at Lucien, who wore the same look of decisiveness as his son.

Lucien leaned forward, his voice low. "I've been in contact with a list of families from all walks of life—aristocrats, collectors, even those whose names would draw no attention. They fear the same thing we do, that their histories will be erased. They're willing to trust us, but we must be cautious. They won't need to know where we're hiding the pieces or even who is transporting them. All they need is assurance that, whether they're here to reclaim them or not, these artworks will survive. They want to know that what they leave in our care won't disappear with them—that it will endure, safe, ready to inspire and connect the future generations who will need these stories as much as we do."

Arnaud's face softened slightly. "This isn't just about us anymore," he said, looking around the table. "It's about preserving the identity of a nation, a people. We're not simply hiding paintings—we're hiding memories, lives, dreams. Each piece of art is a story we're saving for the future."

Nadejda thought of Sergei's words, how he'd once said art was the soul of humanity. Now that same truth had found a new home here, as they banded together to protect what mattered most.

Étienne's expression remained carefully composed, but his eyes showed approval as he listened. He turned to Lucien. "What of the people who won't accept our terms of secrecy outright? Or those who might hesitate to let their works leave their care?"

Lucien glanced at Arnaud, a silent understanding passing between father and son. "Ultimately, this must remain voluntary," Arnaud replied. "If we force compliance, we are no better than the Reich. Some may not see the threat as clearly as we do. Others will need reassurances. But they must understand—this isn't just about the risk of losing their art. Their pieces aren't simply vulnerable; they're targeted."

He leaned back, his fingers brushing the edge of the table, thinking about Eloise. "This is more than just their loss to bear. If these works disappear, it's humanity that loses—a piece of our shared spirit, our history, our very identity. That's why we must remain the invisible hands in this mission. Anonymity isn't a choice; it's a necessity. It's the only way we can ensure these legacies outlast the war, regardless of what happens to any of us."

Arnaud's gaze swept over everyone at the table. "I've started drafting a list of trusted associates who will transport the art—people who will handle it as if it were their own children. We'll keep this number to a minimum. The fewer who understand the details, the safer we will be."

Nadejda nodded, her gaze intense. "We'll also need a secure way to communicate. We can't risk sending messages that could be intercepted. My father and I have contacts in Western Europe—certain couriers who can carry encrypted notes for us."

Étienne looked toward his daughter, and then to the group. "If we agree to this, it must be clear to everyone that there will be no turning back."

The room settled into a silence as they absorbed the enormity of what they were planning. There was no room for hesitation or missteps. One wrong move, one errant word, and everything they were working to protect could be destroyed.

"The stakes are too high for doubt," Arnaud finally said, affirming Étienne's previous comment. "We each have our roles, and we must carry them out with absolute precision. For Eloise, for Sergei, for everything we've already lost."

Nadejda felt a fire ignite within her—a purpose that felt long overdue. She knew now that Sergei's legacy had not died with him. This was her chance to honor everything he had stood for, to finally act on the courage she had held back when the Soviets came for his collection.

"Then it's decided?" Nadejda questioned, her voice resolute. She exchanged a look with Arnaud, Lucien, and her father. No one raised an objection. It was a silent promise of commitment. She continued, "We protect the art, not just as objects but as symbols of our humanity, our resistance. We cannot let the Nazis rob us of who we are."

Arnaud held her confident gaze, feeling a glimmer of hope for the first time since Eloise's death. In Nadejda, he could see a determination that matched his own, mirrored Eloise's, and a fierceness they would both need to see this mission through.

Each person around the table reflected the same conviction. They all understood the dangers ahead, but also the necessity of what needed to be done. Together, they would form an alliance—a secret, silent resistance fueled not by weapons but by ideals. It was an oath to protect the spirit of France and, in doing so, defy those who sought to erase it.

They knew this fight would shape not only their lives but the lives of generations to come.

Chapter 40

Spring nights had finally warmed the narrow streets of the Left Bank. Once, this would have brought bustling cafés and music drifting into the night, a celebration of winter's end. Now, all that liveliness had been smothered by the occupation. The streets lay hushed, disturbed only by the occasional hum of passing trucks and the muffled voices from radios playing behind shuttered windows.

Tucked into the shadows, Arnaud and Nadejda moved carefully, their footsteps nearly lost in the silence of Paris. The operation was meticulously planned, every detail scrutinized, and every route mapped. But no amount of preparation could ease the tension they felt now.

Arnaud led the way, his shoulders tense beneath his coat as he scanned the streets for any sign of trouble. They were moving towards a small, unassuming gallery, tucked away on a forgotten side street. The Bourget family had helped establish this gallery as a haven for up-and-coming artists, and now that cultural investment had paid off.

Despite its outside appearance, inside, works of rare beauty hung on its walls—paintings whose value lay not just in brushstrokes and color but as symbols of identity and courage that the Nazis wanted to silence.

Slipping in through the back entrance, Nadejda took in the dimly lit space. Even in the shadows, the paintings seemed to radiate with meaning, reminding her why they risked so much to protect these pieces. She took a steady breath, focusing on what needed to be done.

Arnaud met the gallery owner at the rear of the room, Bernart, a man whose loyalty to the Bourgets was as enduring as his art collection. "It's an honor to help with this, Monsieur Bourget," Bernart said. "Anything I can do, for Eloise's memory and for France."

"Thank you, Bernart. We won't forget this," Arnaud replied, resting a hand on the man's shoulder.

They worked quickly, wrapping each painting with care. The soft sound of cloth against wood frames filled the silence. Bernart's workers, a few of whom had joined the resistance, handled the pieces with reverence. Arnaud cast a cautious glance toward Bernart, the unspoken question in his eyes clear. Catching his look, Bernart chuckled softly and gave a reassuring pat on his shoulder. "Rest easy, my friend. I trust these men with my life, and you can too."

The room remained silent, filled with the tension of their shared risk. No one spoke of the danger waiting outside the gallery walls. Every cautious glance, every careful movement, showed their understanding of the risk.

Nadejda directed two workers to prepare the covered paintings for transport. She made sure that each one was carefully layered in cloth and placed inside a wood crate, disguised among other crates that could pass as supplies. She glanced at Arnaud, catching his eye with confirmation. This would be their litmus test, a trial run to see if the Alliance could execute the seemingly impossible.

"Be sure to load them in the second truck," Arnaud instructed one worker, voice firm. "We need to know any enemies are watching the wrong prize."

Bernart nodded, signaling his men. As the paintings left the gallery, Arnaud and Nadejda climbed into the second truck, following the first from a cautious distance, and watching for the smallest signs of danger. Every turn felt like a gamble, as the sound of tires against cobblestone amplified in the tense silence of the night. Arnaud kept the windows rolled down, ears trained for suspicious footsteps or whistles, or even glimpses of Gestapo uniforms lurking on street corners, yet the streets remained eerily quiet.

The convoy moved steadily through the winding streets until they reached the edge of Paris, slipping out just before the 21:00 curfew fell over the city like a shroud. Once on the outskirts, the first truck diverted, taking a different route to misdirect any pursuers, while Arnaud and Nadejda continued on in the second vehicle.

They took side roads, avoiding main thoroughfares that might draw unwanted attention at this time of day. Hours passed as they navigated narrow country lanes, each turn carrying them farther from the city's grip. At last, they reached the first safe house—a secluded barn nestled against a grove of trees.

The truck rolled into the barn, where the house's owners, aware of the plan but not the precious cargo inside, quickly shut and secured the doors, sealing Arnaud and Nadejda inside, away from the outside world. Here, they would wait until dawn, hidden within the barn's worn wooden walls.

Inside, the faint scent of hay and soil filled the air, a safe smell in the quiet solitude of the countryside. Arnaud kept watch, tension lingering as he checked the windows, half-expecting the distant rumble of an enemy patrol's engine.

But there was nothing.

Nadejda sat beside him, her gaze steady, betraying none of the exhaustion she felt. In the early gray light, the world seemed suspended in an uneasy calm as it watched them prepare for the next leg of their journey. Only when the first hints of sunrise crept over the horizon did they roll out again, moving swiftly along the roads. With each passing mile, they slipped further from prying eyes and closer to safety.

Days later, they gathered outside the entrance of their hiding space, an unassuming spot known only to the Alliance's inner circle. Its remote location made it ideal, reachable only by a network of winding roads that helped conceal their path. Inside, their cargo was shielded by old walls and silence.

Though the threat still remained close, and one misstep could undo it all, for now, in this place, they allowed themselves a moment to breathe. This art was safe.

Meanwhile, Étienne Vallois, working behind the scenes, had set into motion a series of complex financial maneuvers. With this, he arranged offshore accounts to fund their growing network—money that would cover everything from bribes to secure passage for the art to supplies and safe houses for the couriers. Through discreet transactions and trusted contacts, he wove a protective veil over the funding trails, ensuring the Alliance's activities remained hidden from any who might trace their actions. This is what he was good at.

He also ensured that Arnaud, Nadejda, and their field operatives had forged documents to slip through borders and checkpoints, moving unseen through occupied France—each crafted by his most trusted contacts in both Paris and Vichy. These documents weren't merely falsified papers; they were expertly forged identities complete with detailed backstories, official seals, and subtle signs of wear to pass even the closest scrutiny.

"Everything's in place," Étienne assured them. "Our assets and team members will be protected, hidden behind a dozen paper trails. If anyone follows, they'll lose the scent before they even come close."

"Good," Arnaud said, relieved. The money and papers weren't just for this trip, but for every mission—for all the people who would soon entrust them with their legacies.

Meanwhile, Lucien started establishing an underground telegram network—a hidden line of communication that would allow the Alliance to remain invisible as they solicited their services. The Bourget's deep ties to the art world granted Lucien access to provenance records and other documents that authenticated the history of ownership for countless works. These records, often overlooked by the Reich as bureaucratic waste, held invaluable details that allowed him to discreetly identify and contact families whose art collections were most at risk.

Each message would be encoded, sent through a labyrinthine path, and relayed by trusted contacts and allies. With the network, they could reach out to more families without risking exposure. It was crucial that these solicitations seemed like casual correspondence, not direct pleas.

"Are we certain the messages won't be intercepted?" Nadejda asked as she watched Lucien mark each cipher key on a small pad of paper.

"No system is perfect, but this one will work—for now," Lucien replied. "Each code has a limited shelf life. I'll rotate them to keep everyone on their toes."

Nadejda nodded, satisfied, but the thought of anyone tracing their efforts worried her. She turned her attention to Arnaud, who stood watching with a pensive expression, as though he was thinking the very same concerns.

"The pieces are safe," he said softly. "And if all goes according to plan, they'll stay that way."

Nadejda nodded in understanding. This was still the beginning, and there would be kinks to work out. But as they progressed, each completed mission would be a step in the right direction, each a win against the Nazi threat.

———————

Their second mission also went smoothly, each step carefully execut-ed as if the Alliance was rehearsing a delicate dance.

While Lucien continued to build their backlog, this trip moved the first set of Vallois paintings—a handful of smaller pieces chosen for their historical and cultural significance. Under Nadejda's guidance, they added extra protective layers to the packaging, ensuring these artworks could better withstand the journey. The paintings passed through a series of safe houses and winding roads without trouble, confirming that their system worked.

Back in Paris, Arnaud allowed himself a quick break to relax. He sat at a small café just off Boulevard Saint-Germain, sipping coffee as the warm spring sun lit the street. A few pedestrians strolled by, and a distant murmur of conversation floated from inside the café. For a moment, he let the tension ease. But that relief was short-lived when he noticed some-one approaching from across the street.

As the man drew closer, Arnaud recognized him—Philippe. Eloise had relied on Philippe for his sharp instincts and his unassuming pres-ence. He had been invaluable under the occupation, securing supplies, relaying messages, and even slipping crucial items past German patrols unnoticed.

When Arnaud had expanded the Alliance's network, Philippe was one of the first he reached out to. His knowledge of the city's hidden routes and his natural caution made him the ideal ally. Though they had spoken little since Eloise's passing, Arnaud knew that anyone Eloise had trusted so implicitly was someone he could depend on now more than ever.

Philippe moved with purpose, glancing over his shoulder before reaching Arnaud, trying to catch his breath, his face tense. Leaning in, he whispered, "Arnaud, I've heard talk—The Gestapo. They raided Bernart's gallery while you were gone. They were looking for five pieces that seemed to vanish right under their noses." Philippe's eyes flickered with worry as he leaned even closer. "Arnaud," he said in a hushed tone. "What if they know?"

Chapter 41

Paris, Modern Day

Amelia leaned back in her studio chair, turning the ring over in her fingers as the puzzle began to take shape. The archives had revealed more than she expected. The names Bourget and Vallois surfaced repeatedly, weaving themselves into a narrative too intricate to dismiss. And the deeper she dug, the clearer it became: the key and paintbrush mark wasn't just a crest. It was a symbol—a deliberate signpost of a secret alliance forged in the chaos of war.

She studied the ring, her thoughts racing. The fake diamond and hidden engraving weren't meant to deceive—they were clues, deliberately constructed to lead her here. The ring's value lay not in its materials but in its connection to something far greater: the Bourget-Vallois Alliance and the treasures they had safeguarded. The key and brush wasn't an ornament; it was a guide.

Turning back to the records she had copied at the Archives, Amelia sifted through the fragments of their story. The Bourgets weren't just aristocratic art collectors; they were patrons and curators of French culture, deeply embedded in the Parisian art scene.

But as she flipped through the pages, a new trend emerged. Mentions of the Bourgets seemed to fade from public view as the timeline approached the early 1940s. Their role as patrons of the arts grew more subdued. Fewer exhibitions bore their name; fewer records chronicled their prestige. By the time the Nazis invaded, it was like they had vanished.

What happened?

Amelia paused, staring at the pages before her. She already knew the answer. The war had changed everything. When the Third Reich swept across Europe, their appetite for cultural dominance extended beyond politics and into art. Priceless works were looted, collections dismantled, and families who had spent generations building their artistic legacies were left scrambling to protect what they could. The Bourgets, like so many others, had been forced to act quickly, trying to hide their most valuable treasures from Nazi looters. But how had they managed it?

The Vallois family provided the answer. Wealthy, powerful, and politically entrenched, they had crossed paths with the Bourgets repeatedly. What began as business dealings now seemed like something more calculated. As Amelia dug deeper, a pattern emerged. The Vallois weren't just another family of means. They were experts at wielding their influence, even during the darkest days of the occupation.

Her fingers brushed a letter dated 1942, where she'd first seen the phrase "safeguarded assets." It wasn't specific—nothing about art or paintings mentioned directly—but it hinted at a partnership designed to hide items of value.

Her thoughts whirled as she pulled up more records. Sudden transfers of property, assets moved with little explanation. Estate inventories became curiously absent of the artworks the Bourgets were known for. In one legal document, there was a specific reference to "items of cultural significance" being moved, but again, no specific names or pieces were mentioned. The more she uncovered, the more it seemed this wasn't simply a business partnership—it was a calculated collaboration.

The Bourgets had the art. The Vallois had the means to protect it.

A certainty started settling over her. This was no longer just a theory. Everything she had uncovered pointed to an organized effort to hide art and keep it safe. But they hadn't just hidden it, had they? They tracked it. There was a ledger as well. A list of all the items they safeguarded—to ensure these treasures could one day be reclaimed. She felt a thrill, mingled with determination.

This ledger, if it still existed, could be the key to restoring countless pieces of history. Not just a record, but a lifeline to the past—a way of reclaiming what had nearly been lost.

Amelia drummed her fingers on the desk, eyeing the pile of documents she had painstakingly gathered. Some new questions started bothering her: *So why hadn't this ledger been found yet? Why hadn't these pieces of art been returned? Or had they?*

The more she thought about it, the more the answer took shape. If these families had gone to such great lengths to hide their treasures, then the ledger—the key to everything—would be the most important thing to protect, hidden with the same care as the art it catalogued. *If* someone found it, the world would already know. Yet here she was, decades later, chasing whispers and half-forgotten symbols.

Her eyes drifted to the ring on the table, its engraved symbol suddenly heavy with meaning. It hadn't survived by accident. Whoever had hidden it—and the toolbox—had done so with remarkable foresight, leaving behind the first markers of a carefully laid trail of breadcrumbs. And if something as seemingly inconsequential as a ring and a toolbox had stayed buried for decades, then surely the ledger—far more significant—had also evaded detection, layered with protections to keep it safe.

Further, the war had torn families apart, scattering their secrets. Even the most elaborate of safeguards couldn't account for the chaos that followed. Survivors scattered. Heirs lost track. And without the ledger to piece it all together, the treasures they had hidden would remain just that —hidden.

The more Amelia considered the possibility of the ledger still being hidden, the more it felt... real. And if it was real, one question loomed above all: *Where was it?*

She took a deep breath, her chest tightening as a realization settled over her. Perhaps the people who had hidden these pieces—and their breadcrumbs—hadn't just wanted to protect them. They had wanted them to be found. But only by the right person—someone worthy of their secret. *Could that person be her?*

The thought left her both exhilarated and uneasy. If she was right, if this ledger truly existed, and if she could find it, she could uncover one of the most significant caches of hidden art in history. But she wasn't the only one searching. The shadowy figure at the museum and again at the archives—whoever he was—knew something.

Amelia gathered her notes, stuffing them into her bag as her mind raced. There were more leads to follow, more breadcrumbs to find. But her next move required space—a place where she could sift through everything and map out her strategy. The studio, cluttered with her abandoned restoration projects, felt too stifling. Her apartment would give her the space to think without distractions.

She slung the bag over her shoulder, her heart pounding with the thrill of discovery as unease crept in around the edges. The past was unraveling, but with each thread she pulled, the risks intensified. She wasn't just uncovering history—she was stepping into a game that had begun decades before she was born.

And the players may still be watching.

Chapter 42

What if they know?

Arnaud's relief vanished in an instant. Just moments ago, he had been sipping coffee, trying to find a moment of calm, but now Philippe's warning echoed in his mind. If the Gestapo were already questioning missing pieces, the Alliance's movements might have left more traces than he realized—or worse, someone within their network could be tipping the Nazis off.

The thought tightened his chest. He couldn't do anything about what was already done. But moving forward, they would have to be even more cautious. No mistakes. There was no margin for error. Any slip could mean betrayal, capture, or the end of everything they were trying to save.

Paris, May 1941

The city of Paris seemed overwhelmed, burdened by countless secrets and the watchful eyes of their invading enemy. Arnaud sat in his study at Château Bourget, listening to Nadejda and Lucien outline the newest layers of deceit they would need to safeguard the Alliance's mission.

The stakes had already been high, but now—with a theory that someone in their network could be a Nazi informant—everything had shifted.

Arnaud cleared his throat, his voice calm but intent. "We can't afford another risk like this. From now on, those who transport the art will have no idea what they're carrying. And I think we need some extra mis-direction—more layers to keep anyone from guessing our methods."

Lucien nodded as he considered the implications. "Arnaud is right. Absolute need-to-know. No one outside our inner circle should learn any-thing beyond their own task. Even our communications... we should avoid any mention of the art." He paused, pressing his palms together, his fingertips resting lightly against his lips as a new thought took shape. "Until now, we've been tracking these pieces informally, relying on mem-ory and short notes. But this mission will get too big, too complex... fast."

Étienne folded his hands, now resolute, speaking calmly and clear. "We need a more structured logging system. Simply noting which paint-ings we need to move is no longer enough. As this operation grows, every piece must be thoroughly cataloged and tracked. We need to know exact-ly what's being moved, where each piece is en route, and where it's head-ed, so we can ensure its safety at every stage... especially now that we are limiting details to just us. If our network is ever compromised, this clarity will be what prevents any piece from falling into the wrong hands."

Arnaud paused, feeling the burden of Étienne's suggestion settle over them. Before, they had carried out moves based on a loose under-standing of which pieces were where. Now they needed something more rigorous.

"Yes," he said slowly, the idea taking root. "A ledger, something that will hold everything together, track each piece without revealing too much to anyone who shouldn't know. Coded, and with redundant safe-guards. And for security, only Nadejda and I will know the full system. That way, if anything happens..."

He didn't finish the thought before Nadejda interjected. "We can't leave anything to chance," she agreed, while nodding. "I like this. This ledger will guide us, ensuring we can restore each piece to its rightful place when the time comes. We've been thinking small. We need to think bigger."

She continued, her mind already considering the logistics. "And for each piece, a mark," she said. "If we need to return the pieces to their rightful owners one day, we need to confirm their authenticity and origin. A unique mark, linked to the ledger, will guarantee we can trace each painting back to its true provenance." She reached over and tapped a blank book in front of her. "The ledger will be the heart of our work, Arnaud. It cannot fall into anyone else's hands. We must protect it at all costs."

––––––––––

That evening, Arnaud sat alone in his study, sketching a mark that would identify each piece the Alliance protected. Using one of Eloise's soft charcoals, he drew the outline of a paintbrush intertwined with a key —a simple blending of the Bourget and Vallois family crests, symbolizing both art and protection. The emblem felt like an extension of Eloise's and Sergei's legacies, a union of their lives' work and passions.

Nadejda joined him later, watching as he carved the first lines of the woodcut for the stamp. "It's perfect," she murmured, looking at the sketch, her voice tinged with reverence. "This… it's more than just a mark. It's a pledge."

Arnaud looked up. "Yes, and one we can't afford to break. Each painting we mark represents a life, a story, and a legacy."

––––––––––

The next morning, Arnaud and Nadejda began filling the ledger with their first entries, encoding records of each painting they had already hidden and those they planned to move.

"This work," Nadejda murmured, "it isn't just about preserving beauty. It's an act of resistance—against erasure, against control."

Arnaud glanced at the entries, running his fingers along the fresh ink. "This record is a risk," he said, more to himself than to her, "but it's also our best defense. As long as we hold this, we can prove what was saved."

––––––––––

That afternoon, they met again with Lucien and Étienne to discuss widening the scope of their work. Nadejda listened, aware that every new step took them deeper into morally ambiguous areas. Though she had thrown herself into the Alliance's mission without hesitation, she couldn't ignore a creeping unease. Her mind echoed with a thought that had surfaced more frequently as their plans grew bolder—What would Sergei do?

She wasn't afraid of taking risks to defy the Nazis, but something in her questioned the methods they were beginning to embrace. As Étienne described forging permits and discreet payments, Nadejda spoke up. "We're starting to use tactics that… some might call morally gray. Bribing officials, forging documents, smuggling—these are acts that change us."

Étienne raised an eyebrow, showing a mix of curiosity and confusion. "And… you wonder where the line is?"

She nodded, her thoughts trailing back to Sergei. "Sergei believed in art's purity. He would have done anything to protect it, but without compromising its soul. I worry that if we blur these lines too far, do we risk becoming what we oppose?"

Arnaud, sensing her inner conflict, met her gaze. "We're dealing with an enemy who won't hesitate to erase our culture. If we refuse to use the tools they would, we could lose everything we're here to protect."

Nadejda looked away, considering his words. Perhaps Sergei would have embraced these methods, too. But even as she considered their necessity, she felt one last holdout, a principle she couldn't release.

"Okay… we'll do what it takes to protect these works, but I'm going to be firm about one line we *cannot* cross," Nadejda said, her voice unwavering. "The provenance, the history of these works, *must* remain intact. Each piece must be returned in its true form, to its true origins. And, if, for whatever reason, the original owners cannot reclaim a piece, the art must benefit humanity as a whole." She looked at them while pointing down at the ledger, her gaze steady. "We are preserving, not altering. And if we can agree on that right now, we move forward. Otherwise, we're no better than those we are protecting these from."

Lucien's voice was calm. "We honor the integrity of the art. We don't erase or distort the truth. That's the line we hold," he said, his words settling over the group.

Nadejda felt her resolve solidify. She would go as far as necessary, but not so far as to destroy the essence of what they were saving. This was a price she could live with, a moral line she could defend.

The Alliance continued its mission.

However, every piece of art now carried added responsibility. Their transports were no longer just deliveries—they became calculated maneuvers, requiring even greater secrecy and deception. Couriers were deliberately kept in the dark about what they carried, the cargo hidden in crates disguised as mundane goods. The art slipped through channels as if it were nothing more than routine shipments.

The meticulous planning paid off. Their network worked smoothly; no message was intercepted, no courier questioned. Each step honed their secure process. One that held its own elegance, like an intricate dance of concealment and trust. One by one, the pieces of art found their way to safety, lying dormant, hidden and secure, waiting for the day they could reemerge and breathe life into a freer world.

In this work, they found their purpose, but also their burden. It was a commitment that demanded everything of them—a battle fought not with guns, but with strategy, willpower, and the quiet preservation of history, one secret delivery at a time.

Chapter 43

The dim light of Amelia's apartment flickered in the early morning hours, casting uneven shapes across the scattered documents on her desk. Her coffee cup sat half-full and cold beside her, forgotten as she sifted through estate records and faded papers. She had not gone to bed yet. She *couldn't* go to bed—there was way too much adrenaline pumping through her after her recent discoveries.

It had been just over two weeks since she'd uncovered the false bottom in the toolbox, but time had dissolved into an endless blur of sleepless nights and unanswered questions. Her commissioned restoration projects were all but abandoned, overtaken by a single, consuming purpose: finding the ledger.

Amelia was certain now that this elusive document—if it still existed—held the key to unlocking the Bourget-Vallois Alliance and revealing a hidden trove of art safeguarded during the Nazi occupation. The clues had been cryptic, buried in the vague business correspondences and old legal records, but she'd followed the trail and uncovered their purpose. Arnaud Bourget and Étienne Vallois hadn't left things to chance. They'd hidden something of immense value—something that was meant to survive not just the war, but the passage of time.

But the world was vast, and the ledger could be anywhere. The archives had started to show dead ends; with no further clues to go on, she'd exhausted their usefulness. She needed a fresh approach. *Where would someone hide a ledger that detailed their most precious hidden valuables?* Hiding it with the art itself might have seemed logical, a way to keep the records and the treasures together, but perhaps too risky. If someone found one, they'd find both. The ledger held power as a standalone record, a carefully guarded inventory that could reveal secrets even without the items it documented.

She let her mind wander to the practicalities. A ledger like that would have been crucial, but not something they'd bury beyond reach. They would have needed access to it, if not often, then at least occasionally. Perhaps to update it or to check on their arrangement. Her mind continued to spin. The ledger would need to be somewhere accessible but concealed. A family like the Bourgets or Vallois wouldn't have let something so significant stray too far from their inner circle. Keeping it close, yet hidden within their estate or at a similarly secure location, would have been a calculated decision—a way to safeguard it from outsiders while still keeping it within arm's reach. She reasoned the ledger was likely still in France, possibly close to the family itself—perhaps at Château Bourget or within the Vallois mansion.

But why would it still be hidden? she thought. Eighty years had passed since the war. She quickly returned to a previous realization—*because if it had been found, she would have heard about it*—especially in the circles she frequented. The significance of the ledger may have only been known to a select few in each generation, its existence kept quiet and carefully guarded, even from most heirs. After the war, family members may have been scattered or lost, and with the passing of time, the knowledge of the ledger's true purpose could have faded into obscurity, leaving it as just another old document gathering dust.

Her pulse quickened as she imagined it: a small, ordinary-looking ledger among the records or storage at Château Bourget, left overlooked precisely because it was hidden so well.

Amelia leaned back in her chair, closing her eyes to visualize Château Bourget. She let her memory guide her through spaces she had read about, imagining walking through its grand halls and opulent rooms filled with art and history. *If you wanted to hide something important, where would you put it?* The main house was too obvious—too many eyes, too much activity. The libraries and private offices were possible, but still too open and frequented.

Her thoughts drifted back to an old estate grounds map she'd found a few days ago, a detailed layout of the property cataloged by the French Order of Licensed Surveyors in 1970. She shuffled through the papers until she found it, spreading the large, folded copied sections across her desk. Her eyes traced the familiar outlines: the main house, the gardens, the vineyard, the stables. Then her gaze settled on a small structure at the edge of the property, nearly obscured by the boundary lines and forest—*Le Pavillon d'Artisan*, the Artisan's Lodge.

She dug deeper into her notes about the building and scanned a few historical websites. The lodge had served as a workspace where art was created and restored—a sanctuary for creativity, removed from the bustling activity of the main house.

She scanned through more documents and found a series of purchase orders from 1940 for art supplies—varnishes, brushes, specialized tools—all delivered not to the main house but specifically to the Artisan's Lodge. The orders themselves seemed routine enough, but a small scribbled note beside one caught her eye: *"Items to be kept away from the daily life at the château."* The wording, so intentional and precise, held her attention. It suggested there was a deliberate separation. A sense that these supplies—and perhaps more items—were meant to exist beyond the estate's everyday rhythms.

Away from the daily life at the château. The more she considered it, the more it made sense. *What else could they be keeping in that space?* If the Bourgets wanted to hide something valuable yet keep it within reach, it would need to be somewhere prying eyes couldn't access. This Artisan's Lodge might have been ideal. It was on the estate but *away from daily life*—accessible but inconspicuous, the kind of place few would have a reason to visit. Given they created and restored art there, it was probably safe from the elements, as well. She pulled up satellite imagery of the estate. Her eyes focusing on the tiny outbuilding, which was dwarfed compared to the main house and set back a good distance. *Could this be where they hid their most valuable record?*

Amelia sat back in her chair and considered the idea. *Wouldn't the new owners have cleaned out the space?* she wondered. *What if they threw the ledger away?* But then she considered what the Artisan's Lodge really was—an unassuming, practical workspace. It was a building meant for restoration, repairs, and storage rather than show. For generations, estates like these were acquired by families more interested in their elegance than in cleaning out every dusty corner. The lodge, possibly still filled with old rusty equipment, restoration logs, and paint splatters, might not have drawn much attention at all. It could easily have been dismissed as a storage space or place to house practical tools rather than a place of secrets.

The more she considered it, the more plausible it felt. It was likely the Artisan's Lodge had been left undisturbed, an overlooked relic of the estate's past. *If it's still there,* she thought, *the ledger could be waiting among the layers of dust and forgotten records that no one ever thought to look through carefully.*

But she couldn't rely on theory alone. She needed proof.

And then a memory hit her. The estate inventory sheet from 1935 filed with the Ministry of Finance in the Bourget tax records from the archives. Right next to Eloise's name, the letters "PA." She had assumed they were simply a notation or initials she didn't understand. But now she saw it differently. *PA. Pavillon d'Artisan? What did that line mention, again?* She rifled through her notes, her finger tracing down the list, stopping at "Eloise - PA." The description read: *Household records and financial ledgers.*

Why would Eloise be listed alongside the Artisan's Lodge and household records? More importantly, this was the first mention she'd seen of the lodge as a storage place for such records! Could the Artisan's Lodge, originally a space for creative work, also have housed the family's important documents? Even in a storage capacity? *Kept away from the daily life at the château,* among old tools and supplies? Were there other important things also still waiting to be discovered inside the space?

Her theory was taking shape. Then she recalled a line she'd read in an old exhibition catalog housed in the Bibliothèque Nationale's Rare Books and Special Collections Department. It featured the Bourget family's contributions to art during the early 20th century. The catalog included excerpts from interviews and public speeches, and one quote from Arnaud Bourget stood out when he was asked about his family's wartime preparations. He said, "The finest things needn't be behind lock and key; they remain safe, hidden in plain sight." She'd brushed it off as a casual, philosophical musing. In the catalog, Arnaud had been discussing a case of wine and how, despite the looming threat of Nazi looting, they kept it accessible to enjoy in the present rather than hide it away. But what if that sentiment extended beyond wine? What if it reflected a Bourget strategy, a family philosophy woven into their preservation efforts? With all she'd uncovered, it now read more like a carefully veiled instruction. The Artisan's Lodge—a mundane building *hidden in plain sight*—seemed to align perfectly with Arnaud's thinking.

Amelia leaned back in her chair, replaying her thoughts. The lodge had been used as a workshop for art restoration, far removed from the bustle of the main estate. It was an ideal place to keep something out of sight, buried among mundane family records that wouldn't have drawn attention. What if one of the so-called "financial ledgers" wasn't what it seemed? Could the ledger she'd been searching for be hidden here, disguised as an ordinary household document?

The likelihood that these records had survived unscathed was slim. Time, war, and neglect could have erased most traces of anything left behind. But if the Bourgets were as meticulous as she'd begun to believe, this wouldn't have been a hasty decision; it would have been deliberate and calculated. They would have counted on the idea that the most important things could be overlooked if hidden among the ordinary—*hidden in plain sight.*

Amelia sat up straighter, her mind racing. Looters, historians, even the Nazis might have overlooked the ledger if it was hidden this way precisely because it was hiding in plain sight—camouflaged by the mundane, its significance invisible to the untrained eye. The Artisan's Lodge, with its out-of-the-way location and seemingly ordinary contents, was exactly the kind of place where something valuable could be forgotten.

Her gut told her it was worth the risk. She had to follow this lead. Even if it turned up nothing, at least it would offer a welcome change of scenery from the dim, confined spaces where she'd been buried in documents for weeks. Now, she just had to figure out how to gain access to Château Bourget.

Amelia leaned forward in her chair, her eyes scanning the papers one last time. The ledger was out there—she could feel it. But the memory of the man's gaze at the archives and the museum snapped her back to reality. She wasn't the only one on this trail. The past held its secrets, but so did the present, and as the pieces aligned, the stakes felt higher than she'd first imagined.

And whoever was watching her knew it, too.

Amelia pushed her chair back with a sense of urgency. No more theories. No more speculation. She needed rest, and then she needed to act. Time was running out.

Chapter 44

I begin to write to Étienne with a calm determination, though I can already feel the edges of tension gnawing at me. This letter, these careful words, will probably be intercepted. And that is the point, isn't it? *Vichy pigs.* I've waited for our so-called "defenders of culture" to arrive for so long now, dreading their heavy footsteps through the halls, the way they rifle through history as if it were their own. Let Hitler's stooges come, let them search these walls—take each one if they must—and leave knowing they have what they wanted.

And so I write cautiously, the ink drying as my thoughts shift. I need to tell Étienne enough, *just enough*, to communicate where things are, but nothing explicit. *The key and the brush will guide us.* A small, innocuous phrase that only Étienne would understand, a phrase that will draw the attention of those searching for the secrets they are so certain we are trying to keep from them. For a moment, I almost wish I could see their expressions when they read it, leaning in for some coveted prize.

This letter is a lure. A well-placed hint, vague and suggestive, that will convince them they've outsmarted us, that they've discovered our hidden meaning. But what they won't realize is that they've actually discovered nothing. I will hide nothing in this letter—only an invitation to come and see for themselves, to ransack these rooms once and for all, so that when they finally leave, they'll be satisfied.

Yes. Let them march in, rifles over shoulders, convinced they have the very depths of Château Bourget in their grasps. And when they have turned over every stone, when they have made a show of their search, they will leave, content. Then, we can finally continue our work here in peace, undisturbed and undiscovered, knowing they will not return.

These words will serve two masters—the one who understands, and the one who thinks he does.

Château Bourget, June 1941

The rumble of engines echoed through the château's grounds as a convoy of cars pulled into the courtyard. Moments later, boots crunched on gravel and fists pounded on the grand wooden door.

They were finally here.

The Nazis moved swiftly, cataloging and seizing the artwork from the walls and other spaces. 74 pieces in total. *A small price to pay for the greater good.* Crates were carried out, one after another, as officers barked orders in sharp German. To them, it was a triumph—a conquest of culture.

But it was planned to go this way.

Arnaud watched from the shadows, his expression sad yet resolute. The lure had worked. The ruse was bought. They thought they had the upper hand, but Arnaud had been playing them all along.

Chapter 45

Amelia gripped the steering wheel a little tighter as she drove through the wrought-iron gates of Château Bourget, her emotions a mix of eager anticipation and lingering doubt. The long, winding road led her deeper into the grounds, past ancient oaks and sweeping meadows, until the sprawling house came into view. Once grand, the mansion had fallen into a hushed elegance worn by time and history. But her destination wasn't the main house. It was the small, unassuming lodge at the far end of the property—the Artisan's Lodge—hidden among the trees, far enough from the house to be forgotten.

The estate was now owned by a semi-reclusive couple who had purchased the property from the state in the 1960s, after it had been left abandoned following the war. Amelia had initially assumed she would coordinate her visit with members of the Bourget family, but was surprised to learn that the Moreaus were the current owners. That the Bourget home had remained unclaimed and deserted for so long intrigued her. *What had happened to the Bourget heirs?* This mysterious absence had allowed the state to seize the property and sell it to the highest bidder.

While drawn to the estate for its historical significance, Amelia was confident the Moreaus were blissfully unaware of the *full* extent of the Bourget family's secrets. During a phone conversation with them earlier in the week, she had asked a few carefully crafted questions, and their answers reassured her. Amelia had reached out under the guise of researching the artistic heritage of the Bourgets, and the Moreaus, intrigued by her credentials as an art restorer, had agreed to let her explore the lodge. They hadn't seemed particularly concerned—after all, most of the original contents of the lodge had been taken by the state decades ago, and the lodge itself had become little more than a glorified storage shed.

After hearing this, Amelia's heart sank. The thought that the ledger might have been lost or discarded during the state's clearing was disheartening. All her meticulous research, the sleepless nights spent connecting dots, could be rendered meaningless. She felt a wave of frustration wash over her—had she come this far only to reach a dead end?

But she refused to let despair take hold. Amelia reminded herself that the Bourgets wouldn't have left something so important among items that could be easily discarded or confiscated—especially by the Nazis. The state's officials might have removed the most apparent valuables, but could they have uncovered everything? It was possible that the ledger had been overlooked, especially if it wasn't where anyone expected to find it.

After checking in with a groundskeeper, her heart raced as she parked the car near the overgrown path leading to the lodge. The small stone building looked out of place against the grandeur of the estate she passed earlier. Its humble size and simple design contradicted the secrets it may have once held. She walked toward it, her footsteps crunching softly on the gravel, the world around her eerily still. The lodge had a forgotten air to it, as though it had slipped through time unnoticed.

When she opened the door, a musty smell hit her, heavy with the unmistakable staleness of disuse. The air inside felt thick, clinging to her skin as though the room itself had been sealed away from time. Sunlight streamed through the dirt-hazed windows, cutting through the shadows and creating beams of light that illuminated suspended dust particles, swirling lazily in the air. The space was modest—a 50-square-meter room with a small kitchen area, a fireplace, and a few pieces of worn period furniture that looked untouched since the 1950s. Every surface was cloaked in a thin layer of dust, undisturbed for decades. As Amelia's eyes swept the floor, she noticed the dust lay undisturbed, no footprints breaking its smooth surface. It was clear—no one had stepped foot in this part of the estate in years.

Amelia carefully examined the room. Despite its disuse, the lodge held a warm charm—wood-paneled walls, an ornate fireplace that took up most of the far wall, and the well-preserved furniture hinted at its former purpose. It almost felt like a home, as though it could have been lived in. Not the insignificant storage shed her research had led her to expect.

Her disappointment resurfaced as she noticed the empty shelves lacking any books, documents, or records. According to her research, this was supposedly a storage space for household records and financial ledgers, yet there was nothing of the sort in sight. But it wasn't what she *saw* that interested her. She was looking for what she potentially *didn't* see. What lay *beneath* the surface of the space? If there was anything of significance left here, it would be hidden—*in plain sight*—just as Arnaud had hinted. Amelia's eyes lingered on the details of the room, scanning for anything that seemed slightly out of place, any sign of a concealed compartment or a hollow space.

If there was a mystery here, she was intent to uncover it.

She took her time, running her hands along the walls, tapping gently on the wood, listening for any hollow sounds. She moved cautiously, methodically, her thoughts attuned to the possibilities. She *knew* it was a long shot. Most of the original contents had been moved or sold, and the building had likely been picked over by countless others, leaving it the shell it was today. Every inch of the lodge seemed ordinary. Its simplicity caught her off guard, but Amelia knew better.

As she continued around the room, the fireplace loomed before her, its bricks darkened with layers of soot from fires long forgotten. It appeared to be like any other ordinary fireplace—worn and weathered by time; the mantel adorned with simple carvings that had softened with age. A few stray cobwebs clung to the corners, and a thin layer of dust blanketed the hearth. Yet something didn't sit quite right, a nagging feeling Amelia couldn't shake. Years of experience had taught her to trust her instincts—and her research. There was something here, hidden in this space, waiting to be uncovered.

She stood still for a moment, letting her eyes trace the lines of the structure. The lodge was modest, offering few places where one could conceal something of significance. Her gaze returned to the fireplace—it was central yet unassuming, a fixture that blended into the background of daily life.

Amelia recalled how, historically, fireplaces had been used as secret hiding places. Also, the Bourgets, possibly, had a liking for artful concealment; the hidden compartment in the toolbox had already demonstrated that. Then there were Arnaud's words, which continued to play in her mind: *"The finest things needn't be behind lock and key; they remain safe, hidden in plain sight."* It was almost like he had left a breadcrumb for those astute enough to follow. The convergence of these thoughts led her to a realization: if she needed to hide something important in this space—both accessible and discreet—this fireplace is precisely where she would do it.

She approached it cautiously, her footsteps barely making a sound on the worn wooden floorboards. Almost instinctively, her fingers reached out to brush against the rough stone, as if reacquainting herself with something long forgotten. The stone felt cool beneath her touch, its texture rugged and uneven, yet there was a familiarity in its feel. Running her fingers along the edges of the mantel, she felt for any irregularities. The wood was smooth and showed signs of small disturbances—scratches that didn't match the natural grain—but nothing more.

Then her eyes swept across the hearth, searching for something, anything, that might confirm the pull she felt. But still, nothing seemed obvious. She crouched down to examine it closer.

And then she saw something.

An anomaly so subtle it could have been easily overlooked. But Amelia's trained eye, honed by years of uncovering the things history tried to bury, zeroed in on the slight imperfection. Two bricks near the base of the fireplace, just off-center, sat ever so slightly out of line with the others. For a moment, she doubted herself, convincing her mind it was just age, the natural settling of an old house. But as she leaned in to inspect it more closely, the doubt faded. The mortar around these particular bricks wasn't quite right. It looked crumblier, as though it had been hastily repaired or patched together. Time and the weight of the bricks had taken their toll, causing the mortar to weaken and slowly give way. Unlike the surrounding joints, which had weathered time with uniformity, these two seemed different.

Amelia's fingers moved over the bricks slowly, tracing the edge where the mortar had broken away. The surface gave easily, too easily, crumbling like powder beneath her touch and confirming what her instincts had already told her. This wasn't just wear and tear. Someone had repaired it long ago—just enough for it to blend into the background over the years, yet leaving behind a slight, telling clue.

In the late 18th and early 19th centuries, when secure banking options were scarce and trust in institutions often wavered, families often had little choice but to hide and protect their most precious belongings themselves. For those running businesses from their homes, such concealment was common. Financial records, trade secrets, sensitive information

—or even *ledgers*—hidden in plain sight, tucked behind walls or beneath floorboards, out of reach from prying eyes or thieves.

This discovery couldn't be mere coincidence. In homes as old as this —especially those belonging to families like the Bourgets—such irregularities in the structure often meant one thing: the bricks were deliberately hiding something. Amelia's pulse quickened at the thought.

She reached for a pry tool in her purse, slipping it carefully into the thin gap she opened in the crumbling joints. The bricks shifted with surprising ease, the mortar falling away like dust. She held her breath as she pulled them free, revealing a small, flat, hollow space behind it. Her flashlight beam sliced through the dark and illuminated what lay within. A sudden thrill coursed through Amelia's body.

Placing her hand inside, she felt her fingers brush against something cold—metallic and rusted. She pulled it out slowly as her hands were trembling with anticipation. In her grasp was a small, flat clamshell file box, its edges corroded but intact. It was the kind of box meant to hold something important—papers, perhaps, or something even more significant. The kind of box hidden not out of convenience, but out of necessity. Whatever was inside, it had been locked away for a reason, waiting through the decades for someone to find it.

She positioned the clamshell box in front of her on the floor. Its surface was cold and rough under her fingers, and the rusted and aged lock appeared to be no longer functional. There would be no delicate process here. With a grunt of effort, she wedged her pry tool into the lock and twisted. The metal groaned under the pressure, the rust giving way as she worked at it, straining to pry the lock open.

Finally, with a sharp crack, the lock gave way, and the lid creaked open. Inside, carefully stacked and neatly bound in worn leather, were several documents. Amelia slowly inhaled and paused. Her fingers hovered over the folio for a moment, hesitant, as though touching the papers might break the spell. Then, with a deliberately pursed exhale, she reached for the first bundle as the smell of old parchment rose to meet her. Her fingers lightly squeezed the aged leather. The texture was rough, the edges brittle, but preserved—protected from time, from war, from 80 years of the chaos of history.

This is it!

Her hands shook as she untied the leather cord and flipped open the cover. The pages inside were filled with meticulous handwriting, names, dates, and other unassuming lists. At first glance, they appeared to be ordinary estate and business documents—financial records, household accounts, even a patent design—with dates ranging from 1893 to 1943. But as Amelia continued scanning the entries, her heart raced when she reached one document, dated 1941, towards the middle of the stack.

As she began reading, Amelia immediately noticed the careful language—certain phrases almost coded in their simplicity: "items of cultural significance," "private transfers," "safekeeping." Her pulse quickened as she recognized the deliberate wording designed to mask the true nature of what was being recorded. Her mind raced. She had found it!—the ledger, or at least part of it. Hidden among layers of estate bureaucracy, disguised with everyday documents to protect it from prying eyes.

The fireplace was the safe. It was hidden in plain sight! Concealed in the most mundane of places, its true nature buried under layers of soot and time. No need for a complex lock or heavy vault door—the entire hearth served as the perfect disguise, crafted to blend in and be hidden from the *"daily life at the château,"* as Arnaud had written. Elated, Amelia continued reading the document.

But then a soft sound interrupted her thoughts.

A creak, barely perceptible but unmistakable. Her body stiffened, every nerve on high alert. The lodge had been so quiet, so still, and now... someone was here. *Was it the owner coming to check on her?*

Amelia turned slowly, her eyes scanning the dimly lit room. The shadows seemed to shift, thickening around the doorway. She held her breath, her heart pounding in her chest as she strained to listen. There it was again—a faint sound, like the scrape of a shoe against the floor. Panic surged through her as she realized she wasn't alone.

The figure emerged from the shadows, stepping into the doorway with a deliberate grace. Her blood ran cold.

It was him.

The same man who had watched her in the archives, the same shadowy figure who had followed her from a distance, now stood before her, his expression unreadable. He didn't speak, didn't move—just stood there, watching her with an intensity that sent a wave of fear coursing through her veins.

Amelia's heart pounded in her chest, her mind racing. She had to act—had to do something—but her body felt frozen, her limbs heavy with the weight of the moment. The man's gaze never wavered, his presence both threatening and unnervingly calm.

And then, without a word, he stepped forward, closing the distance between them.

Chapter 46

Château Bourget, Modern Day

I knew it would come to this—the lodge. The Bourget estate had been in my sights for months, ever since I traced the trail of documents that led me back to my family's past. And now, her persistence had brought us both to the same place. I had been following her movements for weeks, watching as she pieced everything together. I couldn't deny her skill. She was methodical, tenacious, and I could tell she was very close to discovering the truth. My truth.

There was only one place left for us to meet. I knew she'd be here, just as I knew I couldn't avoid it any longer. Whatever she was after, it was mine too—it belonged to my family. The Vallois name may have faded from public memory, but the legacy of my great-great-grand father, Clément Vallois, still pulsed through these walls. It was his brother's alliance with the Bourgets that had set everything in motion, and now it was my responsibility to reclaim what was ours. Amelia, whether she knew it or not, was part of that path. I had allowed her to get this far, but now, standing just outside the Artisan's Lodge by her car, I had to decide—was I ready to confront her?

I watch her silhouette in the dim light of the room, my heart pounding with the possibilities of my decision. I step forward over the threshold. It is time to make my move.

Chapter 47

Château Bourget, 1927

Étienne stood by a large window in the Vallois mansion, his gaze fixed on the sprawling French countryside, though his thoughts were miles away. His brother, Clément, paced the room, frustration bubbling just beneath the surface. "We've built our fortune here, Étienne. The Vallois name is rooted in France—but it's stifling. There's more waiting for us across the Atlantic. America is where the future is." Clément's voice was filled with the excitement of new possibilities, but Étienne wasn't swayed.

"Our family's strength has always been in finance, in banking, and the contacts we have in Europe," Étienne replied, his tone cool, measured. "You want to gamble everything we've worked for on a dream in a foreign country? The Vallois name is respected here. I will not abandon that for some reckless pursuit."

The silence between them stretched as the heaviness of their disagreement settled. Clément finally stopped pacing, turning to face his brother with resolve. "Then we branch off," he said. "You stay in France, with the banks and the legacy father left, and I'll take our name to America to build something new. Something lasting. Something that's mine—not just an extension of my older brother." At that moment, the decision was made. The Vallois brothers, once inseparable, would go their separate ways.

Chapter 48

Amelia drew in a panicked breath as the shadowy figure stepped closer. Every muscle in her body tensed as she instinctively reached for the pry tool lying beside her. Her fingers gripped the cold metal handle, her heart hammering in her chest. She couldn't move, couldn't think clearly—only the overwhelming need to defend herself pulsed through her.

"Stop!" she shouted, her voice trembling but resolute, raising the tool like a weapon in front of her. The distance between them now felt entirely too close.

The man froze, his face shifting from initial surprise to a wary understanding. "Whoa!" he exhaled, while lifting his hands slowly, palms outward, his eyes softening as he tried to show her he meant no harm. His movements were measured, deliberate, each gesture meant to reassure rather than alarm. "I'm not here to hurt you," he said, his voice gentle, careful, as though trying to ease her out of her defensive stance. "My name is Gabriel. Gabriel Marceau," he added, keeping his tone low and steady. "I've been wanting to talk with you. I think… we're both looking for the same thing."

He took a slight step back, his posture relaxed, hoping to convey a sense of safety, his gaze never leaving hers as he continued, "I promise, I'm only here to help." He waited for her next move. He didn't want to put her in any more fear than she already was.

Amelia's fingers tightened around the tool, her knuckles white. Her breath came in shallow gasps as her mind raced to process his words. The flickering light from the late afternoon sun coming through the windows threw long shadows across his face, making it hard to fully read his expression. Her instincts were telling her not to trust him, but there was something in the calmness of his voice, the measured way he spoke, that made her pause.

"Why should I believe you?" Her voice was sharp, the suspicion clear.

Gabriel took another cautious step back, sensing her fear. "I understand how this might look," he began, his tone steady, eyes locking with hers. "And I fear, now, I could have gone about this differently. But I'm not your enemy." He paused to let that linger between them before continuing. "My great-great-grandfather… was Clément Vallois. Étienne Vallois' brother."

Amelia's pulse quickened at the name. *Vallois*. She had uncovered the connection between the Vallois family and the Bourgets only days ago, but hearing it from this man—this stranger who had been lurking in the shadows—it made her blood run cold. How did *he* know what she was looking for, what she had found? She didn't lower the tool, not yet.

"Clément Vallois," she repeated, testing the name on her tongue, as if saying it out loud would help her discern whether it was truth or a lie. "And what does that have to do with me?"

Gabriel hesitated, choosing his words carefully. "My family passed down letters. Between Clément and Étienne before he left for the United States in 1927. Letters about the Bourgets, about this estate, about this lodge." His gaze flickered toward the fireplace, towards the two bricks lying on the ground, and Amelia's grip tightened. "I've been following them," he said. "Trying to piece together the connection between our families… and this place."

Amelia narrowed her eyes, refusing to let her guard down so easily. "You've been following me," she said coldly, her voice edged with accusation.

Gabriel met her gaze, his hands still raised in a gesture of peace. "Yes," he admitted, not shying away from the truth. "I had to be sure. I had to know if you were after the same thing I was. I didn't mean to scare you. I promise."

"Scare me?" she shot back, her grip still firm on the tool. "You've been stalking me!"

He exhaled slowly, his eyes softening. "I've been trying to protect what's left of my family's legacy. Clément's letters—they mention this lodge. They allude to a Bourget-Vallois alliance. I've been searching for answers, just like you.

Amelia's heart pounded in her chest. Her mind was a whirl of conflicting thoughts—his words carried truth, but the shadow of his presence still lingered. Could she trust him? Her mind paused. Could she afford not to?

Gabriel slowly turned, keeping his eyes on her as he carefully reached into his backpack. She watched warily, her gaze shifting between the cautious expression on his face and the stack of letters he pulled out. He slowly untied the string around the letters, revealing worn, faded papers. "These letters," he said softly, holding them out to her, "are from my family. They mention this place specifically. The Artisan's Lodge. That is where I hit a dead end."

Amelia's pulse thudded in her ears. Letters… new letters. The very thing she had been tirelessly searching for over the past few days, now right in front of her, offered by the man she still didn't fully trust. Her fingers trembled as she lowered the pry tool slightly, her gaze locked on the letters.

"I didn't come here to hurt you," Gabriel continued, his voice earnest. "I came here because whatever you're looking for—is what I'm looking for, too. My family is tied to this. You may have already uncovered pieces I haven't. And I have these letters. Maybe we can help each other."

Amelia's thoughts spun, weighing the possibilities, the tension in the air thick enough to hold her still. But something shifted as she looked into Gabriel's eyes—a seriousness. An intensity that mirrored her own determination. Slowly and cautiously, she stepped forward, the tight grip on the pry tool loosening just enough as she reached for the letters with a single outstretched arm. Her fingers brushed against the brittle edges of the worn papers, and she felt the tangible heaviness of history pressed into her palms, fragile yet commanding.

For a moment, she hesitated, the trust still very unsteady, like a bridge not fully built. The faded ink hinted at secrets of another time, another era, drawing her deeper. The letters carried the same energy as the documents she had uncovered, the same meticulous care, the same layers of language. Her breath steadied as her eyes scanned the words, trying to further piece together fragments of a story she had been chasing for weeks.

She realized Gabriel *had* figured out much of what she already had —but not everything. Not yet.

Her mind moved between the words on the page and the man standing before her, skepticism still heavy in her chest. The letters felt authentic—old, worn with time—but she hadn't heard of Clément Vallois until now. She was cautious by nature, and the name could easily have been fabricated. Her gaze shifted from the delicate script back to Gabriel, who continued to give her some distance. She searched his expression for any hint of deception, but something in his eyes—a mixture of urgency and sincerity—held her attention.

Amelia's thoughts turned to the information she had studied in the archives. She had come across the Vallois family, but only in reference to Étienne, whose name appeared often in records tied to the Bourgets. Yet, there had been a brief, almost passing mention of a brother who left France before the war—a name she had paid little attention to at the time. Could that have been Clément? It seemed too convenient, but the details Gabriel shared were too precise to be easily faked. He spoke of things she hadn't found yet, references to the lodge, to the Alliance, things buried in the language of history.

Her fingers brushed the faded ink, comparing the handwriting to the old Bourget records she'd seen. It matched. The same loops, the same meticulous style. The letters felt real—genuine. And slowly, as she sifted through the clues, she realized that if Gabriel was lying, he had gone to extraordinary lengths to craft this story. But no…she didn't think he was lying. He knew too much, and as she turned the pages, her suspicions began to wane, replaced by the realization that his lineage was woven into the same tangled web she had been following.

Her wariness lingered, but the grip on the pry tool eased more as she pieced it together in her mind. He continued to remain in place.

She inhaled deeply, feeling the heaviness of the letters and the shared history between them. It wasn't comfort—not yet—but the instinct to keep Gabriel at arm's length was starting to fray at the edges. If he *had* meant to harm her, he would have done it already. *Boy does this guy suck at introductions*, she thought.

Exhaling slowly, she met his gaze. The tension hadn't disappeared, but something had shifted. She could feel it.

Her grip on the pry tool loosened entirely as she let out a sigh, shaking off her lingering nerves.

"Alright," she said, voice edged with caution. "I'll show you what I found."

Chapter 49

Her grip on the pry tool was gone, but the weight of caution hadn't lifted completely. She'd made the choice to let Gabriel in, to allow him a glimpse of the carefully preserved documents—*the ledger*—hidden in the hearth for decades.

But trust, as Amelia knew all too well, was fragile. It could shatter with a single misstep, and she wasn't ready to take that risk just yet.

She kept her eyes on him as they crouched by the open file box, the brittle scent of old parchment mingling with the stagnant air of the lodge. Gabriel's hands rested firmly on his knees, his movements careful, as though he feared disturbing the fragile silence between them. The tension lingered and what remained unsaid pressed down on both of them —but they were allowing each other a chance, especially Amelia. She could see the questions forming behind his cautious expression, but for now, he waited. He could sense her hesitation, her mind still racing through a maze of conflicting thoughts.

The silence was deafening.

Amelia reached back into the box and carefully pulled out the ledger page, squinting her eyes in the dimming light as she scanned its contents once again. The letters and numbers blurred slightly before her eyes, their meaning eluding her just as it had moments ago. She felt Gabriel watching her closely and his gaze adding to the mounting pressure in the room. He opened his mouth to speak, but she raised a hand, silencing him with a single, commanding gesture.

"Wait," she muttered, her voice low and deliberate.

She read the page again, slower this time, her eyes lingering on every word, every phrase that seemed to promise answers but delivered… none. She let out a heavy sigh and her frown deepened as the realization settled in—the document wasn't what she had hoped. The ledger, the one thread tying everything together and the one thing she fully expected to find here, was still out of reach.

Gabriel shifted beside her, his presence a constant reminder that she wasn't alone in this search anymore. Yet for all his apparent sincerity, he was still a stranger to her. And in this moment, the secrets of the past felt more distant than ever. She turned to acknowledge his patience.

"I found these hidden in the fireplace hearth," Amelia said, steady but guarded. "I thought they were… I wanted them to be… *more*. But they're not. They're just ordinary papers—Bourget business records. Probably something they didn't want falling into the wrong hands."

Gabriel glanced at her, curiosity flickering in his eyes. "What kind of records? What were you looking for?"

She hesitated, weighing how much to reveal. Gabriel knew about the Alliance between the Bourgets and the Vallois family, but she didn't think he had figured out the purpose behind it. He didn't know about the ledger or what it could mean if they found it. But if she wanted to keep his trust—if she wanted to further trust him—she couldn't afford to play this too close to the vest. Not now. Amelia inhaled through her nose before speaking.

"The Vallois and Bourgets weren't just working together for business reasons," she began. "This wasn't just about money or politics." She paused, realizing that with her next words, he'd be read in. He would become a partner in the mystery that had fully consumed her. Thirty minutes ago, she'd thought he might be a threat. Now, she wasn't sure if she'd ever be able to shake him loose. She'd always prided herself on working alone, valuing her independence. But now, after this, they'd be in this together, whether she liked it or not.

She sighed and continued.

"There's a ledger," she said, pausing to gauge Gabriel's reaction. "A record that tracks the art the two families smuggled during the war. Priceless pieces they hid from the Nazis—pieces they may have saved from destruction. The ledger was meant to help return the art to its owners after the war, but it's gone missing. That's what I've been searching for. That's why I'm here now."

Gabriel's brow furrowed as he absorbed her words. "A ledger," he echoed slowly. "*Saving* art?" Confusion clouded his eyes, mingling with a hint of disappointment. "I... I thought the Alliance was about something else entirely."

Amelia noticed the shift in his demeanor. "What did you think it was?"

He hesitated, rubbing the back of his neck. "For years, I believed that the Vallois and the Bourgets were involved in a questionable operation—using their influence and resources to manipulate art markets during the war. Quietly acquiring artworks from families in desperate situations, perhaps even taking advantage of the chaos."

She raised an eyebrow. "You thought they were profiteering from the war?"

"Yeah… kinda," he said. "I've come across transactions that suggested they were buying art at fractions of their value and intended to keep them after the war. It seemed like a coordinated effort."

Amelia considered this, her gaze thoughtful. Gabriel's theory introduced a new perspective, but it didn't align with everything she knew about the Bourgets. They were renowned for their unwavering commitment to art preservation and promotion. The Bourget family had, in many ways, created their generation's own Medici effect in France—patronizing artists, funding the construction of galleries, and fostering a cultural renaissance. Exploiting art for profit, especially during a time of crisis, was entirely against their legacy.

"I can see how, from certain records, it might look that way," she said gently. "But the Bourgets were supporters of the arts. They dedicated their lives to preserving and promoting cultural heritage, much like the Medicis did during the Renaissance. They wouldn't have exploited the chaos of war for personal gain—it goes against everything they stood for. The ledger I'm searching for lists the artworks they safeguarded, not hoarded. Their intention was to protect these pieces from destruction and ensure they could be returned to their rightful owners after the war."

Gabriel sighed, a mix of confusion and relief crossing his face. He knew more about the Vallois side of the partnership, being a Vallois descendant himself, and certain questionable actions by Étienne had led him to suspect the worst. But it seemed he'd been wrong. "I suppose I let my cynicism color my research. So many took advantage during those times. I thought you were a reporter. I wanted to uncover the truth first, even if it wasn't flattering. I was nervous about my family's name—for our legacy."

She offered a small, understanding smile. "History is complex, and the lines between right and wrong often blur during war. But in this case, it seems they were trying to do the right thing."

Gabriel sighed, shaking off his nerves, and looked down at the documents between them. A unified sense of purpose was growing between them. "So, you thought this ledger was hidden here?"

"I did," Amelia said softly. "But this… this isn't the ledger." Amelia shook her head as she placed the sheet she was holding back on the pile beneath them.

They turned back to the documents spread across the dusty floor. Yellowed papers, some brittle with age, lay in neat stacks. Amelia carefully picked up one of the older sheets, smoothing the edges as she scanned the text. Her eyes darted over numbers and diagrams—engine schematics, business ledgers unrelated to art or wartime operations. One document in particular stood out, its title catching the dim light: a patent for a modified internal combustion engine. She squinted.

"This is… not what I expected," she admitted, her voice trailing off as she handed Gabriel the patent. "It's not about art. These are business records. A patent for an engine design that never got developed—probably because of the war. It looks like they didn't trust the banks to keep these safe."

Gabriel studied the document, his finger tracing the lines of the technical drawings. "They were protecting this from the Nazis," he muttered in a half-question. "If they got their hands on something like this, they could've exploited it for their war effort."

Amelia nodded, her frustration mounting. This wasn't the treasure trove of art records she had hoped to find. No, this was something entirely different—important, yes, but not what she had spent sleepless nights chasing.

A heavy silence fell between them. Amelia's heart sank as she realized the truth. If the ledger had ever been hidden here, it was long gone now. Swept away with the forgotten remnants of the lodge when it had been cleared out decades ago, probably discarded like a relic, with no one recognizing its true significance. The Bourgets had hidden it "in plain sight," but to those unaware of its value, it would have been too easy to overlook.

She let out a slow, measured breath, her frustration clawing at her insides. The weeks of searching, the late nights spent combing through archives and dusty letters, felt like they had led to this—nothing. "It's probably lost to history," she muttered, the words almost inaudible, almost speaking more to herself than to Gabriel. Her voice carried a tone of defeat. "If it was ever here, someone could have tossed it out, not even realizing what it was."

Gabriel looked at her, his eyes soft but steady. He could see the disappointment etched on her face, the sharp sting of an anticlimactic conclusion weighing on her shoulders.

"Maybe," he said gently, "but maybe not. People don't always know the value of what they have. That doesn't mean it's gone forever. It could still be out there... waiting to be found."

Amelia didn't respond at first, her mind swirling in a tangled mess of doubt, frustration, and a fear she wasn't ready to admit. The ledger, the key that had felt so close, was still out of reach, slipping through her fingers like water. The reality stung, threatening to sever the fragile thread of hope she clung to.

But Gabriel's words lingered, soft but insistent, refusing to be dismissed. Despite her doubts, she couldn't shake the possibility that he might be right. There was still a chance, still a sliver of hope buried beneath her frustration. The ledger, the key to everything she'd been working towards, might not be lost... forever. It could still be out there—hidden, waiting for the right person to discover its true value. After all, she found the ring—the first marker. Perhaps her efforts weren't in vain. Perhaps there was still a path forward, even if it wasn't the one she had envisioned.

"Okay," she said finally, meeting Gabriel's gaze, her voice edged with determination. "We'll keep looking."

His presence, once a source of apprehension, now felt more like an opportunity. He didn't seem to be an obstacle in her way; he had knowledge and a history tied to this enigma that ran just as deep as hers. And even though they hadn't found the ledger, he brought something else to the table—new details and connections she hadn't considered. New things he was offering in good faith. Clément's letters, the history of the Vallois family, the intricacies of the Alliance between the Bourgets and Vallois—it was all connected, and it was all leading somewhere.

Amelia let out a slow breath, her disappointment easing slightly as she carefully photographed the documents, then returned them to the clamshell box and repositioned it in the hearth's hidden compartment. Surveying the crumbled mortar scattered on the floor, she scooped up the loose pieces and gently pressed them back into the joints. It wasn't a perfect fix, but it would conceal the disturbance well enough to avoid drawing attention.

She wasn't ready to give up—not yet. Gabriel's information had opened new doors. Gabriel had offered hope. And while they hadn't uncovered the ledger today, it didn't mean the search was over. They had more work to do, more threads to unravel, and with their combined knowledge, they were closer than ever.

They exchanged a look of mutual understanding. This research would continue—together.

Chapter 50

Researching in the French National Archives was never simple. The vast main hall stretched out before Amelia and Gabriel, lined with crumbling volumes and leather-bound ledgers. Along with its dedicated side rooms, the inside was a labyrinth of forgotten history. Finding anything here wasn't like pulling a book from a library shelf—each record was cataloged only in the broadest terms, offering little guidance for those seeking something precise. Documents were buried in obscure collections, filed away in long-forgotten boxes, and often mislabeled or missing altogether. Each discovery was a matter of patience, intuition, and a lot of reading—a mental game between past and present.

Even armed with Gabriel's letters, the process was painstakingly slow. Containing "all public records of France after 1790," housed on over 480 kilometers of shelf space, the archives offered no obvious path from one clue to the next. Amelia had spent enough time here to know how easily secrets could remain buried. There were no shortcuts, no quick answers. It was a game of persistence, following vague threads until they led somewhere—or nowhere.

Her mind drifted back to her father, William, who had instilled in her an unshakable love for history and research. Before their move to Paris, he had worked at the Isabella Stewart Gardner Museum in Boston, immersing himself in the museum's rich history and sharing its mysteries with her as she grew up. Those after-hours visits to the museum, with its creaky floors and dimly lit rooms, all inside a replicated Venetian Palazzo, had felt like stepping into another world. One where many things lay waiting to be discovered.

He'd taught her early on that understanding art wasn't just about looking at a painting; it was about uncovering the layers of context behind it. "History leaves clues," he would say as they leafed through art catalogues and old records together when she was in high school, preparing her for hours of painstaking research for her senior project. She knew early on she wanted to go into art restoration, largely because of his influence. But restoring art was so much more than removing grime from dirty paintings. It was also research—lots of research. His lessons taught her patience and the value of approaching every discovery with curiosity. He had an almost forensic approach to art, emphasizing that every piece had a hidden story and that every detail, no matter how small, could connect to a larger truth.

As Amelia sat beside Gabriel at a long, worn wooden table, the cold light streaming through the tall, modern transom windows cast a muted glow over their work. Their fingers moved delicately along the fragile edges of Clément's old letters and dozens of estate records, sifting through the relics of two families who had hidden more than just art. The faint hum of the radiators filled the background, unnoticed by Amelia, her focus locked on the shared purpose driving them forward.

She could feel Gabriel's presence next to her, his intensity palpable as he thumbed through a stack of old land grants. Tall and angular, he leaned slightly over the table, the muted stripes of his crewneck sweater catching the light as his fingers moved delicately over the fragile pages. She had been cautious at first, keeping him at arm's length, but now, over the last few days—through conversations and shared discoveries—a fragile trust had taken root between them. Even now, though, that trust felt tenuous, something that could shatter with a single misstep. She wasn't ready to fully let her guard down, but she couldn't deny the connection they shared through this mystery.

She glanced at him from the corner of her eye as she sifted through more Bourget records. His forehead was wrinkled in concentration, his large brown eyes scanning the documents with an almost forensic precision. The clean, polished leather of his brown shoes tapped lightly against the table leg as he shifted his position, lost in thought. Gabriel had brought new pieces to the puzzle—pieces Amelia wouldn't have uncovered without him. She had shared with him the story of finding the brush and the key mark on the painting at the Jewish museum, and Arnaud's cryptic letter to Étienne: *the key and brush will guide us*. Yet, despite the trust they had started building, Amelia still kept some of her thoughts guarded, careful not to reveal *everything*. Not yet.

Clément Vallois, though now living an ocean away, had never fully severed his ties with his family or their legacy. Shortly after his move, the Great Depression hit, disrupting many of the plans he'd envisioned for establishing the Vallois name in the United States. Seeing his brother struggle, Étienne attempted to mend the rift that had formed when Clément left, offering his support and reestablishing a line of trust. While Clément focused on building his own reputation in America, Étienne's letters kept him connected to the unfolding events in France. Despite their differences, Étienne, ever the strategist, still trusted his brother with pieces of the family's intricate dealings, especially as tensions grew in Europe.

The correspondence wasn't explicit—it never could be. In a time of growing surveillance and unease, caution was essential. In the letters, Clément was kept apprised of the Vallois' French-based businesses. It was less about specific details and more about ensuring that should anything happen to Étienne, Clément could act to restore them if needed. Gabriel had uncovered these letters, old and brittle, in the basement of his grandmother's house after her death. Most cold in tone, more focused on business than brotherhood, they had led him to a dead end—until he met Amelia.

As Amelia turned the fragile pages of another estate document, a growing sense of urgency pressed into her mind. They were missing something—something crucial. The letters Gabriel brought to the investigation were valuable, yes, but they felt incomplete. What had Clément known? And how much had Étienne deliberately concealed from him? Did he keep the most sensitive information within the boundaries of France, hidden from prying eyes—even his brother's? The answer hopefully lay somewhere in the archives, woven into the hidden threads of the Alliance that had been shrouded in secrecy for decades. But as she closed another empty file, it felt disturbingly like she'd reached yet another dead end.

———————

As the nighttime attendant announced the approaching closing time, the urgency of Amelia and Gabriel's search intensified. The strain of their efforts grew with each passing minute, and their shared frustration was marked by the rustle of old papers as they searched with increasing desperation. Every document, every faded letter, felt like a false lead, and Amelia could feel her hope slowly eroding beneath the mounting evidence—or lack thereof.

There was nothing new. Nothing that would unravel the secret she was so certain lay within these walls. She exchanged a glance with Gabriel, who looked back with the same frustration. Their unspoken doubts mirrored her own internal struggle. She could feel the realization creeping in, unwelcome but persistent.

Maybe the ledger really was gone.

The thought settled uncomfortably in her chest. How many other hands had touched these same papers, how many other searches had ended with this same silence? Perhaps, like so many artifacts of the past, the ledger had been swept away by time, buried in history, never to be found again.

Suddenly, Gabriel's voice cut through the quiet, an idea filling his words. "You know," he said, his tone low and thoughtful, "these letters from Étienne to Clément never actually mention a 'hidden ledger.' And that makes sense... it would've been far too dangerous to send something so important, so secret, across the Atlantic during the war."

Amelia's attention piqued at the obvious statement. She watched him closely, noticing a shift in his expression as though something had just clicked before he continued. "But what if..."

His words hung between them, unfinished but full of possibility. Amelia could see the wheels turning in his mind, pieces beginning to fall into place. She leaned in slightly, eyes widened, her curiosity igniting once more. "What if what?" she said while shaking her head, eager to know where he was going with this.

Gabriel's fingers sifted quickly through the fragile stack of letters, and his energy was suddenly renewed. "What if the ledger wasn't written *in a ledger,* in a traditional sense?" he said, his voice tight with the excitement of a sudden breakthrough. His eyes shone with enthusiasm, almost like a veil had been lifted from a problem he hadn't even known he was solving.

"All this time, I've been reading these letters—taking them at face value—but now..." His words trailed off as his brow creased in concentration. He pulled out several yellowed pages and carefully unfolded them while looking at Amelia. "...I see them differently."

He laid the pages out in front of her and his fingers scanned the faded ink. His movements were careful and deliberate, but there was an increasing realization that had shifted the way he saw everything. "I thought they were just talking about their daily lives," he muttered, almost to himself, "but these letters… they could be saying something else entirely." Amelia was feeling a surge of impatience—*just get to the point already!*

He paused, his eyes rising to meet hers, seeing the frustration mounting in her gaze. "I didn't realize it before, but I think Étienne was trying to tell Clément something—without actually saying it."

Amelia narrowed her eyes, still not following. She leaned forward as Gabriel laid two letters side by side on the table. He studied the first one with a renewed perspective. "Look at this. It's from 1942. Étienne writes:"

'The recipes coming out of the Bourget's kitchen have been extraordinary! Even Nady can't stop talking about them. The cooks are creating dishes that could rival any chef in Paris.'

Amelia tilted her head, frowning slightly. "That's unusually…personal for Étienne," she observed. She had read a few of Gabriel's letters, and Étienne's tone was always restrained, almost mechanical. "Especially considering how formal he was in his letters to Clément," she added.

"Exactly," Gabriel said, his voice picking up momentum. "For years, these two talked strictly about business—finances, the war, strategies. Then suddenly, out of nowhere, Étienne starts raving about food? It struck me as odd, but I didn't think much of it at the time."

Amelia glanced back at the letter. "Who's Nady?" she asked casually.

Gabriel shrugged lightly. "I'm not entirely sure. Possibly another family member or close friend?"

She nodded as he slid the second letter over, pointing to another passage. "And here, a few months later:"

'Lucien's family recipes are being meticulously safeguarded. The Bourgets are ensuring they'll be passed down to future generations.'

Amelia's head shifted back, her face filled with confusion. "Wait… safeguarded? Why is he randomly talking about preserving recipes in the middle of a war?" She paused, the memory of Arnaud's letter flashing in her mind—*he had used the exact same word*—safeguarded. She looked back up at Gabriel, her eyes widening and expression shifting as it all started to make sense. "You're saying these references to food... Weren't actually about food?"

Gabriel nodded, his voice measured but filled with a growing conviction. "I have had these letters for years and I never thought otherwise —maybe Étienne just wanting a more personal relationship with his brother. But I also never knew about the ledger until a week ago."

"What if 'recipes' was their code? A way of disguising something else entirely. The Vallois and Bourgets couldn't risk openly discussing art smuggling or the Alliance, especially during the Nazi occupation. Any direct mention of hiding valuable items could've been intercepted by the wrong people. But food? No one would question a conversation about recipes—especially in France. It would've seemed like nothing more than casual family talk when taken out of context." Gabriel continued, "But when you look at all the letters combined, this shift in tone becomes quite clear."

Gabriel glanced at her, waiting for her response. Amelia's mind raced, recalling Arnaud's cryptic phrase: *hidden in plain sight*. At the time, it had felt too vague, but now, with Gabriel's insight, its true meaning was becoming alarmingly clear.

Her pulse quickened as her thoughts weaved through everything they had uncovered so far. *Hidden in plain sight*. It was right in front of them.

"So you're saying... the ledger wasn't just stashed away—it was disguised as something ordinary. Something no one would ever question," Amelia said.

"Exactly," Gabriel replied, his eyes gleaming with the thrill of discovery. He paused, making sure Amelia was following his rapid thought process. "What is something that gets passed down through generations, often treated as a cherished heirloom? Something that represents legacy, continuity? Something no one would question sitting on a shelf for years, even decades?

Amelia's breath caught as the answer clicked.

"A family cookbook," she murmured, the realization dawning. Gabriel nodded, his eyes locking with hers.

"All those references to 'preserving recipes' or 'safeguarding culinary secrets'? What if that wasn't about food at all? What if it was their coded way of talking about the ledger, or the artworks they were protecting?"

Amelia's mind turned faster. He was right. Cookbooks, especially in families like the Bourgets, weren't simply collections of recipes; they were part of the family's story. Passed down through the generations, they became symbols of tradition and heritage, just as important as wills or deeds. Amelia thought of her own grandmother's cookbook, with its pages worn and stained from decades of use. She still treasured it, not just for the recipes, but for the connection it gave her to her grandmother's world, her life, her past. A family heirloom like that wouldn't arouse suspicion—it would be the perfect disguise.

She thought about it for a bit. If this theory was true, the Bourgets, then, weren't just clever—they were masterful in their subtlety. Hiding something as significant as *the* ledger amidst the mundane trappings of a family kitchen could very well have been their perfect cover. *Hidden away from the daily life of the château*, indeed. The kitchen, the cooks, the household staff—they would have been invisible to those living in the home. Invisible to visitors. And most importantly, invisible to the Nazi soldiers who had invaded their world. Who would ever suspect something so ordinary, so innocuous?

"They would have known that no one would think twice about an old cookbook," Amelia said, the enormity of the revelation settling over her. "Especially during wartime, when everyone was hiding something. It was the perfect cover. Hidden in plain sight."

The brilliance of it stunned her. In a time when the Third Reich was confiscating art, searching homes for anything valuable, the last thing anyone would look at was a well-worn cookbook. And yet, within its pages, it could have held the most valuable thing of all—the family's efforts to save priceless works of art from falling into the wrong hands.

Amelia looked up at Gabriel, her pulse quickening. "If we're right, the Bourgets hadn't just hidden a book," she said. "They had safeguarded an entire legacy."

She felt the revelation settle in, a mixture of disbelief and excitement rushing through her. It was almost absurd in its simplicity, yet the brilliance of it was undeniable. The ledger—hidden in plain sight all along. "If the ledger was disguised as a cookbook," she whispered, "it could still be sitting on a shelf at Château Bourget, completely overlooked... especially if the current owners bought the home from the state. Everyone assuming it was just another collection of family recipes—something that 'came with the house.'"

Gabriel nodded, his expression mirroring her own awe. "And that's why they kept using the language about recipes—because no one would ever suspect it was anything more than that. It's been right here, hiding all this time, waiting for someone to see the truth."

Amelia's eyes squinted as she processed the revelation. "But if that's true... was Clément in on this? Did he know about the Alliance also?"

Gabriel shook his head, his expression turning thoughtful. "No... I don't think Clément knew the full extent of it. From everything I've read in these letters, it seems like he wasn't part of the Alliance."

"Then why send him coded messages?" Amelia asked, a flicker of confusion in her voice. "If he wasn't involved, why bother sending him anything at all?"

Gabriel sighed, running a hand through his hair. "I was wondering the same thing... I think Étienne was trying to keep Clément connected to the family, to make sure there was a thread tying him to the Bourgets, even from across the ocean. Maybe it was Étienne's way of leaving a trail, just in case something happened to him or the Alliance. If the worst occurred—if Étienne didn't survive the war or their secrets were at risk—perhaps he thought Clément could step in, even without fully knowing what was at stake."

Amelia considered his words, her fingers tracing the edge of one of the fragile letters. "So Clément wasn't part of the inner circle, but he was a backup plan. Étienne trusted him enough to send these veiled messages, even if Clément didn't realize what he was holding."

"Exactly," Gabriel nodded. "To Clément, these letters probably just sounded like normal family updates—raving about the food, the estate, the usual. But in reality, Étienne was sending him breadcrumbs. Crumbs that would only catch the eye if someone knew *what* to look for."

Amelia looked at the letter again, her mind buzzing with the implications. "And now we do."

They exchanged a glance of hope. What had once seemed like an insurmountable dead end was now a new avenue—hidden all along beneath layers of misdirection. It was precisely the kind of clever ruse the Alliance was shaping up to be known for.

She set the letter down, her thoughts already racing ahead: something extraordinary, disguised as something ordinary.

Chapter 51

Amelia and Gabriel returned to Château Bourget together with a renewed sense of purpose. The possibility that the ledger had been hiding in plain sight all along—disguised as a simple family cookbook—fueled their shared determination. The main estate, nestled in the charming town of Saint-Germain-en-Laye, located twenty kilometers outside of Paris, was just ahead of them. Its grand façade, bathed in the warm light of late afternoon, was covered with ivy turned a brilliant autumn gold, clinging to the weathered stone walls. The tall windows, both imposing and alluring, seemed to hint at the secrets waiting inside. This is the first time either of them saw the home up close and it looked every bit the part of a historic French château.

For centuries, this elegant suburb had been a retreat for French royalty and nobility. Its forested surroundings were dotted with impressive estates and each was covered in many layers of history. Château Bourget was no different. It was surrounded by manicured gardens, vineyards, and lush parklands, where visitors from the nearby town often came to picnic and enjoy the serene beauty of the semi-public grounds.

But this time, Amelia and Gabriel weren't here for the peaceful charm that drew so many to its gates. They weren't heading to a secluded lodge or one of the estate's hidden corners. No, today their destination was the heart of the main house—the old staff kitchen. A place that may have been long overlooked, hidden in plain sight, just like the ledger they suspected might still be tucked away within the space itself.

Securing access to the main house hadn't been easy. Earlier that week, Amelia made another carefully orchestrated phone call to the owners of Château Bourget—Christian and Isabelle Moreau, a wealthy, reclusive couple who seemed to have a passion for preserving the estate's historical significance. Amelia grasped onto that knowledge and played the part. The Moreaus had transformed certain parts of the château into a living museum and curated artifacts and stories from its storied past. Amelia already had a rapport with them from her earlier visit to the Artisan's Lodge, where she had been granted permission to explore. This time, her request was more specific, more urgent.

Amelia's reputation as a renowned art restorer once again lent credibility to her request to explore parts of the old staff kitchen at the château. Though she didn't share her full reasoning, she held onto the hope that the Bourgets—like many aristocratic families of the time—had preserved something as cherished as a generational heirloom cookbook. This time, however, it was Gabriel's connection that tipped the scales. Even though his last name was Marceau, Gabriel's lineage traced back to Clément Vallois—Étienne's younger brother—through his mother's mother's father's father, making him a direct descendant of the Vallois family. Though distant, the connection still tied him to Vallois blood.

While Amelia felt confident the Moreaus didn't have knowledge of *the* Bourget-Vallois Alliance, Gabriel's ties to the Vallois family—who the Moreaus knew had once worked closely with the Bourgets—intrigued them. That they might uncover something long-hidden within the house piqued their curiosity just enough to grant Amelia and Gabriel access.

Under the supervision of a house staff member, and with the strict condition that everything be handled with extreme care, they were permitted to explore the original staff kitchen. For Amelia and Gabriel, this was a rare and invaluable opportunity—the access they needed to pursue their theory.

A distinguished butler greeted them at the grand entrance, his demeanor was polite yet unreadable. "Monsieur Vallois, Mademoiselle Beckett," he said with a slight bow. "Monsieur and Madame Moreau are awaiting you in the drawing-room."

Amelia and Gabriel exchanged a brief glance before following him down the opulent main corridor, which was unexpectedly adorned with works by Francis Picabia, Salvador Dalí, and other avant-garde Dada artists. The interiors were a seamless blend of preserved antiquity and tasteful modernity—the Moreaus had skillfully honored the château's rich heritage while adding their own contemporary touches.

Christian and Isabelle rose to greet them as they entered the drawing-room. "Bienvenue!" Christian said warmly, extending his hand.

"We're thrilled to have you here. Any friend of history is a friend of ours."

"Thank you for allowing us this opportunity," Gabriel replied sincerely. "We understand the value of what you preserved here."

Isabelle smiled graciously. "When you mentioned Gabriel's connection to the Vallois family, and your expertise, Amelia, we couldn't resist. That there might be undiscovered pieces of the château's history is simply enchanting."

After a brief exchange of pleasantries and reassurances about the care they would take, the butler led Amelia and Gabriel towards the old kitchen wing. The Moreaus had turned much of this part of the château into a carefully curated museum of its past. Unlike the rest of the estate, which was grand and opulent—and fully remodeled, this section had been preserved to reflect the lives of those who had worked behind the scenes.

As they moved deeper into the château, the atmosphere changed noticeably. The grand, sunlit hallways gradually gave way to narrower, dimly lit corridors where the air grew cooler and carried a trace of damp stone. Ornate tapestries and gilded frames disappeared, replaced by simple, time-worn walls, aged from another era. The transition was stark—a sharp contrast to the opulence of the rooms they had just left. Journeying down these forgotten hallways, parts rarely seen by visitors, felt like stepping back in time—into the domain once reserved for staff and, now, for hidden secrets.

The butler stopped at a heavy oak door and pushed it open with a soft creak. Inside lay the old kitchen, a large, rustic room that seemed frozen in time. Copper pots hung from the walls, and long wooden tables stretched across the space, worn smooth from years of use. The scent of old stone and iron lingered in the air. Though no longer used for cooking, it had been preserved as a piece of the château's history, a reminder of its past. And it was here, amidst the relics of daily life, that Amelia and Gabriel hoped to find what had eluded them for so long.

Amelia felt an awe settle over her. "It's like stepping back in time," she whispered.

"It is!," Gabriel agreed softly. "This place still feels alive."

At the center of the room stood a large oak display cabinet, and its glass doors reflected their curious faces. Inside, various artifacts were meticulously arranged—a hand-cranked pasta maker, embroidered linen aprons, tarnished silverware bearing the Bourget crest.

But what drew Amelia's eye was a weathered, leather-bound book resting on a wooden stand, opened to reveal its elegantly scripted pages.

She approached the cabinet, her footsteps muffled by the worn flagstones. "May I?" she asked, turning to the butler.

"Of course, mademoiselle," he replied, producing a key. "Monsieur and Madame Moreau have given their permission."

With a soft click, he unlocked the lock and the glass doors swung open. Amelia reached in carefully, her fingertips brushing against the aged leather of each side's cover. Lifting the book gently, she brought it out into the light. The scent of old paper and a faint hint of spices greeted her—a sensory echo of the countless meals inspired by its pages.

Gabriel stood beside her, his gaze fixed on the open book. "Is this...?"

Amelia nodded, her voice reverently low. "The Bourget Family Cookbook."

She laid it carefully on a nearby table. The butler, who had been quietly observing, stepped forward with a sense of pride. "Yes, indeed. This is the cookbook the family treasured most. The recipe it's open to—*Coq au Vin*—that was the Bourgets' signature dish. When they hosted guests, it was the most requested meal."

Just as his words settled over them, a small beeping sound pierced the silence, cutting through the moment. The butler glanced at his phone and a flash of apology crossed his face. "Excusez-moi, I'm needed elsewhere in the estate," he said, his voice smooth and formal. "Please continue. I'll return shortly to check on you."

With a polite nod, he gestured towards the book and turned to leave, his footsteps growing fainter as he disappeared down the narrow hallway.

The room seemed to exhale as the door clicked shut, leaving Amelia and Gabriel alone with the cookbook. They both looked at each other with a mix of relief and excitement. Finally, they were alone—no chaperone, no watchful eyes. Their attention shifted back to the open page where the familiar recipe was penned in an elegant, looping script, each letter flowing effortlessly into the next. The thick, slightly yellowed pages showed the signs of aging and their edges were soft from years of being handled. It was clear this book hadn't been tucked away for show—its history was written in the very stains that marked the surface. Splatters of sauce, old dustings of flour, and smudges of oil marred the paper, evidence of countless meals prepared with its guidance. The tiny flourishes in the margins—delicate sketches of herbs, finely detailed vegetables, and ornate borders—added a sense of artistry, like each page had been crafted with the same care as the dishes it held. It was a living document, worn but cherished, connecting the past to the present through the timeless ritual of cooking.

Amelia's fingers moved slowly, almost reluctantly, through the pages. Each delicate turn felt heavier as her eyes scanned the elegant handwriting with increasing urgency. *Potage Parmentier, Tarte Tatin, Cassoulet.* Recipe after recipe unfolded before them and every dish was painstakingly documented with notes on variations and pairings. Each entry was a testament to the care the Bourgets had taken in preserving their culinary heritage—yet there was nothing that suggested the book was *anything* beyond the ordinary.

No cryptic symbols. No hidden markings. Just the preserved memories of a family's meals, passed down through the generations.

Gabriel leaned in, his voice low. "These are incredible," he murmured, his awe at the artistry of the recipes clear, but his tone carried a hint of defeat. "But they seem to be... just recipes."

Amelia's heart started sinking, the growing frustration gnawing at her. They had been so certain they would find the ledger concealed within these pages, cleverly hidden amidst the handwritten notes of old-world cuisine—or perhaps not about cuisine at all. Yet, with every new page she turned, the hope they had clung to unraveled a little more.

Her movements grew faster, more desperate as she neared the final entries. No hollowed-out pages. No secret compartments. No folded slips of paper tucked discreetly between the pages. It was *just* a cookbook.

She paused, her fingers resting on one of the last pages, the weight of disappointment settling in like a heavy stone in her chest. Her eyes drifted over the faded ink, lingering on the familiar loops of the family's handwriting, but all she found were carefully preserved recipes—ordinary and unassuming. Amelia glanced up at Gabriel, who was watching her closely, his expression reflecting the same sinking realization.

Had they been chasing shadows all along?

"This can't be it," she whispered, turning back to the first recipes. "There has to be something more."

Gabriel leaned in closer, scanning the first few pages with her again, both of them searching for any clue they might have missed. But no matter how many times they looked, there was no ledger. The cookbook was exactly what it appeared to be—a well-worn family heirloom filled with recipes. Amelia's heart sank as she closed the book, feeling as though it mocked them by hiding the very thing they sought.

Motionless and defeated, she stared blankly at the closed cover, convinced the ledger was lost to history. *Maybe it had been thrown out years ago… tossed aside with no understanding of its value.*

Everything around her seemed to blur and sharpen in waves, her mind caught between presence and absence. Sensing her stillness, Gabriel stepped closer and gently placed a hand on her shoulder. His touch was light and meant to offer comfort.

"Come on," he said softly, his voice tinged with hope. "We'll keep looking."

But Amelia didn't move. As Gabriel's touch pulled her from her fog, something caught her eye—something she'd overlooked in her haze of disappointment. She tilted her head slightly, her focus sharpening on the object in her hands. The leather cover, worn but beautifully tanned, was adorned with an intricate hand-embossed filigree that gave it an air of elegance. The raised bands along the spine were perfectly spaced and the binding meticulously crafted—every detail precise. It was a stunning book, crafted with care and meant to endure.

But that wasn't what made her pulse quicken.

Amelia blinked, completely in the present now, and her eyes narrowed in on something she hadn't *fully* seen before. She stared down at the book's title embossed on the cover, the gold lettering gleaming in the soft light:

Peindre avec les Saveurs: À la Découverte des Recettes de la Famille Bourget.

"Wait," she whispered. *"Peindre avec les Saveurs…"*

Her pulse quickened, her mind racing as the words connected. She looked up at Gabriel, her heart pounding with realization. "'Painting with Flavor: Unlocking the Bourget Family Recipes'!"

She repeated the words slowly, the meaning dawning on her like a veil being lifted, revealing a hidden truth.

Gabriel's brow furrowed, confusion etched on his face. "Painting with flavor? What does that—?"

Amelia nodded, interrupting him with growing excitement. "It's more than just a clever title—it's a code! *Painting*, like a brush. *Unlocking*, like a key! The book isn't just about recipes; it's about what's *hidden* within them! *The key and the brush will guide us*—what Arnaud wrote to Étienne! The ledger—it's not just hidden within the cookbook. The recipes *are* the ledger itself!" Her fingers quickly opened the cover again, realizing the book *did* contain the secrets they had been chasing.

Gabriel's eyes widened as the realization sank in. The very words in front of them, embossed into the cover of the cookbook, had been the clue they were looking for.

Amelia's breath quickened. "The recipes aren't just recipes; they're a code! The ledger isn't tucked into some hidden compartment—it's somehow… woven into the words themselves!"

Her breathing increased as she turned the pages again, her heart racing with a new urgency. The meaning of each dish, each ingredient, suddenly transformed in her mind. What once seemed like a simple list of family recipes was now revealing itself to be a possible intricate web of coded messages, a secret ledger that had survived the decades. It was *all* here, disguised as something ordinary—*hidden in plain sight!*

She looked up at Gabriel, her eyes wide with realization. "This was their plan all along—hide the ledger where no one would ever think to look. Inside their family recipes!"

Gabriel's gaze locked with hers, the gravity of what they had uncovered settling in. The book they had been searching for, the ledger they thought was lost, had always been here, encoded in the most unassuming way. They just had to find it.

Amelia flipped through the remaining pages, her hands trembling as she reached the final recipe. She paused, and her pulse quickened at the enormity of the moment. "It's all here, Gabriel! The ledger—every transaction, every piece of art, every secret—it's all *somehow* hidden within these words!"

She got goosebumps as the discovery settled over her. The cookbook wasn't just a collection of recipes. It was the Bourget family's masterpiece —a ledger, woven into the every day, waiting to be uncovered.

The words of Arnaud echoed in her mind: *The key and the brush will guide us.*

And they had.

Chapter 52

Château Bourget, 1920

The dining hall of Château Bourget was filled with the soft, golden light of candelabras, their flames flickering as laughter and conversation filled the air. The room was magnificent. Tapestries draped the walls that told stories of centuries past, and the long dining table was set meticulously with polished silver and the Bourget family crest embroidered on the linens. It was 1920, and the Bourget name commanded admiration far beyond the gilded walls of their estate.

On this particular evening, the hall was alive with the excitement of guests who had come from near and far to experience the renowned hospitality of Lucien Bourget. At the center of it all was the promise of their most famed dish: Coq au Vin. Platters of roasted vegetables, bowls of fresh, crusty bread, and crystal decanters of deep red wine surrounded the star of the evening—an aromatic dish that had been perfected over generations.

"Ah, you see, there is no veritable feast without it," Lucien declared, his voice rich and confident. He leaned back in his chair, with a glass of wine in hand, and gestured toward the steaming dish being served. "Our Coq au Vin is the pride of this kitchen. It's a recipe passed down and refined by the most skillful hands."

One guest, a portly lady with an exquisitely crafted dress and an eager smile, raised her fork and nodded. "I've been dreaming of this dish since your last invitation, Lucien. It is said that even in the finest Parisian restaurants, none compare to what comes out of your kitchen."

Lucien's eyes twinkled, and he leaned forward with a grin. "You have my father, Julien, to thank for that. He was a man of great taste—and even greater cunning. Did you know he once managed to poach the chef of the late François-René de Châteaubriand? A feat no less daring than his ventures in the merchant trade. And that chef…," Lucien paused dramatically, "...knew how to prepare Coq au Vin in a way that would make kings weep."

Arnaud, seated to Lucien's left, shared a knowing glance with a few friends gathered beside him. He was barely twenty, but his family's legacy was already familiar to him. The aroma of the rich, wine-infused dish reminded him of the evenings spent in the kitchen as a child, watching the old chef labor over the pot, muttering secrets in low tones as steam billowed around him.

"Papa, does the recipe ever change?" Arnaud had once asked, his voice soft with curiosity.

Julien had only chuckled, placing a hand on his grandson's shoulder. "Some things, *mon enfant*, are perfected and never change. We guard them fiercely... and pass them on so others may enjoy."

Tonight, as the guests savored each bite, closing their eyes to better appreciate the delicate, deep flavors, Arnaud felt a pang of pride and nostalgia. He watched as Lucien recounted stories of their kitchen's glorious past, the room warming with his tales of culinary triumphs and family secrets. The Coq au Vin had become more than a dish; it had become a symbol of the Bourget family, and a testament to their heritage that spoke not just of art, but of home and tradition.

"To the Bourgets," one guest toasted, lifting his glass high.

"To the meals that make memories," Lucien added, eyes bright as he met Arnaud's gaze.

And as laughter echoed through the halls of Château Bourget, the Coq au Vin sat proudly at the center of the table—a savory reminder of all that the Bourget family cherished and protected.

Chapter 53

Amelia's fingers traced the embossed title once again: *Painting with Flavor: Unlocking the Bourget Family Recipes*. The more she studied it, the more the discovery settled into her bones. It *was* the ledger, hidden in plain sight. The recipes themselves—carefully penned with such precision—weren't just meals; they were coded entries. Her heart raced as her mind unraveled the brilliance of it all.

The household staff would have been the perfect mules, passing messages from one estate to another, entirely unaware of the importance of the notes they carried. In a time of surveillance and Nazi occupation, no one would have looked twice at cooks exchanging recipes in the markets. The Vallois and Bourgets might not have ever had to meet in person. The ledger, the one thing that connected their alliance, had been passed right under everyone's nose.

That this cookbook had survived through the years only deepened the genius of Arnaud's deception. During the Nazi occupation, they had looted large estates, just like Château Bourget, but military searches had been focused on vaults, galleries, and treasure troves of art. No one would have combed through a kitchen cookbook with the same scrutiny as the rest of the house.

It had been here all along.

They knew the butler would return soon. The ticking of time seemed louder with each passing second as Amelia and Gabriel's eyes scanned the pages, searching for something—*anything*—that might further validate their growing theory. Amelia's hand paused over the edge of one page, her breath catching. There, nearly invisible in the soft light of the kitchen, was a tiny, darkened dot of ink—an ink splatter, no bigger than the head of a pin—staining the margin of the recipe. At first glance, it seemed nothing more than a blemish, like a careless smudge from a hurried hand. But then her mind darted back to the other pages she had skimmed.

She flipped back to those earlier recipes, eyes sharp, scanning the margins. The *same* faint ink splatter, almost indistinguishable, appeared again. And again. Each one subtly placed, always in the same corner. It was a repetition of an imperfection that now felt far too deliberate to be an accident.

"Gabriel," she whispered with urgency as she pointed to the ink. "Look at this."

Gabriel leaned closer as his gaze followed hers to the tiny mark. "What is it?" he murmured, his voice low but alert, sensing the significance beneath her tone.

Amelia's fingers shook slightly as she turned the page. "It's here too," she said, pointing to another splatter. "And here..." She turned another page, and there it was again—the faint smudge of ink, nearly imperceptible but unmistakably present. She continued, "This can't be a coincidence. It's on a majority of the pages in this book."

Gabriel's eyes widened, the implication dawning on him as he leaned in closer, his breath shallow with realization. "You think it's a marker?" he asked, his voice tense. "A signal or something telling us which recipes contain the coded ledger entries?"

Amelia nodded, her excitement tempered by the unknown. "It has to be. The ink splatter—it's too deliberate to be an accident. Look at the recipes marked by it—they're longer, more detailed. Arnaud wouldn't have used obvious symbols. This... this is deliberate. It's almost invisible, yet it's there, guiding us to these entries!"

Gabriel looked at her, his eyes gleaming with urgency. "Then this book... it *is* the ledger!"

Amelia's mind raced as she quickly flipped through the pages, her hands steady despite the rush of adrenaline. The ink splatters formed a pattern, each one anchoring her belief that the recipes held more than just culinary instructions. But they still hadn't figured out how to decode them.

"We need to get this out of here," Gabriel said quietly, glancing toward the door, his mind already strategizing.

Amelia nodded, but her mind was spinning, calculating their options. They couldn't simply walk out with the cookbook—it would immediately raise suspicion... and possibly send them to jail. And photographing each of the, what seemed like, 200 coded recipes would take time—time they didn't have. Her gaze moved toward Gabriel. *This is it*, she thought. The ledger, hidden in plain sight, coded within the very lines of these recipes. It was all here, waiting to be uncovered.

They had to preserve it. But how?

Just as the gravity of the situation began to settle, the door creaked slightly, sending a jolt through both of them. Amelia's hands froze, still resting on the book's cover. Her pulse pounded in her ears as the butler stepped back into the room, followed closely by Christian Moreau.

The moment shattered. Amelia forced herself to remain calm, her heartbeat quickening as she met Gabriel's glance. Time was running out, and they had to tread carefully.

"Ah, everything going well, I hope?" Mr. Moreau's voice was warm but curious as he glanced between them and the open cookbook, completely unaware of the delicate discovery in their hands.

Amelia smiled, her voice was steady despite the adrenaline coursing through her veins. "Yes, everything's wonderful," she said warmly, casually flipping through a few pages as though admiring the recipes. "It's incredible how well-preserved they are."

The words flowed naturally, but beneath the surface, every move was calculated. One wrong word, one suspicious glance, and everything they had worked for could unravel. They couldn't let the Moreaus know what they had uncovered—not yet. Her mind spun, each thought colliding with the next as she tried to remain composed. Every instinct screamed at her to protect the discovery, but she knew they needed more time to study the cookbook.

Her gaze moved to Gabriel, whose expression remained steady but alert, mirroring her own tension. She had to find a way to gain further access, to delicately slip beneath the surface of casual curiosity while masking the urgent need burning inside her. After a brief hesitation, she forced her smile to broaden while looking up at Moreau, the warmth in her tone carefully crafted.

"Would it be alright if I took a few photos?" she asked, her tone light and nonchalant, as if the request were nothing more than a passing thought. "I'd love to… try some of these recipes myself."

It was a delicate request, and the casual nature of it masked the intensity of her true intentions. Now, all she could do was wait, her heart thudding in her chest as she hoped her words had struck the right balance.

Moreau's face lit up with enthusiasm. "Oh, there's no need for that!" he exclaimed, his passion for the estate's legacy clear. "We actually had the entire cookbook scanned, replicated, and professionally bound a few years ago to preserve the original! We even sell copies to those interested in the dishes made famous by the Bourgets."

Amelia gasped. *Replicated?*

Moreau gestured toward the cookbook, a glimpse of pride lighting his face. "This one right here, for example—*Coq au Vin*—was the most requested dish when the Bourgets hosted guests. It became a signature of the estate, often served at grand dinners and celebrations. Guests from all over would ask for it—specifically—knowing it would rival anything found in the finest Parisian restaurants." He paused, then pointed to another recipe. "And Châteaubriand! The family claimed their chef invented it right here in this very kitchen!"

Moreau's eyes gleamed as he shared the story. "The family chef, Montmireil, used to work as the personal chef to François-René de Châteaubriand, the famous 19th-century writer and diplomat. When he came to Château Bourget, he continued refining his culinary skills. Legend has it that Montmireil created the dish—a thick cut of beef tenderloin, perfectly roasted and served with a rich Béarnaise sauce—as a tribute to Châteaubriand's refined tastes. Some say it was a favorite of Châteaubriand himself, and the recipe became an instant classic... passed down through generations of chefs who worked at the estate."

He smiled, clearly relishing the rich history tied to the dish. "It's a piece of French culinary history, right here within these pages. And to think, it all began in this very kitchen!" He tapped his index finger down on one of the worn wooden tables, pride now beaming from his face.

Before Amelia could respond, Moreau turned to the butler. "Go fetch a copy of *Peindre avec les Saveurs* for our guests."

Amelia's pulse quickened. The ledger—*the* ledger—was now in a mass-produced cookbook, sold to the public as a piece of French culinary heritage. She exchanged a glance with Gabriel, who caught the shift in her expression. He leaned closer, his voice low, meant only for her.

"Do you realize what this means?" Gabriel asked, his tone mixed with urgency. "How many people could already have a copy of this? The ledger's been out there—*for sale*—all this time."

Amelia nodded as her thoughts raced. She forced herself to maintain composure as the butler returned with a pristine copy of the book, identical to the one she had in her hands.

"For you," the butler said, offering the book with a bow.

Amelia took it gratefully, forcing a polite smile on her lips as her thoughts churned. She held in her hands the very key they'd been chasing, but the thrill of discovery was filled with a new anxiety. How many copies of this book were already out there? How many other hands had touched it, unaware of the secrets encoded within? Could someone else be on the verge of uncovering the truth without even knowing it?

"Thank you," she said steadily, though her heart pounded in her chest. Her gaze dropped to the book. "This is... more than I could have… imagined." She looked back at Moreau, her expression carefully composed, masking the uncertainty simmering beneath.

As they exited the château, the heavy door creaked shut behind them. Amelia stared blankly down the perron staircase as she gripped the cookbook tighter, her thoughts continuing to swirl. The ledger hadn't been hidden in some hidden vault or behind a false wall. It had been on display, in plain sight, for years—replicated and sold to anyone curious enough to buy it.

Gabriel's steps fell in sync with hers as they made their way to the car. "What now?" he asked, his voice mixed with both excitement and concern.

Amelia glanced down at the cookbook as her fingers ran over the embossed title. "We decode it," she replied, her voice firm, though a flicker of dread hung to the edge of her thoughts. "But we need to move fast. If anyone else realizes—or already realized—what this is…"

She trailed off, unable to finish the thought. The discovery had been both thrilling and unnerving. The ledger had been hidden in plain sight, and now the challenge was no longer finding it—it was keeping it safe.

As they drove away from Château Bourget, the town of Saint-Germain-en-Laye disappeared behind them, and Amelia couldn't shake the heaviness of the realization. The ledger, the key to uncovering the Bourget and Vallois families' secrets, had been sitting right under everyone's noses for years. Now, it was in their hands, and the race to decode it had begun.

Chapter 54

Paris, August 1943

Two years after the Alliance formed...

A late-summer warmth draped over Paris, softening the edges of the streets and filtering into the calm shadows of Arnaud's study. The Alliance's core members sat around the modest desk where so many plans had been formed. After the relentless pace of recent months—and all they had achieved—the air held a gentle calm now. It felt strange to return to something like normalcy. For years, they had operated in shadows, each member playing a part in their intricate work. They had done so much, yet one final task remained: preserving the ledger.

Arnaud placed the worn, crumpled notebook on the table. Inside, its pages were filled with the records of every artwork they'd hidden—each entry a victory against a relentless enemy. The ledger had been with them through everything—sleepless nights, risky travels, and secret conversations in darkened rooms. But as he looked at its frayed edges and cracking spine, he knew this crucial record could not stay as it was. It needed to be more than just a testament to their work—it had to be something that could endure.

Nadejda studied the notebook, her expression distant, already envisioning what it would take to protect this delicate piece of history. "It's vulnerable like this," she said softly. "A few sheets of paper... one misstep, one discovery, and all of it will be gone."

Étienne nodded thoughtfully. "Then we need to restore it," he said. "But not just with a new cover and ink. To endure safely, it needs to be disguised. Disguised as something ordinary... something that no one would ever question."

A brief pause followed. Étienne's knack for practical solutions had helped the Vallois family thrive. It was also this same thinking that helped the Alliance operate in secrecy for so long.

Arnaud let his thoughts wander, searching for the right idea. Suddenly, his eyes lit up. He snapped his thumb and looked at the others, eager to share his formulating thought.

"Étienne is right. An encoded notebook *does* raise questions," he said. "But what's something that wouldn't? What's something that carries a legacy? Something passed down and treasured from generation to generation, yet so ordinary it could sit on a shelf for decades without suspicion?"

As the idea fully solidified, a sparkle hit Arnaud's eyes. The team looked at him, their expressions a mix of intrigue and uncertainty.

"A cookbook!" he said excitedly. "An unassuming family cookbook! One that's part of everyday life at Château Bourget! The kitchen staff would use it every day, unaware that within its recipes… lies something else entirely!"

Nadejda's lips curved into a smile, catching his enthusiasm. "A cookbook, with our ledger entries encoded inside!" she exclaimed. "The recipes could fill the pages, but each one would have a dual purpose. *No* one would see it for what it truly is! It's genius!"

Arnaud nodded, his mind racing. "The Bourget family recipes are already written out on individual sheets, stored in a box—Coq Au Vin, Châteaubriand, Chocolate Soufflé. All we need to do is bind them together and layer in the ledger's entries, somehow woven into the details of each recipe!"

Lucien, who had been silent until now, leaned forward with a smile. "This new binding would need a good title," he said, with a hint of playfulness. "Something that honors the Bourget heritage but also subtly hints at the art within." He paused, considering, then his eyes brightened. "'Peindre avec les Saveurs'—'*Painting* with Flavor! *Unlocking* the Bourget Family Recipes!' The brush and the key! It's almost a challenge to anyone who dares to look closely!"

Arnaud picked up on the energy flowing through the room, the sense of purpose binding them together. "Yes!" he agreed. "Each recipe entry would correspond to a piece of art, but only someone who knows the full story, knows the brush and the key, would understand its true meaning! Hidden in plain sight! It's perfect!"

As dawn broke, the ledger was finally complete. After working through the night, Nadejda took a moment to hold their new creation one last time before handing it to Arnaud. "The people who use this won't even know what they're protecting," she said with reverence. "But that's exactly how it needs to be."

The leather-bound volume was unassuming, its surface deliberately worn to appear well-used, yet elegant enough to reflect its heritage. The title on the cover, *Peindre avec les Saveurs: À la Découverte des Recettes de la Famille Bourguet*, hinted at nothing more than a family cookbook. *Unlocking secrets, indeed*, Arnaud thought as he ran a hand over its spine.

Inside the bustling staff kitchen at Château Bourget, it would blend seamlessly among other cookbooks. And each day, the staff would turn its pages, completely unaware that their routines sheltered something extraordinary.

As Arnaud placed the book on the shelf, Nadejda stood beside him. "Do you think it's enough?" she asked softly, fingertips brushing the spine.

He nodded, resolute. "It's hidden in plain sight, Nadejda… safe in the rhythm of everyday life. It will survive."

With that, they stepped away, leaving the ledger—and the culmination of their mission—to fulfill its purpose. Endure. In time, when it was safe, someone would open these pages not just to cook, but to reclaim a legacy that had weathered the storm, patiently waiting behind familiar recipes and a quiet act of defiance.

Chapter 55

The soft murmur of Parisian traffic filtered through the open windows of Amelia's studio. Along with it, a gentle late autumn breeze carried in the earthy scent of fallen leaves and damp stone. There was a faint smokiness in the air, likely from a combination of wood-burning stoves and cigarettes, which mingled with the sweetness of roasting chestnuts from a nearby vendor. She rarely kept her windows open while working on restoration projects, so this was a welcome change, helping to offset the intense mental work going on inside. The aroma was distinctly Paris in the fall—rich, layered, and painted with a nostalgia that seemed to settle over the city as the days grew shorter.

The rustling of paper and the occasional scrape of a chair leg against the wooden floor kept the otherwise silent space from falling asleep. Late afternoon light, softened by the curtains, spilled over the long worktable, illuminating a scene of intense concentration. Spread before Amelia and Gabriel were notepads, filled with hurried scribbles and lines of calculations, scattered in disarray. And at the center of it all, like an impenetrable safe, lay the copied cookbook: *Peindre avec les Saveurs.*

Amelia leaned forward while her hands rested on its familiar cover, its title staring back at her like a challenge. Days had passed since their discovery at Château Bourget, and still, the key to unlocking the ledger remained hidden, tangled within the elegant script of recipes that had survived generations. There was no sign that the ledger's entries were written plainly anywhere in the cookbook. They suspected as much but needed to be certain. Having thoroughly searched for any straightforward clues, they moved on to a new assumption—the entries were somehow encoded within the existing recipes.

Gabriel had been an enormous asset in this endeavor. As a structural engineer, numbers and logic were paramount to his profession. He was adept at analyzing complex systems, identifying patterns, and solving intricate problems—skills that were now invaluable. As a child, he had also been fascinated by codes and ciphers, often spending hours with his friends devising secret messages and challenging each other to crack them. They would pass encrypted notes in class using homemade ciphers inspired by books they read. This childhood hobby had instilled in him a love for puzzles, just like Amelia, and the thrill of uncovering hidden meanings—a passion that persisted into adulthood and now found a new purpose in their quest.

Amelia, too, knew a thing or two about ciphers. Her work as an art restorer often required unraveling the stories hidden within paintings and historical artifacts—symbols, markings, and techniques that carried secrets from the past. In college, she'd taken a course on cryptography out of sheer curiosity and was captivated by the interplay of logic and creativity. Her understanding of encoded messages, though not as technical as Gabriel's, was rooted in her ability to see patterns, interpret context, and uncover hidden layers of meaning. Together, their complementary skills made them a formidable team, each bringing a unique perspective to the puzzle before them.

Gabriel sat across from Amelia and thumbed through a notepad as the crease between his brows deepened. His eyes moved back and forth, reviewing the latest round of notes. The cookbook sat between them, its pages waiting, seemingly indifferent to the desperation that had crept into their search.

"We've gone over everything," Amelia said, her frustration actively coming through. "Every recipe, every line. There has to be something we're missing."

Gabriel nodded, tapping a pencil absently against the table. "Maybe we start over from the basics… We've tried everything else."

Amelia sighed and gave a sharp nod. She flipped the cookbook open to the first page and her fingers traced the ink-stained margins. "Okay… Let's try the Caesar cipher again?"

"Sure," Gabriel agreed, pushing his notepad aside to make room. "But let's go through it methodically."

The Caesar cipher was one of the simplest and oldest methods of encryption—dating back to ancient Rome, where Julius Caesar had used it to send secret military orders. It worked by shifting each letter of the alphabet by a fixed number of positions. For instance, with a shift of three,

'A' would become 'D,' 'B' would become 'E,' and so on. The challenge was figuring out what number had been used as the shift—if this was even the cipher they needed.

Amelia ran her finger down the ingredients list for *Bouillabaisse*, one of the recipes marked by the tiny ink splatter. "Let's try shifting the first letters again."

They began with a shift of three—'T' became 'W,' 'O' became 'R,' but as they moved through the list, the letters formed no recognizable word. Undeterred, they tried a shift of five, then six, each time rearranging the letters in their minds.

The letters scrambled into randomness—broken pieces of an unsolvable puzzle. They shifted again and Amelia's finger moved faster now, scanning the page for patterns. But there was nothing.

"No pattern here, again," she muttered, frustration in her voice. The Caesar cipher had seemed so promising, its simplicity appealing. Yet the letters refused to cooperate.

Amelia shook her head. "It doesn't work."

A few minutes of silence passed, and the room was filled with their shared disappointment. Gabriel straightened, running his hand through his hair. "Alright. Maybe the cipher isn't a simple substitution," he said. "What if it's not the letters themselves, but the meaning of the words?"

Amelia tilted her head thoughtfully, considering his suggestion. "You mean... semantic coding?"

"Exactly. Maybe certain words are metaphorical. Like, the ingredients could be symbols for something else entirely. What if we're not looking for letters, but for ideas? Categories, even."

She nodded slowly, turning the idea over in her mind. "Certain recipes could correspond to specific types of art... like paintings, sculptures, or manuscripts? Maybe there's a hidden meaning behind the dishes themselves?"

For the next hour, they dove into this possibility, looking for ways the recipes might be more than just food—they might be metaphors, hidden in plain sight, just as Arnaud had intended. Gabriel flipped to *Potage Parmentier*, his finger tracing the elegant script as he read through the simple ingredients: potatoes, leeks, butter. He leaned back, thinking aloud.

"Could *potatoes* mean portraits?" He wondered, his voice hinting at a mix of hope and uncertainty. "They grow underground, hidden until they're unearthed. Could it be a metaphor for hidden art?"

Amelia, equally invested, flipped to another recipe. "What about *Tarte Tatin?*" she suggested, her eyes scanning the page. "It's layered—like fruit hidden beneath the pastry. Could the layers of fruit represent different layers of meaning, something concealed beneath the obvious?"

They exchanged looks of cautious hopefulness, feeling the spark of a potential breakthrough. With renewed determination, they began analyzing each recipe as though they were decoding an abstract painting, searching for clues buried beneath the surface.

"*Cassoulet,*" Amelia murmured, staring at the list of ingredients. "Beans… they take a long time to cook. Maybe that represents something that takes time to develop—like sculptures being crafted over years?"

"Or *Coq au Vin,*" Gabriel added. "It's slow-cooked, carefully tended. Maybe the wine symbolizes something preserved over time—like the way art is carefully curated?"

Amelia scribbled notes, trying to match ingredients with artistic symbols. But with every dish they analyzed, trying to match culinary terms with categories of art—portraits, sculptures, landscapes—the metaphors seemed to crumble under scrutiny. The connections they were drawing felt tenuous, forced.

As the minutes passed, the effort began to feel hollow. *Potage Parmentier* was just potatoes and leeks. *Tarte Tatin* was nothing more than caramelized apples. The more they tried to twist the recipes into something meaningful, the more obvious it became: these were delicious dishes, yes, but nothing more.

Amelia let out a frustrated sigh, closing the book with a sharp snap. "This is ridiculous! It's not here," she said, her tone edged with irritation. "We're grasping at straws. They're just… recipes."

Gabriel didn't respond immediately. He was just as frustrated, but his mind was already working through a new possibility after quickly dismissing the last. He leaned back in his chair and stared at the ceiling as if the answer might somehow materialize there. After a moment, he rubbed his temples thoughtfully. "What about something in the format?" he said, his voice slower, more deliberate. "The structure of the recipes themselves."

Amelia pulled the cookbook closer, her eyes narrowing as she studied the layout of the text. Gabriel grabbed another notepad, quickly sketching the structure of one recipe, marking out the number of words per line, the number of lines in each paragraph. They spent the rest of the afternoon comparing the formatting of various entries, scrutinizing the alignment of ingredients, the spacing of instructions, the margins and indentations.

"Maybe the code's hidden in the way the recipes are presented?" Gabriel suggested, his tone carrying a thread of hope.

But as they charted the patterns, no hidden structure emerged. The recipes remained elegantly written, meticulously detailed, but frustratingly opaque. The spacing between lines, the alignment of text—none of it yielded any discernible code.

Amelia sighed deeply, rubbing her eyes. "I'm starting to think Arnaud was too clever for us."

Gabriel glanced at her, offering a faint smile of sympathy. "Let's try one more thing. Statistical methods. If there's a pattern, we'll find it in the frequency of letters."

Amelia nodded, though weariness weighed on her movements. She grabbed a blank sheet of paper and began making a frequency chart, listing every letter that appeared in *Confit de canard*. Her pen moved mechanically and her mind was dulled by the tedium of the task, but her hope remained stubbornly alive. Gabriel leaned over, helping tally the results.

Minutes passed in silence as they analyzed the data, but the chart only confirmed what they already knew: the recipes followed no traditional encryption methods. No distinct patterns. No hidden messages waiting to be unlocked.

Amelia leaned back in her chair, dropping her pen with a soft clatter. "It's not a typical code," she murmured, tinged with exhaustion. "Maybe there is no code at all," she said, shaking her head in utter disappointment.

Gabriel closed his notepad, his expression reflecting the same frustration that had settled in her chest. "We've tried everything we know."

The room felt like it was suffocating them, the steady hum of the city outside and the fresh air coming in now offering little comfort. Amelia stared at the cookbook, feeling as though it were mocking them. For all their effort, they had come no closer to unlocking its secrets.

She rubbed her temples, the tension in her head building with every passing second. "There has to be something," she mumbled. "Arnaud wouldn't have made it impossible to decode—*especially* if he purposely left breadcrumbs.

Gabriel looked at her with tired resolve. "Then we keep trying. We'll find it, Amelia."

She glanced at the notepads scattered across the table, the cookbook lying there like an unsolved mystery. Despite the hours they had poured into the search, she refused to accept defeat. Somewhere, hidden within the lines of those recipes, was the answer.

They just had to find it.

Chapter 56

"Breadcrumbs!"

The word burst from Amelia's lips, hanging in the still air of her studio, as she bound upright in her chair, eyes wide with excitement. Gabriel blinked at her, startled by the sudden outburst, but Amelia's mind was already racing, pieces *finally* shifting into place. She hadn't fully understood it before. She hadn't seen the connection. But now, the meaning was clear.

"Wait—what are you talking about?" Gabriel asked, setting his notepad aside.

Amelia's eyes brightened as she flipped open the cookbook once again, the pages seemingly now carrying a new significance. "We've been going about this the wrong way," she said, her voice charged with excitement. "All along, we've assumed that the ledger was coded *into* the cookbook. But look at this…" She ran her finger down the page of *Coq au Vin*, her pulse quickening. "These recipes—they go back decades before the Alliance was even formed! Mr. Moreau said these were the Bourget family's ancestral recipes, passed down for generations. This book pre-dates the ledger."

A look of confusion remained on Gabriel's face as he was trying to catch up. "So… what does that mean?"

"It means," Amelia continued, "that the cookbook came first. The ledger wasn't coded into the cookbook. They coded the cookbook *into* the ledger."

Gabriel stared at her for a moment, the idea sinking in. "So, you're saying the recipes themselves are older... and the ledger used them as the foundation for encryption?"

Amelia nodded, her mind already racing ahead. "Exactly. The cookbook wasn't just used as a cover—it was woven into the very structure of the ledger, hiding the entries within something that already existed, something no one would think twice about."

Her eyes shifted to the toolbox sitting on the floor by the table—the same box that had led her to the cookbook in the first place. The memory of Arnaud's love letter swept through her mind, and the words *"The brush and the key will guide us"* echoed back to her. She had always thought the "brush" referred to something literal in the art world—a painter's tool, perhaps—but now a different possibility dawned on her.

"The cookbook," she murmured aloud, her voice soft but filled with a growing certainty. "The *brush* isn't about painting in the literal sense. It's the cookbook—*Painting with Flavor*."

Gabriel frowned, his confusion deepening. "But if the cookbook is the brush... what's the key?"

Amelia hesitated, looking again at the old wooden toolbox sitting by the worktable, realizing her mouth had outrun her mind. She had been so careful not to reveal everything early on, to keep certain parts of her story locked away, not because it was too personal or intimate, but because she hadn't known if she could fully trust him. *Gabriel's a good guy*. She knew it—and now, with everything coming together, there was no more room, or need, for secrets.

Straightening her posture, her voice suddenly firm with purpose, she said, "The love letter."

Gabriel raised an eyebrow, his expression a mixture of confusion and surprise. "The what?"

Amelia exhaled deeply, feeling the final barrier between them crumble as she prepared to open up. This felt good. No more secrets. It was the last part of her journey she had kept from him, and she knew it was time. Her fingers brushed the edge of the toolbox, its worn wood cool under her touch. Her voice softened by the significance of what she was about to share.

"The love letter I found from Arnaud to Eloise... in this old toolbox," she began, each word slow and deliberate. "I haven't told you everything about how I got here, Gabriel. About how I even began this search."

Gabriel's confusion shifted into curiosity, his eyes never leaving hers. He'd sensed her withholding. He sensed some residual guardedness that lingered between them. Until now, he hadn't pressed her, respecting the unspoken boundaries. After all, he had terrified her when they met. He knew trust was slow. But hearing her say it aloud and watching her as she stood before the toolbox, he realized she was finally letting him in.

Amelia knelt down beside it and her mind flashed back to the day she had first pried it open. She remembered the rush of emotions—the blend of excitement and uncertainty. "It was hidden in here," she continued, "along with a ring, an old photo, and a handkerchief." She took a moment to expand on each item, carefully detailing their significance before resting her hand gently on the pages. "But this letter... it was different. Everything else in the toolbox had a purpose, a connection to this search, like breadcrumbs leading me here. But the letter... I always thought it was something personal, something Arnaud Bourget—" she looked up at Gabriel, emphasizing the name to make him understand its importance—"wanted to protect for sentimental reasons."

She held the letter up, the fragile pages of paper rustling softly between her fingers. "But now, I'm wondering if we missed something. Why would Arnaud hide it here with the other breadcrumbs if it wasn't a breadcrumb itself?"

Gabriel studied her carefully, sensing the importance of the moment. "Why didn't you tell me about this before?" His voice was gentle, not accusatory, but laced with curiosity.

Amelia hesitated, her gaze switching between the letter and Gabriel's eyes. "Because I didn't know if I could trust you," she admitted. "I've been careful—this search is dangerous, and I wasn't ready to share everything with anyone. But now..." She looked back at the letter in her hands. "Now I think this is the final piece. I think Arnaud hid something in this letter that I missed. Why else would he place it here, with all these other clues? Why else would he tuck it away if it wasn't meant to guide us? If it wasn't a... *key?*"

Gabriel took a step closer, the distance between them closing as his curiosity grew. "You think the love letter holds the key to deciphering the recipes?"

Amelia nodded slowly, her grip on the letter tightening. "I think the letter *is* the key to 'unlocking the Bourget family recipes'—*À la Découverte des Recettes de la Famille Bourget*. We've already found the brush in the cookbook itself—'Painting with Flavor.' But the key... I think the *literal* cipher key for the encoded recipes is hidden within this letter. It's not just a love note—it's something more!"

Gabriel exhaled, her revelation sinking in. He could feel the gravity of the moment, the way everything in their search seemed to pivot around these eight fragile pieces of paper. He reached out and his hand rested on the letter over hers. His voice was low but filled with determination. "Show me," he said, his tone steady, his eyes locking with hers. "Let's figure this out together."

Amelia looked up at him, her heart thudding in her chest. For the first time, she allowed the final wall of trust between them to fall away. Gabriel wasn't just a part of the search anymore—he was a part of her story, of the journey she had been on since the beginning.

———

Without another word, Amelia stared down at the pages, her eyes narrowing in deep focus. The familiar words of affection, written in the faded ink, remained just as they had the first time she read them—fragile, worn, and ordinary. But this time, something nagged at her, a faint irregularity beneath her fingertips. She had read the letter before, even scrutinized it, but she hadn't been looking for anything beyond the sentiment behind the words. Now, with the possibility that the letter was more than it seemed, everything felt different.

She turned the pages carefully, her fingers brushing over the delicate paper. There it was again—something subtle, like a whisper just below the surface—almost imperceptible, yet undeniably off. The texture wasn't quite right, as though the paper had been altered in some way. It wasn't obvious, but her years as an art restorer had trained her to notice even the smallest inconsistencies—especially now that she was *looking* for something. She had spent years handling fragile artifacts, manuscripts, and paintings, learning to detect hidden layers beneath surfaces, finding what others might overlook.

Amelia paused, holding the letter up to the light streaming in from the window and tilted it slightly. Her fingertips brushed over the back of the page, tracing the minute differences in texture again. *What am I missing?* she wondered. The surface felt just slightly rougher in certain places, almost like indentations that had been worn smooth with time.

Her heart quickened as techniques from her restoration work surfaced in her mind—methods used to uncover what eluded her. She turned the page over again, her fingers more purposeful in their search, tracing the delicate irregularities she now recognized as intentional. Could it be?

Invisible ink.

The thought struck her suddenly. It was an ancient technique used to conceal sensitive information. What if Arnaud had used it here? What if there was something more hidden beneath the seemingly innocent love note?

Amelia's pulse quickened as the idea solidified in her mind. It wasn't just about the words written *in plain sight*; it was about what had been *hidden* all along, waiting to be found.

Amelia stood up suddenly, rushing to the small kitchenette in the corner of her studio. Gabriel watched in confusion as she rummaged through the cupboards until she found what she was looking for—powdered dish detergent.

"Amelia, what are you doing?" Gabriel asked, his curiosity piqued. He had been watching her in silent focus, careful not to disrupt her, but this sudden burst of action was impossible to ignore.

"Sodium carbonate," Amelia muttered, holding up the container. "It's the main ingredient in dish detergent—and it's exactly what we need to reveal iron sulfate ink."

Gabriel's eyes widened in realization. "Iron sulfate ink?"

Amelia nodded while her excitement grew further. "It was a common technique in the 19th and early 20th centuries. Iron sulfate ink is invisible to the naked eye but becomes visible when treated with sodium carbonate."

Gabriel leaned in, his gaze fixed on the letter. "You think there's invisible ink on this letter?"

Amelia paused for a moment, considering her next words. She glanced up at him, a smirk forming on her lips. "We're about to find out!"

She handed the detergent to Gabriel. "Here, dilute the powder with water—just enough to create a thin paste." He moved quickly, following her instructions, and soon enough, a small bowl of the mixture was ready.

Amelia grabbed a clean cloth and dipped it into the solution, her hands steady despite the anticipation building. The room fell into a tense silence as Gabriel leaned in closer, both of them holding their breath while Amelia carefully applied the solution to the back of the letter.

They watched, eager to see something, but nothing happened. The paper stayed blank, and doubt quickly crept into Amelia's mind. Had they been wrong—*again?* Seconds continued to pass and she felt her heart sink, the disappointment closing in on her—on both of them. But just as she was about to pull away, something caught her eye—a faint line began to emerge.

"Wait," she said quietly.

Slowly, like ghosts rising from the past, tiny, precise numbers emerged—written in iron sulfate ink, concealed for decades beneath the surface, hidden in plain sight.

Chapter 57

Amelia gasped as more numbers appeared, forming rows upon rows across the back of the letter's pages after she applied the solution to each.

Gabriel blinked in disbelief. "That's... that's a *lot* of numbers!"

Amelia nodded, feeling a surge of excitement. "It's not just a love letter! It's a key! We literally found the brush"—she pointed to the cookbook, then back to the letter—"and the key!"

Gabriel skimmed the tiny, intricate rows. "There must be over 500 lines!"

Amelia's lips curved into triumphant smile. "It was never *just* a love letter," she said. "Arnaud hid the key to the ledger *within* it, designed to be uncovered by someone who understood its significance!"

Gabriel nodded, energized by the discovery. "Like us! And now we have the key to unlock the ledger—to unlock the recipes!"

Amelia's gaze drifted back to the cookbook, her mind already spinning with possibilities "The key and brush *will* guide us! Now we just need to decipher them!"

The desk lamp cast a steady light over the worktable, illuminating the scattered notepads, cookbook, and the love letter's densely numbered pages. Hours had passed since their discovery, and the initial rush of excitement had given way to determination. Outside, the once present hum of Parisian traffic had now dulled into the late night, leaving only the rustle of paper and the occasional scrape of a pencil against the table to break the silence.

Amelia sat hunched over in concentration as her finger traced the rows of invisible ink markings. Each one was a potential clue waiting to be deciphered, but as the night dragged on, it became clear that solving the cipher was far more complex than they had expected.

"There are *hundreds* of lines here," Gabriel muttered, rubbing the back of his neck. "Each line has something like 50 numbers. How are we supposed to figure out what they all mean?"

Amelia glanced at him, her lips pressed into a thin line. "Okay… We've ruled out the usual suspects—this isn't an Ottendorf cipher or a Trist cipher. The numbers don't correspond to page-line-word patterns." She paused, flipping through her notes. "There's no obvious link to any traditional book ciphers either. If there were, we'd be able to see groupings of numbers that correlate to some sort of sequence, but here…" She trailed off while shaking her head, staring at the long strings of digits.

They had spent hours combing through various cryptographic techniques, cross-referencing the numbers with any cipher they could think of using books, computers, and calculators—but nothing materialized. The frustration was showing in both their expressions as the minutes stretched into hours. Amelia leaned back in her chair, staring at the ceiling to clear her thoughts.

After a minute of silence, she lifted her head and started piecing together everything they had uncovered so far. "We're looking for a cipher that uses something from the cookbook," she said, steadier now, but still laced with uncertainty. She paused, mentally organizing the scattered fragments in her mind—the ink splatters on the pages, the recipes, the numbers hidden on the love letter. It all pointed to something complex.

"And I believe," she continued, her brow furrowing as the thought crystallized, "we're looking for a cipher that might… adapt—something dynamic, not static. We've had no success with frequency analysis, which means it's not a simple letter substitution. And since there is no clear pattern—the key…" she paused, considering her words. "*If there is a key,* must be shifting. There's something here we haven't unlocked yet."

She stood as her words hung between them, a spark of inspiration igniting somewhere in her mind. Something she just said resonated with her, but she wasn't quite sure how. She paused, letting the thought simmer.

Whenever she faced a difficult problem alone in her studio, she had a habit of talking things through with an inanimate companion—a small rubber duck perched on her desk. Simply voicing the issue aloud often helped her see connections she hadn't noticed before. Now Gabriel seemed to serve the same purpose. She glanced at him, noticing the weariness on his face as he looked up from his notepad. His eyes, still searching but curious, met hers.

Amelia's thoughts continued to meld as she searched for the connection. Then, it clicked—a memory surfacing from her early university days at the Sorbonne, in her *Art as a Language* course. She had studied a piece of art that had fascinated her not just for its beauty, but for its hidden layers of meaning. That puzzle, encoded in a sculpture, must have stayed with her all these years.

The *KRYPTOS* sculpture by James Sanborn in Washington, D.C., vividly surfaced in her mind. She could almost see it: tall, winding copper panels cut with layers of coded text that had stumped cryptographers and curious onlookers for decades. Designed with four sections of encrypted messages, the sculpture had captivated Amelia during her studies. The way Sanborn blended art and cryptography—each section hiding different layers of secrecy—had inspired her, showing how the *hidden* could be so intertwined with the *visible*.

She excitedly voiced her thoughts aloud to Gabriel, their eyes still locked. "I'm thinking back to a sculpture I studied at university—the *KRYPTOS* sculpture," she began, her voice growing stronger. "It's an artwork in Washington, D.C. that's famous for its layers of encrypted text—something no one's fully solved yet. But in those parts that *have* been solved, *KRYPTOS* uses a cipher called the Vigenère cipher to encode its messages."

Gabriel's eyes widened with recognition. "The Vigenère cipher! That's a polyalphabetic cipher. It uses a keyword to encrypt the message, making it more secure than simple substitution."

"Exactly!" Amelia nodded, stepping closer to the table where their notes and the cookbook lay scattered. "So instead of shifting all the letters by the *same* amount—like in a Caesar cipher—it uses that keyword to determine how much to shift each letter. The keyword creates a repeating pattern of shifts, making it much harder to crack."

Gabriel leaned forward, his interest piqued. "But we've found no repeating patterns... And we're dealing with numbers, not letters."

"Right!" Amelia agreed. "But what if the numbers correspond to letters after applying the shifts?" She paused, considering her next words carefully.

"And to your first point… a Vigenère cipher has its limits. It uses a single, repeating keyword, which means it's still vulnerable to pattern recognition—as you said, something we could not detect. I think we might be dealing with something more advanced. *Like* a Vigenère cipher… but instead of using a *single*, unique keyword, what if the key… changes?"

Gabriel's analytical mind kicked into gear. "The ink splatters in the cookbook! What if they're not random? What if they're marking the specific recipes we need to use for decryption?"

Amelia's pacing quickened as the realization solidified. "Yes!" she said, her voice growing more animated. "And… what if the key isn't just a single word? What if it's an entire block of text? Think about it: by using sequences longer than the row of numbers, like sentences or even paragraphs from these recipes, it prevents patterns from forming—the cipher becomes dynamic!"

Gabriel eagerly nodded, matching her enthusiasm. "Each row of numbers would have its own key, pulled from different parts of the cookbook! It continually evolves!"

"Right!" Amelia said, her pulse quickening. "The ink splatters in the cookbook mark which recipes to use, and the numbers in the letter are a running key—somehow telling us where to start within those recipes."

Gabriel smiled, impressed. "That's why we haven't been able to crack it! We're not dealing with a fixed code; this is a moving target!"

Amelia hurried back to the table and started flipping through the cookbook, her eyes scanning for only the ink-splattered recipes. She mentally counted each and stopped at the last one. "156," she said, confirming her count. "There are 156 recipes with this ink marker."

She picked up the love letter again and carefully parsed the rows, stopping on a line near the middle of one page. "156! Right here!" She turned the page to show Gabriel. "It's too much of a coincidence to *not* be true!" she said with confidence, pointing to the first number in the row:

156 32 19 15 20 13 24 4 18 20 11 3 5 4 18 19 18 8 8 12 4 4 13 15 15 16 22 22 7 23 18 6 25 5 7 19 2 17 2 20 21

Her excitement grew as the connection solidified. "156 is the key! It tells us which recipe to use for this row—*Bouillabaisse!*"

Gabriel leaned closer, intrigued but still cautious. "Okay, but this recipe looks pretty long. How do we know where to start the key? What part of the page do we use to begin deciphering?"

Amelia glanced down at the numbers again as she thought through the possibilities. Her eyes narrowed in focus, and her finger pointed to the second number in the sequence—32.

"Here," she said, her voice gaining momentum. "If the first number gives us the specific ink-splattered recipe, then maybe the second number, 32, tells us where to start within that recipe. Like, the sentence or the line that begins the key phrase."

Gabriel nodded in agreement. "So these first two numbers aren't encoded—they're plain text coordinates. Nice work!"

He leaned over the cookbook, with some concern on his face. "But is it the 32nd sentence? Or the 32nd line? How do we know?"

"Sentence," Amelia replied confidently, her eyes scanning the *Bouillabaisse* recipe. "There aren't 32 lines of text here, but there are well over 32 sentences."

She counted quickly, her finger moving down the recipe until it stopped at the 32nd sentence, nestled within the recipe's pairing suggestions. She exhaled through pursed lips as she read the words:

"Un Bordeaux blanc, généralement dominé par le Sauvignon Blanc, offre un excellent accord."

"A white Bordeaux, typically led by Sauvignon Blanc, provides an excellent match," Gabriel translated. "An excellent match indeed!" he said. "Looks like we've found the key phrase!"

Amelia smiled and nodded. "Yep! We've found the brush *and* the key," she said, filled with excitement. "Now we just have to decode the ledger!"

She took a deep breath and wrote the row of numbers in her notebook so Gabriel could see:

156 32 19 15 20 13 24 4 18 20 11 3 5 4 18 19 13 8 8 12 4 4 13 15 15 16 22 22 7 23 18 6 25 5 7 19 2 17 2 20 21

"So the first two numbers in the row are our plaintext coordinates," Gabriel confirmed. "156 corresponds to the recipe we need—*Bouillabaisse*…"

Amelia nodded. "And the key phrase for this row of numbers begins with the recipe's 32nd sentence, '*Un Bordeaux blanc…*'" she said, running her finger along its text, counting carefully, until stopping on the 39th letter—the exact number of digits remaining in the row after the two coordinates.

"…and ends with '*par le S*'," she confirmed, her voice steady.

She wrote the 39-letter key phrase in her notebook, directly beneath the row of numbers after the two coordinates, removing all spaces and punctuation, and pairing each letter with a single number in the row:

156th RECIPE, 32nd SENTENCE → KEY PHRASE: FIRST 39 CHARACTERS OF THE SENTENCE

156 32 | 19 15 20 13 24 4 18 20 11 3 5 4 18 19 13 8 8 12 4 4 13 15 15 16 22 22 7 23 18 6 25 5 7 19 2 17 2 20 21

U N B O R D E A U X B L A N C G E N E R A L E M E N T D O M I N E P A R L E S

She glanced at Gabriel with a faint smile. "Don't mind me if I think out loud for a bit. It helps me process complex ideas."

Gabriel nodded, curiosity showing in his eyes. "By all means, go ahead!"

Amelia took another deep breath, grounding herself for the work ahead. "We'll start with the number right after the first two coordinates—19. From there, we decode each number, one by one."

She continued, "Each number in the row corresponds to a letter: we'll say A = 1 and Z = 26. So, to decode, we subtract the numerical value of the key letter from this encoded number."

Gabriel held up a hand to stop her. "Wait, we should be using A = 0 and Z = 25 instead."

Amelia frowned slightly. "Why does that matter?"

"Well," Gabriel said, leaning forward. "If there's no shift, the letter should stay the same, right? If A = 1, then A could never remain A because it would always be shifted by 1. Using A = 0 keeps everything consistent—letters shift based on their position relative to 0."

Amelia nodded thoughtfully, understanding the logic. "Got it! That makes sense. So, A = 0, and Z = 25," she repeated. "And if the result is negative, we'll need to add 26 to loop it back into the alphabet range, like wrapping around a clock."

"Exactly," Gabriel said with a small smile. "It keeps the math clean."

"Okay," Amelia said, after quickly scribbling the alphanumeric conversion chart in her notebook. "Our first encoded number is 19, and it is matched with the key letter 'U'." She quickly glanced at the chart. "Which is the 20th letter when A = 0. So we need to subtract the key letter from the encoded cipher number: 19 minus 20 equals -1."

Amelia continued. "And, since we can't have a negative, we need to add 26 to -1, giving us 25. This corresponds to the letter 'Z' if A = 0. That's our first decoded letter!"

She jotted down 'Z' with a hopeful excitement and moved to the next pairing.

$$156 \quad 32 \mid 19 \ 15 \ 20 \ 13 \ 24 \ 4 \ 18 \ 20 \ 11 \ 3 \ 5 \ 4 \ 18 \ 19 \ 13 \ 8 \ 8 \ 12 \ 4 \ 4 \ 13 \ 15 \ 15 \ 16 \ 22$$
$$- \quad U \ N \ B \ O \ R \ D \ E \ A \ U \ X \ B \ L \ A \ N \ C \ G \ E \ N \ E \ R \ A \ L \ E \ M \ E$$
$$(A{=}0, \ Z{=}25) \quad 20$$

$$= \ -1$$
$$(if \ neg, \ +26) \quad 25$$
$$Z$$

"Next is the number 15 and the letter 'N', which is the 13th letter. So we take 15 minus 13 and that gives us 2, which is positive, so we don't need to add 26," Amelia said, her voice steady but eager. "And 2 corresponds to the letter 'C'."

Amelia wrote 'C' next to the 'Z' as both of them excitedly waited for a word to reveal itself.

"The next number is 20," Amelia said. "And subtracting 'B' from it gives us 'T'."

Following, she added another 'Z' to the encoded text for 13. Then 'H' for 24. Gabriel stood beside her watching the process unfold.

```
156 32 | 19 15 20 13 24  4 18 20 11  3  5  4 18 19 13  8  8 12  4  4 13 15 15 16 22
        -  U  N  B  O  R  D  E  A  U  X  B  L  A  N  C  G  E  N  E  R  A  L  E  M  E
(A=0, Z=25)  20 13  1 14 17
       ___________________________________________________________________________

        = -1  2 19 -1  ?
(if neg, +26)  25        25
             Z  C  T  Z  H
```

"Z…C…T…Z…H," Amelia muttered as she stared down at the first five letters, her confusion quickly moving to frustration. "What does that even mean?"

She let out a sigh and rubbed her temple with one hand. "Maybe we missed something? Or maybe there's another layer?"

Gabriel's jaw tightened, but he encouraged her to continue. "Let's keep going. We might start to see a pattern in the rest."

Amelia nodded and moved to the next number. "4 paired with 'D'… 4 minus 3 is 1, which is 'B.'"

She continued methodically, her voice gaining momentum.

"18 minus 'E' equals 'O'."

"Then 'U' for 20… and 'R' for 11."

Amelia paused, and they both stared at the letters now laid out before them.

"B…O…U…R?" Gabriel spoke, his eyebrows lifting slightly. "It looks like—"

"Bourget!" Amelia finished, filled with excitement. "It has to be!"

The next number—3.

"3 minus 'X' is 'G.'"

Amelia's hands trembled as Gabriel gripped the edge of the table. "Keep going, Amelia!"

She exhaled sharply as the next two decoded numbers fell into place.

```
156 32 | 19 15 20 13 24 4 18 20 11 3 5 4 18 19 13 8 8 12 4 4 13 15 15 16 22
       -  U  N  B  O  R  D  E  A  U  X  B  L  A  N  C  G  E  N  E  R  A  L  E  M  E
(A=0, Z=25)  20 13 1 14 17 3 4 0 20 23 1 11
______________________________________________________________________

       =  -1  2 19 -1  7  1 14 20 -9 -20 4 -7
(if neg, +26)  25        25              17 6    19
          Z  C  T  Z  H  B  O  U  R  G  E  T
```

"BOURGET!"

They both stared down at the letters in silent disbelief. For a moment, neither of them could move. Their discovery was so monumental, it felt almost unreal.

Amelia was the first to break the silence. "We've done it, Gabriel!" Her voice was shaking with equal parts joy and disbelief. "We've cracked code!"

Gabriel let out a shaky breath, and a huge grin spread across his face. "This is it, Amelia! The ledger—*it's real!*"

———

Excitement surged through them as they continued decoding the first line of numbers, both on the edge of their seats. "Bourget" had been hidden for decades within the ledger's code. But there was more. Methodically, they pressed forward, eager to reveal the secrets still concealed in the ledger.

"SGL…" Amelia muttered as the next letters unfolded, but no immediate connection formed. She glanced at Gabriel, who shook his head. It didn't make sense yet, but they continued.

And then another name began to surface in the row.

```
156 32 │ 19 15 20 13 24 4 18 20 11 3 5 4 18 19 13 8 8 12 4 4 13 15 15 16 22
       -   U  N  B  O  R  D  E  A  U  X  B  L  A  N  C  G  E  N  E  R  A  L  E  M  E
(A=0, Z=25)  20 13 1 14 17 3 4 0 20 23 1 11 0 13 2 6 4 13 4 17
       ────────────────────────────────────────────────────────────────────
       =  -1  2 19 -1 7 1 14 20 -9 -20 4 -7 18 6 11 2 4 -1 0 -13
(if neg, +26) 25      25            17 6  19              25   13
              Z  C  T  Z  H  B  O  U  R  G  E  T  S  G  L  C  E  Z  A  N
```

Gabriel leaned closer to the page, his voice tightening with anticipation. "Cézanne?" he repeated, barely able to contain his excitement.

Amelia's pulse quickened again. "It has to be!" she said. Her fingers moving faster now, writing the remaining letters as they formed. The code was no longer a string of abstract symbols—it was unraveling into something tangible, something extraordinary.

```
156 32 │ 19 15 20 13 24 4 18 20 11 3 5 4 18 19 13 8 8 12 4 4 13 15 15 16 22 22 7 23 18 6 25 5 7 19 2 17 2 20 21
       -   U N B O R D E A U X B L A N C G E N E R A L E M E N T D O M I N E P A R L E S
           20 13 1 14 17 3 4 0 20 23 1 11 0 13 2 6 4 13 4 17 0 11 4 12 4 13 19 3 14 12 8 13
       ────────────────────────────────────────────────────────────────────
       =  -1 2 19 -1 7 1 14 20 -9 -20 4 -7 18 6 11 2 4 -1 0 -13 13 4 11 14 18 7 -12 20 4 -6 17 -8
          25    25          17 6 19          25 13                    14       20 18
          Z C T Z H B O U R G E T S G L C E Z A N N E L E S J O U E U R S
```

As *"LESJOUEURS"* slowly appeared next to *"CEZANNE,"* Amelia felt a thrill course through her, its significance taking form in her mind even before it was fully decoded. *"Les Joueurs de Cartes!"* she exclaimed with awe.

Gabriel's eyes widened as he shoved his chair back and shot to his feet. "The Card Players!" he exclaimed, his voice tinged with disbelief. "It's one of Cézanne's most legendary masterpieces!"

Amelia nodded enthusiastically, barely able to contain her excitement as she focused to finish unmasking the remaining numbers in the row.

```
156 32 | 19 15 20 13 24 4 18 20 11 3 5 4 18 19 13 8 8 12 4 4 13 15 15 16 22 22 7 23 18 6 25 5 7 19 2 17 2 20 21
    -    U  N  B  O  R  D  E  A  U  X  B  L  A  N  C  G  E  N  E  R  A  L  E  M  E  N  T  D  O  M  I  N  E  P  A  R  L  E  S
    20 13 1 14 17 3 4 0 20 23 1 11 0 13 2 6 4 13 4 17 0 11 4 12 4 13 19 3 14 12 8 13 4 15 0 17 11 4 18
    ──────────────────────────────────────────────────────────────────────────────
    = -1 2 19 -1 7 1 14 20 -9 -20 4 -7 18 6 11 2 4 -1 0 -13 13 4 11 14 18 9 -12 20 4 -6 17 -8 3 4 2 0 -9 16 3
       25       25            17 6 19              25  13                  14     20 18            17
       Z  C  T  Z  H | B  O  U  R  G  E  T | S  G  L | C  E  Z  A  N  N  E | L  E  S  J  O  U  E  U  R  S  D  E  C  A  R | N  D
```

"We've just decoded a ledger entry, Gabriel!" she said, her voice filled with emotion. "The Bourget family hid one of the paintings from *Les Joueurs de Cartes* by Cézanne!"

She sat back in her chair, staring at the decoded message, mouth agape, the weight of their discovery pressing down on her like a physical force.

```
Z  C  T  Z  H | B  O  U  R  G  E  T | S  G  L | C  E  Z  A  N  N  E | L  E  S  J  O  U  E  U  R  S  D  E  C  A  R | N  D
```

Paul Cézanne's *The Card Players* was a monumental series of five paintings, five masterpieces that had profoundly influenced countless artists and movements.

Her mind raced, recalling everything she knew about the paintings. *Les Joueurs de Cartes* was not just a simple depiction of peasants playing cards—it was an iconic series of paintings, representing Cézanne's mastery of composition and form, his ability to elevate the mundane into the profound.

The figures, their stillness, their focus—Cézanne had perfectly captured a human still life, and now, here one of them was—one that had gone missing—hidden within the Alliance's ledger, waiting to be uncovered after all these years.

Amelia's voice was soft, almost reverent, as her eyes stayed locked on the decoded text. "This series, Gabriel... it contains some of the most important works of Cézanne's entire career. Maybe even the entire Post-Impressionist Movement. *Les Joueurs de Cartes*. These paintings shaped the course of modern art!"

Gabriel leaned forward, his phone in hand as he quickly searched for details to confirm what they'd uncovered. His eyes widened as he read aloud, "One version of *The Card Players* sold at auction for over $250 million." He looked up at Amelia. His voice was a mixture of awe and disbelief. "We've just possibly uncovered a missing Cézanne!"

Amelia nodded, her hands shaking as she let the enormity of their discovery sink in. The possibilities hidden in the ledger were now more than they had ever imagined—it was more than just a record of transactions or a simple list of hidden art. It was a window into history, a carefully preserved catalogue of treasures that had been kept hidden for decades.

"The Bourget family…," Amelia said, "they were safeguarding this painting. They must have known the significance of it."

Her mind spiraled with questions. What else could be hidden in the ledger? What other masterpieces lay coded in these pages, waiting to be uncovered? She felt the significance of history closing in on them, the enormity of their discovery growing with every breath.

They had found the ledger. They had cracked its code. But now, as the decoded letters stared back at them, Amelia realized they were still nowhere near solving this.

Chapter 58

Amelia's eyes lingered on the decoded number string before them, her heart still racing from their breakthrough:

ZCTXH BOURGET SGL CEZANNE LES JOUEURS DE CARTES ND

Bourget. Cézanne. Les Joueurs de Cartes. It was all there.

But not *everything* made sense.

Gabriel leaned back in his chair, letting out a long, measured breath. "We've kind of cracked the code," he said, rubbing the back of his neck. "But what do those mean?" He pointed at the first five letters. "'ZCTZH'… and what about 'SGL'? And the 'ND' at the end?"

Amelia leaned in as she considered the letters. In the enthusiasm of their triumph, she had willfully ignored them. But now, these remaining fragments demanded attention. Her eyes focused on the "ND" at the end of the decoded message. It seemed out of place at first, but then something clicked.

She straightened her back with the idea. "Wait a second," she murmured, hurrying to her bookshelf. Pulling out a book on Impressionism, she flipped through the pages until she found what she was looking for. Returning to the table, she placed the open book in front of them. "Cézanne completed this painting series in 1892!" she said, pointing to the date in the book. "Eighteen *ninety-two*… nine, two… *neuf, deux*, in French… 'N, D'." She paused, letting the revelation sink in. "'ND' could refer to the year the painting was created?"

Gabriel's eyes widened. "The painting's year! Of course!"

Amelia nodded, running the idea through her head. "It makes sense, right? The ledger would want to record the date when each artwork was created or cataloged. So 'ND' *must* refer to 1892. It checks out!"

She quickly turned her attention to the next string of letters: "ZCTZH"—running her finger over the unfamiliar sequence. The pattern wasn't immediately clear. But with the breakthrough on "ND," her mind went right back to the theory.

"If 'ND' is a shorthand for the year the painting was created, what if 'ZCTZH' represents digits also? Maybe *zero cinq trois zero huit*," she said, slowly sounding out the numbers in French. "Zero five three zero eight—could be a catalogue reference number, maybe?"

Gabriel leaned back, considering it. "A catalogue number for the painting?"

Amelia nodded, the new theory taking root. "Yeah! It could be the specific identifier for this painting within the ledger—or the physical piece itself!"

Gabriel's eyes widened with affirmation. "That makes sense! Good thought!"

The puzzle was coming together, with each decoded piece feeling like a revelation. But there was one more fragment left to figure out.

Amelia bit her lip. "So, what about 'SGL'?" She repeated the letters under her breath, trying to decipher their meaning. "It doesn't seem like a code for numbers. Maybe it's… a location?"

Gabriel leaned over the table and narrowed his eyes at the letters, slowly reciting a thought. "Saint-Germain… de Laye?" he suggested, his voice uncertain but hopeful.

Amelia's eyes widened as realization dawned. "Yes! Saint-Germain de Laye!" she exclaimed. "The Bourget family *lived* in the French arrondissement of Saint-Germain de Laye. That is where Château Bourget is! 'SGL'—it has to be!"

She glanced at Gabriel, and their eyes met in a moment of shared excitement. They had just fully deciphered their first row of the ledger—but with the inclusion of locations, it was clear they had stumbled upon something far bigger than they had initially realized.

"If 'SGL' stands for Saint-Germain de Laye," Amelia continued, "then they weren't just recording paintings—they were recording where families lived. And if this ledger includes *addresses*…"

Her thoughts raced, but her words came slower and more deliberate. "This isn't just about a single family's hidden treasures," she said, staring down at the coded letters.

Gabriel leaned forward, the realization dawning. "The Alliance wasn't just protecting *their* art," he murmured. "They were protecting *everyone's* art!"

Silence settled between them as they took in the magnitude of their discovery.

Gabriel finally spoke. "This list, Amelia—it's a map! An entire network of hidden art—across families, across France… maybe even across Europe!"

Amelia's gaze locked with his, her pulse racing. "Then let's find out where it leads!"

Chapter 59

Château Bourget, March 1941

Two years before the ledger would be hidden in a cookbook...

An early spring coldness settled over Paris like a shadow, its icy grip creeping into every corner of the city. But the Alliance could not afford to pause. In the infancy of their mission, each meeting carried a tension and urgency as Arnaud, Nadejda, Lucien, and Étienne plotted in secret to protect the cultural treasures slipping ever closer to Nazi hands. The stakes were rising, and with each passing day, the need to find a secure hiding place for the art they would soon protect became urgent.

They gathered around a table in Arnaud's study at Château Bourget, a map of Europe spread out before them. Pins and handwritten notes covered its surface, marking potential sites where the art could be hidden—remote places, carefully chosen to evade detection. Arnaud traced his finger along the map, pausing at distant, inconspicuous locations far from occupied France. As his finger hovered over a region in northern Yugoslavia, just south of Austria, his expression shifted, his mind already picturing a secluded spot that could serve their purpose.

"We're seeking places not just hard to reach," he said, "but also places where the pieces will remain undisturbed." He glanced at Nadejda, a shared understanding passing between them. These artworks needed protection beyond the immediate danger—they needed a sanctuary that could resist the elements, the wear of time, and, if necessary, the destruction of war.

Nadejda nodded, leaning forward, her eyes on the map. "I can think of many places," she murmured. "Old spaces, natural spaces... places untouched by modern development. They could be difficult to access, but they offer a kind of safety no building can match." Her voice held a determination, one to find something impenetrable, something even the most vigilant eyes might overlook.

Lucien adjusted his spectacles, the faint creases around his eyes deepening as he studied the map with care. "The conditions matter," he added, tapping a location they were considering. "We need environments that can preserve." He pointed to a few other pins on the map. "Think of the issues we'd find in some of these places—the wrong environment could be as dangerous as the Nazis themselves."

Étienne nodded, voice calm but resolute. "Seclusion is vital. A place no casual wanderer would stumble upon. These pieces must sleep in silence."

They continued, each member offering insights based on their unique skills and experience. Lucien spoke of atmospheres best suited for preserving oil paintings, suggesting certain geological characteristics that would naturally protect. Nadejda, meanwhile, referenced locations she had learned about through Sergei—remote places he had once considered for his own collection, places that alluded to resilience.

Gradually, their criteria sharpened. The site would need to meet exacting standards. Security, accessibility, and preservation. All had to align. No exceptions.

As they reviewed the possibilities, a single hiding place emerged as the best choice. It would not be easy to reach, but that difficulty would also work towards their benefit.

Arnaud leaned back, meeting each gaze in turn. "Only the four of us will know of this location. Nobody else—the couriers, the transporters, even those who help along the way. It's the only way we can ensure safety. Nadejda and I will handle the last legs ourselves."

Nadejda met his eyes, her voice steady as she addressed the group. "And if we must hide some pieces and never return, we'll do so knowing the art is safe. We're not guarding it for ourselves—we're preserving it for a future we may never see."

The room fell silent with the heaviness of her comment. They all realized this was no small task they'd taken on, no modest ambition. But it was necessary. They were weaving a web of secrecy so intricate that even they might become lost within. And in that moment, they understood, perhaps more clearly than ever before, this path would demand not only resilience but sacrifice.

Chapter 60

Row after row of decoded numbers slowly revealed a catalog of master-pieces—Cézanne, Renoir, Miró—each name a revelation, each detail a bridge to a lost world.

Though Amelia and Gabriel had been awake for nearly 24 hours, the room felt alive with excitement and curiosity as pencil scratches and the occasional rustle of paper punctuated the stillness.

But beyond its famous names, the ledger held even deeper secrets.

Near the end of the entries, while Gabriel researched the provenance of a previously unknown Delacroix painting, Amelia froze mid-line. Her pencil halted and she quietly gasped as a name appeared—one she never expected to see again: Henri Vallin.

The memory of her graduate school restoration project surfaced with startling clarity—the enigmatic woman in the emerald dress, *The Portrait of Eloise*. It was Vallin's only known work, shrouded in mystery. Until now, no one alive had heard of him or seen any other paintings attributed to his name. And now there were more.

Four more.

Her pencil hovered over one of the rows mentioning him. *Who was this artist?*, she wondered, blinking in disbelief. His name appeared next to four additional titles: *Lady by the Window*, *The Violinist's Muse*, *Garden by the Vineyard*, and *Twilight at Montmartre*. Each name conjured images so vivid she felt she could see the scenes unfolding beneath her fingertips. She couldn't hold back any longer.

"Gabriel!" she exclaimed, her voice filled with excitement. He jumped up from his chair, startled by her sudden outburst, and looked at her with concern. "There are more Vallins! Four more paintings! The portrait in the Jewish Museum isn't the only one!"

He stared at her, eyes narrowing with curiosity but still not fully understanding. "Is that good?"

Amelia's breathing increased as she tried to convey the significance. "Is that good? You don't understand! Vallin was practically a ghost! When I restored the portrait of Eloise in grad school, it was the *only* piece of his anyone had ever seen. And now, there are four more listed here!"

Gabriel's expression shifted as comprehension dawned. He leaned forward, eyes widening as he absorbed the magnitude of what she was saying. "So these could help discover who the artist is?"

"Yes!" Amelia said, her excitement palpable. The ledger was no longer just an archive—it was a guide to new discoveries, and they were on the brink of uncovering another story hidden by time.

Her eyes returned to the pages spread before her and the inked numbers that had become their obsession.

She was nearly done. 476 entries decoded, and only 10 more remained. In total, that meant the Alliance had hidden 486 paintings, carefully shielding their existence from the world. Amelia had heard stories of resistance groups saving one or two pieces before, but never anything remotely on this scale. Yet, despite the magnitude of this discovery, a lingering question gnawed at both of them.

"Where are they hidden?" Amelia whispered to herself, staring down at the list. *We've found everything except the one thing we need the most,* she thought.

As she began decoding the 477th row, Gabriel now by her side, Amelia's attention snagged on a detail that kept surfacing. Her eyes narrowed as the word revealed itself again. This and several other ledger entries all referenced "Trubetskoy"—a word that felt deliberate, yet its significance eluded them.

"Trubetskoy..." Gabriel muttered, glancing up from the notebook, his finger pointing to the name. "Why does this keep coming up?"

Amelia leaned in, her mind trying to piece together the clue. "It's strange," she said. "It's not a family name or a painting. And it doesn't seem to link with the other entries." She pointed to the ledger, "Most of these are from Western Europe—France, Spain, Amsterdam... But this... I don't think it is."

Gabriel tapped his pen against the table, thinking it through. "There has to be a reason. What connection could it have to all of this?"

Amelia's mind raced. "I'm not sure…" Her voice trailed off in thought. "Trubetskoy… I've heard that before," she said slowly. Torn between pursuing the memory and continuing decoding, she hesitated. Then it clicked. Her eyes widened. "Trubetskoy Palace! It's in Moscow! I think it was a nationalized mansion? Or something like that?" The memory was hazy.

"Moscow?" Gabriel echoed, surprise flashing across his face. "What would Russia have to do with this?"

Amelia shook her head, her mind churning. "I don't know yet, but it's a thread we haven't fully unraveled." She stared at the entry again, knowing this was something they'd have to revisit. For now, they had more immediate concerns with the 9 remaining entries. They also still hadn't found the one thing they needed the most: a location.

———

As they finished decoding the last page, Amelia noticed something unusual at the bottom. She had always assumed it was a line wrap from the final ledger entry, but that row was fully decoded and these numbers remained. Unlike all previous entries, which had roughly 40-50 numbers each, this row only had 16.

She squinted, her curiosity sparked by the odd break in the pattern. "Gabriel, look at this," she said softly, pointing to the peculiar sequence.

16 2 16 4 19 25 25 20 20 16 20 3 20 20 25 3

Gabriel, still dazed with the fatigue of their long night, leaned in closer. His exhaustion momentarily lifted as his eyes scanned the numbers. "This doesn't look like the other row," he said, rubbing his eyes to focus. "It's too short… it can't be a ledger entry, right? There's no space for the usual details."

Amelia stared at the page, the numbers blurring together before her as she tried to make sense of them. "It breaks the pattern," she muttered, while uncertainty started creeping in. "Why here? Why at the end of the ledger?"

Her thoughts spun as she stared harder at the sequence. If it was different from the others, then there had to be a reason. The ledger had been precise, meticulous—nothing so far had been left to chance. Her gut told her this deviation wasn't a mistake, but an intentional decision. Yet the reason eluded her.

"It might be a continuation of the cipher?" Gabriel suggested, reaching for the cookbook. "Let's try using the first two numbers of the line to find a recipe and sentence, like before."

Amelia nodded. To rule out the obvious, she flipped to the 16th ink-marked recipe in the cookbook—*Beurre Noir*. She found the second sentence and applied it to the numbers, hoping for a breakthrough. But the result was incomprehensible gibberish, a jumbled mess of letters that offered no clue. It didn't fit.

"No… nothing," Amelia said, her frustration mounting. "The sentence doesn't produce a meaningful key for this set of numbers."

Gabriel frowned, staring at the numbers as if willing them to reveal their secret. "So it's not a ledger entry, and it's not using the same cipher."

Silence fell between them as the tension built. Amelia sifted through possibilities, each one tumbling away before she could grasp it. The number sequence was a puzzle—one final riddle, taunting them at the very end of their search. "There has to be something we're not seeing." *What would you do, dad?* she thought.

Amelia paused before sitting back in her chair. "Let's try a simpler approach," she said after a moment, her tone steady despite her frustration. "What if we assign each number to its corresponding letter? Maybe it's trying to spell something."

She quickly scribbled out the letters that matched the numbers when A = 0:

16 = Q, 2 = C, 16 = Q, 4 = E, 19 = T, 25 = Z, 25 = Z, 20 = U,
20 = U, 16 = Q, 20 = U, 3 = D, 20 = U, 20 = U, 25 = Z, 3 = D

Q C Q E T Z Z U U Q U D U U Z D

They stared at the sequence of letters, tilting their heads.

"Doesn't seem to spell anything," Amelia said, tapping her fingers on the edge of the table. "Could be an anagram?"

She and Gabriel spent several minutes trying to rearrange the letters, but nothing meaningful emerged. The sequence remained stubbornly cryptic.

Then Gabriel sat up a little straighter, his eyes narrowing. "Wait," he said slowly, "this reminds me of something… remember how the decoded numbers in the ledger entries for the catalogue and painting dates didn't spell words? They corresponded to the first letters of the French numbers they represented!"

Amelia's eyes widened. "Yeah! 'Z' was *'zero,'* 'U' was *'un,'* 'D' was *'deux'*…"

Her voice trailed off as the realization took hold. "You're right!" she said. "This *isn't* an anagram! The letters represent numbers! It's the same pattern as before! Nice work, you!"

They quickly decoded the sequence, using 'I' for six *(six)* and 'E' for seven *(sept)* since both start with 's,' just as they had with the ledger entries:

Q = 4, C = 5, Q = 4, E = 7, T = 3, Z = 0, Z = 0, U = 1
U = 1, Q = 4, U = 1, D = 2, U = 1, U = 1, Z = 0, D = 2

4 5 4 7 3 0 0 1 1 4 1 2 1 1 0 2

4547300114121102.
They exchanged a look, their eagerness mounting.

"This feels deliberate," Gabriel said, his voice filled with anticipation as he looked at the numbers again. "But what do they mean?"

There was a long pause until Gabriel's eyes suddenly widened. "Wait... 45..." he said softly. "Could this be a coordinate?"

Amelia's gaze snapped to the page. "A coordinate?"

"Look at it," Gabriel said, still processing the idea. "It looks like the start of a geographic coordinate—45 degrees, 47 minutes..."

His voice quickened as the realization seemed more obvious. "These numbers could represent latitude and longitude!"

Amelia leaned closer, scanning the numbers again, and spoke to confirm, "45 degrees, 47 minutes... and 30.01 seconds?"

"Yes!" Gabriel said, his eyes shining with excitement as he continued. "And 14 degrees, 12 minutes, 11.02 seconds!" He quickly grouped the numbers into two sets of coordinates:

$$45° \ 47' \ 30.01"$$
$$14° \ 12' \ 11.02"$$

He looked up at Amelia, his heart pounding. "These are coordinates, Amelia! We've just found coordinates! A location!"

"Latitude and longitude!" Amelia said, trembling with anticipation. "We need to input this into a map."

Gabriel nodded, his fingers flying over the keyboard as he brought up a map on the computer. "Alright!" he said enthusiastically. "Let's try North and South for latitude, and East and West for longitude. We'll have four possible combinations."

They both leaned in as Gabriel typed in the first combination with South for the latitude coordinate and West for longitude coordinate.

"Nothing," he said. "The coordinates point to the middle of the ocean."

He tried South and East next.

Still nothing—another location lost at sea.

"Try North and West!" Amelia urged frantically.

Gabriel entered the next set of coordinates. But once again, the map zoomed in on a vast expanse of ocean.

Amelia's foot fidgeted restlessly. "It has to be North and East," she said carefully, edged with doubt. "Please, let it be North and East."

Gabriel's fingers rested over the keys, hesitating for the briefest moment before entering the final set of coordinates—North for latitude, East for longitude. Each keystroke felt like a final step into the unknown. This had to work.

They both leaned in, eyes locked on the screen as the map zoomed in, pixel by pixel, the familiar blue of the ocean shrinking away.

Amelia held her breath. The silence in the room thickened, and the only sound around them was the faint hum of the computer. Her nerves continued with every millisecond that passed and the tension stretched until it felt unbearable.

And then the screen revealed something.

Land.

For many seconds, neither of them moved. Amelia's breaths were deep, trying to calm her rapid pulse. She leaned closer, her wide eyes scanning the screen again as if trying to convince herself it was real.

Gabriel's hand stayed over the keyboard, his own heart thudding in his chest. "Is this…?" he murmured, his voice rough with disbelief.

Amelia swallowed hard, a mix of awe and relief settling over her. "It is," she said, barely audible.

"We've found it. We found the location of the hidden art."

Chapter 61

It was early summer in Paris, and though the air was warmer, the city's mood had not brightened. The Alliance gathered again in Arnaud's study, well aware that the threats were evolving. For months, they had focused on saving France's artistic treasures, smuggling them from occupied cities, and hiding them safely. Yet, as the team sat around the table, Nadejda's mind shifted beyond the borders of France.

"We've been working to ensure France's art is safe," Nadejda began, looking from Arnaud to Lucien and Étienne, "but the Nazis don't stop at our borders. They're targeting every country they occupy—Belgium, the Netherlands, Spain. They've already made their way into collections across Eastern Europe."

Arnaud leaned forward, studying her. "Are you suggesting we should extend our scope?"

Nadejda nodded. "Yes. *And* beyond just Europe—there's also the Soviet threat. In the regime's effort to 'reclaim cultural works,' they've been absorbing private collections for years. Sergei's was seized by the state, dismantled and scattered." She stared off into the distance with an angry scowl before continuing. "It's not just about preserving French art anymore; it's about protecting our shared culture, our collective human legacy. These pieces aren't just *ours* to defend—they belong to the future, to everyone."

Lucien studied her with care, his eyes narrowing as he considered what she was proposing. "Reaching into Soviet territory would be dangerous. I'm assuming you have connections, Nadejda, and experience in that world that none of us can claim. But the risks are high, and that network is beyond our control."

Nadejda's voice remained steady. "That's why I would be the only one making contact. Sergei's family still holds some influence there; I know people who could quietly connect us with families looking to safe-guard their pieces. They're facing the same threats we are, and they're just as afraid of losing the things they cherish to political whims."

Étienne nodded slowly. "If you're serious about taking on this role alone, Nady, the rest of us can keep our focus here in Western Europe and expand to some other countries. We'll handle the transport and cover on our side."

Arnaud frowned slightly, still thinking about her request. "But how will you manage secure pickup routes inside Russia?" he asked. "Tracking individual locations there would be an entirely new risk. The region's oversight is intense… Europe is challenging enough."

Nadejda's expression softened as she explained her idea. "Instead of retrieving from each family's location, the families will bring their art to us. It would be simpler and safer for all Soviet pieces to be brought to one central location. From there, we'll coordinate a single, secure passage into Europe."

Étienne nodded, considering her plan. "That's good. It makes sense —using one central location simplifies logistics and keeps the families protected. We avoid the risks of a scattered trail," he said, thinking aloud. "And though I no longer hold an official title, I still have contacts. I can reach out discreetly to diplomats who would support this cause without drawing attention. If I can arrange it, we could transport a full truck of art from the single location under diplomatic immunity—no inspections, no restrictions!" He allowed himself a brief, satisfied smile. "That's actu-ally more freedom than we have here in France!"

Arnaud, who had listened silently, finally spoke in confirmation. "So we expand to other countries in Europe and modify our approach for So-viet art." He looked up at the group, pausing for rebuttal, and then to Nadejda with a trace of admiration in his eyes. "It's bold… But I like it!"

Chapter 62

Paris, Modern Day

The glow of the map filled the room, its stark coordinates pulsing softly on the screen.

45° 47' 30.01" N
14° 12' 11.02" E

"Postojna Cave," Amelia said softly, finally breaking the silence. Her tone hovered between disbelief and confirmation.

Gabriel glanced at her, still leaning over the keyboard. "In Slovenia?" he asked cautiously. "You've heard of it?"

Amelia nodded slowly, her thoughts racing. "It's more than just a cave. It's a network of caverns, one of the largest in Europe." Her voice contained a mix of excitement and apprehension. "But why there? Why does a cave in Slovenia connect with the Bourget-Vallois Alliance?"

For a moment, neither of them spoke. The coordinates, once cryptic numbers on a page, now possibly linked the hidden paintings to a place buried deep within the earth. Despite the unknown, Amelia could feel the pull of history calling them forward.

Her mind spun, trying to piece together the reason why this cave, of all places, would hide the ledger's 486 missing masterpieces. She quickly stood and moved to her bookshelf, fingers dashing over the spines of old volumes, searching for something she had read long ago. It didn't take her long to find it—a book on the history of art theft during World War II.

"Here," she murmured, flipping through the pages. "Postojna Cave was used during World War II." Her finger stopped on a passage she'd once skimmed but now read with new intensity. "It was a storage site…

by the Nazis. They used it to hide supplies, weapons—anything they wanted to keep safe from Allied bombings."

Gabriel straightened in his chair, his brow lifting. "But art?" he asked, curiosity evident in his voice. "Did they store art there too?"

Amelia looked up from the page. "It's not confirmed. But there are rumors—rumors that art looted by the Reich was hidden in these caves. Paintings, sculptures, and other treasures that were never recovered after the war." She paused, a hint of irony in her smile. "It's possible the Alliance hid their paintings there as well—right under the Nazis' noses."

Gabriel's eyes widened as the significance hit him. "Hiding art in the same place the Nazis were using... the best way to protect something... hidden in plain sight!"

Amelia nodded with a mischievous grin on her face. "Yep! What better place to hide something you didn't want found? If the Nazis were using Postojna Cave to store their stolen loot, no one would have thought to look for anything else there. The chaos of the war provided the perfect cover."

She sat back down, her fingers moving over the text in the book. Postojna Cave was more than just a hiding place; it was a labyrinth of caverns twisting deep underground. Stories of missing art were nothing new, but many historians had dismissed them as speculation. Yet now, with the coordinates pointing directly to this very location, the possibility felt real.

Gabriel leaned forward, rubbing his chin thoughtfully. "If that's true," he murmured, "then Postojna Cave could hold the Alliance's entire collection... hidden alongside history's greatest theft!"

A silence fell between them as the significance of their discovery became clear. They had the coordinates. They had the history. Everything pointed to this hidden labyrinth in Slovenia. It was a secret that had been concealed for decades, buried beneath layers of war, time, and legend. And now it was theirs to uncover.

But as the thrill of the moment settled over them, another realization took root—neither of them knew the first thing about spelunking.

Amelia leaned back in her chair and grappled with the next step. "So... we're not exactly equipped for this, Gabriel," she said with a small, nervous laugh. "Exploring a massive cave system like Postojna... it's dangerous. We don't even know where to start. What if we get lost down there?"

Gabriel nodded with concern crossing his face. "Yeah… I was just thinking that. We can't just walk in there with flashlights and a map. We need proper equipment, training, and guidance. And… I don't know about you, but I've never been inside a cave like that before."

Amelia bit her lip, thinking through the logistics. They couldn't abandon this lead now—not when they were so close. But the dangers were real, and the thought of venturing into a cave with no experience felt reckless.

"I don't want to bring more people into this, but I hate to admit it— we'll need help," she said finally, determined. "We can't do this alone."

Gabriel nodded with relief crossing his face. "Agreed. Exploring an unknown cave is way beyond my expertise. But where do we even find someone for that? A cave that's been used for military storage, possibly booby-trapped or unstable… we'll need professionals."

Amelia considered the options, her thoughts churning. "There must be caving experts—local guides in Slovenia who know the terrain. If this cave has historical significance, I bet there are researchers, geologists, even adventurers who've explored it."

Gabriel's eyes widened. "You're right. We could reach out to them, hire a guide. We'll need proper equipment too—climbing gear, head-lamps, GPS trackers… everything to make sure we're prepared."

Amelia nodded, but her expression turned thoughtful. "We'll have to keep why we're there under wraps… at least for as long as possible." Her voice trailed off, a new consideration forming.

She looked back at the screen. "Wait," she said, her tone shifting. "The coordinates—they're not at the main entrance of the cave. Look."

Gabriel leaned closer, following her line of thought. "You're right… it's not in the main complex. It looks like it could lead to a side passage, maybe an offshoot?"

Amelia's pulse quickened. "Exactly. This isn't a general search—we don't need to explore the *entire* network. These coordinates are precise… maybe an 'X marks the spot' kind of thing? It's not as if the Alliance would've strolled into the main entrance of Postojna Cave with 486 pieces of art. They would've chosen a specific location. We should check this spot first."

Gabriel eagerly nodded at the thought. "That could save us from having to hire an entire caving team."

Amelia smiled, excitement sparking in her. "Yes, we start with the coordinates. If it takes us deeper or if we need more equipment, we re-group—hire a guide, if necessary. But for now, we follow the lead right to where it's pointing. We're not walking in blind."

Gabriel exhaled, his tension easing as the plan solidified. "That makes so much more sense. We've got a target. We'll be smart about it, but this gives us a starting point." He grinned, a new energy lighting his face. "We can do this, Amelia!"

Amelia met his gaze, her heart pounding with anticipation. "We're *going* to do this. Let's start arranging transportation to Slovenia. This is happening now."

Chapter 63

The low drone of the airplane engines filled the cabin as Amelia and Gabriel sat side by side, their laptop screens illuminating their faces in the dim light. The plane cut steadily through the sky as they made their way to Slovenia. It had been a whirlwind few days, and now, on this flight, they finally had a moment to process everything—to dig deeper into the work of the Alliance.

Gabriel leaned back in his seat, stretching his arms as he let out a pursed breath. "We've got everything ready for when we land. Local contacts, equipment… all that's left is to check the site," he said, his voice steady but edged with anticipation.

Amelia barely nodded, her focus locked on the screen in front of her. The ledger had been their obsession for weeks, each decoded line unraveling another layer of mystery. But one particular detail lingered persistently in her mind. She glanced at Gabriel. "Before we get to Postojna," she began thoughtfully, "there's something we set aside. We didn't have time to focus on it earlier, but it kept resurfacing in the ledger."

Gabriel looked at her curiously. "Trubetskoy?"

"Yeah," Amelia said, her fingers hovering over the keyboard as she pulled up the relevant digitized ledger entries. "It's referenced multiple times here, but we haven't figured out why. The name isn't linked to a specific family—it's just… there. Again and again. Like breadcrumbs."

Gabriel leaned closer to her screen. "Right… We tabled it. So, why *would* Trubetskoy or *any* references to Moscow keep appearing? It doesn't fit with the French, Spanish, and Dutch entries we've been working through—specifically those that have a family name attached to the painting. These entries have no names associated with them."

Amelia squinted her eyes as she scanned the lines again, her thoughts racing as she tried to recall what she knew of Trubetskoy Palace.

Then, after a quick search, the connection snapped into place.

"Trubetskoy Palace…," she said softly, her tone steady with certainty, as though recalling something she had long known. She glanced at Gabriel. "That's where Sergei Shchukin lived."

Gabriel's eyes widened. "Sergei Shchukin?"

Amelia nodded, her pulse quickening. "Yes. He was a Russian art collector with a huge affinity for western culture—one of the most famous art collectors of his time. His collection was massive—Monet, Cézanne, Matisse, Degas. He practically built the foundation of Impressionism with what he curated."

Gabriel's mind paced to catch up. "Okay. But how does that connect to the Alliance?"

Amelia's fingers flew over the keys, pulling up more historical documents she had scanned from the Archives, her mind whirling with possibilities. "Nadejda Shchukin," she said slowly, piecing the name together with care. "She was Sergei's wife." She paused for a minute, deep in thought. "But what if there's more to her than just being his spouse?"

Gabriel leaned in, his curiosity piqued. "What do you mean?"

Amelia paused, chewing on her pen as she scanned the notes she had been compiling—genealogical charts, historical records, small clues they had collected along the way. "It's the name, Nadejda. It's the Russian form of Nadia, right?" she asked rhetorically. "And Nadia… that name has come up before, hasn't it?" She scrolled through her notes, searching for something that was nagging at her memory.

Gabriel anxiously watched as she flipped between documents, searching for what had sparked the thought. Then she immediately paused, her gaze looking forward into a blank stare. The leap felt tenuous, almost improbable. "Could it really be?" she muttered, doubt creeping in as the possibility teased at her mind.

She found the Vallois family tree she had been curating, a web connecting key players through history. Amelia's pulse quickened as her finger moved down the line, following it to the generation beneath Étienne. She stopped on a name she knew she had seen before, now holding a deeper significance: "Nadia Vallois." she said aloud. "The 'Nady' in your letters." Gabriel's expression shifted to surprise.

Amelia blinked, the thought almost too perfect. "Could she really have just… changed her name?"

"This can't be a coincidence," she said, her hesitation giving way to realization as Gabriel encouraged her with his eyes. "Nadia Vallois, Étienne's daughter. We hear little of her… but she would have likely been an integral part of the Alliance. And look at this—Sergei met Nadejda, his future wife, in a Moscow museum in 1928. That's the same year *Nadia* accompanied her father, Étienne, on a diplomatic trip to Moscow! Then, in 1930, when Nadejda married Sergei Shchukin, all records of Nadia Vallois in France vanish. What if she adopted the Russian form of her name to honor her new husband?"

Gabriel blinked, processing the revelation. "Wait… so you're saying Nadejda Shchukin is actually Nadia Vallois?"

Amelia nodded, her excitement building as her thoughts aligned. "Yeah! Records of her don't stop because she died or disappeared from the Vallois family—she simply changed her name when she married Sergei. The timeline matches perfectly, and so does the connection to the art world. It all adds up!"

She quickly tapped the screen, bringing up scant records on Nadejda. "There's almost nothing about her, outside of her name engraved on Sergei's tombstone. But the dates don't lie. Nadejda—formerly Nadia— didn't just move to Russia and fade away. She stayed deeply connected to her family. Sergei died before the Alliance was formed, so he wouldn't have been able to help. But *she* helped carry on his work *and* her family's."

Gabriel leaned back, his eyes wide. "So she was a key figure all along, but her name change and the times erased her role."

Amelia nodded. "Exactly. At the time, women weren't openly recognized in business matters, especially not in something as clandestine as art smuggling. Even though the Alliance operated in secrecy, mentioning Nadia's involvement would have risked exposing their entire operation. But that doesn't mean she wasn't a key player behind the scenes."

She paused, her mind racing. "After the Russian Revolution, most of Sergei's collection was seized by the Soviets. We know the ledger is tied to art hidden from the Nazis. But if the 'Trubetskoy' in the ledger is *Shchukin's* Trubetskoy, then the Alliance may have been hiding art from the Soviets as well! Nadejda could have expanded their mission to protect what was left of her husband's legacy—and possibly others in Russia, too!"

The cabin lights flickered as the plane began its descent into Slovenia. Amelia closed her laptop, but her mind raced with possibilities. The Alliance hadn't just been hiding art—they'd been waging their own silent war against two of history's most oppressive regimes, protecting culture itself from those who would destroy it.

And somewhere in Postojna lay the truth of just how far they'd gone to succeed.

Chapter 64

A damp chill lingered in the narrow paths of Montmartre Cemetery as Nadejda stepped silently through the wrought-iron gates. Fallen leaves muffled her steps, and the towering crypts and winding paths offered a perfect place for secrecy. In any other setting, she might have felt vulnerable, but here among the tombs, where grief cloaked her visits in unassuming silence, she felt invisible. No one would question a widow visiting her husband's final resting place.

At Sergei's tomb, she saw a single candle left by an unknown mourner, casting a faint glow on the inscriptions etched into the stone. It was here, hidden in plain sight, that the Alliance had established one of their most discreet dead drops. Beneath a patch of loose earth near the headstone, they would exchange coded messages, instructions, and updates for their network. It was a quiet sanctuary, a place where secrets could pass undisturbed.

Moments later, Arnaud emerged from the darkness, his arrival purposely staggered from Nadejda's. His footsteps were soundless on the damp ground, and they exchanged a nod, moving into their roles with practiced efficiency. He knelt by Sergei's tomb, reaching beneath the loose earth to retrieve a small envelope. Inside were a set of coded messages—updates from their network confirming recent shipments and introducing new routes for guiding artwork out of danger. The contents were brief but vital, a fragile lifeline of communication.

They reviewed the notes quickly, adjusting a few details. Then a sudden noise broke the silence: footsteps. Heavy, hurried, and too close.

Arnaud froze, his eyes snapping to Nadejda's, alarm flashing between them. In that instant, the somber peace of the cemetery transformed into a trap. Without a word, they tucked the papers back under the loose earth and covered them over.

"Go!" Arnaud whispered with urgency. "We'll meet later!"

Nadejda hesitated only a moment, then slipped into the shadows. Her heart pounded as she melted into the maze of tombstones trying to get away. She moved swiftly but carefully, keeping low, her senses hyperfocused on every sound, every shift. A sharp voice—authoritative and unmistakably German—cut through the air, sending a jolt of fear through her. The Nazis were here. They must have discovered the dead drop.

Arnaud had vanished in another direction, blending into the darkness. Nadejda forced herself to stay calm, to trust her logic and instinct. But the cemetery, once a place of solemnity, now felt like an oppressive maze closing in around her.

Just before she reached the perimeter, she heard more boots on the damp ground. Slipping behind a towering statue, she willed herself to steady her rapid breaths, fighting against everything in her body that threatened to betray her presence. She waited, watching as the shadows of two soldiers passed only meters from her, their eyes scanning the darkness. She clutched her coat tightly, her heart racing.

Finally, after what felt like an eternity, the soldiers' footsteps faded. She waited until she could no longer hear them before slipping through a side exit and disappearing into the streets of Paris.

Just before dawn the next day, Nadejda returned to the cemetery, moving silently between the graves. Her nerves were on edge, but her mind remained resolute. There was an eerie stillness to the place, as if unaware of the chaos that had unraveled hours earlier. She retraced her steps to Sergei's grave, inspecting every shadow for signs of disturbance.

How did they know? she wondered, a bitter thought taking root. *We had been so careful.* But as she moved, each step brought a mounting awareness that clawed at her. The timing of the raid, their precise arrival—too many details fit together, each one another confirmation. They'd planned every step to be untraceable, invisible. But last night's ambush could mean only one thing: betrayal. Someone within their network had turned on them.

With a steady hand, she knelt by Sergei's grave, reaching into the loose earth. Her fingers searched for the hidden papers, but her heart sank as the realization set in.

They were gone.

The key notes intended for their extended network—notes that contained references to their operations, to the art, and to Postojna—had vanished.

Part III

Restoring the Future

Chapter 65

Slovenia, Modern Day

The descent into Slovenia from the airplane window offered a stunning panorama of jagged mountain ranges that gave way to rolling valleys. Amelia stared out the window, her fingers absently tracing the cool glass, her mind already lost in the task ahead. The green and rocky landscape of Slovenia stretched beneath them like a quilt, woven together by time and nature. It was so unlike the Parisian skyline she was accustomed to, with its carefully planned streets and historical façades. This was rugged, untamed land—almost Eastern Europe, edging away from the refined elegance of Western Europe.

The capital, Ljubljana, unveiled itself through taxi windows on their journey from the airport, revealing its simple charm. The streets were peaceful, almost sleepy, and the buildings, though lovely, seemed to carry an air of modesty, as if content to remain unassuming. It felt humble, a far cry from the grandeur of the City of Light. But as the car wound through the roads leading toward Postojna, the scenery shifted. The further they traveled, the wilder the landscape became with every passing kilometer.

Before reaching their final destination, they stopped at their small, rustic hotel nestled on the outskirts of the town. It was unpretentious but cozy, its stone walls blending into the mountainous backdrop. The innkeeper greeted them warmly, and after checking in, Amelia and Gabriel took a moment to settle into their rooms, gathering their thoughts for what was to come. The task ahead weighed on them as they unpacked only the essentials, their minds already racing to the coordinates, the cave, and what they might find.

Leaving the hotel behind, Amelia again found herself captivated by the stark contrasts. Here, the land seemed ancient, untouched in a way that felt almost primal. The forests thickened, their dense trees stretching like arms reaching for the sky as the mountains in the distance grew nearer. The dark peaks loomed ahead, towering over the land, almost like they had witnessed centuries of history unfold in silence. With each turn of the road, the distance from modernity became more pronounced, and Amelia could feel the pull of the unknown calling them closer.

Gabriel sat beside her in the cab, his gaze moving between the GPS on his phone and the scenery outside. "We're almost here," he murmured, a note of anticipation in his voice.

Amelia nodded, though her thoughts still lingered. She had lived in Paris for decades and before that Boston, immersed in both cities' carefully maintained histories and cultures. But here, everything felt raw—untouched by the need for perfection. Slovenia was a different world, more subdued and shadowed, as though it held secrets even older than the people who walked its streets. And now, here they were, on the verge of uncovering one of those secrets lost for decades.

The taxi slowed as they approached the entrance to Postojna Cave, where the familiar signs of a tourist hotspot began to appear. A crowd of visitors gathered near the entrance, their chatter filling the air as they snapped pictures and wandered in and out of the small, kitschy gift shops that lined the pathway. Trinkets of Slovenia—fridge magnets, postcards, and little carved figurines—glinted in the afternoon light. Families and travelers alike posed for photos in front of the large signs welcoming them to one of Europe's most famous cave systems—completely oblivious to the fact that beneath their feet, hidden within the shadows of history, was one of the largest caches of forgotten masterpieces. The entrance itself loomed, grand and imposing, like a gaping mouth in the rock, leading to a vast underground world that had enticed adventurers and explorers for centuries.

Amelia and Gabriel exchanged a glance, knowing their path diverged from the one laid out for tourists. While others shuffled toward guided tours and cute shops, their destination was something far removed from the well-lit paths. The coordinates they had uncovered led them somewhere different—somewhere hidden. Far from the crowds, the noise, and the polished experience of the main cave, their journey was taking them into a part of Postojna that few had probably ever ventured to. As the taxi rolled to a stop, they both felt the gravity of the moment settle in. This was the threshold of the unknown.

They paid the driver and thanked him as they stepped out into the crisp, cold afternoon. From this point on, they were on their own—no visible roads led to the coordinates they were tracking. The woods ahead of them marked a clear boundary between the familiarity of the known world and the secrets that awaited. As they stepped into the trees, the contrast between their surroundings and the bustling tourist area was stark. The first thing Amelia noticed was the sound—the soft, rhythmic rustle of leaves underfoot, dense and golden-brown, carpeting the forest floor. The late fall air was sharp, and its biting chill stung her skin after the warmth of the cab. A profound stillness settled over the woods, as though it were holding its breath.

The deeper they ventured, the further the quiet surrounded them, the familiar sounds of civilization slowly fading. The wind moved through the trees, carrying with it a sense of the ancient and unknown, and each crunch of leaves beneath their boots seemed louder in the hushed forest. With every step, the eerie stillness heightened the sense that they were no longer in a place meant to be seen by just anyone.

Amelia glanced around. The woods were darker here, the trees thicker, their gnarled branches creating a web of darkness. The map showed the coordinates about 3 kilometers from the main cave entrance, leading them deeper into the forest.

———————

"This is it," Gabriel murmured, his voice subdued by the surrounding silence. He gestured to the GPS screen. "The coordinates should be just ahead."

The tension was building now. Amelia felt it too—a knot forming in her chest as they continued their trek. The forest was beautiful, yes, but it also felt isolating. The further they walked, the more the world seemed to close in around them, with the canopy of trees overhead blocking out most of the light. It was peaceful, but unsettling at the same time.

They pushed past a dense thicket, the undergrowth scratching at their legs, and then it appeared—so subtle, so well-hidden, it was almost part of the landscape itself. The coordinates had led them to a nearly invisible entrance, if one could even call it that. The small opening was tucked into the side of a rocky hill, completely obscured by deep layers of ivy and overgrown brush that seemed to have grown undisturbed for decades. If they didn't *know* the opening was there, it would be very easy to miss. Amelia *had* nearly missed it, but Gabriel's sharp-eyes pointed out a shallow depression in the ground. The earth had sunken just enough to reveal the faint, jagged outline of a cave mouth hidden beneath nature's veil.

They climbed a short way up the hillside, and the world around them felt still—eerily still. The sounds of crunching leaves and their labored breaths from the climb had faded, leaving only the rushing of blood in their ears. Gabriel knelt down, his fingers sinking into the cool, damp earth as he carefully pulled back the thick vines and layers of leaves. The low rustle of foliage was the only sound. "It's here," he said, his voice low and reverent, as though he had uncovered something ancient and sacred.

Amelia crouched beside him, her heart pounding as she helped clear away the layers of tangled vines and leaves. Slowly, the entrance emerged, and with it, a cold exhale of wind drifted from within, sending a chill through her. They both knelt at the narrow opening, humbled by the realization that while all they could see was this small, unassuming entrance, what lay beyond was far more immense—a hidden expanse, like the unseen mass of an iceberg. The opening itself was no more than a meter wide, just under three-quarters of a meter high, the kind one would have to crawl through to enter. Its rocky edges, worn smooth by centuries, seemed ancient—hidden in plain sight for untold years. Amelia stared into the darkness, her mind racing.

The first thing that struck her was the size of the opening. It was so small, so tight—far too narrow for anyone to carry large objects through. Amelia's thoughts turned to the paintings they had seen listed in the ledger. Many of them were grand in scale, some measuring as much as 1.5 to 2 meters on their narrow side. She shook her head, her brow creasing in concern as she looked at Gabriel. "This doesn't seem right," she said softly, doubt creeping into her voice. "How could they have brought *anything* through here, especially those massive paintings?"

Gabriel paused, glancing at the entrance and then at her, weighing her words. "Canvases," he said, his voice questioning but steady. "They can be removed from their frames, right? Rolled up, maybe? They could've transported them that way?"

Amelia nodded slowly, her mind turning over the possibility. "It's not ideal," she murmured, staring into the darkness beyond the opening. The cave mouth led horizontally into the hill, a long, narrow tunnel that disappeared into the earth. "But it's possible."

Gabriel leaned closer to the entrance, shining his flashlight into the hole. The beam illuminated a straight passage that cut deep into the rock. It didn't look treacherous—at least, not yet—but the claustrophobic tightness of the space sent a shiver down Amelia's spine.

"We can do this," Gabriel said, his breath visible in the cold air. He knelt at the entrance, ready to go in. "Let's just take it slow. We'll turn back if it gets dangerous."

Amelia nodded, her pulse quickening, both at the thought of what lay inside and the creeping sense of unease that came with venturing into this unknown. But they had come too far to turn back now. Swallowing her fear, she followed Gabriel as they crawled through the entrance.

———————

Once inside the opening, they could finally stand upright. The walls of the cave seemed to press in close around them, but the floor beneath their feet felt solid—firm, despite the loose pebbles and thick dust scattered along the path. Their flashlight beams cut through the near-perfect darkness, bouncing off the rocky surfaces, casting long, dancing shadows as they ventured deeper into the shaft.

The air was heavy and damp, clinging to their skin like a cold mist. It smelled of earth, a musty, ancient scent, mixed with the slight hint of decay—the kind of decay that comes from something long abandoned. There was a stillness to the cave, a silence that made Amelia feel like they had crossed some invisible threshold, leaving the world they knew behind.

As they moved cautiously, Amelia's skin prickled with a mix of excitement and unease settling deep into her bones. This wasn't just a cave —it was an untapped mystery, a hidden chapter of history that had been kept out of reach for decades. Each step carried her closer to what could be the greatest discovery of her life—even her generation—a treasure trove of masterpieces that the world believed lost. The ledger's entries were more than numbers and names—they were symbols of lives interrupted, of cultures that had been looted and erased by war. She imagined what lay beyond these stone walls: the brushstrokes of Monet, the vibrant colors of Matisse, the hidden beauty of stolen history waiting to be revealed. The mere thought sent a thrill coursing through her veins. *We're close.*

But with that thrill came a sudden, almost crushing awareness of how exposed they were to the unknown. She shivered, though she couldn't tell if it was the cold or the sheer magnitude of what they were walking toward. The darkness beyond their flashlight beams seemed endless, like the cave was swallowing their light, eager to keep what it knew hidden for just a little longer.

"I don't know if I like this," she whispered, for fear of disturbing the silence of the cave. "We don't know what's in here… but it feels like we're stepping into something bigger than ourselves."

Gabriel glanced back at her, his flashlight creating fleeting patterns of light along the jagged cave walls. His expression was serious, but there was a determination in his eyes. "I know," he said. "But we're here now. We've come too far to turn back. Let's just go a little further—see where this leads. We'll know if it's time to turn back."

Amelia nodded, her breath steadying as she followed him deeper into the shaft. Gabriel had a way of pushing ahead without hesitation, unbothered by rules or protocol. She had sensed this about him from the start, during their first meeting at the Artisan's Lodge—a visit he hadn't exactly secured permission for. He was far more comfortable bending boundaries than she was. In a way, it was very "Vallois" of him. Yet, she trusted his instincts, his expertise as a structural engineer, and despite her apprehension, she felt a growing pull—a feeling that they were on the verge of something monumental.

The tunnel stretched endlessly ahead, a straight, narrow path carved deep into the earth. The walls were rough and jagged in places, but smooth in others, worn down over time. It was a strange, almost unnatural space, but not impassable.

She imagined what it must have been like for those who had hidden these works—the fear, the urgency, the hope that someday someone would find them. This was their legacy, and now it was hers too—waiting to be uncovered.

As they moved forward, Amelia could sense the rocks above them, a heavy, looming presence that made her acutely aware of how far beneath the surface they were. Every sound they made—the crunch of their boots on the gravel, the soft exhales of their breathing—was swallowed by the silence of the cave. The beam of her flashlight flickered slightly, momentarily illuminating nothing but the cold stone walls, before steadying again.

Her thoughts swirled between fear and anticipation as the significance of their discovery loomed large in her mind. But above it all, she felt they were not ready for this moment yet. They needed to regroup. She opened her mouth to speak, to voice the tension building inside her, but before she could, Gabriel stopped abruptly.

"Look!" he said, his voice tense.

Amelia's pulse quickened as she stepped closer to him, following his line of sight. Her flashlight flickered again, her beam moving down the tunnel. Ahead, the light from the entrance had almost completely faded, leaving them in near-total darkness. But there, just beyond the reach of their light, something caught her eye.

At first, she thought it was just the uneven ground, but as her beam steadied, it became clear—there were scuff marks. Disturbances in the thick dust and pebbles that coated the cave floor, like someone—or something—had dragged or moved across it. Not fresh, not crisp like recent footprints, but the faint, almost ghostly remnants of movements from long ago.

The passage before them split into two, a fork leading deeper into the darkness. The marks—almost imperceptible—seemed to trail off to the right.

Amelia held her breath in thought. The entrance had been sealed, hidden for years under layers of overgrowth. How could there be marks left behind? But as her mind raced, another thought settled in: these traces could have survived for decades, undisturbed and frozen in time by the very isolation of the cave.

She crouched down, her fingers hovering just above the disturbed ground. "These aren't fresh, Gabriel," she said softly, a mixture of awe and unease in her voice. "They could've been made after the war."

Gabriel scanned the dim path ahead, his light steady. The tunnel, untouched for years, now felt crowded with history.

"They could have been made *during* the war," he murmured, his voice tense and thoughtful. "But whenever they were made, one thing's clear."

Amelia glanced up, sensing the gravity of his words, the truth settling between them before he even spoke.

"We're not the first ones here."

Chapter 66

The cave's atmosphere shifted as Amelia and Gabriel crouched close to the ground, their eyes fixed on the dust before them. It had clearly been disturbed, yet, when was impossible to tell. Amelia's flashlight beam flickered over the prints and followed them as they trailed off toward the right fork of the tunnel. To her, the cave felt alive with anticipation, like it was holding its breath, waiting for their next move.

Every instinct told her to turn back, to take a step away from the unknown danger that seemed to lurk in the darkness. But something stronger kept her rooted to the spot. The thought that these markings could have been left by someone from the Alliance pulled at her, along with the idea that the lost art—masterpieces missing for decades—could be just a few steps ahead.

Beside her, Gabriel crouched in silence, looking down the right tunnel. Finally, he broke the silence. "Do you think someone found it?" he asked, his voice low but laced with genuine concerned.

Amelia swallowed hard as she pondered the question. What if someone had already beaten them to it? What if, after all their painstaking research and countless hours spent following clues, the artwork was already... gone?

"We won't know unless we check, will we?" she said steadily, despite the uncertainty racing through her mind. Even she was surprised by her own response.

Gabriel hesitated, glancing back down the tunnel toward the now faint light of the entrance. "Maybe we should turn back," he said, his voice low, almost conspiratorially. "We could regroup, get the guides, come back with more—"

"No." Amelia's voice was firm, echoing sharply through the tunnel, stronger than she intended. *She* had been the cautious one, the scared one. But now, something had shifted. The fear was still there, but so was a growing sense of determination. She steadied her flashlight, meeting Gabriel's gaze with a resolve she hadn't felt before. "We've come this far. What if it's just a little further?"

Gabriel nodded, though concern washed over his face. "Alright," he said, his voice cautious. "But we *need* to be careful."

Amelia turned her gaze back to the markings on the ground, her mind running with possibilities. They had followed the cookbook clues and decoded the ledger—*everything* had pointed them to this place, this moment. The thought of turning back now felt unbearable. They couldn't leave. Not yet. Just a little bit more. They needed to see this through.

They pressed forward, the tunnel narrowing as they followed the scuffs in the dust. The cave was silent except for the sound of their boots against the stone. The air grew colder and damper, and the walls seemed to close in tighter with every step. Amelia's chest tightened as the heaviness of the earth above became impossible to ignore.

Gabriel's flashlight flickered, and his beam caught on something. The narrowing tunnel forced them to walk single file, and now the light illuminated a hollow space carved into the rock just ahead. A chamber, opening up from the constricting walls of the cave. Gabriel slowed and raised a hand to signal Amelia to stop. His voice was hushed and laced with anticipation. "Look!"

Amelia stepped forward, trying to stifle her deep breaths, and looked over his shoulder. Squinting into the dimness, through the cave's damp, stale air, she could barely see the opening. From there, the walls seemed to curve inward in a way that made it feel like they had stumbled upon a secret room.

Her breath caught. *This is it!* she thought, her pulse quickening with a blend of excitement and fear. The place they had been chasing for weeks—the spot where the Alliance had hidden their treasures—loomed before her. She raised her flashlight and swept its beam across the rough stone walls, shivering slightly at the realization that they were on the verge of discovering something monumental.

She searched desperately, yearning for something—anything—that would confirm they had finally reached the right place. The flashlight's beam moved in slow, deliberate sweeps, casting long shadows in the eerie darkness, illuminating each crevice with painstaking care.

And then she saw it.

Amelia froze. There, scratched in the stone above them, barely visible beneath layers of time, was a mark she knew all too well. The same mark she had seen over and over again—on the painting of Eloise, on the ring, in the words from the archives—a small skeleton key topped with a paintbrush. The mark of the Alliance. Though weathered by the years, it was unmistakable. The key and the brush. They *had* been here!

"Gabriel," she gasped, pointing above them, her voice trembling with excitement. "This is it! The mark—it's the Alliance! They were here!"

Gabriel's light joined hers, falling on the same lines above. His mouth dropped as he inhaled slowly, the gravity of the discovery settling over him. "We found it!" he whispered loudly, eyes wide, as his gaze locked with Amelia. "This *is* where they hid the paintings!"

Hope and disbelief passed between them as they stood on the verge of unlocking a piece of forgotten history. Everything they had worked for —the research, the decoding, the chase across Europe—it all seemed to lead them to this moment. *This* was the culmination of their effort.

Amelia squeezed past Gabriel, anticipation bubbling beneath her skin as she stepped into the open space. Her flashlight cut through the darkness, gliding over rough stone walls and sweeping across the uneven floor. She moved quickly, eager to uncover how the paintings were stored. The air grew denser with each step she took, but the thrill of discovery still moved through her veins. *This has to be the place*, she thought. *It has to be!*

Their beams bounced, illuminating jagged rocks as shadows danced along the crevices and cracks. Amelia's eyes strained in the dim light, searching for crates, tarps, or any sign that suggested this was the hiding place they had been chasing. For a moment, the chamber seemed alive with possibility, the silence heavy with potential. Yet, nothing appeared.

Could there be another passage? Another vault? Something deeper? Her stubborn optimism clung to the hope that they were just on the brink of something monumental.

But as her light moved across the space, the entirety of it, a sense of unease began to settle in. It started as a flutter in the back of her mind, barely perceptible but insistent. The space wasn't just smaller than she imagined—it felt... wrong. Too empty. Too still. With each step she took, the unease deepened, and her thrill gave way to the sharp edge of doubt.

The shadows cast by her flashlight now seemed less like hints of hidden treasures and more like dark, hollow spaces, devoid of life. There was nothing here. No crates. No tarps. No grand masterpieces waiting to be uncovered. Just stone.

Her heart sank.

The excitement that had filled the room moments earlier drained away, leaving only a void of silent disbelief. She glanced at Gabriel, her voice faltering as reality crashed in. "It's… empty."

Gabriel didn't respond at first. He just stood there, his gaze sweeping the space, almost trying to will something into existence. "It can't be," he finally said, his voice filled with defeat. "This was supposed to be the spot. The ledger… the coordinates… it all led us here."

Amelia felt a heaviness settle in her chest. She stepped further into the chamber, running her hand along the cold stone. *How could this be?* After everything they had been through, had someone found the artwork already? Could it have been moved? Had they been too late? Questions flooded her thoughts. She felt the emptiness around her, suffocating in its finality.

Gabriel's frustration was palpable. "This doesn't make sense," he muttered, shining his light over every inch of the chamber, desperate for something they might have missed. "There has to be something here."

Amelia's thoughts mirrored his. It didn't make sense. The chamber was here, the etching was here, the coordinates—this *had* to be the right place. She crouched down, inspecting the floor closely, still hoping to find a hidden passage, a concealed door—anything that could lead them to the treasure. But the stone was solid, undisturbed.

The thrill they experienced only moments ago was now replaced with crushing disappointment. It was as if the cave itself had tricked them, drawing them in with the promise of hidden wonders, only to reveal nothing but emptiness.

She stood slowly, brushing the dust from her knees. "Gabriel," she said softly, filled with resignation. "We're in the right place… but there's nothing here."

He didn't want to believe it. Neither did she. But the truth was staring them in the face. They had followed every lead, every clue, and still, they had come up empty-handed. Amelia felt her heart ache with the finality of it.

Gabriel sighed deeply, running a hand through his hair. "If someone took it," he began, "then we would have heard about it. We would have known if someone found it, right?"

Amelia shook her head, the question hanging in the air like an unanswered riddle. "I don't know," she finally admitted. "But I don't think they did."

They stood there in silence, the moment pressing down on them like the stone ceiling of the cave itself. The cold air now felt hot, subtly mocking their presence. Everything they had hoped for—months of research, hours of painstaking decoding, every risk they had taken—was slipping through their fingers.

Gabriel moved to the center of the chamber and swept his flashlight across the rough, empty walls again. His shoulders sagged and the excitement that had fueled him was now draining away. "Was it ever here?" he murmured, his voice hollow, the sound barely audible in the stillness. His question seemed to hang in the air, unanswered and heavy with uncertainty.

Amelia didn't respond. She couldn't. Her mind was racing, the moment now eclipsed by a thousand nagging questions. The paintings they had revealed in the ledger—masterpieces that had survived the chaos of war, hidden from the eyes of both the Nazis and Soviets—were massive, fragile, priceless. And yet, as she thought back to the small entrance they had crawled through, she felt a rising tide of doubt. How could they have possibly stored something so large and delicate in here? How could those towering canvases, some nearly two meters wide, have been squeezed through such a tight, constricted opening?

Her fingers brushed absently against the cold stone wall, searching for answers that refused to reveal themselves. It didn't make sense. Why would the Alliance—an organization dedicated to protecting these treasures—choose a place like this? The cave was damp, cold, and its atmosphere was thick with decay. She knew how temperamental art could be, how much care and finesse it demanded, even under ideal conditions. And after experiencing this space firsthand, it now struck her as the *last* place anyone would want to store fragile, irreplaceable masterpieces. Was this ever truly meant to be the hiding spot? And if it was, how could they have moved the paintings without damaging them?

She swallowed hard. The marking they had seen—the brush and key—had led them to this spot, but the emptiness of the chamber now felt like a cruel trick, a false lead in a mystery far bigger than either of them had expected. The scuffs on the ground—*could* they have been left by someone who had already come and taken the artwork? The thought sent a shiver through her.

Gabriel turned to her, his face etched with disappointment. "What now?" His voice cracked, like all the air had been let out of him.

Amelia's thoughts swirled, the weight of their discovery—or lack thereof—settling like a stone in her chest. The chamber felt too quiet, too final, and yet... her instincts wouldn't let go. Something about it felt unfinished, like the puzzle wasn't quite complete. She didn't know if it was the oppressive stillness, the damp air, or the sheer magnitude of what they had set out to find. But her gut told her there was more to this than what they were seeing.

She took a slow breath, steadying herself. "I don't know," she said, voice low. "But this doesn't feel right. The art... it couldn't have been stored here. It wouldn't have survived in this place."

Her fingers tightened against the rock. The doubts, the frustration, and the fear of being so close to a truth that kept slipping through their grasp all swirled in her mind. The paintings... someone could've taken them. But when? How?

She turned her gaze back to Gabriel, meeting his eyes, and in that moment, they both knew—this wasn't the end. It couldn't be. There were too many questions left unanswered, too many pieces that didn't quite fit. And yet, the silence of the chamber offered nothing in return.

Gabriel shook his head slowly above the dim beam of his flashlight, his frustration palpable. "We've been following the ledger—every clue, every symbol... But this place—" he gestured around the empty chamber, his voice echoing eerily off the stone walls, "You're right. It doesn't feel right—not for all that artwork."

Amelia nodded, her thoughts spiraling. The scuff marks in the dust —they weren't fresh, but they weren't ancient either. Someone had been here, but whether they had found anything remained a troubling question.

She stepped toward the chamber's exit, her boots scraping softly against the gravel floor. Her thoughts pressed forward, already turning over their next move. But before she could glance back to catch Gabriel's eye, a sharp snap echoed through the space, cutting through the stillness like a whip.

Amelia froze, her breath held in her throat. Slowly, she looked down, her heart hammering against her chest as her trembling flashlight beam flickered over the ground.

A thin wire, barely visible in the dim light, was pressed taut against her ankle, unmoving. Her pulse quickened as she traced the wire with her flashlight, the beam revealing its path toward the far side of the space.

There, half-buried in dust and debris, was a small, rusted metal box. Its corners worn with time, the surface encrusted with grime. But it was the faint lettering, barely legible, that sent an icy wave of fear rushing through her.

Achtung.

Amelia's heart stopped. She knew the German word. *Danger.*

Gabriel's eyes followed her flashlight, widening as the reality of the situation dawned on him. His face paled and his voice was tight with alarm. "Amelia... do not move!"

She couldn't. She stood frozen in fear, her throat dry as she stared at the rusted box. Her mind raced through every possibility, every scenario —none of them good.

They hadn't just stumbled upon a forgotten hiding place. They were standing in the middle of a trap.

A slight creak echoed from the box, like ancient metal finally giving way. Then came a sharp, hollow click.

The wire slackened against her ankle.

A deafening crack split the air. Blinding white light erupted through the chamber, consuming everything in its path. The flashlight clattered from Amelia's hand as the cave disappeared into a searing void of impossible brightness. Her world dissolved into a silent, blazing nothing.

Then everything went black.

Chapter 67

The silence inside the cave was broken by the rhythmic whirring of dynamo flashlights, their pitch rising and falling with each squeeze of the handle. Batteries, once plentiful, were now a luxury the Third Reich could no longer afford, forcing ingenuity to replace convenience. These small, hand-powered devices, though noisy, brilliantly converted manual effort into light and provided an endless source of illumination for those strong enough to keep squeezing. Their practicality came at a price, though, and the constant noise served as a reminder of how even the Reich's vast resources had been worn thin by the war.

The whirring mingled with the crunch of heavy boots on loose gravel. The men inside advanced, with labored breaths, towards their singular, grim purpose. Postojna Cave resisted their intrusion—it was damp, suffocating, and clung to the skin like a cold, wet sheet. Flickering beams from the flashlights cast shadows on the jagged walls, their light barely holding the darkness at bay. The tunnel that led into the heart of the mountain yawned before them, a gash in the rock that seemed to swallow the light.

"Keep moving," snapped a harsh voice, rough with authority. The command echoed off the walls, flattening against the rock before disappearing into the black depths of the cave. Three soldiers advanced, their movements precise, their faces set in expressions of steely determination.

The youngest soldier paused as they stepped into a hollow chamber, the narrow passage giving way to a broader, more open space. This place had once served as a hidden cache for munitions during the Reich's strategic retreats from the Allies. But all the crates filled with bullets, artillery, and grenades had now been moved elsewhere to support their final, desperate efforts. Yet, even stripped bare, this part of the cave held strategic value. If the Allies found it, they could repurpose it as a stronghold or a supply station.

They were here now to ensure that would never happen. If they couldn't use it, then no one would.

"Hard to believe we're leaving it like this," the youngest soldier muttered, the words slipping out before he could stop them. The officer's gaze cut to him, sharp and unyielding.

"Don't be so down!" the officer corrected, his voice menacing and deliberate. "Think of it like we're leaving a little welcome present… for anyone foolish enough to follow our path."

Another soldier crouched near the entrance, hands steadying, as he laid a tripwire across the uneven floor. His fingers trembled as he adjusted it, the thin line vanishing beneath a layer of pebbles and dust. The wire stretched taut, leading back to a small crate nestled discreetly against the wall—its contents, a deadly payload designed to bring the cave down on any who dared to trespass.

"Make it seamless," the officer said, low and commanding. The soldier nodded, moving the last stones into place until the tripwire all but disappeared into the cave's natural chaos. Every movement was precise and deliberate. They had been trained for this—a mission of deception and destruction.

They exchanged no more words. One by one, they retreated from the narrow passage, boots grinding softly against the gravel and loose stones as they left their deadly handiwork behind. After exiting, the last soldier paused and looked back at the entrance to the cave—just wider than a man's shoulders, barely tall enough to crawl through. It was swathed in shadows, tangled with ivy and creeping tendrils of brush, just as it had been when they first discovered it. Easy to miss. But if anybody did find it, he thought, they'd be sorry.

Chapter 68

Postojna Cave, Modern Day

The ringing in Amelia's ears slowly faded as consciousness returned. She lay sprawled on the damp cave floor, her body tense, her heart pounding. Spots of light swirled behind her closed eyes, and when she finally dared to open them, she saw Gabriel leaning over her—his silhouette framed by the faint outline of his flashlight. She tried to breathe, to steady herself, but her chest felt tight.

He sounded distant, his voice muffled as though speaking underwater. "Amelia!" Gabriel said urgently. His beam cast across her face as he scanned her for injuries. "Are you hurt? Can you hear me?"

Amelia blinked slowly and winced, disoriented, but she managed a small nod. Her chest rose and fell with shallow, uneven breaths, but she was alive. Relief washed across Gabriel's face, but it was short-lived. His mind was already churning.

"A flashbang," he muttered, rubbing a hand across his face. "Those weren't explosives—it was a damn flashbang." He glanced around the chamber, his expression darkening. It was the kind of device designed to blind and disorient with a burst of light and sound, not to kill. He paused, struggling to comprehend. "But why would they...? That doesn't make any sense. The Nazis wouldn't have..." He let the thought trail off, voice filled with confusion and something darker.

Moments ago, Amelia had braced for an ending—the deafening blast, the force that knocked them off their feet, the darkness closing in. Yet they were still alive. The flashbang had rattled her senses, but it hadn't killed them.

Gabriel's flashlight darted around as he crouched down next to her, his hand settling gently on her shoulder. "Take it slow," he said softly, fighting to steady the tremor in his own hands. She didn't need to move yet—she needed a moment to regain her composure. He caught her gaze

—her eyes wide, body rigid with fear. He could see she was scared. He was too, but he had to remain calm—for both of them.

He forced himself to breathe, to think through the panic that was threatening to cloud his mind. But he couldn't shake a dark question. The Nazis didn't build traps for mercy. They didn't build traps merely to stun. They built them to kill. So *why* a flashbang? The realization hit him like a punch to the chest. *Because the flashbang wasn't meant to kill—it was meant to stun, to bait its victims into something worse.*

This was a *Doppelblitzfalle*—a "double flash trap." A fragment of a documentary he'd seen resurfaced in his mind, the details sharpening in his memory. Its purpose wasn't just disorientation. The flashbang was designed to lure in others—soldiers rushing to help the stunned victim— only to be caught by the main charge themselves. A short delay, created by a secondary trigger or a timed fuse, ensured the second explosion would hit when *everyone* was inside the space. Death wasn't just a weapon to the Nazis—it was a game.

And this trap still had another turn.

His flashlight moved over the cave floor, catching on the thin wire stretched taut beneath Amelia's leg. When the flashbang had knocked her down, she'd landed directly on it, pressing it into the ground.

"Don't move," Gabriel said sharply. His voice was steady and firm, but inside, his mind was racing. "The wire is still engaged. It might still be attached to a secondary trigger."

Amelia stayed frozen, her breath catching, eyes wide. "I'm not moving," she said, her voice trembling with fear. Her breaths came in shallow, ragged gasps. She was scared, more scared than she had ever been, and yet, somewhere deep inside, she clung to Gabriel's presence. He was calm. He *had* to be. "Gabriel… what do we do?"

Gabriel moved his flashlight along the wire's length. It led away from them, vanishing into the small, rusted box embedded in the ground. It looked ancient, covered in years of dirt and neglect. But he knew appearances lied. Inside, someone had once set a deadly intention.

His mind churned through the details, replaying what had just happened. The flashbang had gone off first, blinding and disorienting them, yet the box showed no signs of having contained it. No soot, no shattered seams. That meant the flashbang must have been positioned somewhere else in the cave, out of sight. A separate device tied into this same tripwire system, triggered by a shift in tension when Amelia's ankle first caught the wire. It had rattled them, knocked them off balance, and if they had moved recklessly afterward… well, that was likely the point.

Gabriel swallowed hard. The two parts were separate but connected by the same trigger line and gears. The first stage had succeeded—the flashbang had fired perfectly. The second stage, however, seemed to have failed to follow through. Why? Was it a bad fuse? A broken trigger? Simply the age of the device? He needed to confirm what had gone wrong inside the box, because that malfunction was the only reason they were still breathing.

He crawled over to the box, trying to steady himself. His fingers felt the old, corroded edges, and he shined his light across its face, looking for a clue—a sign, anything that might tell him what was going on.

Amelia's voice broke through his concentration. "What do you see?" Her voice was small, tight with fear, and Gabriel could hear the tremble in her words.

He didn't answer immediately. He couldn't afford to give her false hope until he knew for sure. His mind worked frantically, his hands moving with careful precision as he examined every centimeter of the wire, the gears, and the worn-out parts of the device. His heartbeat echoed in his ears, with pressure building as he realized how much was riding on these next few moments. There was no room for mistakes.

You're an engineer, he reminded himself. *So think like one.*

The wire was old, its surface discolored from time. Gabriel followed it carefully into the box, knowing that in the tight confines he would have to let his fingers serve as his eyes. He followed the gear chain, feeling the teeth weathered in places, but still interlocking with precision. The mechanism felt deceptively delicate, which was a testament to the craftsmanship of its time.

His fingers moved slowly, brushing past the gears until they found the striker assembly—the piece that would initiate the secondary detonation. Just beyond it, he felt the small, rusted spring buried deep within the mechanism. He froze as his thumb pressed lightly against the coil. It was corroded, snapped clean through in the middle.

He gasped sharply. *Broken.* The spring, once under tension, was now useless—it lacked the elastic potential energy needed to expand with enough force to activate the firing sequence. If the spring had been intact, they would already be dead. Relief washed over him in an instant, crashing through the tension like a wave, leaving him breathless but grateful.

"The spring mechanism," he almost shouted. "It's broken. It's not operational anymore!"

Amelia didn't dare move. She hadn't blinked for what felt like minutes, her breathing still rapid as Gabriel examined the trap. *Was he sure? Was it really safe?* She felt her arms start to wobble, but she remained as still as possible. Her pulse thudded in her ears as she waited for Gabriel to confirm what she desperately needed to hear.

Gabriel leaned back slightly, his flashlight steady as he took one last look at the wire, the box, and the rusted mechanisms that no longer posed a threat. *Thank God.* He looked at Amelia, his voice more certain now, more sure of what needed to happen next. "I think we're okay," he said, then caught himself, realizing she needed more assurance. "We *are* okay," he corrected. "But we still need to be very careful."

Amelia's body tensed, but she managed a tiny nod. *Careful.* She could do that. Her legs felt like lead, but she would move—if it was safe. "What do I do?" she asked.

"Get up very slowly," Gabriel said, his voice calm. Though the mechanism was broken, he couldn't be certain what other surprises might lurk inside the box. He kept his flashlight trained on the wire. "Just move off the wire… carefully. I'll watch it. If it pulls differently, I'll stop you."

Amelia nodded again, her throat too dry to speak. Her muscles screamed in protest, locked tight from the terror that had gripped her body. Slowly—painfully slowly—she began to shift, lifting her body onto all fours, her pulse racing with every slight movement. Gabriel's flashlight followed her every motion, with his beam focused intently on the wire. He didn't blink, his breath held as he watched her rise, the wire staying in place.

Almost there. Centimeter by centimeter, she got up, barely breathing as she moved her second hand over the wire. The tension in the air was suffocating, the silence between them filled with the awareness of how much could still go wrong.

And then—she was free.

Gabriel exhaled sharply, his shoulders sagging with relief, but his eyes remained fixed on the trap. "We're not out of this yet," he said cautiously, now next to her, and motioning toward the exit. "We need to get out of here. Now."

Amelia didn't argue. Her legs felt weak beneath her, but she followed Gabriel, moving quickly but carefully as they made their way out of the chamber. Every sound—every breath, every step—felt too loud in the darkness around them. The shadows seemed to press in closer as they hurried down the narrow tunnel, the cave walls looming over them.

With each step, the fear of what they had narrowly escaped clung to them—a reminder of how close they had come to losing everything. Gabriel's thoughts churned, replaying their near miss over and over. The image of the wire around Amelia's ankle, the ancient trap poised to spring, refused to leave his mind. Ahead, the light from the entrance grew steadily brighter, pulling them toward safety. They just kept moving towards it.

The cold air hit them like a slap to the face as they emerged from the cave. A small breeze drifted past, evaporating the sweat from their foreheads and carrying away the staleness of the underground. Amelia's legs buckled beneath her, and she stumbled forward, gasping for breath. The fear that had held her rigid inside the cave finally broke, leaving her body weak and trembling. Gabriel caught her just before she collapsed, guiding her to a nearby rock where she sank down, her hands shaking uncontrollably. The surge of adrenaline overwhelmed her, and she vomited, her body releasing the tension it could no longer contain.

For a moment, the serenity of the world around them felt overwhelming. The soft rustle of leaves in the wind, the distant calls of birds, even the faint trickle of a stream somewhere nearby—it all felt too loud, too real after the suffocating silence of the cave. It was like the forest was trying to remind them they were alive, though only moments before, the threat of death had seemed almost certain.

Amelia sat hunched over, clutching her knees, her breath still coming in ragged bursts. Her mind was racing, but not with fear—there was something else now. Something beyond the terror that had nearly paralyzed her inside. The adrenaline slowly ebbed away, leaving behind exhaustion, but within that fatigue was a stirring of something more. *Why had the art been hidden in such a dangerous place?*

Gabriel, pacing nearby, raked his fingers through his hair, his expression filled with frustration and residual fear. "That was too close," he said, his voice lower than usual but still mixed with panic. "Way too close."

Amelia nodded absently, staring down at her hands, still shaking from the lingering adrenaline. "I thought…" she trailed off, her throat tight, unable to finish the thought. The magnitude of what had just happened was too much to fully process. They had nearly died. If time and decay hadn't worked in their favor, they would have become just another story swallowed by the cave.

But as the fear slowly receded, the nagging thoughts pushed their way back through the haze of panic. Something was off. The pieces weren't fitting together like they should. Amelia looked up slowly, confused, as the logical part of her mind took over. "Gabriel," she said, much steadier now. "Something doesn't make sense."

Gabriel stopped pacing and turned towards her. "What do you mean?"

Amelia took a deep breath, forcing her racing thoughts to slow down enough to form a coherent sentence. She wiped her palms on her jeans and tried to stable herself. "The Alliance. The Bourget-Vallois Alliance… they wouldn't have hidden priceless artwork in a cave used by the Nazis—let alone one they booby-trapped. It doesn't make sense."

Gabriel nodded, sharing her frustration. "I know. But we followed the ledger. The coordinates… they led us here."

"I know… That was stupid," Amelia said, her voice firmer now, as her thoughts aligned. "We let our excitement impede logic. We *wanted* it to be true. Think about it. If the Nazis had set traps here, they must have thought there was something worth protecting. And when they found the cave, they would have confiscated *any* treasure stored inside. The Alliance was too careful for that. They knew the risks—they wouldn't leave their art in a place where the enemy could stumble upon it and claim it for themselves."

Gabriel's frown deepened as realization set in. "So you think this was never the hiding place? But the ledger… why would it lead us here?"

Amelia straightened, a sudden clarity hitting her. Her mind raced back through all the clues they had followed—the layers of misdirection and careful planning. The pieces were fitting together. "What if they led us here on purpose?" she said slowly, her eyes meeting Gabriel's. "What if this was… a decoy?"

Gabriel's eyes widened as the full implication of her words sank in. "A decoy? You mean... to mislead anyone who came across the ledger?"

Amelia nodded, the certainty in her voice growing. "Exactly! It makes sense. Think about it. The Nazis were searching for treasures, just like we are. They were already using this cave to hide their own stolen items. So they already considered it secure. The Alliance must have known that and turned it to their advantage. By pointing the ledger here, they could mislead the Nazis into thinking *this* was the hiding place of a great treasure—just like they did with us."

She paused, glancing at Gabriel with a wry smile. "And we fell for it, didn't we?"

Amelia continued, her tone more thoughtful now, working through the theory aloud. "But the Nazis would never have imagined the Alliance could deceive them right under their noses. Their overconfidence would have blinded them to the possibility that the real hiding place was somewhere they'd never think to look. Their arrogance would lead them to believe the artwork was already in their grasp, and their hubris would prevent them from questioning it further. They'd assume this cave *was* the location and would keep searching here, convinced it was only a matter of time. *That's* why this was the perfect decoy."

She hesitated for a moment, her gaze dropping to the ground as her tone softened. "I don't think the Alliance would have risked their treasures being so easily discovered here. We let ourselves be fooled by what we wanted to believe. But if that's true, then it can only mean one thing —the hiding place, the *real* hiding place, is somewhere else."

Gabriel's pacing slowed, his voice heavy with disappointment as he repeated, "So... we've been chasing a false lead this whole time."

Amelia shook her head, her voice soft but sure. "Not exactly. I think the ledger brought us here for a reason. This cave, this place, these coordinates—I think they're part of the riddle. But it was never meant to be the final destination. I think the Alliance set this up to mislead anyone chasing them, to make them believe they'd reached the end. The real hiding place is still out there. But they wanted anyone following the trail to believe they had found it—or, more likely, that somebody *else* already had."

Gabriel stopped pacing, standing still as the full realization settled over him. "They tricked us," he muttered, half to himself. "They tricked everyone."

Amelia nodded, her mind spinning with possibilities. "The booby traps... the Nazis must have thought they'd already found everything. But the Alliance was one step ahead. They knew how high the stakes were. They wouldn't leave their treasures here, in such a vulnerable place."

Gabriel's shoulders sagged, the emotional crash hitting him hard. "So we've been chasing shadows," he said with a tinge of defeat. "All this time..."

"No," Amelia said firmly. "We've been following the trail they wanted us to follow, but this isn't the end. We need to find where that trail deviated and get back on the right path. The *real* location is still out there—we just have to find it."

Gabriel looked at her, his face a mix of exhaustion and disbelief. "How do we do that? We've followed every clue, every lead..."

Amelia looked back at the cave entrance, her mind racing with the enormity of the revelation. "We go back to the ledger. We missed something. There's another clue hidden... somewhere."

Her gaze hardened as she continued, her voice resolute. "And this time, we're not chasing a decoy."

Chapter 69

Postojna, Slovenia, Modern Day

The sun was already sinking low as Amelia and Gabriel packed up their things, preparing to leave Slovenia. Their time in the country had been a short whirlwind—filled with tension, near-disaster, and what felt like endless uncertainty. The coordinates to Postojna had been a dead end, but neither of them was ready to admit defeat. There had to be something they missed, a clue, something buried in the details that would point them to the real hiding place of the Bourget-Vallois cache.

Back in their modest hotel rooms, Amelia sat at a small wooden desk, the late afternoon sun streaming through the window, casting a warm golden light over the pages of the ledger and the old family cookbook. Gabriel stood by the window, absently watching the street below, his mind no doubt racing through every clue they had uncovered so far. But Amelia's focus was on the reproduced pages of the cookbook that now lay open before her.

"We've been over this a hundred times," Gabriel murmured from across the room, with a sigh of frustration escaping his lips. "What are we missing?"

Amelia didn't respond immediately. Her eyes remained locked on the pages, flipping through them slowly, her fingers tracing the delicate script of each recipe. She had been reviewing the ledger and cookbook side by side, searching for any thread that might lead them back on course. A clock on the nightstand ticked steadily, providing just enough rhythm to underscore the silence.

Minutes slipped by as she immersed herself in the faded ink and worn pages, the late afternoon sun drawing longer shadows across the desk. Gabriel shifted by the window, his gaze drifting from the scene outside to Amelia's steadfast focus. Though his last question was somewhat rhetorical, he held back from speaking further, sensing that interrupting her might break whatever connection she was trying to make.

Amelia turned another page, then another, each one a step deeper into the family's history *and* the mystery. She drew in a breath, ready to sigh in resignation, but froze mid-inhale, her breath holding. On the final page of the book, a recipe she had barely noticed before now caught her eye in a completely new way.

"Schlissel Challah Badigeonné de Sel," she murmured aloud, staring more intently. This recipe had never really come up in their deciphering process. It didn't have the ink splatter mark, so they had paid little attention to it. But now, after going over the other recipes so many times, something about *this* one seemed… off.

Gabriel turned from the window, curious. "What?"

Amelia squinted at the page, her eyes flicking between the last recipe's handwriting and that which accompanied the others. "This recipe… it's different. The handwriting—it's not like the others. It looks more… hurried, like whoever wrote it didn't care about the precision of the rest of the recipes. It's not as meticulous as the others. Almost… like it was added as an afterthought."

Gabriel came over, leaning against the desk, peering over her shoulder. "That's odd. Why would this one be different?" he said, trying to figure out where Amelia was going with her thought.

"I don't know. But look at this footnote." Amelia pointed to a strange passage at the end of the recipe, her finger hovering over the words:

"Pour révéler plus de saveurs cachées: Ajoutez zestes de bergamote, zestes yuzu, ananas, abricots, bananes, xérès. Battez beurre. Yaourt utilisez avec beurre."

She translated aloud, her voice filled with confusion as the words tumbled out. "To reveal hidden flavors: Add bergamot zest, yuzu zest, pineapples, apricots, bananas, and sherry. Beat the butter. Use yogurt with butter."

Gabriel chuckled softly, confused as well. "That sounds like a strange bread to me."

"Exactly!" Amelia said, affirming the thought, her tone serious. "This isn't like any of the other recipes. It's… odd. And these 'extra' ingredients make *no* sense for a challah recipe. Bergamot? Pineapples? Banan—" She stopped suddenly, her eyes widening. "Wait."

Gabriel leaned in closer, sensing her shift in focus. "What is it?"

"It's not just the odd ingredients," she said enthusiastically. "Look at how salt is referenced throughout. The title includes 'de sel'—'with salt.' And here, next to the salt measurement, there's a side note that translates '...*more salt unlocks flavor.*' Then there's this other line in the instructions: '*Salt preserves all that is precious.*'"

Gabriel's eyes narrowed as he took the book from her hands, flipping through the earlier pages. "That's strange. None of the other recipes focus on salt like that. They just give a specific amount and that's it—no more mentions."

Amelia nodded, her thoughts racing. "Exactly. I don't think this is just about seasoning. It's too specific—too deliberate. *Salt preserves all that is precious,*" she repeated, her voice quiet as the words sank in. "Why would they use this line in instructions to make bread? It's almost like... a clue."

"Preserves...," Gabriel muttered, pacing slowly, his mind turning over the possibilities. "Salt preserves food, sure. But what else is it used to preserve?"

Amelia spoke through her thoughts as they clicked into place. "Salt was used to protect things from decay. Meat, fish, even wood. But even more than that..." she continued, trailing off on different routes in her mind. "The *reason* it preserves things is because it reduces water activity, inhibiting microbial growth and extending life... It was used in ancient tombs—mummies, for instance—and it's still used today to keep so many things from deteriorating. Salt *preserves* things, Gabriel."

For a moment, they were both silent, her realization filling the room.

"So what does that mean?" Gabriel asked, his voice cautious but curious. "Where are you going with this?"

Amelia began pacing the room, her mind spinning through the possibilities. "We've been thinking too literally, Gabriel. We've been following coordinates, but what if the clues aren't just pointing to a specific place? This recipe—its too unusual not to take a second look. If this recipe *is* a clue, what if *salt itself* is part of the answer? Salt has always been used to preserve valuable things—even in ancient times, it protected against decay."

She stopped, looking at Gabriel. "The Romans valued salt so much they paid their soldiers with it—it's where the word *salary* comes from. That's how essential salt was for people's daily lives."

Gabriel frowned, trying to keep up with her scattered thoughts. "Preserving things is important, yes. But again, how does that connect to what we're searching for? Why would we need to think about salt *now?*"

Amelia's expression brightened as a realization clicked. "We need to find a place where salt isn't just used, but where it's critical for *protecting* something valuable—like a large cache of hidden paintings. A place designed to preserve things naturally. Not the ocean, not a kitchen... it has to be more specific than that. A place where salt is used for *storing* or *protecting...*"

Gabriel's eyes suddenly lit up—a large gasp quickly interrupting Amelia, causing her to stop mid-thought. "Or mining!"

Amelia stopped, turning to face him, her heart racing. "Mining?"

Gabriel nodded, his excitement building. "The Vallois family! I heard about this from my grandma. They invested in salt mines in Switzerland at the end of the 19th century! It was part of a diversification strategy, or something—one of their many investments. I think they owned a fairly large one there!"

Amelia stopped pacing, thinking carefully about what Gabriel had just said. "Salt mines," she murmured. "That could make sense..."

She looked at Gabriel, excitement sparking in her eyes. "Think about it—salt mines would be naturally cool, dry, and stable environments. Salt in the air would prevent decay and bacteria. It would be a perfect way to preserve things—canvases, wood... paintings!"

Her thoughts were racing now. "And Switzerland," she continued, her voice picking up, "was neutral during the war. The Nazis couldn't just waltz in and take whatever they wanted there. The Vallois family would've known that. They wouldn't risk hiding their priceless artwork in a vulnerable location—like Postojna Cave," she said, shaking her head. "But a salt mine, in a neutral country? That would be perfect for long-term preservation!"

Her voice grew more certain as she affirmed herself. "A salt mine would be a natural vault. It could store anything valuable—gold, documents, artwork—and it would be preserved. *Salt preserves all that is precious,*" she repeated, the phrase taking on new meaning.

Gabriel's eyes widened as Amelia's revelation sank in. "This all makes sense now! The artwork... it was never meant to *just* be hidden. It was preserved. In a place no one would think to look!"

Amelia's thoughts converged as she pieced it together one more time for confirmation. The odd phrases in the recipe—the emphasis on salt, the cryptic instructions about preservation—suddenly made perfect sense. She rushed back to the desk, flipping to the final page of the cookbook. The words that once seemed strange and out of place now resonated with purpose, each line revealing itself as part of the puzzle they'd been missing all along.

"'Preserve with salt,' 'timeless recipe,' 'layers of flavor,'" she read aloud, her fingers trembling with excitement. "These aren't just cooking instructions, Gabriel. They *are* clues," she said, now with assurance in her voice. "Hidden beneath layers…"

"Layers of salt," Gabriel finished, chuckling, his voice heavy with realization.

Amelia nodded, her pulse quickening. "The ledger pointed us to Postojna Cave as a decoy, but this… this feels different. This isn't just a random recipe. It was left for a reason—it was *added* for a reason—to point us to the salt mines. The Alliance *did* modify the cookbook!"

Gabriel's eyes met hers, his excitement tempered by a wary caution. "We have to really be sure this time, Amelia. The cave taught us that today. We can't let our excitement cloud our judgment. We can't jump to conclusions."

"I know," Amelia said softly, still shaking off what had happened to them earlier. She trembled for a second before regaining composure, her voice now steadying. "But this feels right. The Alliance wouldn't have risked the artwork being discovered by the Nazis, not in a cave that they could easily access. But a salt mine in Switzerland? Neutral territory, naturally protected… it makes sense."

Gabriel sighed, rubbing the back of his neck. "We've been misled once already, but… this fits, doesn't it?"

"It does," Amelia agreed. "But we have to play it carefully. No more running headfirst into the unknown. We'll need more information, more research… and a plan."

Gabriel nodded, his mind already working through the logistics. "Agreed. We'll take this one step at a time. When we get back to Paris, I'll start gathering anything I can find from my family's records on the Vallois Salt Mine."

Amelia's fingers hovered over the final recipe of the cookbook—
"Schlissel Challah Badigeonné de Sel." It was Jewish, she realized, but mixed
with French—just like the Bourgets!

"Badigeonné de sel," she murmured the French words under her
breath. "Brushed with salt." There was a brief second of silence as the
translation hung in the air. Then, a shiver ran through her, goosebumps
rising on her arms. The brush! She thought of the familiar emblem, the
brush and the key that they had seen carved into the stone in the cave,
marked on the painting of Eloise, and even etched on the ring. The brush
had been staring them in the face this whole time! Right here in this
recipe! But *Schlissel…* what did that mean? Even with her native fluency,
she had never encountered that French word before.

Her breath quickened as she grabbed her phone, her fingers shaking
slightly as she typed the word into the search bar.

The screen loaded, and the answer quickly popped up.

It *wasn't* French.

"Schlissel: Hebrew for 'Key.'"

Amelia gasped, another shiver running down her spine as the realization hit her like a jolt of electricity. She whispered loudly, "The
brush… and the key!" Her voice trembled with awe. This really *was* the
clue. This *was* the message the Bourget family left behind concealing the
hiding place of their smuggled artwork! A Jewish family, using a Jewish
recipe, to say a resounding 'fuck you' to the Third Reich! They had hidden everything in plain sight, daring anyone to find the true meaning!
"Damn, Arnaud! You were a bad ass!" she chuckled.

Gabriel looked up sharply from the other side of the room and
laughed, his curiosity piqued by her sudden shift in tone. "What did you
find?"

Amelia turned toward him with excitement, her pulse racing. "Gabriel… *Schlissel* means 'key' in Hebrew. It *is* a clue. The brush and the key
—it's right here, hidden in this challah recipe! *The brush and the key will
guide us!"*

Gabriel crossed the room quickly, peering over her shoulder at the
recipe. "The brush and the key… It's been right here the whole time," he
murmured, almost in disbelief.

"Yes," Amelia said, as she returned to the odd side note at the bottom of the recipe again. The words still felt strange, out of place, as
though they didn't belong. "Add bergamot zest, yuzu zest, pineapples,

apricots, bananas, sherry. Beat the butter. Use yogurt with butter." It wasn't just the ingredients—it was the way it was written, the unusual order of the words. Her instincts buzzed, telling her there was something more to this note. Something hidden in plain sight, just like the rest of the clues.

She ran her fingers over the page, mumbling the words to herself again. "This isn't right... The way this is written—it's off. It doesn't flow like this or any of the other recipes."

Gabriel watched her closely, his brow creasing with concern. "What are you thinking?"

Amelia's eyes darted back and forth between the lines, her heart pounding in her chest as she counted each word in the side note. "Sixteen," she said, almost to herself. "There are sixteen words!"

Gabriel blinked, not understanding yet. "Sixteen?"

"Yes!" Amelia said, her tone rising with urgency. "There are sixteen words... just like there are sixteen digits in the Postojna coordinates. And look at this." She flipped back to the notes they had made on the ledger. "When we found the Postojna coordinates in the ledger, we didn't have to decode them—we just used the numbers to get the first letter of each word. But there was no key. No additional layer of decryption."

Gabriel's eyes widened as he began to understand. "Wait... are you saying that this side note... is a key?"

Amelia nodded excitedly. "It has to be! Sixteen words, sixteen digits... I think we've found the key for the coordinates... for the *real* coordinates!"

They exchanged a quick, eager glance before Amelia grabbed her notebook and hastily jotted down the first letter of each word in the side note:

"A—Z—D—B—Z—Y—A—A—B—X—B—B—Y—U—A—B," she read aloud.

Gabriel leaned closer, his mind racing as he processed the letters. "That's... the key?"

Amelia nodded, unsure but driven to test it. "Let's try it with the Postojna coordinates," she said, her voice steadying with determination. She quickly wrote down the numbers and key phrase:

4 5 4 7 3 0 0 1 1 4 1 2 1 1 0 2
- A Z D B Z Y A A B X B B Y U A B

Together, they worked in silence, the tension in the room thickening with every second. Amelia's heart pounded as she focused, her fingers trembling as she applied the key to the numbers, slowly transforming the digits into what she hoped would reveal something monumental. One by one, the new decoded numbers revealed themselves.

"4… 6… 1… 6… 4… 2… 0… 1… 0… 7… 0… 1… 4… 7… 0… 1…" she read aloud, her voice wavering with a mixture of anticipation and uncertainty.

Gabriel's eyes widened as their pattern began to take shape. His voice quickened with excitement. "It's a new location!"

They sat there for a moment in shock. The realization that Postojna had been a decoy, that the real coordinates had been hidden in the cookbook all along, left them both silent. Still. The salt, the key, the brush—it had all been leading them here.

"We found it," Amelia finally spoke, the words tasting like victory on her lips. "We found the real coordinates."

Gabriel said nothing. He didn't need to. The look on his face said it all—disbelief, awe, and a dawning realization that they had just placed the final piece of the puzzle. Slowly, without breaking eye contact, he reached for his phone.

He began typing the new numbers into a GPS, his thumbs moving quickly but deliberately, each click like a distant thunderclap, echoing through the stillness as they waited for the result that could change everything.

Once the new coordinates were entered, he hit "search." They both froze, staring at the phone as the seconds stretched into what felt like hours. The screen was initially blank, teasing them with what it knew.

And then the location popped up.

"Bex," Gabriel said softly, his voice filled with both disbelief and thrill.

Amelia inhaled sharply as she looked up at him, her heart hammering against her ribs. "Bex?"

"Switzerland," he finished, a rush of awe in his voice. He turned the phone to her, and for a moment, they just sat there staring at each other,

the enormity of the discovery sitting between them with the location staring right back.

    Bex, Switzerland.

Chapter 70

The sound of a crackling fire filled the room, its warmth pushing back against the cold evening outside. Frost rimmed the windowpanes, and distant mountain peaks stood dark against the fading sky. Inside, the room glowed with a soft amber hue, and the flicker of candlelight cast shadows across the faces of three men near the hearth.

Antoine Vallois sat back in a leather armchair, his posture relaxed but his gaze sharp. Across from him sat his eldest son, Étienne, and by the fireplace stood his younger son, Clément. Antoine was a tall figure, his hair streaked with age and neatly slicked back, his eyes clear and calculating. In his hands, he held a glass of cognac, the amber liquid reflecting the flames from the fireplace. Étienne, both his son and a trusted business associate, leaned forward slightly, his expression thoughtful, as he swirled the glass in his hand.

"So," Antoine began, his voice measured, "you believe this investment is worth pursuing?"

Étienne nodded, a smile appearing on his face. "Yes, I do. The Bex Salt Mines have been operating for centuries, but they are far from reaching their full potential. The current owners are struggling—they lack the vision and, more importantly, the capital. I see an opportunity here, Father. If we acquire the rights, we could turn those mines into something truly profitable."

The fire crackled, filling the brief silence that followed. Antoine's eyes narrowed slightly as he considered Étienne's words. "And what makes you so certain that this is the right move?" he asked. "We have done well in textiles, banking… what makes salt worth our attention?"

Étienne took a slow sip, savoring the warmth before answering. "Salt, Father, is not just a seasoning. It's a necessity, and demand for it is growing. Industries need it for preservation, for chemicals, and for leather tanning. This isn't just about selling salt as it is; it's about controlling a supply chain that touches so many aspects of daily life." Setting his glass aside, he leaned in with confidence. "If we can secure the Bex mines, we would not only gain access to one of the most reliable sources of salt in the region, but also have a stronghold in a market that will never fade."

Antoine listened carefully, his fingers tapping absently against the armrest. "Go on."

"The location is ideal," Étienne continued, his eyes bright with the excitement of his idea. "The mines are nestled in the mountains, easily defensible and difficult to access without proper knowledge of the terrain. This means minimal risk of theft or sabotage. And given Switzerland's neutral stance in all matters, it's a haven—safe from political unrest and conflict. The salt mines themselves are stable, naturally cool, and dry. It's not just a business; it's an asset we can rely on through any storm."

Antoine's lips curved into a faint smile as he swirled the cognac in his glass, watching the liquid catch the firelight. "You've given this a great deal of thought, Étienne."

"I have," Étienne replied without hesitation. "We can modernize the extraction methods, improve production efficiency, and expand our distribution network across Europe. Salt is essential, but few truly appreciate its value until they need it. And when they need it, we will be the ones they come to."

The room hushed for a moment, broken by the occasional snap of the fire. Clément stood quietly, taking in the conversation. Antoine weighed the risks in his mind. The Vallois family had always been cautious, but they had also built their fortune on bold moves, on seizing opportunities that others might overlook.

"Tell me about the current owners," Antoine said finally, his voice thoughtful. "Why are they selling?"

Étienne's expression darkened a bit. "They're struggling to keep up. The mines are old, the equipment outdated. They lack the resources to modernize, and with other ventures failing, they're desperate for capital. They're willing to sell the rights at a fraction of their true value because they can't see the long-term potential. But we can."

Antoine nodded slowly, eyes distant. "And you're confident we can turn this around? That it will be worth the investment?"

"Yes," Étienne said firmly. "Absolutely. With the right leadership, the Bex Salt Mines could become one of the most lucrative parts of the Vallois portfolio. It's not just about mining salt; it's about diversifying our assets, securing a stable revenue stream, and establishing a foothold in a market that will never fade. We could corner the market on salt distribution across the region. No matter the state of the economy, no matter the conflicts that may arise, there will always be a need for what these mines produce."

Intrigued, Antoine raised an eyebrow. "And how do you propose we handle the modernization? It's not a small undertaking."

"We'll bring in engineers, update the equipment, and streamline the process. I've already begun making inquiries. The technology exists—we just need to invest in it. Once we control the flow, we can regulate supply, stabilize prices, and ensure that no one can undercut us. We will be in control."

Antoine let the words settle before taking another sip of cognac. It was a gamble, certainly, but not without its merits. And if Étienne was right, it could offer the Vallois family a good source of income for generations to come.

"And what of the future?" Antoine asked. "If we do this, if we invest in these mines, how do we ensure they remain profitable in the long run? How do we safeguard our investment?"

Étienne's smile widened. "By diversifying within the market. We won't just sell raw salt; we'll produce refined products, invest in chemical industries, supply contracts for municipal needs. We can even expand into export markets. And should the need arise… well, the location is remote, secure, and easily guarded. It's an asset that can be used in ways beyond what we plan today."

Antoine's eyes met Étienne's, and a silent understanding passed between them. "You're thinking strategically, Étienne. That's why I trust you. If we do this, I want it managed carefully. The investment must be sound, the operations efficient, and the returns substantial."

"You have my word," Étienne said, his tone earnest. "This isn't just a business venture, Father. It's a foundation, something that will keep the Vallois name strong no matter what storms come. We've weathered many changes over the years, and this will be our anchor."

Antoine set his glass down, the decision solidifying in his mind. Turning to Clément, he asked, "And you, Clément? What are your thoughts?"

Clément hesitated for a moment, surprised his father sought his opinion, but quickly composed himself. "I've reviewed everything with Étienne, and I agree—it's a sound investment."

Antoine nodded, a slight smile tugging at the corner of his mouth. "Very well. Let's proceed. Begin the arrangements, make the offers, and acquire the mines. If we're going to do this, we'll do it right."

Étienne nodded, a sense of triumph flashing in his eyes. "You won't regret it, Father. This is exactly what our family needs."

The three men fell silent for a moment longer. Outside, the night deepened, reducing the mountains to dark silhouettes. But, within the warm confines of the room, the future seemed bright, filled with promise and potential.

Chapter 71

Château Bourget was thick with tension as Arnaud dropped a small envelope on the table, the familiar crinkle of the thin, worn pages from within breaking a heated conversation between Lucien and Étienne. Nadejda's gaze fell immediately to the documents, her face a mix of disbelief and relief.

"They're here," Arnaud said, both words deliberate. "I managed to pull them from the dead drop just before we had to scatter. The chaos gave me just enough time."

Nadejda looked up, her expression softening with gratitude, though a trace of fear lingered. "They knew exactly where to go, Arnaud. They came too close. If the Nazis were aware of Sergei's grave, they may know far more than we've hoped."

Étienne, now sitting across from them, leaned forward to speak. "We have to assume they could be watching you, Nadejda. You've been the heart of our work in many ways. But any trace back to the Vallois family would be dangerous—not only for you, but... for all of us."

Nadejda looked at Étienne, the calm in his gaze a contrast to the unease growing within her. "Am I endangering our mission?" she asked.

Étienne shook his head. "I anticipated this risk. I removed every possible connection you had to the Vallois name before we even took on the first mission. As far as the Reich knows, you are a Shchukin. Your French identity, your history, has been erased where it matters." His voice softened as he added, "But our next steps must be calculated. You should consider taking precautions."

She nodded, taking in his words. They were nearing the end of their mission, but each day now felt like it carried twice the risk. Without another word, she turned toward the mirror on the far wall, her reflection steady and determined. The transformation would be simple, yet necessary. A short cut and a dark dye—one last measure to ensure her movements remained untraceable. With her heart pounding, she imagined Sergei's approval, knowing he would understand the impulsivity of her choice.

Arnaud's eyes met Nadejda's through the mirror. "It's not just you," he said gently. "We need to assume this level of caution across our entire network."

She turned back to the others. "Agreed," she replied. "This might not be the last time this happens. We need to be prepared for it again, to expect it." She glanced at the notes on the table sitting next to the ledger with its layers of ciphered entries. "From now on, we rely solely on ourselves for the transport. We'll remove any reliance on outsiders."

Lucien, nodding in agreement. "And any remaining art will need to be brought to us. No more pickups, no more individual routes."

Étienne added, "The fewer people involved, the less risk of leaks. By using a central location, we'll create a bottleneck… a controlled environment." He met Arnaud's eyes. "Like we've done with Russia."

Arnaud smiled. "Exactly. We follow that model moving forward." He paused, the smile now fading. "But there's more we can do to secure our work."

He gestured to the recovered pages from Sergei's grave, tapping lightly over one line that referenced Postojna Cave in northern Yugoslavia. "We've spoken of Postojna before, as an option we eventually set aside. But recently, our network learned the Nazis have started using it to store some of their *own* caches."

Lucien muttered under his breath, "Their precious pieces won't last a month in that damp cave."

Arnaud allowed himself a faint smile before continuing, "If the Reich comes across our ledger or any plans, Postojna would be the perfect misdirection—a believable decoy that would make it appear we'd stumbled on the same *brilliant* idea." His eyes sparkled with inspiration as he added, "We'll encode Postojna as a more accessible layer in the cipher… just complex enough to lead them there if they think they've outsmarted us."

Lucien's eyes lit with a menacing playfulness. "They'll *think* they've found the actual location. A wild goose chase! I like it."

Nadejda caught the glimmer of satisfaction in Arnaud's face. "It's clever," she said. "A deception within the deception. Let them search the cavern while our work remains untouched."

Arnaud's gaze grew distant as he absorbed their evolving strategy. "Then it's decided. We'll embed Postojna, and any further entries will be modified to fit this new approach. Ironically, the more breadcrumbs we leave, the less vulnerable we are."

After a pause, Arnaud took a deep breath and looked around the room. "One last thing," he said. "I'll be vacating this château until the war is over. This place has been raided already and it could happen again. Our Alliance's work needs me closer, more integrated—especially now. An unassuming apartment on the Left Bank will keep me within reach and give me a chance to remain vigilant over our remaining operations."

The room stayed silent as Arnaud's decision settled over them. Château Bourget had been their sanctuary, the birthplace of plans that had kept their mission alive against impossible odds. But he was right—this was the right move. It wasn't just a necessary tactical shift; it was a reminder of the risks ahead, a signal that even the most steadfast strongholds could no longer be taken for granted.

Chapter 72

Bex, Switzerland, Modern Day

The air was cool and crisp as Amelia and Gabriel stepped off the train at the Bex railway station, the towering Alps standing as a silent backdrop with their peaks dusted in snow. The sun was low and cast long shadows over the peaceful village, which was quaint and almost untouched by time. Narrow cobblestone streets wound gently between centuries-old buildings, each adorned with shutters painted in bright blues and greens. The chimneys puffed soft trails of smoke into the evening sky, and the scent of wood-burning fires mingled with the crisp, alpine air.

Amelia's gaze kept drifting past the village to the distant silhouette of the Bex Salt Mines buried deep within the mountain range ahead. From where they stood, it was just a dark, looming shape against the rugged outline of the mountains. Even from afar, she sensed its historical pull, as if the land itself guarded an ancient secret.

It was a postcard-perfect scene, but neither of them was here to sightsee. Armed with their theory and a new sense of purpose, they had come to Bex for one reason: to uncover what they believed the Alliance had hidden away decades ago.

Her mind was alive with the possibilities and hope of what they might find hidden under those peaks. She could almost see the untouched rooms, with artifacts buried for decades under layers of salt, forgotten by time and preserved in silence.

But first they needed proof.

"Do you think they're still there?" Gabriel asked, his breath visible in the cold air. There was a hint of something wistful in his voice. "Hidden somewhere, waiting for us?"

Amelia glanced at him, and for a moment, she saw the same excitement, the same determination she felt reflected in his eyes. It was a look that made her feel like they were truly partners in this. Two people chasing the same dream, driven by the same need to uncover the past. She was glad he was here with her. Her expression grew resolute, and she nodded, her voice firm. "If the Alliance was as meticulous as we believe, then yes. I think it's out there…"

They both turned back to the sight of the mine. Its sheer size could have made Amelia feel insignificant. Instead, it fueled her resolve. Something was waiting there, something hidden and precious, calling to her, daring her to unlock its mysteries. "We just have to find it," she added, the words carrying a promise.

As the evening chill settled in, they made their way to their hotel. It was a modest inn with a warm, inviting glow that spilled onto the cobblestone street from its windows. It was cozy inside and filled with the pleasant aroma of wood smoke. They checked in at the small counter, where the innkeeper greeted them with a friendly smile and handed over their keys. "It's quiet this time of year," he said warmly, his tone welcoming. "But I think you'll find the village has its own charm."

Amelia smiled back, but her mind was still on the mine, and she barely noticed as they made their way to their rooms. She could hear Gabriel's footsteps behind her, and for a brief moment, she felt a strange comfort in knowing he was there. As she unlocked the door to her room, she hesitated, glancing down the hall at him. "Tomorrow," she said softly, "we start early."

Gabriel nodded, a smile tugging at the corner of his lips. "Tomorrow!" he echoed, before disappearing into his own room.

Amelia closed her door and the solitude of her room enveloped her. She set her bag down and moved to the window, pulling the curtain back just enough to catch one last glimpse of the dark shapes in the distance. It was barely visible now, swallowed by the night, but she could still feel it— like a shadow waiting to be brought into the light.

The Municipal Administration Office on Rue Centrale in Bex was a blend of old-world charm and modern updates. The white stone building, with its quaint blue and white shutters and traditional spruce tavillon shingles, exuded a sense of timelessness. The shingles layered like the scales of a pine cone and each carried the distinct, uneven grain of hand-hewn craftsmanship. Window boxes were filled with dried berries, seed pods, and twigs, their earthy tones complementing the crisp white stone of the façade. As Amelia and Gabriel approached, the sleek, modern glass door slid open automatically with a muted hiss, a contrast to the building's classic exterior.

Inside, it was warm, a welcome change from the crisp chill outside, and carried the faint, familiar scent of aged paper and polished wood. Despite the modernized entrance, the interior felt frozen in time, like a forgotten library, filled with whispers of the past, its secrets waiting to be uncovered.

Behind a small desk near the back of the room, an elderly woman looked up from her paperwork, her glasses perched low on her nose. She wore a dark, neatly buttoned cardigan, and her silvery hair was pulled back into a tidy bun. Her expression was stern, but not unfriendly, as she regarded the two strangers who had just entered, their presence a disruption to her usual routine.

"Bonjour," she greeted, her voice firm. "How can I help you?"

Amelia stepped forward, offering a warm smile, her hands slightly outstretched to convey they meant no trouble. *"Bonjour, Madame.* We were hoping to look through some of the historical records you might have concerning the Bex Salt Mines." She paused, carefully choosing her words. "It's for a research project on the region's industrial history. We've come from France and have heard so much about this place's importance."

The woman adjusted her glasses, her sharp eyes scanning Amelia's face, then Gabriel's. "France, you say?" There was a hint of skepticism in her tone, as if weighing whether to indulge their request. "We rarely get visitors from outside the village asking for such records. They're quite old… delicate."

Gabriel, sensing the hesitation, stepped closer and spoke in a respectful tone. "We understand, and we really appreciate your time. This is a part of a larger project we're working on, one that aims to document how industries shaped the lives of communities in the region." He paused, observing her reaction. "We know it's an unusual request, but we've been following the history of certain families who were involved in these industries, particularly during the 19th and 20th centuries. The Vallois family, for example, played a significant role, and we would love to learn more."

The mention of the Vallois name seemed to catch the woman's attention. She raised an eyebrow, tilting her head slightly as if trying to recall a distant memory. "Ah, the Vallois," she said, almost to herself. "I haven't heard that name in a long time."

Amelia took the opportunity to press further. "Yes, exactly. We've found some documents in Paris that suggest the Vallois family owned part of the mines here, but there are gaps in our information. We were hoping to fill those gaps by looking at any old ledgers or property records you might have. We promise to be careful, and we'd be grateful for any assistance."

The woman's eyes softened, and a small smile tugged at the corner of her lips, though it didn't quite reach her eyes. "You're quite determined, aren't you?" she said, more amused than before. "Very well. I can give you access, but there are rules. No food, no drinks, and no ink pens —only pencils. And you handle the documents with care. Some of these papers are older than you and I combined."

"Of course," Gabriel said, nodding sincerely. "We'll be careful."

She stood up slowly, the chair creaking as she did, and motioned for them to follow her down a narrow corridor that led to a small room at the back of the building. It was dimly lit, with shelves lined floor to ceiling with thick, leather-bound folios and stacks of yellowed documents. The scent of paper and dust grew stronger, and the air felt still, like it hadn't been disturbed in years.

The woman retrieved a set of keys from her cardigan pocket and unlocked a glass-fronted cabinet, revealing a set of older books. "These are the records from the late 1800s through to the mid-20th century," she said, carefully pulling out a heavy, leather-bound book and placing it on the wooden table in the center of the room. "These will have information on property ownership, transactions, maintenance records, and anything else you might find of interest about our mines."

Amelia glanced at Gabriel, a flicker of excitement passing between them, but they kept their composure, not wanting to appear too eager. "Thank you so much," Amelia said, her voice sincere. "We truly appreciate your help."

The woman's gaze lingered on them for a moment before she nodded, satisfied. "I will be just outside. If you need anything, let me know."

"Thank you. We'll be very careful with these," Gabriel assured her.

As the door closed behind her, Amelia and Gabriel exchanged a quick, hopeful glance. The room was silent, except for the background hum of the heating system, and the stillness felt almost reverent. Amelia ran her fingers over the worn leather of one of the folios from the 1880s, then carefully opened it, the pages crackling softly as she turned them.

Hours passed in concentration, the two of them tracing through line after line of faded ink, scanning maps and property records from the case, and piecing together a story from the past. Every so often, Amelia would find a name or a date that seemed significant, and she'd quickly jot it down in her notebook. Gabriel would murmur his findings, and they'd cross-reference, slowly building a picture of how the Vallois family had come to own a section of the Bex Salt Mines.

"I found it!" Gabriel said excitedly, pointing to a particular entry from 1892. "The transfer of ownership... from the previous owner to the Vallois family. That's the confirmation we needed!"

Amelia leaned in and Gabriel gave her the stack of pages, her pulse quickening as she read the faded ink. "If this date is correct, then Antoine would have passed away not long after the purchase." She carefully turned to the next page. "After he died, it looks like ownership of the mine was split between his sons... But when Clément moved to the US, everything was left to Étienne."

She continued skimming through the stack of documents while Gabriel watched her piece together what he found. "Then, in the 1950s, the mine was claimed by the state and eventually sold off to private owners. This *definitely* ties the mine to the Vallois family! Nice find!" She offered Gabriel a warm smile, but a thought nagged at the back of her mind. "But it doesn't give us any sign of where the art could be hidden inside."

Amelia sat back, her gaze drifting to the array of records spread across the table. Earlier, while Gabriel delved into ownership documents, she had been poring over maintenance logs from the 1940s. Something about those logs had unsettled her—a small inconsistency she couldn't quite put her finger on.

She stood abruptly, her chair scraping softly against the floor. "Give me a minute," she said, her voice thoughtful.

Returning to the pile of logs she'd set aside, Amelia felt a familiar stir of anticipation as she flipped through the pages again. Her eyes scanned the columns of meticulous handwriting—dates, signatures, notes on equipment repairs. Every entry reflected the miners' and Cantonal Authority's commitment to compliance, documenting every detail with painstaking precision as required by cantonal law.

Except for one area.

Her finger paused over an entry—or rather, the absence of one. 'Chamber 226B' was listed, but the notes were sparse, almost nonexistent compared to the exhaustive records from other chambers.

Her heart beat a little faster. Could this be something?

Amelia gathered the logs and walked back to Gabriel, who looked up with curiosity. "While you were confirming the ownership, I was reviewing these maintenance records," she began, laying the documents between them. "I assumed the Vallois family owned the mine during the 1940s, and your find confirms that."

She flipped through more records, her brow furrowing. "However, while looking, I noticed an anomaly..."

Gabriel's eyes sharpened, catching her shift in tone. "What do you mean?"

Amelia scanned the documents again, her finger trailing over the neat lines of text. "I'm still piecing this together, but these records are detailed—there are logs for maintenance, inspections, and routine safety checks," she said slowly, her eyes narrowing. "Most chambers of the mine have extensive notes. But there's something strange after 1941. Look here," she said, pointing to the log. "'Chamber 226B.' Its records seem to abruptly stop. After that, there's almost nothing—just brief mentions, far less than any of the others."

Gabriel looked thoughtful. "Maybe it wasn't a priority? Some areas might not have seen much activity or needed regular upkeep."

"Possibly," Amelia agreed, though her tone was cautious. She flipped back through the pages, her finger pausing at a sparse entry. "But even sections listed as 'inactive,' like this old mined-out area, still have regular logs—basic inspections, safety checks, the kind of routine oversight you'd expect with local ordinances. '226B' is different. There's barely anything, just vague mentions... and then nothing at all after 1941.

And look at this—" she tapped the edge of a plat map. "I can't find '226B' listed anywhere on the official records filed with Bex. It doesn't fit."

Gabriel leaned in, studying the pages with her. "1941… During the war. So you think it was intentional? To keep it under the radar?"

Amelia nodded slowly, a spark of excitement rising in her chest. "Exactly. It's like they wanted it acknowledged just enough to seem irrelevant, but not enough to raise any suspicion. *Hidden in plain sight.*"

They exchanged a look, the hint of a shared understanding sparking between them. It was a subtle, almost hidden detail, but it felt significant. Amelia felt a rush of hope, a sense that they were closer to uncovering something crucial.

They continued digging through the documents, searching for anything that might reveal more. Hours passed, the room hushed except for the steady shuffling of pages, until Gabriel's hands paused on a sheet buried beneath a stack of old mining reports.

"Amelia, come look at this," he said, his voice hushed, like he was afraid to disturb the delicate balance of their find.

Amelia leaned over, squinting to see a rough, worn, hand-drawn map—dated 1904, its lines faded but still discernible. Scribbled notes crowded the margins, cryptic and barely legible, hinting at something out of the ordinary. But Gabriel pointed to the more relevant object that caught his eye—a small, tucked-away area, separated from the rest of the more clearly defined sections. "Look… '226B!'"

Amelia gasped as she held the fragile sheet while Gabriel quickly fetched the official plat map from the table. They compared the two, side by side, under the soft, yellow light. "That section isn't on the newer mine plans. They either excluded it on purpose... or didn't even know it existed!"

Amelia's heart quickened as she studied the old map, her finger tracing the aged lines around the mysterious section. "You think this could be it?" she said softly, her voice tinged with awe. "A part of the mine purposely excluded from modern records? Could '226B' just have been dried up?"

"That is what I wondered too," Gabriel spoke, his expression serious. "But look here." He tapped the modern map spread beside them. "There are other areas clearly labeled as 'closed sections.' Yet there's no mention of '226B' anywhere on this map."

He leaned back slightly and scanned the two maps again. "If these paintings are still missing, it means nobody from the Alliance was around to recover them—especially after the mine passed to the state in the 1950s. If this section really *was* used to hide them, it would have likely been hidden well enough to prevent snooping eyes. And if that's the case, it might have also been hidden well enough to escape detection, even during a modern survey!"

His voice gained a note of excitement as he gestured toward the old map. This... this feels like a breadcrumb to me!"

They exchanged another look filled with cautious optimism. These were subtle clues, barely more than suggestions, but they *could* lead them exactly where they needed to go. Amelia's pulse quickened, sensing they were on the verge of something monumental.

As they carefully completed their notes and began reassembling the folios, the woman from the front desk reappeared, glancing at the open book on the table. "Did you find what you were looking for?"

Amelia gently closed the remaining books and nodded. "Yes, we did. More than we expected, actually."

The woman smiled, a glint of curiosity in her eyes. "Good. It's nice to see the old records being of use. And to such a beautiful young couple. So many stories here, just waiting for someone to find them."

Amelia smiled at the woman's comment, feeling a faint blush creep up her cheeks. "Thank you," she said, her voice soft but sincere. "We'll be back tomorrow, I'm sure."

As they stepped outside, the crisp evening greeted them, sharp and invigorating after the warmth of the archive room. The sun was now low on the horizon and cast the village in a soft amber light. Amelia and Gabriel fell into step beside each other, their footsteps crunching lightly on the cobblestones, the excitement from their discovery still vibrant between them.

For a moment, neither of them spoke, both lost in thought. Then Gabriel glanced over at Amelia, his expression warm, a hint of a smile tugging at his lips. "A beautiful young couple, huh?" he teased, his tone light, but his eyes searching hers.

Amelia laughed, shaking her head, though she felt the blush deepen. "She must have meant you and the books," she said, trying to sound casual, but her voice held a playful edge.

Gabriel chuckled, and for a brief second, their eyes met, the teasing giving way to something deeper, unspoken. It was just a flicker, a moment suspended between them, but it lingered, even as they turned their attention back to the path ahead.

"We're onto something," Amelia said, her voice filled with eagerness. "This isn't just a theory anymore. We have proof. Now we just have to find what we're looking for."

Gabriel glanced up at the darkening silhouette of the mountains, the mine hidden somewhere within. "Then tomorrow we head to the mine," he said, with certainty hardening his voice.

"But first, we need to figure out how to get inside."

Chapter 73

The next morning, Amelia and Gabriel took a taxi to the Bex Salt Mines' field offices, just a short drive from the village center. The offices, nestled at the foot of the mountains, were housed in an unassuming mobile building that blended well into the rugged landscape. A sleek, relatively new sign out front read "Keller Group AG," marking the Swiss corporation's recent acquisition of the property from the Montrose family in an all-cash deal. Despite the change in ownership, most of the original staff had been retained, maintaining continuity in the mine's operations.

As they stepped out of the taxi, the crisp morning air was sharp with the scent of pine and cold, and the rising sun cast a pale, diffused light across the scene, making the frost sparkle like tiny crystals underfoot. They exchanged a glance, silently encouraging themselves for what would be an important, and likely challenging, conversation.

Inside, the offices were quiet, the kind of stillness that comes with early morning routines not yet disrupted by the day's work. The reception area was small, with a few mismatched chairs lining the wall. A counter was cluttered with safety pamphlets, maps, and a stack of worn, laminated brochures detailing the history of the mine. There was a faint smell of coffee mingling with the scent of dust and old wood, and Amelia could hear the low hum of machinery somewhere deeper within the building.

After checking in, they didn't have to wait long before they were greeted by Dieter, a gruff, middle-aged man who clearly wasn't in the mood for small talk. He emerged from an adjoining room, wiping his hands on a rag, and his eyes narrowed slightly as he took in their appearance. His hair was graying at the temples, cut close to his scalp, and his lined face bore the unmistakable look of someone who had seen his fair share of schemes. He folded his arms across his broad chest in an almost defensive gesture, as if daring them to make their case.

"So, what can I do for you two?" Dieter asked, his Swiss accent thick as his eyes darted between them with a mix of curiosity and suspicion. "You're researchers, huh? Don't see many of those poking around my mines—especially this time of year."

Gabriel stepped forward, trying to project a calm, professional demeanor. He had rehearsed this in his head, knowing that any slip-up could shut the conversation down before it even started. "We appreciate you taking the time to see us," he began, his tone measured. "We're historians, working on a broader project documenting regional industries and their impact over the last century. Part of our research has led us to the older sections of the Bex Salt Mines, and we were hoping to gain supervised access to the 200 Deck, just to explore a few specific areas for historical context."

Dieter's eyes narrowed, and he shifted his weight, leaning against the counter as he assessed them. "This is a commercial operation," he said flatly, not bothering to mask his skepticism. "The chambers you're talking about have been closed for years. There's a reason for that—safety. We don't just open up those areas for curious visitors."

Amelia could feel the resistance in his voice, but she stepped in, her own tone calm but firm. "We understand the safety concerns, and we're not asking to disrupt anything or put anyone at risk. We've done our homework, and we believe there are parts of the old mine with significant historical value, particularly related to the Vallois family's involvement. We're just requesting a chance to look around—under your supervision, of course."

She carefully avoided mentioning anything that might raise red flags—no hints of hidden treasures, no allusions to wartime secrets. They were just two historians, seeking to uncover a piece of forgotten history. It was a delicate line to walk, and she knew one misstep could make Dieter suspicious of their plans.

Dieter's expression remained impassive, but there was a hint of curiosity in his eyes when she mentioned the Vallois name. "The Vallois?" he repeated, almost testing the name on his tongue. "I've heard of them. Old mining family. But that was decades ago... What exactly are you expecting to find? Because if it's valuables, you're better off looking elsewhere. Anything worth anything would have been removed long before now."

"Our interest is academic," Gabriel said, carefully keeping his tone steady and professional. "We're trying to piece together a historical narrative that hasn't been fully explored. Any findings would be part of our broader research, and we'd be happy to credit the Keller Group in any publications. Plus," he added, "highlighting the mine's role in the local history could be good publicity, especially if we uncover something that adds to the story of the canton."

Dieter's eyes remained narrowed, his expression unreadable. The idea of free publicity seemed to have caught his attention, but there was still caution in his gaze, as if he was waiting for the catch. "It's not just a matter of opening a door," he said slowly. "The 200 Deck hasn't been maintained for years. We'd have to take precautions, limit your access, and it would be under strict supervision. I'm not even sure if the new board would allow it."

Gabriel nodded, sensing a small opening. "We understand, and we're willing to abide by whatever conditions you set. We won't take any unnecessary risks, and if at any point it seems unsafe, we'll stop. We're here to learn, not to disrupt."

Dieter regarded them for a long moment, his eyes searching their faces as if trying to see past their words to their true intentions. The room felt suddenly smaller, the air thick with doubts. Finally, he let out a slow breath, unfolding his arms. "I'll see what I can do. No promises, but I'll talk to the board and let you know."

Amelia felt a small sense of relief, but it was quickly tempered by the uncertainty hanging over them. "Thank you, we appreciate it," she said, maintaining a polite smile, even as her mind raced ahead, wondering what their next move would be if the answer was no.

As Dieter turned away, already moving to the back offices, Gabriel caught Amelia's eye, his expression momentarily slipping from the calm professionalism he'd maintained. There was a silent exchange between them—hinting at everything they'd planned for, everything they'd hoped to uncover, hinged on a decision that was now out of their hands.

They stepped out of the office, the chilly morning air biting at their cheeks again as the door swung shut behind them. For a moment, they stood still, letting the chill settle around them, neither one willing to break the silence. Then Gabriel exhaled a slow, measured breath. "If they say no—"

"They can't say no," Amelia interrupted, her voice firmer than she felt. "This is our best lead, Gabriel." She glanced back at the building, her gaze narrowing with persistence. "We're so close."

Gabriel gave a small, tight nod, but his unease lingered. As they walked back to the village, their steps fell in sync, each echoing the other. Yet in the heavy silence between them, one thought loomed: if the board refused, the answers they sought—and everything they were chasing—might slip beyond their reach forever.

Chapter 74

The days of waiting felt endless, each one stretching into the next as Amelia and Gabriel tried to keep their minds occupied. They pored over old maps and documents, double-checking coordinates and re-reading notes, preparing themselves for what they hoped would be their next step. When the call finally came, it was late in the afternoon, and Dieter's voice was as short and no-nonsense as ever. "You've been granted limited access. One hour, supervised, and you'll follow all safety protocols. If there's any sign of instability, we're pulling you out. Understood?"

"Yes, thank you!" Amelia replied, her relief noticeable. "We appreciate it!"

The following morning was colder still, the frost thicker on the ground as they stood at the entrance to the mine, a mix of anticipation and nerves hanging between them. They were provided helmets, headlamps, and heavy jackets, and the gear was both cumbersome and oddly comforting. The weight of it reminded them of the seriousness of what they were about to do. This wasn't just a theory anymore. This was real. They were going in.

Gabriel adjusted his helmet while giving Amelia a reassuring nod. "Ready?" he asked, his breath visible in the cold morning air. Then, with a playful glint in his eye, he added, "Just remember, if you hear me scream, it's probably because I saw a mouse or something."

Amelia couldn't help but chuckle at the comment, meeting his gaze and feeling her nerves soften a bit. She tightened the strap under her chin, feeling the chill of the metal buckle against her skin, and nodded back with confidence. "Let's do this."

After a brief chat with a few workers, they were directed to the shaft entrance. Lukas, the guide assigned to them, was already waiting, his expression a mix of boredom and impatience. He was a stocky man, his face weathered from years of work underground, and he didn't seem thrilled about the assignment. "You've got one hour," he said, his tone curt. "Stick close, and don't touch anything you don't have to. This isn't a museum tour."

———————

The descent into the mine was slow and deliberate as the narrow shaft seemed to close in around them. Though it had been cold outside, the temperature here, influenced by the geothermal gradient, grew slightly warmer—still chilly, but no longer freezing. The metallic clang of their boots against the grated stairs rang out in the silence, occasionally joined by the distant bass drone of mining equipment coming up from under them. With each step, it felt like they were descending into a hidden world, one that had been forgotten by time but was still very much alive with secrets.

Amelia could feel her heart rate increasing as they walked, each step bringing them closer to the truth she hoped lay hidden in this space. She glanced at Gabriel, who gave her a reassuring nod with the same blend of excitement and caution. They couldn't afford to fail—not this time.

As they left the shaft behind and ventured deeper into the mine, Lukas led them down a series of winding tunnels. Their headlamps cast narrow beams of light that illuminated the salt-encrusted walls with a ghostly shimmer. When the light hit the salt crystals just right, it refracted, scattering into tiny patterns that gave the eerie impression of a subterranean disco ball. Each turn was a step further into a labyrinth as the paths continued to narrow and then widen again. It felt almost like the tunnels were breathing. Lukas occasionally paused to consult a worn, laminated map, its edges nicked from years of use.

"Most of these tunnels haven't been used in decades," he said, his tone almost indifferent. "Back in the day, they used to haul salt from every corner of this place, but now the active decks are mostly deeper. Some of these sections don't even show up on modern maps. Anything that doesn't produce anymore? The company doesn't bother maintaining it. If it's not making money, it's not worth the effort."

Amelia's pulse quickened at the mention of the neglected areas. "Not on modern maps," she repeated, trying to sound casual, though the excitement behind her words was hard to conceal. "That makes sense for a place that's been around this long. Old sections get forgotten, I suppose."

"Yeah," Lukas replied with a nonchalant shrug. "Most of it's probably just empty shafts, dead ends, or old equipment left to age."

As they continued walking, the tunnels began to slope downward and the atmosphere inside started to feel thicker. Their path seemed to weave through the mountain itself, twisting through levels that were stacked like the floors of an underground building. Lukas guided them toward what he called the "200 Deck," a term that seemed both official and cryptic. Amelia couldn't help but ask.

"What exactly is the 200 Deck?" she said, glancing at the map in Lukas's hands.

Lukas didn't look up. "It's just a name for this level of the mine. Think of it as the second major depth or tier. Salt mines are layered, with different decks or levels where different veins of salt were extracted over the years. The numbering helps keep track of which sections are where. The 200 Deck sits about two hundred meters below the highest point of the old shaft. That's where they started mining back when this place was in full operation."

Gabriel listened intently, nodding as he took in the information. "So each deck would have its own network of tunnels?"

"Yeah," Lukas confirmed. "You've got main shafts that run vertically, and then the decks branch out horizontally from them." He adjusted his headlamp, the beam catching the salt-encrusted walls. "The 200 Deck is one of the older ones, mostly carved out in the late 18th century. It's been inactive for a while, so it's a bit of a relic. But that's where you'll find some of the more interesting, older sections... I guess like the ones you're interested in."

The deeper they went, the more the mine felt like a relic of a forgotten time. The walls were rough and veined with streaks of salt that glittered under their headlamps, creating a strange, ethereal glow. Old wooden supports, darkened and warped with age, lined the tunnel at intervals, occasionally creaking slightly under the weight of the rock above. Here and there, metal tools lay abandoned, like the miners had just set them down one day and never returned.

Amelia's thoughts brimmed with everything they had read and cross-referenced over the past few days. She kept her eyes peeled, searching for anything that might signal they were on the right track.

They reached a junction where the tunnel branched into two paths. Lukas paused to study his map, tracing his finger over the laminated surface. "We'll take the left fork," he said, glancing up. "It should be close now."

Amelia's headlamp swung instinctively toward the right fork, her curiosity piqued as she tried to peer into the shadows. "What's down there?" she asked, motioning toward the right.

Lukas followed her gesture and glanced down at his map before responding. "It's an old maintenance shaft," he answered, pausing briefly and expecting her next question. "But it's too narrow for our equipment, so we don't use it much anymore." His gaze shifted back to the path ahead as he finished speaking.

They continued down the left path, and after another minute, spotted an old, galvanized metal sign attached to the wall. It was barely legible under layers of sediment and a fine crust of salt. Lukas brushed away what he could with the back of his glove, revealing the faded numbers beneath.

"201," Lukas read aloud, glancing back at them. "That's the start of this section."

Amelia felt a jolt of anticipation as she looked at the sign. "We need to get to the 226 markers," she said, trying to keep the eagerness out of her voice. "How far is that?"

Lukas checked his map, squinting slightly. "It's a bit of a walk, but not too far. We'll pass a few other chambers on the way—205, 210, 218 —and then we should hit 226."

They followed him deeper into the tunnel, passing the chambers as they increased gradually, their numbers stenciled onto metallic signs that clung to the walls. Each step brought them closer, each turn heightened the suspense, and Amelia's heart raced a little faster as Lukas announced the numbers.

"210," Lukas said as they passed a junction where the path split towards the chamber. "We're getting closer."

They kept moving, the tunnel curving and narrowing, their footsteps muted in the enclosed space. "218," he said, brushing off a layer of dust from a faded sign. Amelia and Gabriel exchanged a hopeful glance. The numbers were climbing, and so was their excitement.

Finally, as the anticipation was about to reach a maximum, they turned a corner, and Lukas slowed down. "226," he read aloud, his voice absorbed by the salt-coated walls. "Here you go."

Amelia's headlamp illuminated the sign, and a surge of enthusiasm shot through her. "226!" she exclaimed. Her voice was bright with hope, though a mix of confusion crept in as she scanned the area. She turned to Gabriel, catching the way his eyes were already darting around, searching for something. He was looking for it, too.

She turned to Lukas, her voice steady but curious. "There's supposed to be a 226B. Do you know where that is?" Her gaze shifted back to the walls, scanning them eagerly, her thoughts racing to understand why it wasn't immediately visible.

Lukas shook his head and joined in, his headlamp sweeping across the smooth, featureless walls. Apart from the single sign, there was nothing else to indicate another chamber. He walked a bit further down the tunnel, stopping just shy of the next marker at 232, before turning back with a slight shrug. "If there is a 226B, it's not marked," he said, his voice neutral while referencing his laminated charts. "And I don't see it on my map, either. Could've been sealed off or collapsed a long time ago."

Gabriel's eyes met Amelia's, a silent understanding passing between them. This was exactly what they had hoped for—and feared. A section without a clear mark, something hidden just out of reach, yet almost within grasp. "If it's not listed, there's a chance no one's touched it in years," Gabriel said out of earshot of Lukas, his voice hushed, almost covertly.

Lukas kept looking at his map. "If there was a 226B, it *probably* would have been documented somewhere, but not everything was always recorded accurately back in the day. Things get lost, especially when sections were decommissioned or forgotten."

Amelia's thoughts spun. They were close, but, once again, they felt like everything was on the verge of slipping through the cracks. She stepped closer to the wall next to the 226 sign, her headlamp illuminating the rough, uneven surface, looking for any signs that something might have been covered or obscured. But there was nothing—just the same cold, featureless wall staring back at her, refusing to give up its secrets.

She glanced over at Lukas, trying to sound casual, though her heart was pounding. "Would you be able to unlock 226? Just so we could have a quick look inside—for our research? I'm curious to see what it looks like in there."

Lukas raised an eyebrow, a hint of amusement creeping into his otherwise neutral expression. *"Es git kei Schlösser a dene Türe, Weib,"* he said with a dry laugh in Swiss German, his voice echoing slightly in the tunnel. "There aren't any locks on these chamber doors, lady," he repeated, shaking his head like the idea was absurd. "Nothing in there worth locking up. The doors are mainly for airflow and safety, to control the environment within different chambers. The only locks are on the shaft doors at each deck. Once you're in, you have access to everything on that level."

Seeing they were not amused with his snarky comments, he stepped forward and placed a hand on the cold metal of the door, exchanging a quick, silent look with them. "I can open it, but don't get your hopes up. If 226B is an actual chamber, it would've shown up on these maps."

Without waiting for a response, Lukas gripped the handle and gave it a firm tug. The hinges protested, creaking loudly, and the noise echoed down the tunnel. It was like the door itself was fighting against him, groaning with age and neglect from decades of disuse. With a final, reluctant screech, it gave way, and they all stepped inside.

The 226 chamber opened up before them, in striking contrast to the narrow, confining tunnels they had just navigated. Their headlamps pierced the darkness, and the beams bounced off the light-colored walls, scattering to create a soft glow. It almost appeared the space was lit by an unseen source. The chamber was vast and its tall walls curved gently upwards, almost imperceptibly, giving the impression of a massive dome overhead. Amelia exhaled in awe and her breath echoed softly in the stillness. For a moment, the silence was so profound that it felt like they were the last three people left in the world.

Lukas stood in the doorway while Amelia and Gabriel moved forward cautiously, their footsteps echoing in the silence. Each crunch against the salt-flaked floor was amplified in the still air—like walking on a snow dusting that had partially melted and frozen over again. Except for this, the room was eerily quiet. Amelia's breath was shallow, and she could hear the soft rustle of her jacket as she inhaled. She glanced at Gabriel, who was sweeping his light across the chamber, methodically tracing the outlines of the walls, the floor, and the ceiling, searching for something familiar to anchor to.

Amelia's headlamp flickered, catching a glimpse of old, rusted equipment abandoned near one wall—buckets, rusted pickaxes, and a heavy, dented wheelbarrow that looked as though it hadn't been touched in decades. She imagined the miners who had once worked here, their briny sweat mixing with the salt in the air, clinging indistinguishably to their skin. Their voices must have echoed through this space, now silent and long forgotten. A thin layer of salt coated the tools, its crystals glinting faintly under the beam, as if nature had slowly begun reclaiming them, pulling them back into the earth.

Gabriel's light shifted upward, catching the remnants of wooden beams crisscrossing above. They were splintered and sagging under the weight of time, but still standing after a century—there was a good chance they would continue to hold for another hour or two. Amelia followed his light, her eyes tracing the way the beams disappeared into the darkness. The whole chamber felt alive, like it had been sleeping for years, now waking up for this very moment.

As they ventured further in side by side, their lights swept over patches of wall coated in thick salt deposits. Jagged and crystalline, the formations shimmered, catching the light in dazzling, almost hypnotic patterns. Amelia moved slowly, intimately, as her beam bounced and shifted across the rough, uneven surfaces. She half-expected to find another abandoned piece of equipment or maybe some remnants of old mining work, but the wall was mostly bare—a rough, pockmarked canvas that told no stories.

Then, her light illuminated something different, and she stopped in her tracks. Gabriel must have seen it too because he immediately swung his headlamp back, catching on the same patch of wall that stood out—oddly smooth, almost unnaturally so, like a thin layer of ice had started to melt and flow down its surface. Unlike the rest of the chamber, this section was glossy and reflective, almost like it had been polished. Amelia's pulse quickened as she stepped closer, her hand reaching out instinctively.

"What is this?" she whispered, more to herself than to Gabriel. She moved the light slowly, tracing the contours of the strange, sleek patch, noting how it seemed to glisten, almost wet, in the light. What she saw was subtle, but definitely there—a hint of a line running vertically down the wall, just visible under the thin sheen. She leaned closer, squinting, and saw that the salt here was different, smoother, more compacted, as if it had been carefully layered and fused.

Gabriel joined her, his light focused on the same spot. "It's not natural," he murmured, his voice tight with anticipation. "This isn't like the rest of the wall. It almost looks... sealed."

Amelia's mind raced, her heart pounding against her ribcage. "What if this is 226B? A sub-chamber of 226, hiding behind here?" she breathed, barely daring to believe it. They exchanged a look, a flicker of shared excitement tempered by the reality of their situation.

"We can't do anything right now," Gabriel said, glancing over his shoulder, where Lukas's silhouette loomed in the dim light far behind them. "Not with him here."

Amelia's eyes looked at Lukas and then darted back to the glossy patch of wall, the urge to reach out and start chipping away almost overwhelming. "What if we can't come back? What if this is our only chance?" she whispered, the fear of missing their moment creeping into her voice.

Gabriel's jaw tightened, his mind visibly racing as he considered their options. "If we want to keep this a secret, we can't have Lukas or anyone else watching us," he said, his tone resolute. "We need to come back alone. Somehow."

Amelia's gaze lingered on the wall, her pulse pounding in her ears, a mix of frustration and urgency bubbling inside her. She knew he was right, but the thought of walking away now, without knowing, felt impossible. They had to find a way. She turned to Gabriel, her eyes determined. "Then we better figure out how," she said, her voice tight with defiance.

The sound of Lukas's footsteps approaching snapped them back to the moment. "Everything okay?" he called out, his tone casual but laced with impatience.

Gabriel glanced at Amelia one last time, then forced a smile as he turned to Lukas. "Yeah, we're good," he said, his voice steady. "Just... interesting patterns on the wall. We're done here."

Lukas nodded, and all three began heading back toward the door.

But as they followed Lukas out of the chamber, the strange, smooth wall stayed with Amelia, like a puzzle piece that didn't quite fit. They needed to see it again, and this time, they couldn't afford any interruptions. Breaking rules had never been her way, but now it felt almost inevitable. They would have to do whatever it took.

As they entered the main shaft, Gabriel slowed and turned back to Amelia while Lukas continued ahead. His voice was low, almost conspiratorial, as he mouthed each word deliberately for emphasis. "We'll come back," he said, reassuring her.

Amelia met his gaze and replied softly but firmly, leaving no room for doubt.

"Yes, we will."

Chapter 75

The steady hum of machinery faded as the team descended into the lower decks of the Bex Salt Mines. Each step took them deeper into a world of rock and salt, their headlamps revealing glittering deposits in some places and rough, dark stone in others.

They reached the entrance to the 200 Deck, and Arnaud gave a single nod to the others, signaling it was time. For two and a half years, the Alliance had secretly preserved a massive cache of cultural treasures here, all while spreading carefully constructed rumors that the salt veins in this section had run dry. As expected, few questioned such claims—salt mining was dangerous enough, and no one would dare venture down to the 200 Deck without good reason. Today, they would seal the chamber—and their secret—ensuring their work remained buried in both salt and silence.

Approaching the 226 chamber, Lucien paused to inspect the surrounding tunnels. "You chose well," he said to Arnaud, a hint of fatherly pride in his voice. "Close enough to the mountain's edge for a quick escape, but far enough to blend into the maze."

Arnaud nodded, placing a gloved hand against the entrance wall. "It had to be 226B," he replied. "From here, we can reach the air shafts if we need an alternative exit. If anything goes wrong... if there's even a hint of discovery, we can dig in from the mountainside and move everything out. We have options!"

Étienne studied the deck with reverence, the very heart of the venture—his venture—that had brought the Vallois family a steady flow of capital over the past four decades. The toll of the last two years was etched deeply into his face, and he knew, with a finality, that this was likely the last time he would stand in this place.

He slowly traced the wall with his fingers, feeling the rough salt and stone before looking up. "Let's finish this," he said to Lucien. Nadejda and Arnaud had already closed off the other sections of the 200 Deck, securing each door to make the area appear fully abandoned. Now, only 226 A and B remained—its 486 paintings safely stacked inside, hidden away in a quiet, dormant sleep.

After returning, Nadejda gave a signal and everyone gathered at the B chamber's entrance. She closed the door and Arnaud carefully began layering dampened salt dust over the doorway, detailing each application to match the rugged texture of the surrounding chamber walls. The scrape of metal tools echoed through the stillness as the group worked to pack and spread the salt like plaster, patting it firmly to mimic the natural contours of the rock. After the last layer was applied and troweled, Lucien stepped forward with a water sprayer, misting the fresh salt until it shimmered under the droplets. They watched in silence as the salt dried and fused, blending seamlessly into the rock, and obscuring any trace of the hidden chamber behind it.

"Unrecognizable," Étienne remarked, with satisfaction in his tone. "If anyone enters, they'll see nothing but the sides of this chamber. A solid, natural wall." He looked at the others with a drop in his tone. "Even after we're gone."

Nadejda's gaze lingered on the sealed wall, absorbing the gravity of what they had accomplished. They had done it. They had protected the paintings, and with them, the legacies and stories captured in each brushstroke. For the first time since Sergei's death, she felt a sense of resolution. This was his legacy—a promise she had once made to him. Yet, with this protection came the cost of their silence—a silence they all must carry until a better tomorrow.

Arnaud's voice broke the stillness, steady and certain. "We've held this secret under threat of capture and death. But even when the war ends, when the world no longer needs to hide, we may still need to carry it. There are no guarantees." He paused, letting his words sink in. "Until these treasures are returned, until our fight ends... we remain silent."

He looked at Étienne, Nadejda, and Lucien, each showing a shared understanding that their efforts were meant for a future they might never see.

As they prepared to leave, Lucien stepped forward, carefully spreading the final layer of salt paste over the last visible seam. He worked methodically, troweling the surface until no hint of a crack remained. By the time he stepped back, the wall was smooth and solid—a silent guardian of their hidden legacy.

One by one, they turned and made their way out of 226A.

And as the chamber door swung shut behind them, they exited, leaving behind nothing but the impenetrable silence of a salt mine.

Paris, August 1943

Nadejda felt a calm as she returned to her study on Rue de Rivoli at the Vallois mansion, the familiar walls and shelves grounding her as she reflected on their last mission. The art was safe now, hidden away, secured from the world. Yet the memory of their work lingered heavily as she settled back into her routine.

A stillness filled the room as she leaned back in a chaise, her mind drifting over the cataloged entries and names she had come to know so well. Through them, they had preserved more than just art. These pieces carried fragments of history, lives, and legacies that might have otherwise been lost to the war.

Sergei had always believed that art was humanity's voice against oblivion, a declaration that beauty and individuality could endure even in the face of oppression. In these safeguarded masterpieces, his voice—and theirs—would live on, guiding a future they might never see but had dared to believe in.

With that, Nadejda took a steadying breath and allowed herself a moment of peace.

But her eyes had barely closed when muffled voices drifted up from downstairs, followed by the faint sound of footsteps in the hallway outside her door. She tensed a bit, her eyes snapping to the entrance. It was late, and no one was expected. Rising cautiously, she moved to the door, opening it a crack to peer into the hall.

A figure in the shadows stepped forward, his face obscured by the dim light. "Madame Shchukin?" he asked.

"Yes," she replied, her voice steady but wary.

"I'm sorry to disturb you, but your housekeeper let me in." The man slipped a thin envelope from his coat pocket, holding it out to her. "An important message," he murmured, his eyes darting down the hallway. "From an associate of your late husband."

Her heart leapt, a rush of cold racing through her veins as she took the envelope. She could feel the importance of the words within, the sense of something vital, something dangerous.

With a quick nod, the man turned and disappeared, leaving her alone in the quiet hallway, the envelope heavy in her hands. She slipped back into the room, breaking the seal, her hands trembling as she unfolded the letter.

She scanned it, her eyes darting over the hurried scrawl—until she froze, eyes locked on the last line:

"I think we've located Sergei's collection."

Chapter 76

The chill of the night air clung to Amelia's skin, seeping through her jacket as she and Gabriel stood at the entrance to the mine's supplementary maintenance shaft. She glanced at her watch: 20:00—8 p.m. The automatic lights had finally turned off, just as they had planned. After days of careful preparation, Amelia had stepped far outside of her comfort zone, agreeing to something she never thought she'd do. Now they were alone—no Lukas to watch over their every move, no sharp eyes to scrutinize their motives. But getting to this point hadn't been easy.

Dieter hadn't approved this particular visit; in fact, he'd been very adamant about not granting any more access after their first tour. "You've had your look," he'd said, his tone curt. "One hour with Lukas, and you're done. No more special access." But Amelia and Gabriel weren't ready to give up. They *had* to get back in—somehow.

Over the next few days, they spent their evenings in a small, dimly lit Beiz in Bex, the local tavern where the mine workers often gathered after their shifts. Working on a hunch, it was here, over the clink of beer glasses and low murmurs, that they overheard the kind of conversations they'd hoped for. Several mine workers were grumbling about the new Keller Group's cost-cutting measures—longer shifts, reduced breaks, and the feeling that they were being squeezed dry to maximize shareholder profits.

"They don't care about us," one of the older men had said, shaking his head. "It's all about the bottom line. We're just numbers to them."

Gabriel caught Amelia's eye, a trace of understanding passing between them. This could be the opening they needed. If the workers felt undervalued and overlooked, maybe they'd be willing to bend the rules for a little extra cash.

The next evening, Amelia and Gabriel returned around 7 o'clock, blending into the background as they watched the miners filter in after their shifts. It was smoky and loud, a refuge where the workers could unwind, their laughter and complaints mixing with the clink of beer glasses.

Gabriel specifically noticed a younger man—one of the shift workers they'd met on their guided visit of the mine. He seemed isolated, hunched over his drink, staring into the amber liquid as if lost in thought. Over the past few days, they had seen him in passing in the Beiz, always with the same weary, detached look, and always leaving just a bit earlier than the others. This was the moment Gabriel had been waiting for.

He signaled to Amelia, who gave a small nod of encouragement, and slowly made his way over. It was crucial not to seem too eager, too desperate. Sliding onto the barstool next to the man, Gabriel took a moment before speaking, casually ordering a drink and glancing around the room like he was just passing the time.

"Long day?" he said eventually, his tone light, almost sympathetic.

The man turned, clearly surprised to be addressed by a stranger. But he recognized Gabriel from their polite interactions at the mine a few days ago, a fleeting acknowledgment that now served as a thin bridge. "Yeah," he said, voice low and flat, like the day had drained him. "Always is."

Gabriel sipped his drink, nodding slowly. "I can't imagine it's easy," he said, his words chosen carefully, "especially with the way things have been lately. Heard the Keller Group's made a lot of changes. Tough for the people who've been around longer, I'd guess."

The worker's expression darkened, but he didn't respond right away. Gabriel let the silence hang, giving him the space to speak if he wanted. Finally, the man scoffed, shaking his head slightly. "Yeah, well... they care more about squeezing a few more francs out of the mine than about us. We're just here to keep the gears running, far as they're concerned."

Gabriel caught the bitter edge in his voice and leaned in slightly, lowering his own voice. "I've been noticing that. Seen it before, too—new management comes in, and suddenly the people who've been holding the place together are the ones getting squeezed." He paused, letting his words sink in. "Not fair, is it?"

The man glanced at him, a glimmer of curiosity crossing his tired eyes. "You seem to know a lot about it... for an outsider."

Gabriel offered a small smile. "I've been around enough to know when people are getting a raw deal… And that's why I wanted to talk to you." He hesitated, as if debating whether to go on, then continued. "I'm not looking to cause trouble, just… hoping you might help us out. *Off* the record."

The worker looked confused, suspicion creeping in. "Help you? How?"

Gabriel shifted, leaning in closer, his tone calm but sincere. "I know this is asking a lot, but we were only given an hour in the mine, and we need more time. Nothing that would cause any issues, just a couple of hours to finish up our research—without interruption… with no one looking over our shoulders. I understand any possible concern, but I can make it worth your while." He slid an envelope from his pocket, letting the man catch a glimpse of the cash inside, enough to hint at a generous offer.

The worker hesitated, his eyes darting between the envelope and Gabriel's face, as if trying to gauge the seriousness of his intentions. "And what exactly do you need from me?" he murmured, almost reluctantly, under the chatter around them.

Gabriel leaned in slightly, keeping his tone steady, casual, like he was asking for nothing more than a small favor. "To borrow your shaft keys," he said. "Just for a few hours tonight. We'll be in and out—two, maybe three hours, tops. No mess, no problems. You'll have them back before sunrise."

"I could lose my job!" he said, his voice low but edged with anxiety, his eyes darting around the room as if expecting someone to overhear. Despite the protest, Gabriel noticed a bit of doubt. It was a subtle shift in the man's posture that suggested he was considering it, caught between caution and curiosity.

"I understand," Gabriel said softly, leaning in just a bit closer. "And I wouldn't ask if it wasn't important. But let's be honest, the Keller Group isn't exactly bending over backward for its workers. I've heard the talk— the longer shifts, the tighter rules. They're squeezing every bit of profit they can, and it's you who feels the strain. What I want to do… it won't affect them, won't even be on their radar. It's just a few hours, and it could make things a bit easier for you. No one else has to know."

The man's eyes lingered on the envelope, his fingers twitching as he weighed the decision. "And if anyone finds out?" the man asked, still skeptical but now curious.

"No one will," Gabriel assured him, his tone earnest. "We're not here to cause trouble, just to finish what we started. You'll have the keys back by tonight. No fuss, no mess. This is just between us, and it'll stay that way. You're helping me, and I'm helping you. That's all."

Gabriel could see the struggle—the worker's eyes darting around the room, searching for an excuse to refuse. But after a tense pause, he reached out, took the envelope, and slipped it into his pocket with a small, almost imperceptible nod. Carefully, he passed a key ring with three keys on it to Gabriel. "You've got three hours," he said, his voice low. "I'll be here until 23:00… 11 p.m. And you better be careful. If you get caught, I don't know you. If you don't return, I will call the police myself."

Gabriel's heart pounded, but he managed to keep his expression calm, offering a steady, appreciative smile. "Understood. Thank you," he said softly. "We'll be careful, and no one will know." They exchanged a brief, almost wordless understanding, as Gabriel slipped the keys from his closed fist into his pocket. He knew they'd just secured their chance—but it was a slim, fragile thing, and they couldn't afford to waste it. Their clock started now.

As he walked back to Amelia, who had been watching from a distance, he could see the question in her eyes, the hint of anxiety. He gave a slight nod, and she exhaled, the tension easing slightly. They had what they needed—access to the mine, and this time, they were going in alone. Now, all they had to do was make it count.

Chapter 77

While figuring out a way to get back into the mine, Amelia and Gabriel had planned carefully, noting the shift changes and activity patterns over the past few days. They knew the 200 Deck was officially closed to new digging, and the likelihood of anyone venturing down there was slim. As for cameras, they observed surveillance was mostly concentrated around the active shafts and central office areas—not the forgotten sections like the 200 Deck. The mine's camera strategy seemed to be based more on safety than security, which played to their advantage. Even so, they needed to avoid detection.

They decided to enter through the maintenance shaft. The information Amelia had learned from their earlier conversation with Lukas proved invaluable. Not only was the maintenance shaft closer to 226B than the main shaft, but it also allowed them to bypass the cameras in the busier areas. Still, they remained cautious, choosing to act when the mine was at its quietest, with only a skeleton crew working above.

Just like it was now, at 8 p.m.

As they stood at the entrance to the shaft, Gabriel fumbled with the borrowed keys, trying to steady his hands against the cold metal. If they were caught, they'd have a lot more than questions to answer. But if they didn't do this now, they might never get another chance to uncover what had been hidden here for decades.

"Got it," Gabriel whispered as the lock clicked open. They slipped inside and softly closed the door behind them, the keys now heavy in Amelia's pocket as they began their descent. The narrow staircase twisted and turned, and the air grew thicker with each step. Amelia kept glancing nervously back up the dark shaft, half-expecting to see Lukas or Dieter appear, their flashlights cutting through the gloom.

They had left their mobiles back at the hotel. It wasn't just the lack of reception in the mine—there wasn't a single bar of signal to be found —but the thought of being tracked made her stomach churn. Even a stray ping to a nearby cell tower could betray their movements, triangulating their location in a way they couldn't afford. Gabriel had been firm: "No phones, no exceptions." Still, it felt strange not having the familiar weight of her phone in her pocket—a tether to the outside world, now abandoned in favor of stealth.

Though Lukas had mentioned the maintenance shaft wasn't used often, the staircase seemed remarkably sturdy. Each step, though coated with a thin layer of dust, held firm under their weight. It was clear the structure had been built to endure, even if time and neglect had left their marks in the form of rusted edges and faint creaks that echoed in the confined space.

Once inside the main tunnel of the 200 Deck, the silence around them felt fragile, like it could shatter at any moment. Amelia's headlamp flickered against the salt-crusted walls, sending fragmented beams of light into the dark, narrow corridor ahead. Her heart pounded as each step brought them closer to the chamber they were so desperate to access. Beside her, Gabriel's headlamp swept across the walls, searching for any signs of what they hoped lay hidden just out of sight.

As they approached the door to the 226 chamber, Amelia steadied her breath as the anticipation tightened in her chest. She glanced at Gabriel, who gave her a reassuring nod, though his eyes were sharp, focused. They had waited for this moment, planned it down to the smallest detail, and now that they were here, it almost felt surreal.

The door, which had groaned and protested during their earlier visit with Lukas, now gave way with unexpected ease. It creaked open, the hinges still squealing but not as loudly as before, almost like the metal had resigned itself to their persistence. They slipped inside and the chamber opened up before them again, vast and shadowy, with curved walls stretching out into the darkness.

The space felt different this time, heavier somehow, like it was now eager to share its secrets with them. They made their way back to the spot where they had first noticed the strange, glossy patch on the wall— the anomaly that had been both a beacon of hope and a source of endless speculation. The chamber was as still as they remembered, with the scent of earth and minerals lingering in the background.

Amelia's headlamp caught on the smooth, reflective surface again, sending a rush of excitement through her, tinged with a sliver of fear. This was it. They were back—alone, without Lukas's watchful eyes on them, which was both liberating and unnerving. But also without any assurance that they would find what they were looking for.

She stepped closer, her beam illuminating the sleek, almost polished section of the wall. It glistened as if perpetually wet. Slowly, she reached out, her fingers brushing the cool, smooth surface. The salt felt slick and strangely pliable, almost like it had been recently molded, yet she knew it hadn't been touched in years. She could feel a slight give, like there was something beneath, pushing against it.

"It's still here," she whispered, more to herself than to Gabriel, her voice echoing softly in the cavernous space. "We weren't imagining it."

Her mind raced, sifting through the fragments of information they had pieced together from old documents, maps, and cryptic notes. Every step of their journey had led to this moment, each clue pointing them here, to this hidden corner of the mine. She remembered how the Alliance operated, always one step ahead, concealing things within intricate layers of deception. If they were right, if what they suspected was true, this could be the key to everything—the place where something precious had been sealed away, undisturbed for decades.

"Someone definitely used salt to seal this wall—to make it look like part of the natural cavern," Amelia said, reaffirming their earlier suspicions. She leaned in closer, her face just inches from the surface, examining the slight curve where the salt seemed to sag, a small depression that set it apart from the rest of the wall. "Almost like a patch job," she added, her breath hitting the wall and condensing into tiny droplets.

Gabriel stepped closer, his headlamp casting a more focused beam on the spot she was studying. The light illuminated faint, almost invisible cracks spidering around the edges, creating an outline that was both unnatural and deliberate. "You're right," he murmured with a mix of excitement and disbelief. "They fused salt and water to cover something up. Like plaster on a wall!"

Amelia's hands trembled with anticipation as she picked up a rusted pickaxe they had found earlier, near a stack of forgotten mining equipment. Gripping it by the head for better control, she carefully positioned the point at the edge of the glossy salt façade, near one of the fissures, and began chipping away. Small, brittle flakes crumbled off under the pressure, gradually revealing a darker, denser material beneath.

Amelia gasped.

It wasn't rock. It was metal—cold, smooth, and unmistakably man-made.

They both exchanged a look, with a mix of awe and exhilaration passing between them. Without a word, Gabriel grabbed another tool and joined her. Soon, the space filled with the rhythmic sound of metal striking salt as they worked in tense silence. The salt initially resisted, stubborn and solid, but as they chipped and pried, larger chunks began to fall away, gradually revealing a blurry, rusted outline beneath the encrusted surface.

They were uncovering something that had been hidden for decades—maybe even longer. Every bit of salt that fell was another step closer to uncovering the truth.

They worked methodically, careful not to rush, not wanting to damage whatever lay hidden beneath. Bit by bit, the salt crumbled, revealing more of the dark metal underneath. The outline became clearer—a rectangular shape with corroded edges that hinted at something mechanical.

Amelia inhaled sharply as the realization hit her. The shape was now unmistakable. "It's a door!" she exclaimed, barely believing what was before them. "They sealed off a door!"

Gabriel nodded, his eyes wide with a mix of wonder and exhilaration. "It has to be! They hid it behind the salt! Made it blend in so well that no one would think to look twice!"

He ran his fingers along the rusted edge, feeling the cold, rough metal beneath the thin, stubborn layer of salt still clinging to it. "It's brilliant, really," he said, almost to himself. "To hide something so important by making it seem so ordinary, so natural. *Salt preserves all that is precious!*" he added, repeating the line from the old cookbook that had led them here in the first place.

The phrase echoed between them, heavy with significance and everything it implied. They had followed that cryptic clue through dusty archives, forgotten ledgers, and now, into the cold, dark depths of this mine. It had been a leap of faith, but now the truth was literally in their hands.

Together, they brushed off the remaining flakes of salt, working carefully, almost reverently. As the last bits crumbled away, it revealed a small metal plate on the door, faintly engraved but still legible.

"226B."

Amelia's mouth dropped, and for a moment, all she could do was stare. The number gleamed softly back at them under their lights, and the metal, darkened with age, was still defiant against the years that had passed. Her voice came out in a hushed tone, almost disbelieving. "We found it," she said, half-turning to Gabriel. "We actually found it!"

After a silent acknowledgment of the significance of what lay before them, Gabriel's hands slowly reached out to grasp the handle. He looked at Amelia one more time, almost searching for permission, before attempting to twist it. As he did, the latch resisted, its stiff metal groaning in protest, reluctant to give up its secrets.

He tried again, putting more weight into it, but the handle barely budged. "It's stuck," he muttered, frustration creeping into his voice. Amelia stepped forward, her heart pounding, and together they braced themselves against the old, rusted door. She grabbed a nearby tool—an old iron pry bar they'd found discarded earlier—and wedged it into the narrow gap between the door and the frame.

"On three," she said, her voice low but firm. "One... two... three."

Chapter 78

Their muscles strained as they worked in tandem on the rusted door, each movement deliberate and forceful. The metal creaked and groaned, stubbornly resisting after decades of being sealed shut. Small flakes of rust and salt crumbled away, dusting their hands and the floor, and with each push, the door frame separated from the door a little more.

The effort was slow and difficult. The pry bar bent dangerously under the pressure, bowing as they leaned into it, with their combined strength barely enough to force a gap. The harsh strain of their work unnervingly echoed around them, and amplified the tension in the still, dark space.

Finally, after what felt like an eternity, there was a loud cracking sound as the door latch broke. They exchanged a quick, breathless glance, and moved to get their fingers wedged in around the door edge to pull it open. Centimeter by centimeter they pulled, each movement accompanied by an ear-piercing screech, sharp and grating, like the chamber itself was protesting their intrusion.

Finally, the door shifted slightly, creating a narrow gap—just wide enough for them to slip their bodies through.

They aimed their headlamps into the opening and the beams cut through the darkness, revealing a narrow, curved passageway that led deeper into the mine.

As Amelia stepped through, Gabriel's hand instinctively shot out, catching her shoulder. She turned back toward him, startled. "Careful," he said, his voice low, afraid to disturb whatever lay beyond. "We don't know how stable this is."

Amelia nodded with an affirming smile, then shifted her gaze back to the passage. She slipped through the opening cautiously, scanning the darkness ahead, trying to make out any shapes or obstacles. "We have to see what's down here," she said, the urgency in her voice betraying her restraint. "This might be it, Gabriel!"

He followed behind her as the tunnel gradually widened. Each step they took was muted, echoing softly before being absorbed by the layers of salt that coated the floor. Finally, the rough, salt-encrusted walls curved outward, opening into a vast, darkened chamber untouched by time. The air was filled with the scent of earth, salt, and a faint, resinous smell that seemed to cling to the back of their throats.

Amelia's pulse quickened as her headlamp panned the space. Her beam stretched out many meters before fully dissolving into the darkness. Beyond the light's reach, nothing emerged clearly enough to reveal what lay ahead.

They moved forward cautiously, mindful of both their past missteps and the state of the space around them. Gabriel kept his focus on the ground ahead, alert for any signs of traps. At the moment, he was less concerned with the expanse of the chamber and more with ensuring each step was safe.

After many cautious steps, they paused. Gabriel raised his light, sweeping it across the chamber, trying to make out the far end. The beam stretched into the distance, dissolving into shadow—until it didn't. His light caught something, faint but distinct—a hazy outline in the dark. Amelia's eyes followed his, narrowing as she strained to see. For a moment, it seemed like nothing more than a trick of the light. Then, the shapes began to solidify—rows of angular forms, stacked neatly in lines, emerging from the darkness. Her stomach clenched, and she swallowed hard.

As they edged closer, Gabriel continued to keep his light low, scanning the ground for hazards. Meanwhile, the beam from Amelia's headlamp was fixed on its target, illuminating its edges with a cold, stark clarity.

Wooden crates. Hundreds of them.

After the first row, more came into view, then even more, extending back into the darkness and disappearing into the far corners of the chamber. Amelia gasped, her eyes wide as she crept forward. Her heart pounded with a mix of fear and exhilaration, and each step felt like it carried with it everything they had been searching for—everything that had led them here.

Gabriel stepped beside her, his own headlamp now fixed on the line of crates as well. They moved together, their lights overlapping, revealing more and more of the hidden space as the chamber slowly gave up its secrets, reluctant to reveal everything at once.

Approaching one of the crates, Amelia's fingers trembled as she reached out, her hand hovering over the weathered wood. She hesitated, almost afraid to disturb this remnant of history that had lain hidden for so long. Then, with a gentle, reverent touch, her fingers moved across the edge of the crate, feeling the rough grain beneath her fingertips and the fine layer of salt dust that had settled in over the years.

She glanced up, taking a step back, and looked over the darkened chamber with her light. "There have to be hundreds of these," she said, her voice tight with anticipation. "This... this is it, Gabriel! The hidden paintings… everything they fought to protect!"

Gabriel moved closer, his own breathing shallow and eyes wide with awe. Kneeling beside another crate, he brushed away a stubborn layer of dust clinging to the surface, and a sharp scent of pine resin filled his nostrils. There were no markings, no writing—just the rough, aged wood, acting as a final barrier to whatever it guarded. "This *has* to be it," he murmured, his voice hushed as he rose to meet Amelia's gaze.

They stood there in silence, letting the reality sink in. This was the culmination of months of research, dead ends, near death, and vague clues that had led them halfway across Europe. Amelia felt the weight of history on them, the echoes of those who had risked everything to keep these treasures hidden. It was a moment of reverence, almost sacred in its intensity.

She took a step back, letting her light sweep across the chamber to take in every row of crates in the hidden space, each one stacked with precision. There was a stillness here, a calm dignity, like a tomb filled with relics from a lost era, patiently waiting to be discovered.

Amelia's pulse raced as a surge of triumph rose in her chest, snapping herself out of the trance she was in. They had found it! She could hardly believe it, but here it was, right in front of them. Realizing they hadn't yet confirmed if these *were* the paintings, she turned to Gabriel and spoke, sharp with urgency. "We can't just stand here! We need to open one! We need to see what's inside! *Now!*"

Gabriel nodded, quickly pulling out a small crowbar from his pack. He moved to the nearest crate, his hands steady as he slid the metal under the lid edge. With a slow, deliberate motion, he applied pressure. The wood creaked and groaned as the nails released their hold, reluctant to be disturbed after all this time. The sound echoed through the chamber, sharp and unsettling in the stillness.

With a final, low crack, the lid gave way, lifting just enough for them to peer inside. Amelia leaned in, holding her breath as Gabriel set the tool aside and carefully eased the lid off, placing it gently on the ground. Inside, a dark covering stared back at them, concealing whatever rectangular object lay beneath. They exchanged a quick, tense glance, their eyes wide with anticipation, before turning their attention back to the mysterious contents.

In an almost reverent manner, Gabriel's hands moved slowly as he started peeling back the fabric. Beneath it, a glint of color emerged—deep, rich hues shimmering under the harsh beams of their headlamps. Amelia's eyes widened as she caught the first glimpse of Cobalt Blue peeking from underneath the dark cover. The colors were intense, almost luminous, like a hidden world that had been kept safe in the dark. She moved closer, her heart pounding, eyes locked on the fabric as it slid further back. The moment felt suspended, every second stretching like time had slowed to witness the reveal.

More colors appeared as Gabriel continued to pull—soft greens and warm ambers, blending together in a way that suggested movement, life. She could make out a patch of sky, a ripple of water, hints of delicate brushstrokes that seemed to shift and shimmer in the light. The anticipation built with every centimeter that was revealed, teasing her with glimpses of the scene beneath, making her desperate to see it fully.

With a final, gentle pull, Gabriel slid the dark fabric away, revealing the painting beneath. It was stunning—bold strokes of blue, green, and amber swirled across the canvas, the colors vivid and untouched by time. Light seemed to dance across the surface, illuminating the delicate textures that made the scene come alive.

Amelia gasped as she took in the scene: a serene landscape, the brushstrokes capturing the gentle ripples of a river under the dappled light of a summer sky. Two silhouetted figures stood at the water's edge, their backs turned, watching boats paddle slowly in the distance. Each detail was exquisite, painted with a precision and sensitivity that brought the entire scene into sharp, beautiful focus.

She recognized the style immediately—early Impressionist—the soft yet confident lines, the vibrant play of colors. For a moment, she couldn't move, couldn't speak. Time had truly stopped, and she was caught in the painting's spell, lost in the delicate interplay of colors and light. Her eyes drifted down to the lower corner of the canvas, searching. And there, hidden among the layers of color, she saw it—a signature, painted with a flourish, almost hidden in the play of shadows.

"Monet," she whispered, her voice not much louder than a breath.

Her heart skipped, the word hanging in the air between them, heavy with awe and disbelief. They had found it—a painting by one of the most celebrated artists of all time, hidden away, untouched by the chaos of the world outside.

Amelia pulled a pair of white gloves from her bag and carefully slid them on, her hands trembling with a mix of excitement and reverence. She gently lifted the painting, tilting it to catch the light, admiring the vibrant colors and delicate brushstrokes. After a moment, she turned the framed canvas over to inspect the back, her eyes scanning every detail. There, on the lower left corner of the canvas, just where it wrapped around the stretcher frame, was a small mark—black, faded, but unmistakable.

She gasped, recognizing it instantly. It was the same mark that had started this entire journey—the mark she had first seen on the painting of Eloise, the one alluded to countless times in their search. She brought the frame closer, her eyes narrowing to make out the details. There, clear as day, was the mark of the Alliance:

A paintbrush and a key, merged as one.

"Oh my god," she breathed again, tears stinging at the corners of her eyes. "This is it! They're here... all of them!"

Gabriel's voice was tight, filled with the same awe and emotion that she felt, as he blinked back the tears also welling up in his eyes. "We did it! We really did it!"

Wiping his eyes, he reached into his bag and pulled out the copy of the ledger they had painstakingly deciphered. With steady hands, he scanned down the list of entries, his finger moving quickly over the lines until it stopped at catalog number 32176—the same number stamped below the mark on the canvas. He read aloud, his voice quick at first, then slowing as the significance of the words sank in.

"River Landscape with Two Men and Boats, 1894. Van den Bergh Family. Willemspark, Amsterdam."

He glanced up at Amelia, his eyes wide as the discovery dawned on him. "This... this is one of the paintings from the Lost Art Database marked as 'Nazi-confiscated property,'" he said. "They thought it was gone forever!"

The Van den Bergh family, a Dutch-Jewish family, had appeared several times in the ledger. They had entrusted the Alliance with their artwork, knowing the Nazis could raid their home at any moment and seize everything. Tragically, the Nazis did exactly that, and it was rumored that many valuable pieces were confiscated before they could be moved. Until now, neither Amelia nor Gabriel believed the Alliance had managed to smuggle any of the family's works out of the Netherlands before the raid. Yet here, against all odds, was one of them.

Amelia leaned in closer, scanning the ledger entry, then returned to the painting in front of them. She spoke, her voice steady despite her emotions. "If the Alliance hadn't saved this, it *would* have been lost—maybe even destroyed, like so many others."

Her fingers traced the edge of the canvas, with the realization of what they had uncovered washing over her. "They risked everything to keep it safe," she said softly. "And it's been here, hidden away, waiting to be found all this time."

The silent room seemed to grow quieter. The painting, vibrant and alive, stood as a testament to the lengths the Alliance had gone to preserve it, and Amelia couldn't help but feel a deep, overwhelming sense of gratitude—not just for the art, but for those who had fought to protect it.

Amelia and Gabriel stood there, side by side, their lights dancing across the crates, knowing that behind each one lay another piece of history, another secret that had been hidden away, waiting for this moment. And for the first time, Amelia allowed herself to believe that they had finally uncovered what they had been searching for, the lost paintings of the Alliance, preserved against all odds.

Her eyes started glossing over with tears again as the enormity of it all sank in. "They didn't just hide the art... they safeguarded history—culture itself! The Alliance made sure no one would forget what these pieces meant, preserving not just the art, but the spirit and meaning they carried—something far greater than the canvases themselves!" She ran her fingers over the edges of another crate, feeling the worn wood again under her touch, and for a moment, she could almost see the hands that had carefully placed it there, knowing it might never be found.

"This is bigger than we thought," Gabriel said with a mix of wonder and disbelief. "If we can get these out... the stories they'll tell..."

Amelia's head snapped up. "We have to!" she said, her determination hardening. "We *have* to get them out… and we have to make sure *everyone* knows what the Alliance did!"

Before Gabriel could respond, a sudden, piercing beeping shattered the stillness, cutting through the space like a siren. The sound echoed off the chamber walls in a relentless, jarring rhythm. They froze, wide-eyed, the noise jolting them violently out of the sacred silence that had surrounded their discovery. For a second, they stood there, paralyzed, the magnitude of what they had just uncovered suddenly colliding with the stark reality of the situation.

"Gabriel!" Amelia hissed, her voice breaking the spell. Gabriel snapped out of his trance, quickly glancing down and frantically fumbling with his wrist to silence the noise. His hands shook as he looked at his watch. "The alarm... it's almost 11 p.m!" His voice was tight, panic edging every word.

"We have to go—*now!*, he urged. "If we don't get the keys back to the bar, he'll call the police on us!" Amelia's eyes widened as his words hit her like a jolt. Gabriel quickly replaced the cover over the Monet and grabbed her hand. He looked directly into her eyes, his expression intense. "We need to move before anyone realizes we're down here!"

Chapter 79

The chill night air bit at their faces as Amelia and Gabriel rushed through the dark, empty streets, their footsteps quick against the cobblestone. What they had just uncovered still hung over them, but there was no time to dwell on it. The clock was ticking, and they had only minutes left before the bar closed. They needed to return the shaft keys to the worker before he called the police.

Gabriel's heart pounded as he glanced at his watch: 22:53—10:53 p.m. "We're cutting it close," he muttered, while shaking his head. They picked up the pace. Amelia was right beside him, clutching her bag tightly, her mind racing. She could still see the painting in her head, every brushstroke vivid and clear, but she forced herself to focus. They had one more thing to do before this night was over.

As they turned the corner, the warm glow of the tavern's lights came into view, cutting through the fog. Through the windows, they could see a few patrons lingering over their drinks, the low hum of conversation barely audible from the stillness of the street. Most importantly, the worker was still seated at the bar, his back to the entrance, still nursing a drink as they'd left him earlier.

"We've got seven minutes," Gabriel said with urgency in his tone. "Do you have the clay ready?"

Amelia nodded and pulled a small, flat tin from her bag, snapping it open to reveal a soft, grayish lump of clay. "Just one quick press," she said, handing it to Gabriel. Her voice was calm despite the tension crackling between them. "We can't afford to mess this up."

Gabriel pulled the maintenance shaft key from the ring. With steady hands, he pressed both sides into the clay, making sure to imprint every groove and ridge. The clay molded perfectly around the key, capturing its shape in sharp, precise detail, just as they had hoped. He carefully pulled the key out and examined the impressions to make sure they were clear. Satisfied, he handed the key back to Amelia, who quickly wiped off any residue before slipping it back onto the ring. Gabriel snapped the case shut and passed it to her.

"Done," she said, tucking it back into her bag. "Let's go."

They took a moment to catch their breaths before stepping into the bar, the warmth and scent of stale beer hitting them immediately. Their hearts were still racing, but outwardly they appeared as calm, like they had just stopped in for a nightcap. Gabriel scanned the room, making sure no one was paying them too much attention. The worker glanced up as they approached, his eyes narrowing slightly, but he didn't say anything. Gabriel slid onto the barstool next to him, casually pulling the key ring out from his pocket.

"Right on time," the worker said, a hint of a smirk playing on his lips. "I was starting to wonder."

Gabriel forced a smile, trying to keep his tone light. "Told you we'd be quick. No trouble, just like I promised."

The worker reached out, taking the keys from Gabriel's hand, and his fingers brushed over the metal as if checking to make sure everything was there. He gave a small nod and slipped the keys into his pocket. "Good," he said, his voice low. "Because if anyone asks, I never saw you. And if this comes back to me…"

"It won't," Amelia cut in, her voice firm but quiet. "We're done, and you'll never hear from us again."

The worker's eyes lingered on them for a moment, searching their faces for any sign of deceit. Finally, he shrugged, turning back to his drink. "Gute Nacht."

Gabriel exhaled, relieved. "Good night," he replied. He gave Amelia a quick, knowing glance before they turned and headed for the door.

As they stepped out into the cold night, with the imprint of the key safely hidden in Amelia's bag, they knew they had bought themselves a little more time—but at a cost that was still unfolding.

The door to the bar creaked shut behind them, leaving them alone in the empty street. Amelia looked over at Gabriel, the tension in her chest finally beginning to ease, but she could see in his eyes that the night was far from over.

"What now?" she asked, her breath fogging in the cold air.

They had closed the doors to both 226B and 226 before racing up the maintenance shaft. With the 200 Deck decommissioned, it was likely enough to keep things hidden, but all it would take was a random worker wandering down there to stumble upon 486 priceless works of art. They had hesitated over whether to lock the maintenance shaft door. Leaving it open risked an inspection if anyone found out, but locking it meant they might never get back in. They finally settled on the latter.

Gabriel glanced down the empty street, the shadows stretching long and dark. "Now, we figure out how to go back without borrowing any more keys."

Chapter 80

The salt mine seemed to swallow them as Amelia and Gabriel descended the narrow maintenance shaft, their breaths forming small clouds in the cold, stale air. Dim, flickering bulbs lined the walls, casting an eerie, pale light that was barely enough to see by. But they didn't need much—they had memorized the route by now. Chamber 226B lay buried deep, hidden from the world for decades, and tonight, they were about to bring its history back to life.

Amelia felt the key in her pocket, a replica of the original they had borrowed and returned, cast from the clay mold. It had been a gamble, but the resin reproduction worked perfectly on the first try. She marveled at how simple it had been to create, yet when the key slid into the lock, there was still a split-second of doubt—what if it didn't work? But the maintenance shaft lock clicked open, just as it had two nights ago with the real key, and the heavy, reinforced door swung wide to reveal the yawning darkness of the mine beyond.

Gabriel had whispered, "It's Saturday. We have until dawn before anyone else comes around here. Let's make this count."

They slipped inside and sealed the door behind them, knees already aching at the thought of another 81 story trek.

Now, as they zigzagged down the shaft to the 200 Deck, their headlamps cut narrow paths through the darkness, illuminating the familiar, salt-crusted walls.

At 200 meters deep, the shaft door opened to an outstretched tunnel, leading them back to Chamber 226B. Amelia's mind raced, replaying the plan over and over—there was no room for error. Over the last two nights, they had debated every angle, every possibility, until they were sure. The trucks were parked near the maintenance entrance, hidden from the main access points, engines cooling under the chilly night sky. It had been risky to rent two 7.5-tonne lorries in Monthey, just west of Bex, but the cover story Gabriel provided had been believable enough—they were a newlywed couple moving to France to be closer to his in-laws. Still, using his actual passport to secure the rentals added another layer of risk. They had to be cautious—*any* driving near the mine had to avoid cameras, keeping the trucks off the radar and out of sight.

As they walked down the tunnel toward 226, Amelia felt her heart quicken, a tightness settling in her chest that hadn't eased since they made the decision to return. Two nights ago, she had been overwhelmed by the sight of the crates, neatly stacked and sealed, just waiting for them —remnants of a history that felt both distant and immediate. The dim light from their headlamps had moved across the weathered wood, drawing shadows that stretched and distorted, making the crates look like sentinels standing guard over the past. Each one represented a piece of history—a story that had been hidden away, waiting for someone to care enough to uncover it.

In that moment, she knew they had been entrusted with something bigger than themselves—something that couldn't afford to be lost again. But as they approached the door to 226B, reality settled over her and the full responsibility of it all gripped her even tighter. These weren't just paintings; they were lives, memories, and legacies that had been nearly erased.

Taking a steadying breath, Amelia opened the door to 226B and stepped inside. The scent of pine resin once again enveloped them, and with a renewed purpose, she and Gabriel moved toward the rows of crates. The Monet was still lying on the ground, just as they had left it, its protective cover carefully re-affixed. Amelia's gaze lingered on it, and time seemed to slow again. It had been the first painting they'd uncovered—the first confirmation that what they were dealing with wasn't just a myth or a rumor, but a reality. Priceless works of art, tucked away for generations in this forgotten corner of the world.

She glanced at Gabriel, his face lit only by the pale, wavering glow of his headlamp. His expression was focused, and a silent determination mirrored in his eyes. They both knew why they were here—to finish what had been started decades ago.

Yet even as they stood there, fully aware of what needed to be done, doubt crept back into Amelia's mind—an internal voice that questioned everything they were about to do. She had always prided herself on being a professional, someone who followed the rules, respected the process, and worked within the boundaries of the law. Breaking it—no matter how noble the cause—went against everything she had been taught, everything she had built her career on. Her parents had always instilled in her the importance of integrity, of doing things the right way, even when the right way was the hardest path.

But now, she wondered: what if doing things the "right" way wasn't enough? What if, this time, the hardest path wasn't a slow and careful process, but acting decisively, even recklessly, to protect what mattered most? The thought terrified her, but it also sparked a steady confidence.

She thought of the ledger they had uncovered, the meticulous records of each piece, the names of families listed beside them. Those names were the only link left to people who had once loved and cherished these works, who had been forced to let them go under the cruelest of circumstances. If they handed everything over to the authorities, there was no guarantee those connections would be honored. The paintings could end up locked in a museum vault, tied up in legal disputes, or, worse, disappear into the hands of opportunistic collectors who cared only for the prestige and profit.

Gabriel, being a Vallois descendant, could lay claim to his family's artwork without going through too many formal channels. That was one small comfort. But what about all the other pieces that *didn't* have clear heirs? She thought of the Van den Bergh family and the other names they had seen. Families who had been scattered and destroyed. Those whose descendants might not even know that a part of their heritage still existed, hidden here. Would they ever have a chance to reclaim what was rightfully theirs, or would the art be swallowed up by endless bureaucratic procedures, tied up in red tape until no one remembered why it mattered in the first place?

If she hesitated—if she left this to "the right way"—they might be lost again, suffocated by the system she had spent her life trusting. For the first time, the boundaries she had clung to felt less like anchors and more like chains.

Amelia's hands tightened into fists at her sides before relaxing again, the motion almost instinctive as she wrestled with her thoughts. She had always believed in following the rules, but standing here now, she wondered if those rules had ever been meant to protect people like this. The law was supposed to serve justice, but would it? In this case? Could she trust the system to do right by these families, by the history that had been hidden for so long? Or would it fail, as it had failed so many times before, letting the powerful dictate the fate of what didn't belong to them?

Her gaze drifted back to the Monet, thinking about the delicate brushstrokes she knew were inside the crate. She remembered the feeling she had when they had first uncovered it—the awe, the sense of standing on the brink of something extraordinary. It had felt like a gift, like a piece of history was reaching out to them, asking to be remembered. And she realized, with a kind of desperate clarity, that she couldn't let that be taken away, not again.

"What now?" she asked, her breath fogging in the chilly air, the question more to herself than to Gabriel. She needed to hear it, to say it out loud, to make sure she still believed in what they were doing.

Gabriel's voice was steady, grounded. "Now, we finish this. We get them out, and we make sure they end up where they're supposed to be."

Amelia nodded, but the tension didn't fully ease. She knew they were crossing a line they could never uncross, and she knew there could be consequences. But as she looked around the chamber, at the silent, waiting crates, she felt a sense of resolve harden within her. If they did nothing, the story would end here, buried in the dark, the art lost to those who had every right to it. And she couldn't let that happen.

"Do you think we'll be able to get them all out?" she asked, genuinely concerned.

Gabriel nodded, though his jaw was tight. "We have to. If the authorities get involved, it could take years to sort this out, and who knows how many will ever see the light of day again." He didn't say the rest, but Amelia heard it anyway—*they had no time to waste*.

Amelia swept her light across the crates, still neatly stacked, as if waiting for this very moment. She had counted them twice before, but she couldn't help but count again. Four hundred and eighty-six. She took a deep breath, the enormity of it sinking in once more.

"We'll move them ten at a time," Gabriel said. "It's the only way."

Amelia nodded, already picturing the process in her mind. They would need to load the crates onto the electric crawlers they had seen near the 300 Deck—compact, treaded machines designed for carrying heavy loads through narrow mining tunnels. If they could get one or two of those, they could transport the crates to the conveyor belt at the main shaft and send them up to the surface. The thought of climbing a thousand stairs with a crate under each arm had crossed her mind, and it made her laugh now, albeit nervously. It wouldn't come to that.

Gabriel checked his watch. "It's nine o'clock. We have six hours."

The hardest part had been planning around the mine's security. During their first visit, while waiting for Dieter to greet them, Gabriel had discretely snapped a quick photo of a map hanging in the field office. It was a crude, laminated sheet, creased and faded at the edges, but it revealed everything they needed to know. The map showed how the shafts and diagonal tunnels connected the various decks, weaving a complex web of routes through the mine. The 200 Deck was mostly decommissioned, a forgotten corner that had long since ceased to be of interest, except perhaps to a few maintenance workers. But it was still connected to the 300 Deck, where salt was actively mined, and from there, to the main shaft.

That connection was crucial. It meant they had a path—discreet, efficient, and, with any luck, unnoticed. If they could navigate those tunnels, they could bypass most of the security checkpoints, steering clear of the active mining areas. But more than just the pathways, they found the map had provided something even more valuable: it showed where the cameras were. Every small, black lens marked on the diagram was a potential obstacle, and they had spent hours poring over the image, memorizing which areas were monitored and which weren't. The plan was to keep to the blind spots, to hug the walls of the unmonitored sections, using the mine's own design against it. It was a delicate dance, and there was no room for missteps.

Armed with all the knowledge they had gathered, Gabriel took the lead and guided them towards the 300 Deck. As they crossed into the deeper section of the mine, their headlamps illuminated three old mining crawlers parked just above their intended location. Each was coated in a thin layer of dust but otherwise appeared intact. Gabriel ran a hand over one of the machines, inspecting the controls.

"Looks like it's ready to go," he said, a small smile tugging at the corners of his mouth. "We'll take turns. One of us loads, the other drives."

Amelia couldn't help but feel a surge of amazement as she watched Gabriel. He had been the one to spot the machines during their tour, and it was his quick thinking that had made this part of the plan possible.

Without them, there would have been no way for just the two of them to transport 486 wooden crates over 200 meters, all in a single night.

"Let's hope they still run," she said, a hint of a smile breaking through her otherwise tense expression, her gaze lingering on him a moment longer. She admired how he always seemed to know just what to do, how his confidence in their abilities inspired her own. His presence in this—it made her heart race a little faster, reminding her just how lucky she was to have him by her side.

Gabriel flicked a switch on the first machine, and then the others, the crawlers humming softly to life. Each was fully charged, ready for use. If one happened to run out of power, they had two more at the ready to take its place. He climbed on the front one and eased its joystick forward, testing its movement, listening to the treads creak slightly as they adjusted to the weight. It wasn't smooth, but it was steady. "Looks like we're in business," he said, his voice low but assured.

Amelia gave a nod, and they each climbed onto a crawler, guiding them back up the diagonal tunnel toward the 200 Deck. The machines moved slowly but surely and their low hum reverberated through the narrow space, echoing off the salt-coated walls.

Back in 226B, they began the slow, methodical process of loading the crates into the crawler. They had agreed not to open or disturb the rest of the crates. For now, the Monet was proof enough—its presence validated everything. The other crates would remain sealed, with their integrity preserved for the journey ahead.

Though the crates held only stretched canvases, each one felt unnaturally heavy, like the weight of history itself had solidified within them, pressing down with every lift.

After a few trips from the chamber to the crawler, Amelia settled into a rhythm and her movements became efficient and controlled. They had spent the past two nights discussing the logistics, the risks, and the consequences. But now, as they worked in silence, she felt a strange sense of calm. They weren't just smuggling art; they were preserving history— restoring a piece of humanity—rescuing treasures that had been buried and forgotten for far too long.

With the first ten crates loaded, Gabriel climbed onto the crawler and eased it forward, steering it through the narrow tunnel that led to the maintenance shaft and from there, the main shaft. The machine crept along at a steady three kilometers per hour—just as they had calculated.

Each trip would take roughly six minutes of travel time, not counting the loading or unloading, and with 49 trips ahead of them, it was going to be a long night. But the rhythm of the work would keep them focused, each task flowing into the next: load, drive, unload, drive, repeat.

Chapter 81

The Keller Group's Bex Salt Mines Field Office, Saturday, 9:07 p.m.

Adam Dupont leaned back in the squeaky office chair, rolling his shoulders to ease the tension that had been building for hours. The wall clock ticked steadily: 21:07, Saturday. Nearly eight hours until the first crew arrived at 05:00 Sunday morning. Eight hours of watching absolutely nothing happen. Being posted here on a Saturday night, manning the security feed when there wasn't a soul scheduled to work, was just shy of torture. But The Keller Group's new insurance policy demanded a warm body in the booth, no exceptions, so here he was.

He cranked up the volume on the battered radio perched beside the bank of monitors, letting the rhythm of a bluesy American guitar solo echo through the cramped room—now loud enough to drown out the oppressive silence. With one hand idly flipping through an outdated sports magazine and the other drumming on the desk, he let his gaze lazily drift across the rows of black-and-white feeds displayed on the monitors.

Most of the screens showed the same thing they always did: still, empty corridors, inactive machinery, and the seemingly endless walls of salt. Nothing moved. Nothing ever moved. He'd been here long enough to know better than to expect otherwise. But just as his focus dipped back to a recap of last year's Tour de France, something in the top right corner of the screen labeled MAIN SHAFT (300/200) caught his eye.

It was a flicker—a momentary flash of movement. His spine stiffened, and his hand froze mid-drumbeat. Leaning forward, he narrowed his eyes at the monitor. For a moment, everything looked as it should. The conveyor belt appeared to be off and the shaft was still and empty. But something had moved. He was sure of it.

Adam reached for the screen and clicked to rewind the feed. The grainy footage jerked back a few seconds, and his heart kicked up a notch as he hit play. The screen replayed the same moment, frame by frame. *There*—a quick blur in the corner of the frame. It was faint, just the edge of something dark sliding upward between the beams of the tunnel walls. A shadow. A shape.

He leaned closer, replaying it again, slower this time. A crawler? But the angle was bad—just a glimpse of, possibly, the machine's tread as it disappeared out of view? It was impossible to tell. Adam frowned, chewing the inside of his cheek. He knew those crawlers were parked near the 300 Deck. Maintenance used them occasionally for inspections, but on a Saturday night? With no staff scheduled?

He shifted his gaze to the other feeds, scanning each one carefully. All still. His mind scrambled for an explanation. Maybe one of the mechanics forgot to log an inspection, or—hell—maybe even a stray cat had triggered something. Animals occasionally found their way into the mines. He had heard stories. That made sense. At least, it made enough sense to calm the flicker of unease creeping up his neck.

Adam shook his head and leaned back in his chair, muttering, "Damn cats," before tossing the sports magazine onto the desk. He reached for his thermos and took a long sip of lukewarm coffee, keeping one eye on the screen.

"Still," he thought, as if justifying his actions to the empty room, *"better be safe than sorry."*

The radio continued to hum with distorted guitar riffs as Adam leaned forward again, tapping his fingers lightly on the control panel. The single sweeping camera feed from **MAIN SHAFT** (300/200) filled the larger central screen. His gaze lingered on the monitor for a moment, scanning the grainy footage for any sign of movement. But the screen remained steady—quiet and empty, as always.

But this time he'd keep watching. Just in case.

Chapter 82

Bex Salt Mines, Sunday, Early Morning

It was just after midnight when Amelia and Gabriel completed their twenty-fourth trip—almost halfway there. Amelia's hands were sore, her fingers stiff from gripping the edges of the crates even with gloves, and her muscles were aching, but she didn't let herself slow down. The thought of failure was enough to keep her moving. They had to finish.

Gabriel was just returning from another round and he turned off the crawler with a sharp twist of his wrist. The sudden silence that followed was almost deafening after hours of the mechanical whirring. "I think we need a break," he said, his voice low and heavy with fatigue. He rubbed a hand over his face, trying to shake off the hypnotic trance of the constant noise. He glanced down the dark, empty tunnel, then back at Amelia before sighing. "And we need to figure out the cameras," he added, with urgency.

Amelia's stomach clenched. They had known this moment would come, but now that it had arrived, the risk hit her harder than she'd expected. Up to this point, though nerve-wracking, things had gone relatively smoothly. They had a plan for nearly every step. But this was the one thing they couldn't plan for. It had been a "we'll figure it out when we get to it" decision—a gamble based on the hope that necessity would spark a solution. And yet, standing on the edge of action, they both couldn't help but dread what came next.

The main shaft was under constant surveillance, with cameras positioned to monitor the conveyor belt and the entrances to the active decks. Before they started moving crates, they had scoped out the setup. Unfortunately, the camera in the main shaft was placed in the worst possible spot for them. If someone was watching the feed—even casually—they might catch a glimpse of the crates being moved through the door, and the entire operation would unravel.

Fortunately, there was a glimmer of hope.

She took a deep breath, forcing herself to think clearly, and tried to keep her voice steady. "I think we can time it between rotations. We've watched how the cameras pan—there's about a twenty-three-second gap when the shaft door is out of frame. If we're quick, we can move the crates during that window without being seen. And the conveyor—" she paused, thinking it through, "we don't need to stop it every time. If it keeps running, that motion should barely register on the feed. It'll look normal."

Gabriel nodded, his eyes dark and serious, and his jaw set with determination. "It's risky, but it might be our only shot. We'll have to be precise, no hesitating. As soon as the camera swings away, we move." He glanced down the tunnel again, picturing the path they would have to take, then back at Amelia. "If we mess up, even once…"

Amelia didn't need him to finish the thought. They both knew the stakes. She swallowed hard, steeling herself. "We can do this," she said, firmer now. "We've come this far. We're definitely not stopping now."

They made their way to the main shaft, crouching in the shadows while studying the camera movements. The slow, mechanical sweep of each lens felt like a predator scanning for prey, and Amelia could barely hear the hum of the mine's machinery over the pounding of her pulse.

Every pan seemed to stretch longer than the last, the seconds dragging on as the cameras moved back and forth, back and forth. Amelia forced herself to breathe evenly, keeping her count steady. She had to resist the urge to rush, syncing her rhythm with the precise sweep of the lens. With each pass, she could seemingly predict the exact moment the camera would reach the end of its arc, pause, and begin its slow return.

And yet, no matter how predictable it became, her heart lurched every time the lens swung toward their position.

Fortunately for them, the cameras did not appear to have visible microphone holes—a conclusion Gabriel reached after inspecting their design earlier. While it was possible for some to integrate audio internally, he reasoned that in a mine filled with constant mechanical noise, audio would be redundant and unlikely to be included.

They stood motionless, watching and waiting, while their minds rehearsed every movement to fit within the narrow window. There was no margin for error—every action had to be precise, threading the eye of a needle. Gabriel positioned the first set of crates to load on the conveyer, his movements careful but tense. Beside him, Amelia kept her eyes fixed on the camera's rotation, counting the seconds under her breath.

"Twelve… thirteen… fourteen…"

She glanced at Gabriel. His eyes were glued to her—focused and filled with urgency—waiting for her cue, and gripping the cart's handle so tightly his knuckles had turned white. Adrenaline coursed through both of them, spiking as the lens crept closer to their position, just daring them to make a mistake.

"Twenty one… twenty two… twenty three."

"Now!" Amelia whispered sharply. The camera began its pan away. The corridor was clear—for the moment.

Gabriel didn't hesitate. He wheeled the stack of ten crates through the main shaft door, moving as quickly and carefully as he could. The crates slid onto the conveyor belt without issue, their faint scraping sound barely noticeable amid the hum of machinery. He started the conveyor and confirmed movement before slipping back into the shadows to ready the next set.

Amelia's eyes darted between the crates and the camera, holding her breath as the belt carried the stack up and into the dark tunnel above, maintaining her count the entire time.

"*Eighteen… nineteen…*"

Her heart skipped when one of the crates tilted slightly, teetering on the edge. She clenched her fists, willing it to stay steady. If even one slipped, if one of those wooden boxes tumbled off the belt, it could trigger a disaster that would send everything crashing down—quite literally.

As the crates finally disappeared into the shadows, her muscles relaxed slightly—*they made it.*

"*Twenty two… twenty three… one…*"

The camera has already begun its slow arc back, and she instinctively started counting up again at one, preparing for the next run.

Gabriel stepped back, his expression tense, and Amelia could see he needed a moment.

"I'll handle the next set," he said, his voice low but resolute. "You're gonna need to go up to the top and make sure they come off smoothly. We can't afford any slips."

Amelia hesitated. They had only completed one run so far, but she knew Gabriel was right. The crates had to be offloaded when they reached the surface roller platform. If they were left to pile up and tumble off, there could be significant damage to the art, not to mention the noise it would make. She took a breath and nodded. "Okay. Be careful."

Gabriel turned back and resumed the count.

With one last look, Amelia turned and made her way back to the maintenance shaft. The climb was steep, and her legs burned with the ascent, but she pushed up. Ironically, the chill grew as she neared the top, biting at her skin despite the effort.

After reaching the surface, her headlamp cut through the dim light, and revealed the conveyor exit between her and the main shaft. The belt whirred steadily, its low, rhythmic hum seeming unnaturally loud in the night's stillness. *It's late. Could anyone have heard this?* Amelia wondered, her heart beating faster. For now, the conveyor was still empty—the crates hadn't yet completed their longer, winding journey up from below.

But as she approached, Amelia hesitated. She remembered there was a camera at the top, positioned to monitor the area around the unloading platform. They couldn't rely on the same gaps they used below— the angles didn't line up here. Glancing around, she spotted a small control panel set against the wall, barely visible in the shadows. Her mind raced, trying to think of a way to buy them time.

She hurried, her hands fumbling slightly as she removed a black scarf from her neck. Amelia stretched it taut and stepped up to the control panel, masking her movements with her body. She draped the scarf over the lens of the camera, securing it with a double knot, hoping it would be just enough to obscure the view without drawing suspicion. She knew she was creating a short window—eventually, someone would notice, but it might give them the few hours they needed. *It had to.*

Amelia positioned herself at the conveyor's end, her hands hovering just above the belt, ready to catch the crates as they arrived. Moments later, the first stack of ten appeared and tilted slightly before sliding onto the flat unloading platform. She reached out instinctively to steady the load, then began stacking the crates neatly on the ground beside her. For a moment, relief washed over her—it had worked.

Her eyes darted around, checking for any signs of movement, but everything remained still. She could only hope Gabriel was managing the cameras below as carefully as she had above. They needed to keep the rhythm smooth, to stay invisible. If anyone caught even a glimpse of those crates on the surveillance, it would raise questions they couldn't afford to answer.

She glanced down the shaft, imagining Gabriel below, readying the next set. "Send them up," she whispered, though she knew he couldn't hear her. There was no room for breaks or mistakes; they had to keep moving, keep the rhythm. The clock was ticking, and every moment counted.

Chapter 83

Adam Dupont jolted awake, the faint creak of the office chair beneath him snapping him out of a restless nap. He blinked groggily at the monitors, trying to shake the fog of sleep. The big screen in front of him still displayed the sweeping feed of MAIN SHAFT (300/200)—empty, steady, and uneventful. His gaze darted to the smaller screens surrounding it, a wall of identical monotony.

It was the same as it had been all night, except…

Adam frowned, sitting up straighter. One of the screens was black. TOP CONVEYOR EXIT, the label read in small, white text. He leaned forward, squinting, as though the darkness might reveal something he'd missed. But the feed didn't flicker, didn't even hint at movement. Just a blank, lifeless screen.

"Great," Adam muttered, running a hand through his hair. A broken camera. Of course. He glanced at the clock—02:52. No way was he calling his boss at this hour over something like this. Not unless he wanted an earful about "wasting resources" or "panicking over nothing."

Instead, Adam reached for the landline on the corner of the desk, flipping through the laminated directory taped beside it. He found the number for Keller Group's on-call maintenance and dialed, the receiver cool against his ear as he waited through several rings.

"Yeah?" A groggy voice finally answered, heavy with sleep.

"Hey, this is Adam Dupont, night security at Bex," Adam said, keeping his voice low. "Got a busted camera on my end—Top Conveyor Exit. Screen's gone black. Thought you should know."

There was a long pause, followed by a muffled yawn. "Black screen? No feed at all?"

"None. Dead as a doornail." Adam drummed his fingers on the desk, glancing back at the monitor as if it might suddenly spring back to life. "Everything else is working fine. Just that one's out. Probably needs a reboot or something."

The maintenance tech sighed, and Adam could almost hear him scratching his head. "Okay, I'll head over. Should be there by 04:45 at the latest."

Adam grunted in acknowledgment. "Thanks. I'm stuck in the booth, so I can't check it myself. Just give me a call if you need anything from me."

"Will do," the tech replied, the line clicking dead a second later.

Adam hung up the receiver and stared at the black screen again, his brow furrowed. He hated when equipment failed. Made him feel like he was flying blind, even though the other cameras showed nothing but the same still corridors and dormant machinery. He scanned the feeds one by one, double-checking each for any hint of movement, but everything remained as docile as ever.

He leaned back, crossing his arms over his chest. "Just a stupid camera," he muttered to himself, though the unease from earlier still lingered in the back of his mind. He reached for his thermos and took a swig of cold coffee, his gaze flicking between the black screen and the others.

The office settled into silence again, broken only by the soft hum of the radio and the occasional creak of the chair. Adam sighed, forcing himself to relax. Maintenance was on the way. The rest of the feeds were fine. He just had to wait it out.

Chapter 84

Hours passed, and Amelia and Gabriel's work blurred into a repetitive, exhaustive routine. They moved in silence, precise and calculated, as each ascent chipped away at their impossible task. By 03:20, only the final ten crates remained, and Amelia rejoined Gabriel back underground. Her entire body ached, and she felt exhaustion settling into her bones.

Gabriel wiped the sweat from his brow and his eyes met hers. "Last run," he said optimistically, and Amelia nodded, barely able to muster a smile.

"Twenty two… twenty three," he mouthed to himself before making his final push.

They both stood in the shadows of the shaft door, watching as the final crates disappeared up the conveyor. For a moment, Amelia allowed herself to believe they might actually pull this off.

But then she remembered the trucks still waiting at the surface—and that the hardest part of the journey still lay ahead. For now, though, this was a win.

Climbing onto their crawlers, they started the machines one last time. Amelia led the way, guiding them back down the winding tunnel to the 300 Deck. Once there, they returned the crawlers to the exact spots they had found them. Gabriel pulled a tarp over both machines, making sure they looked undisturbed, before hopping down and brushing the dust off his hands.

He turned to Amelia with a tired but triumphant grin. "We did it!"

Then, with a wry smile, he added, "Now, we just have to get them over the border."

Amelia let out a half-chuckle, meeting his eyes. "You make it sound so easy!" She glanced back up the dark tunnel, thinking about the hidden chamber, now empty, its secrets laid bare. They had carefully closed both doors and swept the excavated salt chips close up to the wall's edge, hoping no one would know the wiser.

She exhaled. "We're not done yet." Her mind was already racing ahead, mapping out their next steps. "But we're close!"

Gabriel nodded, and together, they made their way back to the maintenance shaft, the resin key still pressing lightly against Amelia's thigh in her pocket. As they climbed up for the last time, the air felt lighter, as if the mine was finally willing to let them go. Yet, an awareness lingered in her mind—it was only a matter of time before someone noticed... *something*. They still had to be quick, precise, and, above all, invisible. The world couldn't know what they did—at least, not yet.

When they emerged into the cold night, the sky was already beginning to lighten, a hint of dawn on the horizon. Amelia looked over at Gabriel and he had exhaustion etched into every line of his face. But there was something else too—relief, and maybe even hope.

They crossed to the conveyor exit and their steps crunched slightly on the frost-covered ground. The belt whirred steadily, its low hum blending into the stillness of the early morning. Gabriel crouched by the controls, his fingers lingering for a moment as though considering something. Then, with a final glance at the last ten crates on the conveyor, he flipped the switch, and the mechanism came to a gradual halt, the silence it left behind feeling almost deafening.

Amelia watched him as he stood, brushing his hands against his jeans, and followed his gaze to the other stacks of crates waiting on the ground.

"We have to get moving," Gabriel said, breaking the silence as his eyes moved toward the trucks. "Before anyone sees."

Amelia nodded, but her heart was pounding. The last leg of their journey was about to begin, and its stakes were even higher. She could only hope they had thought of everything, because after everything they had just done, there was no turning back.

From somewhere in the distance, a faint sound carried on the early morning air—a low rumble echoing off the mountain sides, growing steadily louder. Amelia's breath caught as she exchanged a sharp look with Gabriel in alarm.

"Do you hear that?" she hissed, the fear in her voice unmistakable.

He nodded slowly, his expression tightening as he scanned the faint light.

"It's a truck," he said, edged with concern. His eyes met hers, wide and alert.

"And it's coming straight toward us."

Amelia felt a chill race down her spine. They might have run out of time.

Chapter 85

The low rumble grew louder, vibrating through the crisp morning air. Amelia and Gabriel stood tense beside the crates, eyes fixed on the horizon as the sound intensified. The first light of dawn moved over the mountain tops, casting blurry, elongated shadows that seemed to reach toward them like silent warnings.

Amelia held her breath, straining to listen, but her quickened pulse thundered in her ears, making it nearly impossible. "It's getting closer!" she said with fear.

Gabriel strained to listen, his expression grim. The rumble grew, echoing off the mountainsides, and enveloping them in uncertainty. For a moment, it seemed like the sound was coming from all directions.

Amelia's thoughts spun. *Had they been discovered? Was someone coming for them?* The urge to grab the crates, to shield them from some inevitable disaster, clawed at her. Her instincts screamed to run, to somehow carry all of them to safety, even though she knew it was impossible.

The engine was getting louder and louder... closer and closer.

But then, as suddenly as it had amplified, the noise faded. The rumble softened and veered away, until it became clear the truck was passing by on a nearby road, oblivious to their presence.

Relief flooded through Amelia. She exhaled slowly and her shoulders eased. "It's not coming here," she said, more to convince herself, still with some concern on her face.

Gabriel nodded while his gaze stayed fixed on the fading sound. "Maybe just an early delivery heading into town?" he offered, though his clenched jaw betrayed his lingering tension. "But it's a reminder—we have a little over an hour before the first staff comes in."

Amelia agreed, and they turned their attention back to the task at hand, the scare injecting a renewed urgency into their movements. She had done a masterful job stacking the crates into neat columns beside the conveyor's end. Each box held a piece of history—artworks hidden away for decades, sealed in darkness, now waiting to see the light of day once more.

She ran her fingers over one of the lids and the wood was cool beneath her touch. She needed this tangible proof it was real—that they had actually done it. They had brought every last one up from the depths. But now came the most dangerous part—getting them out of the country with no one noticing.

She met Gabriel's eyes, with her determination hardening. "We can't afford any more close calls."

He nodded, then paused to look around. His face was pale in the dim pre-dawn light, but his eyes were sharp and focused as he looked back at her. "This is it," he said. "The Alliance returns... it's up to us now."

The Alliance returns. Those words echoed in Amelia's mind, and she felt a surge of responsibility wash over her. It felt as though they were walking on a tightrope, with everything balanced precariously, ready to fall with the slightest wrong move. This wasn't just about the paintings. It was about the people who had risked everything to save them, to hide them away so they wouldn't fall into the wrong hands. And now, she and Gabriel were the ones carrying that legacy forward—finally completing a task that started over 80 years ago.

As they stood close together, ready to move the crates, Amelia felt the warmth of Gabriel's presence beside her; their shoulders brushed lightly, sending a flutter of nerves through her. Instinctively, she stepped away, seeking to ground herself in the reality of their accomplishment. "Let's get these loaded," she said, breaking the silence. "We don't have much time!"

The two trucks were parked nearby, their engines off, shrouded in the darkness. It had been a risk renting them in Monthey, but a necessary one.

Now, every second that ticked by felt like a countdown, and the sooner they were across the border, the safer the paintings would be. As far as Amelia and Gabriel knew, they were still the only ones who knew about the cache. They wanted to keep it that way.

Working side by side, they quickly loaded the crates into the trucks. A 7.5-tonne lorry was spacious, but it was still a puzzle to fit all the paintings securely in both trucks. As they lifted and stacked, Amelia's mind drifted to the names listed in the ledger, each recorded with meticulous care. The Blochs, the Cohens, the Van den Berghs, the Abramovich and Zaslavsky families in Russia—all these families had entrusted their treasures to the Alliance, hoping against hope that their heritage would survive. Tyranny had tried to erase their histories, their cultures, and their stories, but the Alliance had fought back, hiding these pieces to preserve a legacy that could have been lost forever. Now, decades later, Amelia and Gabriel found themselves part of that same effort, trying to keep those stories alive—to give that hope in humanity back—even if it meant risking everything.

The minutes flew by, and by the time they finished, the first full sun rays were starting to creep over the mountains, painting the sky in shades of purple and orange. Amelia's muscles ached, and her hands were raw—she and Gabriel were both exhausted—but the sight of the two loaded trucks, their precious cargo safely secured, made it all worth it.

Gabriel closed the back of the second truck and wiped the sweat from his forehead. "It's almost 05:00," he said, glancing at his watch. "We need to move."

Amelia nodded, and they climbed into the cabs of their respective trucks. She adjusted the rearview mirror, catching a glimpse of the crates stacked tightly behind her. It was a sobering sight—a visual reminder of everything they were risking, and everything they stood to lose. "Stick to the plan," she said to herself. "Just stick to the plan."

Amelia's hand froze on the ignition, her mind suddenly flashing to the camera at the top of the conveyor. She gasped, her heart skipping a beat, and quickly opened her door. Gabriel, already seated in his truck, noticed her sudden movement and rolled down the passenger window, concern etched on his face.

"What's wrong?" he called out, his voice low but urgent.

"The camera at the top of the conveyor! My scarf is still covering it!" she whispered sharply, her eyes wide with realization. "If anyone sees it, they'll know something's up!"

The light outside was growing stronger, and the darkness that had been their shield was fading. If someone spotted a camera lens draped with a scarf, it would be a clear sign that something had gone terribly wrong. Amelia's mind raced—*had they been careful enough?* The mine staff would have no reason to review the footage unless they discovered something unusual—like something covering a camera—and that alone could unravel everything. She had to retrieve it, and quickly.

"I'll be right back," she said, not waiting for Gabriel's response as she jumped down from the cab. She hurried back towards the conveyor's exit, with footsteps light and quick, and adrenaline driving her forward. But as she neared the building, she stopped abruptly and gasped.

Standing by the main shaft door, just a few yards further from the conveyor, was a mine worker. He was wearing a dark blue coverall and a helmet, and the reflective strips on his clothing were glinting in the early morning light. Amelia's heart pounded as she quickly ducked behind a stack of barrels, peeking around the edge to get a better look. He must have arrived early for his 05:00 shift, and now he was lingering near the entrance, checking something on his phone.

Why was he standing there? Did he see something suspect? she worried.

For a moment, Amelia considered abandoning the scarf—just leaving it and hoping no one would notice. But she knew better. A covered camera was the kind of thing that would prompt questions, and questions led to investigations. She couldn't risk it. She had to get that scarf.

She took a deep breath and tried to steady her nerves. The worker appeared to be distracted, scrolling through his phone, his attention completely absorbed. She had to move now, or she might lose the opportunity. Amelia crept out from behind the barrels and moved as quietly as she could. The frost underfoot crunched slightly, and she winced, pausing to make sure the worker hadn't heard. He didn't look up.

Step by step, toe to heel, she edged closer to the conveyor, keeping her head low, and using the shadows cast by the machinery to stay hidden. Her pulse thudded in her ears, each beat echoing like a drum, and she kept her eyes on the worker. If he moved, she was ready to duck back at the slightest sign that he could notice her. As she got nearer to the conveyor exit, she could see the dark fabric of the scarf, still knotted over the lens, a stark contrast against its lighter-colored casing.

Just a few more meters, she thought, willing herself to stay calm. The worker let out a sigh, still engrossed in his phone, and Amelia seized the moment. She lunged forward, reaching up and gently tugged the scarf free from the camera. It slipped off easily, and she quickly balled it up in her hand, tucking it into her jacket pocket.

She backed away while keeping an eye on the man, her movements slow and deliberate, trying not to make a sound. But then he shifted, stretching his neck and glancing around like he sensed something was off. Amelia quickly ducked and held her breath with every muscle tensed. He looked in her direction, and for a split second, their eyes almost met. She was pressed low against the far side of the conveyor, hidden just below his line of sight.

The seconds stretched out, painfully slow, but then the worker's gaze drifted back down to his phone, and he resumed scrolling. Amelia took one last, careful step back, then turned and slipped away, making her way back towards the trucks. She could feel the sweat trickling down her back, cooling relief washing over her as she put more distance between herself and the building.

When she reached Gabriel, he was still leaning out the window with a worried look on his face. "What happened?" he asked in awe as she climbed back into her seat, slightly breathless.

"There was a worker," she said, glancing over her shoulder to make sure no one had followed. "But I don't think he saw me. I got it." She pulled the scarf out of her pocket, holding it up briefly before shoving it back inside. "But we can't risk going out the main way. We need to use the rear entrance."

Gabriel nodded. "Alright. Let's move."

Amelia shut her door, and her hands trembled slightly as she gripped the steering wheel. She glanced at the side-view mirror, seeing the light of dawn growing brighter, and took a deep breath. They weren't out of this yet, but they were close. And as she turned the key in the ignition, she knew there was no turning back.

Chapter 86

Just outside the main shaft entrance, Keller's on-call maintenance worker, Marco Lemoine, leaned against the frosted wall, tapping on his phone to start the work order for the *Top Conveyor Exit* camera. He yawned, his breath visible in the cold air as he entered the details. A busted camera wasn't how he'd hoped to spend his Sunday morning, but it beat dealing with an oil spill or some grimy mechanical failure.

As he stood there, the stillness of the mine entrance was broken by a faint snap, like the sound of brittle wood cracking underfoot. Marco froze, his eyes lifting from his phone to scan the area. The dim light spilling from the entrance illuminated nothing but the shadowy outlines of machinery and a few stacked pallets near the conveyor. *Probably a mine cat,* he thought. The little creatures always seemed to show up just before dawn, scrounging for food.

Stuffing his phone into his pocket, Marco walked toward the camera. As he neared the conveyor, a low rumble cut through the quiet morning air. Engines? He paused, frowning, and turned back toward the platform, scanning the area. Trucks running this early? That didn't make sense. Operations usually didn't start for another hour, and the platform had been empty when he arrived.

Marco listened for a moment, the sound growing weak before fading completely. He shook his head, dismissing it. Maybe some overeager workers had shown up early to warm their engines—or perhaps security had mixed up the shift schedule. Either way, it wasn't his problem.

Reaching the camera, Marco climbed up onto a small control panel set against the wall and inspected the device. The casing looked perfectly intact, no damage to the lens, no obvious issues. He pulled out his tablet, fingers stiff from the cold, and tapped into the remote feed from the field office. The connection looked… stable? Everything appeared normal. He could see the shaft, the conveyor—nothing seemed out of place.

He sighed, shaking his head. Security said the feed was dead? *Proba-bly should have checked it first before I drove all the way out here*, he thought. Hop-ping down from the panel, he brushed some salt dust from his hands and gave the camera one last glance. Everything looked fine. He grabbed his radio and called the field office to report back. "Looks like a temporary glitch," he said, his tone dry. "Camera's working fine now."

He paused for a moment, scanning the quiet platform out of habit before heading back toward his truck. Just another wasted trip, he thought, but at least it wasn't a bigger issue.

Chapter 87

The trucks rumbled to life, breaking the stillness of the early morning. Any noise now would likely be dismissed as part of the soon-to-begin shift—if anyone noticed at all. Amelia and Gabriel drove slowly at first, winding their way out of the mine's rear maintenance road and onto the back roads, keeping to the shadows as best they could. Amelia's knuckles were white as she gripped the steering wheel. Every bend in the road, every flicker of movement in the distance, made her chest tighten. They were still moving under the cover of darkness at ground level, but dawn was fast approaching from above, and they had to get across the border before the world woke up.

The usual route from Bex to France would take them along the A21 through Monthey, westward toward Saint-Gingolph on Lac Léman. But that wasn't an option. As a main artery between the two countries, it was too exposed—too many chances for random customs checks. Any inspection of their cargo would lead to confiscation at best, and prison at worst.

Instead, they planned to turn off the A21 in Monthey and take the Route de Morgins, a hair-raising, winding road that climbed the steep side of a mountain to the border town of Morgins. From there, they would cross into France via the Pas de Morgins, a high mountain pass known for its narrow, twisting curves. What made the Pas de Morgins ideal, though, was its absence of a border crossing station. Still, it was a challenging 45-minute drive under normal conditions. In a 7.5-tonne truck, it promised to be nothing short of terrifying.

Every muscle in Amelia's body ached from hours of relentless work, the weariness compounded by minimal sleep. The exhaustion was bone-deep, a constant weight pressing on her shoulders. But she couldn't afford to let it take hold—not now. She needed to stay alert, sharp, fully aware of every move, every turn, because this next part would demand everything from her. As they began the climb, Amelia felt every shift and dip in the road beneath her tires, with the early morning frost adding a treacherous slickness that made the truck slide just enough to keep her on edge.

Her headlights cut through the darkness, illuminating the sharp, jagged edges of the mountain road, and each turn demanded her full concentration. Just ahead, Gabriel's taillights glowed like steady beacons, a small comfort in an otherwise difficult situation. The incline grew steeper with each turn, punishing the truck's engine, and every time she rounded a corner, she had to fight to keep the vehicle steady. Though exhaustion clung to her, adrenaline coursed through her veins, pushing her past the limits of fatigue and keeping her grip firm on the wheel.

The air grew colder as they ascended, seeping in through the cracks of the truck cab and fogging the windows. Amelia had the defogger on high, but it struggled to keep up. Mist clung to the mountainside like a shroud, thickening as the dew point dropped and further reducing the already poor visibility. She gripped the steering wheel tighter, her eyes flicking to the edge of the road where a sheer drop waited, hidden in the dark. She didn't dare think about what would happen if either truck lost control, if the brakes failed, or the road gave way. Her heart lurched every time she heard the tires squeal, and she found herself holding her breath as they navigated each frost-coated hairpin curve.

Ahead of her, Gabriel's truck suddenly slowed, his brake lights flaring. For a moment, Amelia's heart jumped, thinking he might have spotted something—another vehicle, a patrol, anything that could ruin their escape. But then she saw it. The road ahead snaked sharply to the right, a hairpin turn so tight it looked like it was designed to catch someone off guard. It wasn't just a curve—it was a knife edge, with a near-vertical drop on one side.

Gabriel's truck inched forward, the massive vehicle now creeping as he attempted the turn. Fully stopped behind him, Amelia shut off the heater to sharpen her focus and rolled down both windows. The cold air rushed in, but she barely noticed, her attention fixed on the grating screech of his tires against the frost-slicked pavement. For a sickening moment, Amelia saw the entire frame of Gabriel's lorry tilt, his cab leaning precariously toward the drop-off. Her hands tightened on the steering wheel, knuckles white, as she watched in helpless terror. It was almost like the mountain itself was pulling the truck over, coaxing it closer to the abyss. Gabriel's headlights swung out over nothing, illuminating only darkness and the faint outline of jagged rocks far below.

Amelia's breathing increased as his truck continued its slow turn, the trailer swinging wide behind it, the back wheels perilously close to slipping off the edge. The entire frame swayed, teetering on the brink, like gravity itself was deciding whether to hold or let go. The image flashed through her mind—one wrong move on the frost-coated asphalt, one extra push on the gas, and the truck would tip. It would tumble end over end down the mountain, smashing against the rocks below, and scatter Gabriel and the paintings like shards of broken glass.

Her pulse spiked, hammering in her ears, and she had to fight the urge to close her eyes, almost like not seeing it would make it less real. The seconds felt like hours. Each heartbeat stretched out as she watched the truck cling to the road while Gabriel struggled to navigate the turn. She saw the glint of his side mirror angled down, trying to gauge just how close he was to the edge. For a moment, the back wheels seemed to slip, the trailer shuddering, and her heart stopped. "Stay with me!" she said to herself, willing Gabriel to hold, to make it through just one more turn. Then, with agonizing slowness, the truck began to straighten out, the wheels finding grip, the trailer easing around the bend.

Amelia exhaled a breath she hadn't realized she was holding, her hands shaking as she wiped her palms against her jeans. She saw Gabriel's truck come to a stop on the road above. But her eyes moved back to the narrow ledge he had just cleared, daring her to try the same. She could barely swallow against the dryness in her throat. She knew she had no choice. There was no going back. She would have to make that same turn, and if she didn't do it perfectly, it could be *her* and her truck that disappeared over the edge.

Steeling herself, she eased forward, gripping the wheel tighter while navigating the bend. She aligned the cab with the curve and every muscle in her body was taut as the trailer followed around the bend. The edge loomed closer, and for a gut wrenching moment, she felt the truck's balance shift slightly to the left. She froze, her breath catching, until the swaying stopped. Her instincts screamed at her to brake, but she forced herself to hold steady, knowing a sudden stop could tip the truck over the side.

When she finally cleared the hairpin, relief flooded through her, but it was short-lived. The climb was far from over, and the road wound higher and higher, with each new curve presenting a fresh test of their endurance and nerves. The sun was peeking over the horizon, spreading a pale light over the mountains, and Amelia could feel the mounting urgency. They were running out of time—soon, the world would wake, and the pass, still ahead, was their only shot at slipping through unnoticed.

Finally, the road leveled out, and the climb eased as they neared the top of the mountain. The air was thinner here, colder, and the altitude itself was testing them. Gabriel slowed, his brake lights flaring briefly in the dim pre-dawn light, and Amelia followed as they both pulled off to the side to check their trucks before crossing through. The hum of their idling engines was the only sound breaking the stillness of the early morning.

Amelia climbed down, and the crisp, biting air hit her face as she stepped onto the smooth pavement. The cold carried a sharp, clean scent, and cut through the lingering smell of diesel from the idling trucks. Her legs trembled from the grueling drive and the tension of what they'd just endured. She hobbled over to Gabriel, who had also stepped out of his cab, his face tight with worry but his eyes sharp and focused. "Gabriel, I..." Her thought trailed off right into him.

"You okay?" he asked, his voice low, glancing over her shoulder at the road they had just conquered. "That was... intense."

Amelia nodded, attempting a smile, though her heart was still pounding. "Yeah, I'm fine. I just... I thought... I almost lost you back there." She caught herself, the words slipping out before she could rein them in. A flush of warmth rushed to her cheeks, and she quickly tried to backtrack, glancing away. "I mean, the paintings," she added, her voice a bit too quick, the attempt to cover up her slip painfully obvious.

She stole a glance at Gabriel, half-expecting to see confusion or maybe amusement in his eyes. Instead, she found his gaze steady, searching hers, and for a brief moment, the world around them seemed to fall away. She felt exposed, her heart beating faster, not from fear this time but from the sudden, raw vulnerability of what she had just let slip.

Amelia swallowed, forcing her eyes back to the road ahead. "We just need to make it across now," she said, her tone firmer, but softer than before. "I'll take the lead. We go slow, stick to the plan. If there's any trouble, we keep driving. No stopping, no hesitating."

Gabriel didn't respond right away, and she felt his gaze still on her, like he was trying to decide whether to address what she'd said or let it pass. After a beat, he nodded, his expression thoughtful but determined. "Alright. I'm right behind you," he said, and there was a warmth in his voice that hadn't been there before, like he understood more than she'd meant to reveal.

As Amelia turned back to the wheel, a new layer of tension settled over her—one that had nothing to do with the border ahead. Yet beneath it, she felt a sense of relief, like something had finally surfaced, even if only for a moment. She eased back into the driver's seat and tried to focus on the road. Up ahead, she could see the small, dimly lit border sign, a Swiss flag fluttering on one side and a French flag on the other. They had chosen this crossing for a reason—no guard posts, no customs checks, just a quiet road slipping from one Schengen Zone country to the next. Seeing it now, though, twisted her stomach with anxiety. The plan had always been to cross without stopping, to blend in with the early morning, but even this late in the game, anything could still go wrong.

She glanced at her side-view mirror, catching sight of Gabriel's truck idling behind her, his headlights shining softly, waiting. They were almost there—just a few more minutes, and they would be across, out of Switzerland and into France. *Free.* The thought steadied her nerves, if only for a moment.

Easing back onto the road, she squinted into the dim light ahead, her eyes narrowing as she tried to focus on the stretch leading to the border. But something moved in her vision. She blinked, half-convinced it was just the dim light of dawn playing tricks on her exhaustion.

But then her heart skipped, and a chill washed over her. This wasn't a trick of the light.

Ahead, about 50 meters from the border sign, a silhouette emerged from the shadows.

The figure stood by the side of the road next to a car, barely visible against the dawn light. But then a faint glint caught her eye—a badge. The uniform followed, now unmistakable in the growing light. It was a Swiss patrol agent.

Panic surged, tightening her chest. He wasn't supposed to be there. There were *never* supposed to be guards at this crossing, especially not this early. Why was one here now?

A terrible thought seized her: Was the agent waiting for… *them?*

Amelia's mind spun with possibilities, each more alarming than the last. She could see the agent's head turn slightly, tracking their approach. His posture seemed casual, but there was a readiness about him that set her nerves ablaze.

She had seconds to decide what to do. Slow down? Speed up? Anything but hesitate. If he flagged them, even gave them a second look, the entire operation would be over.

She glanced in the mirror again, locking onto Gabriel's silhouette in his truck. Her pulse quickened. There was no time to stop and establish a plan—they couldn't risk it. She was leading, and if Gabriel saw the guard, he would be waiting for her signal, trusting her to make the call.

Amelia took a deep breath, trying to suppress the rising tide of fear inside. *Blend in,* she reminded herself. *Look like any other driver passing through.* The plan was simple, but the stakes were impossibly high. Her hands tightened on the wheel, and she forced a small, practiced smile, even though no one could see.

"Just a routine drive," she said to herself. "Like we're supposed to be here… *smuggling 486 priceless works of art across an international border.*"

With a shaky exhale, she kept her foot steady on the accelerator, continuing to move forward at a deliberate pace. The patrol agent was leaning against his car, his posture relaxed but purposeful. His eyes scanned the road ahead, sharp and observant, making her feel as though he'd been waiting for this exact moment.

Amelia kept her gaze forward, refusing to look at him as she approached, like she was just another driver heading over the pass. She could hear her heart beating so loud it drowned out the engine's hum as she kept tight just waiting for him to step out into the road to stop them.

Wait, am I supposed to acknowledge him? The thought hit her like a jolt. *Would ignoring him look suspicious? But if I wave, does that draw attention? Too friendly? Too obvious?* Her hands tightened on the wheel, her mind spiraling as she tried to anticipate his reaction. She decided to keep her gaze fixed on the road, her grip rigid, her pulse hammering in her ears. *Just keep driving. Just another driver.*

As the truck approached, she caught the slightest glimpse of his face out of the corner of her eye. His expression was neutral, his focus elsewhere—as though he was scanning for something but hadn't yet decided what. For a moment, she almost believed he wasn't paying attention to her. *Almost.*

But then, his head turned, just enough to track the truck's movement. Amelia's pulse spiked violently, her grip tightening on the wheel as she fought the urge to slam the brakes, to stop and explain, to do anything but drive. *No. Keep going. Steady. Normal.*

Her breath stayed locked in her chest as the truck rolled past, the tension tightening with every passing meter. She couldn't know if the agent's gaze lingered or if he had already turned away. But she didn't slow down, didn't dare to check the mirror, even as she thought of Gabriel's truck following behind. She could only hope he would keep his nerve also, that his approach would appear just as routine as hers—and that the agent wouldn't take a second look.

Amelia kept her breath held until she saw the Swiss flag in her side mirror, fading behind her as she crossed into France, the road ahead blessedly clear.

The tension that had gripped her body began to ease, and she could finally breathe again. It felt like they had slipped through a crack in reality, an impossible moment where everything lined up just right.

She kept driving until they reached Châtel, the town just across the border, and pulled over on the side of the road. Moments later, Gabriel's truck rolled up beside hers, his passenger window already down, relief etched across his face.

"We're in France!" he said, his voice shaky, but mixed with unmistakable relief. He leaned over the passenger seat, and even though exhaustion was sculpted into his features, Amelia could see his eyes gleaming with triumph.

Amelia nodded. Taking a deep inhale through her nose, she held it for a second before exhaling slowly. As the tension gripping her chest finally began to loosen, a smile crept onto her face—a genuine, unguarded smile. "We made it," she said softly, the words carrying a mix of disbelief and overwhelming relief.

For a moment, they just looked at each other, the still dawn settling around them. Gabriel's grin softened, and his eyes held hers, lingering a little longer than she expected. "Let's get out of here," he said, his tone light but with an edge of something deeper. "We've still got a long way to go."

Amelia felt a sudden warmth pulse through her body. It may have been the lingering endorphins, but there was something in his gaze—something that made her heart skip, a warmth that seemed to reach out to her, even across the distance between their trucks. She didn't need him to say it; she could feel it in the way he looked at her, the way his smile lingered, almost reluctant to fade. He wasn't just talking about the journey ahead, but about them, and the bond that had grown between them through all of this.

"Yeah," she said softly, her smile widening. "Together."

Gabriel's grin deepened, and he nodded, as if her word had confirmed something he hadn't dared to say out loud. "Together."

The road wound down, descending deeper into France, and Amelia's hands finally relaxed on the steering wheel. The adrenaline still surged through her veins, but she allowed herself another slow, deep breath. "We made it," she whispered again, barely daring to believe it. "We actually made it."

The trucks rumbled onward towards Paris, and as they entered the rolling French countryside, the sun broke fully over the horizon, casting a warm, golden light across the landscape. The mountains that had seemed so foreboding were now softened by the dawn, and the distant towns were just beginning to wake. Amelia felt a profound calm wash over her. They still had a journey ahead, and more obstacles to face, but they had achieved the impossible. They were no longer fugitives in the dark—they were protectors, guardians of history. And as long as they had each other, she knew they could see this through to the end.

Chapter 88

Paris, Modern Day

The first days back in Paris felt like a whirlwind. Amelia and Gabriel moved through the city like shadows, keeping their operation as discreet as possible. They didn't announce the discovery, didn't make grand gestures. Nobody could know what they found or where they found it. Instead, they worked secretly behind the scenes, reaching out through trusted channels to the families they believed had rightful claims to the artworks, as indicated by the ledger entries. But it wasn't enough to simply make contact with these families; they knew they had to be meticulous and careful.

Every name in the ledger was a starting point, but confirming legitimate heirs was no easy task. Amelia and Gabriel sifted through genealogies, old letters, and public archives, piecing together fragmented family trees that had been torn apart by war. All in all, they had about 300 families to research and contact. They traced lines of inheritance across continents, reaching out to descendants who had scattered far from their European roots. For many of these families, the war had been a cruel divide, separating generations by loss, distance, and, in the worst cases, death. Yet, whenever they found even a faint connection, Amelia and Gabriel followed it, intent to find someone with a rightful claim.

It was painstaking work, and time was not on their side. They had to move quickly, knowing that once word got out, their careful plans could unravel. The cache of paintings would attract attention from art traffickers, treasure hunters, and even authorities like Interpol. Each conversation was a delicate balance—sharing just enough to build trust without revealing too much. But they kept pushing forward, knowing that each verification brought them closer to fulfilling the promises the Alliance had made decades ago.

Gabriel spent long hours reviewing the ledger, carefully examining the entries, each a small clue that could unlock a family's lost story. Amelia's contacts in the art world proved invaluable, helping to trace family lines, find names, and connect paintings to their rightful heirs. Some families, like the Blochs in Paris, were easier to find; when their paintings were returned, they were met with a tearful gratitude. Others were much harder to trace, with names faded and connections lost to time and tragedy.

Through word-of-mouth, old letters, and even DNA services, they gradually reconstructed a web of relationships that had been severed long ago. Charlotte Hawthorne, Gabriel's shrewd lawyer, worked tirelessly to handle the paperwork, ensuring the transfers were discreet and legally secure. Given the world didn't know about where the paintings had been found yet, the documentation needed to imply the art had "been in private storage" for over 80 years.

They were always mindful that the Swiss authorities or the Keller Group would not be pleased to learn that 486 priceless works of art had been smuggled from sovereign territory. Such a revelation could lead to international legal battles, seizure of the artworks, and possibly severe repercussions for everyone involved. And the Keller Group, with its vast resources and influence, might stop at nothing to reclaim the paintings, seeing them as assets unjustly taken from their control.

But despite these challenges, Amelia and Gabriel were unwavering in their goal. The paintings had rightful owners, and they saw themselves not as smugglers but as facilitators of justice, returning the art to those it truly belonged to. Their task wasn't just about the act of return—it was a race against time, ensuring the rightful owners reclaimed their legacies before anyone else could stake a claim.

Each family was approached privately, and many were astonished to discover that a part of their past had survived all these years. For Amelia, it wasn't just about returning art; it was about reconnecting people with a piece of themselves they thought was lost forever.

In the flurry of uncrating and cataloging the artworks they had recovered from Bex, Amelia finally came face-to-face with the four newly discovered Henri Vallin paintings. Upon seeing them—*Lady by the Window*, *The Violinist's Muse*, *Garden by the Vineyard*, and *Twilight at Montmartre*—it felt like a piece of her own past was opening up before her.

She remembered her time in grad school when she'd painstakingly restored the *Unknown—The Portrait of Eloise*, the only Vallin painting the art world had ever known. Now, there were four more, their luminous brushstrokes unmistakably matching the style she'd studied all those years ago. The artistry was truly a masterwork and a mixture of awe and gratitude washed over her as she finished unwrapping each canvas. The colors and faces—long buried beneath layers of salt and secrecy—spoke to her, reminding her how art could transcend time. And just then, she understood how much remained hidden in the world, and how vital her mission truly was.

As they continued down the ledger, Amelia and Gabriel were reminded of a recurring reference: Trubetskoy, the grand estate once owned by Sergei Shchukin and his wife, Nadia Vallois. Initially, they thought these entries might be about artworks hidden by Sergei, whose collection had been confiscated by the Soviet regime. But as they investigated further, they realized the original masterpieces from his collection were still missing, likely lost forever. Instead, the entries tied to Trubetskoy pointed to a different act of preservation.

Nadejda had used her influence and the estate's relative safety to protect art on behalf of Soviet Jews and other persecuted families. These weren't her works to save, but her actions ensured that pieces of cultural and personal significance endured, even as their owners faced unimaginable fates. It was a quiet resistance, carried out with meticulous care, and the ledger had preserved this legacy for decades, waiting for someone to uncover the truth.

Unlike other entries, which often had family names and traceable locations, the Russian pieces only had "Trubetskoy" as a point of reference. This vague detail made it incredibly difficult to find direct heirs, especially since many original owners' fates were lost in the chaos of Soviet purges and forced relocations. To unravel this part of the puzzle, Amelia and Gabriel took a different approach. They reached out to historians familiar with Soviet displacement and art confiscation, and Gabriel used his family's diplomatic connections to access archives in Russia. They examined emigration records, consulted genealogists, and connected with descendants of Soviet expats across Europe. It took months of research, but slowly, they uncovered stories of those who had fled, those forced into exile, and those who had disappeared, leaving their art as a lasting testament to their lives.

Despite these successes, there were still unresolved issues. As they worked, a nagging question continued to linger in Amelia's mind. Who really owns art? Who decides what should be seen and what remains hidden? She had spent her career bringing paintings back to life, breathing new life into colors that had faded, and textures that had crumbled. But as she watched the pieces being returned, she felt a deeper, more complicated issue. Art wasn't just a commodity, not to her. It was a piece of culture, of humanity's collective expression. Could it really belong to anyone, or was it something that should transcend ownership altogether?

Amelia found herself grappling with these questions late into the night, as she stared at the paintings still stacked in her studio, waiting to be claimed. Does anyone have the right to possess something that represents a collective human experience? Should art be returned to its origins, even if those origins are fractured, lost in the haze of history, or does it belong to everyone—to the world that once sought to destroy it and is now trying to reclaim it?

Despite her philosophical doubts, Amelia understood that art also carried personal histories and familial legacies. In the case of Gabriel's family, the connection was deeply personal. They had a clear claim to the 28 Vallois paintings in the ledger, directly linked through his lineage as descendants of Étienne and Clément Vallois. The documentation was meticulously prepared, with Charlotte ensuring every legal detail was secured, leaving no room for dispute. Amelia began to see that returning these pieces wasn't just about ownership—it was about restoring a family's lost heritage.

She realized while art transcends ownership in its ability to touch all who experience it, there is profound value in returning it to those whose histories are intertwined with it. Perhaps ownership wasn't about possession, but about connection. By restoring the paintings to Gabriel's family, they weren't just handing over canvases; they were rekindling stories, memories, and a sense of identity that had been lost to time and turmoil. The process felt seamless, almost natural, as the art found its way back under the Vallois name, sidestepping any potential legal challenges that might have arisen.

Yet, while the Vallois claim was straightforward, the situation involving the Bourget paintings—including the four Vallins—and several others on the list, particularly a few from Russia, proved far more delicate. Without direct heirs to claim ownership, these pieces lingered in a fragile state of uncertainty, their fates still hanging in the balance.

But as word of Amelia and Gabriel's discovery in the Swiss mine began to spread, that fragile state was threatened. Distant relatives, some with the faintest trace of a bloodline or none at all, started emerging to stake claims. None of them could be proven or verified and Amelia could already see what they were—treasure hunters. They didn't see the Bourget pieces for their historical value, their artistry, or what they represented. They saw them as a windfall, a way to cash in, and sell to the highest bidder. They had no intention of preserving the legacy, only exploiting it. And if those paintings ended up scattered in private homes, the world would never see them again, the light of their history snuffed out by greed.

Amelia's hands clenched as she thought of it. No. She couldn't let that happen. She had worked too hard, risked too much to let the Bourget collection disappear back into the shadows. Those paintings were meant to be seen, to remind the world of what had been lost and what had been saved. They weren't trophies to be stashed away by collectors who cared more about their own wealth than the stories behind the art. But without clear legal ownership, any attempt to donate them to museums would almost certainly be challenged, possibly even dragged into court, tied up in legal disputes for years.

It was Charlotte who voiced what Amelia had been fearing. "They're already organizing a class-action suit," she said, her voice crisp, yet tinged with frustration. "They want to make a claim on the Bourget estate and challenge any transfer of ownership to museums. If they succeed, those paintings will be stuck in limbo for years, maybe decades, hidden away, just as they were before."

Amelia felt a sick twist of anxiety in her gut. "I get it, Charlotte. I mean, if someone was staring at a million-dollar painting, especially if they were struggling, who wouldn't think about selling? But these people aren't even direct heirs. Their connections are flimsy, half of them barely even related. Under French law, unless you're a direct descendant or named in a will, you don't just get to claim an estate. It's not like you can just say, 'Oh, my cousin's uncle's neighbor once owned this,' and expect to walk away with it. They have no more right to this art than I would have to anything from their families."

She paused, her frustration giving way to a deeper sense of urgency. "But it's not just about the legal stuff. These paintings... they're not just objects. They're stories, memories, pieces of people who were almost erased. You can't put a price on that. If these pieces end up sold off to private collectors, they'll vanish, and everything they stood for will disappear with them. That's what scares me. We can't let that happen."

Charlotte nodded. "I know. But we're running out of time. Once this goes to court, it's going to be nearly impossible to resolve it quickly. We need to find a way to invalidate their claims."

Amelia's mind raced, trying to think of a way out. There had to be something, some loophole or strategy that could protect the paintings, and keep them from vanishing into private collections. But the law was murky, the arguments complex, and she felt like she was fighting against a tide that was already beginning to pull her under.

Amelia glanced across the room at Gabriel, who was deep in conversation over the phone with a representative from the Dzidkowicz family in Malopolskie, Poland. They were finalizing the transfer of a Manet from the ledger, a piece the family had chosen to donate to the Warsaw Museum in memory of their relatives who had perished in Auschwitz. She watched the determination in his eyes, and something more   a flicker of the same passion that had driven her throughout this entire journey. It was a reminder of why they were doing this, why they had risked so much from the very beginning.

The Alliance returns. The words echoed in her mind again, resonating with a strength she hadn't felt in a long time. This wasn't just about rescuing art; it was about preserving the memory of those who had once risked everything to save it, hiding these works so they could endure through a darkness that sought to erase them.

But now, as she stood over their operations desk, Amelia felt that strength wavering. How could they keep it from slipping away again? She watched Gabriel end the call, and the sight of him pacing the room deep in thought only deepened her anxiety. They were running out of options, and she finally gave voice to a fear that had been ever-present in her mind. "What if it's not enough?" she said to him. "What if everything we've done still isn't enough to protect them?"

Gabriel suddenly stopped and turned to her, his eyes intense, a glint of energy cutting through his exhaustion. "We'll find a way," he said.

"There has to be a clause, a loophole—something about how they were stored or cataloged. We can't give up. We have to try."

Amelia's heart clenched. She wanted to believe him, to feel the same certainty he seemed to be clinging to, but the reality of what they were facing felt crushing. "Even if we find something, it might not be enough," she said softly. "And if we can't..." Her voice trailed off, the unsaid fear hanging between them. She didn't want to say it, didn't want to admit that failure was even a possibility, but it lingered in the silence.

Gabriel stepped closer, closing the space between them, his gaze softening as he looked down at her. "We're not giving up," he said, his voice steady, but with a slight tremor that mirrored her own uncertainty. "We've come this far. We're not giving up." He reached out, his hand resting gently on her shoulder, and for a moment, the world around them seemed to fall away, leaving just the two of them standing there, holding onto each other for support.

Amelia felt her heart pound as she met his gaze, seeing the same fear, the same hope reflected back at her. It was as if, in that moment, all the chaos and uncertainty had distilled into a single, clear connection between them. She hadn't realized how much she needed that—needed him. And before she could second-guess herself, she closed the distance, her lips brushing his in a soft, deliberate kiss.

Gabriel's hand tightened slightly on her shoulder as his other hand moved to her cheek, and he kissed her back. It was a slow, tender meeting that carried all the words they hadn't dared to say. It was brief, a moment that felt suspended in time, but when they pulled apart, the air between them seemed different—charged with a new kind of focus.

Amelia blinked, a smile tugging at her lips. "We're not giving up," she echoed, her voice stronger now, almost like that kiss had reignited something inside her. "No matter what."

Before Gabriel could respond, the door burst open, and Charlotte hurried in, her cheeks flushed and her breath slightly ragged, like she'd been running. "I'm sorry to interrupt," she said, glancing between them and then quickly looking away, realizing she had stepped into an intimate moment. But there was an urgency in her eyes, an excitement that hadn't been there before. She took a breath, her gaze locking onto Amelia's, and a small, knowing smile crept up the sides of her mouth.

"I have an idea."

Chapter 89

The gathering took place in a discreet, elegant salon tucked away in the heart of Paris, a place where the city's aristocratic charm still lingered, untouched by time. The sun had dipped below the horizon, draping warm, orange hues across the streets as Amelia and Gabriel stepped into the space. Inside, the room blended history with modernity. Paintings lined the walls, each carefully illuminated to reveal its detail and craftsmanship, and the atmosphere radiated the significance of the moment.

Among these works were the four newly discovered pieces by Henri Vallin. Seeing them displayed here felt surreal. Amelia stepped closer, drawn to the depth and light in each painting, marveling at the delicate brushwork that somehow carried hints of both Impressionist whimsy and classical precision—a voice resurrected decades after it had gone silent. These paintings weren't just masterpieces; they were fragments of history brought back to life.

The atmosphere buzzed with anticipation. This wasn't just another art event; it was the culmination of the Alliance's mission—a promise made decades ago to preserve cultural treasures from destruction and exploitation. Tonight, that promise would be fulfilled and the secrets unearthed from the depths of the Bex Salt Mines would finally come to light.

Representatives from the Louvre, Rijksmuseum, Prado, and other renowned institutions moved among the paintings, their conversations blending with the faint echo of footsteps on marble floors. These works had not been seen publicly in over 80 years—if ever.

At the front of the room stood a polished wooden podium bearing a glass case. Inside lay two unassuming objects: the eight-page love letter—now the fully decoded ledger—and the *actual* Bourget Family Cookbook.

Amelia had reached out to the Moreau family to explain everything, including her and Gabriel's earlier misdirection with the book and what they found in the Artisan's Lodge. Despite the deception, the Moreaus were thrilled to support the cause. They graciously lent the cherished cookbook, even sending it via armored courier to ensure its safe arrival as part of the event.

Though humble in appearance, the significance of these objects was monumental. Together, they held the key to verifying the provenance of every piece in the room, documenting how each painting had been entrusted to the Alliance—not to be sold, but to be protected and preserved.

Amelia's gaze swept the room as she stood beside the podium. Though the preparations for this event had been meticulous, a subtle wave of unease lingered. What if, after all their efforts—all the near disasters, sleepless nights, and risks taken—some last-minute complication still unraveled everything? She wasn't usually one to dwell on worst-case scenarios, but she was also a realist. The very fate the Alliance had sought to prevent *could* still befall these works and she couldn't bear the thought of it.

She took a deep breath, trying to steady herself. Beside her, Gabriel was talking with Charlotte, who, along with her team of lawyers, had helped to set this up, with much of her work offered pro bono. Amelia leaned toward him and whispered, her voice low and tense. "What if someone contests this? Have we missed something?"

Gabriel looked back at her and shook his head. "We can't think that way," he replied softly, his gaze steady. "This *has* to work. After tonight, the art will be where it belongs—preserved, protected, and seen."

His assurance eased her nerves, and she allowed her gaze to drift across the room, taking in the faces of some of the most respected figures in the art world—people dedicated to preserving history and restoring what was lost. *The Alliance returns*, she thought, with hope stirring in her. It was comforting to know they *all* shared the same goal.

The plan was straightforward yet delicate, requiring a careful balance of legal strategy, historical respect, and moral clarity. This event wasn't an auction where participants would bid against one another to claim valuable assets. Instead, it was a dedication designed with a singular purpose: to place these works in public institutions best equipped to preserve them for future generations.

With no legitimate heirs to claim tonight's paintings, representatives were here to accept a unique responsibility: to become stewards of these works. By formalizing the transfer legally, they established a clear chain of provenance, supported by the ledger and historical records.

However, the ledger didn't *explicitly* outline the original owners' wishes for the artworks in the absence of heirs, presenting a potential legal challenge. Anticipating this, Charlotte turned to established legal doctrines and collaborated with experts in art and inheritance law. By focusing on principles of cultural property protection and heritage preservation, they worked to address this thoughtfully and responsibly.

Central to their strategy was the "cy-près" doctrine—a legal principle allowing courts to interpret the intent of a gift or trust when the original purpose could no longer be fulfilled exactly as intended. By showing that the families had entrusted their artworks to the Alliance to safeguard them from loss or exploitation, Charlotte argued that placing the pieces with public institutions dedicated to preservation, education, and public access was closely aligned with their original intent. To solidify this position, they obtained a declaratory judgment from a judge, affirming that this course of action was legally sound.

Her team meticulously crafted agreements that detailed each museum's responsibilities, with an emphasis on preserving the artworks' historical context. This documentation would establish a clear line of custody, deterring any distant relatives from making frivolous claims.

In the weeks before the event, Amelia and Gabriel reached out to museums renowned for their ethical leadership—places more concerned with education than profit. Amelia personally spoke with curators from institutions such as the Musée d'Orsay, the Metropolitan Museum of Art, and the National Gallery, sharing the remarkable histories behind each painting. Rather than viewing these pieces as mere acquisitions, she invited the museums to become part of a broader narrative of resilience and cultural preservation. A story of humanity—both at its worst and greatest.

Amelia knew they had to be thorough. The thought of the paintings being tied up in court for years haunted her. As a temporary steward of these works, she was determined to do what was best for them, and she knew Gabriel shared her resolve. Together with Charlotte, they spent long nights drafting plans, revising contracts, and considering every possible scenario to ensure that nothing could derail the dedication. Still, an uneasy sense of anticipation lingered.

As she glanced around, her gaze caught on a man standing near the back, half-hidden in the shadows. Unlike the others who moved easily from painting to painting, engaging in conversation, he remained still, his eyes fixed on the proceedings with an unsettling intensity. For a moment, their eyes met, and she felt a chill. There was something calculating in his stare, a quiet scrutiny that felt out of place amidst the reverent atmosphere. Gabriel must have noticed too, because she saw his expression tighten as he glanced in the same direction. It was only a moment, but it stirred an uneasy feeling, a hint of trouble looming just out of sight.

As the event began, Amelia stepped to the podium. The conversations quieted, and all eyes turned to her.

"Thank you all for being here," she began, her voice steady. "These paintings are more than just art; they are symbols of hope. The Alliance began as a promise to protect them against forces that sought to erase our culture. Tonight, we stand at the end of that journey, and we ask you to be the guardians who carry it forward."

She glanced at the ledger, resting her fingers on the glass case. "This document holds the records of families who were determined to safeguard these works for the future, no matter what that future might look like. Tonight, we are not here to debate ownership. We're here to celebrate *stewardship*—to affirm that these pieces belong to everyone, and not disappear into private hands. This ledger isn't just a list. It's a map of hope and defiance, a story of how far people will go to protect what mattered to them."

"In speaking with many of you tonight, I've heard similar stories, and they made me realize how deeply intertwined our histories are and how vital it is to honor the connections that bind us. Even though these paintings' original owners are no longer with us, their stories, their memories, and their resilience endure through these works."

The room remained hushed as Amelia spoke, but she could see nods and glances among the attendees—signs of their willingness to embrace the responsibility ahead. She felt a sense of calm wash over her, knowing that these works would be in the right places, with the right people.

When she finished, the silence lingered for a moment before a curator from the Rijksmuseum rose to speak. "We are honored to accept stewardship of these pieces," she said, her voice trembling slightly with emotion. "They fill gaps in our cultural story and allow us to reconnect with a shared past." Her eyes shone, betraying the depth of her feelings.

Next, a representative from a museum in Warsaw stood. "For us, this is about more than art," he said solemnly. "It is about preserving the stories of resilience and loss that shaped our history. We pledge to honor the families' trust and ensure these works remain accessible to all."

Amid these pledges, Gabriel stepped forward, glancing briefly at Amelia for reassurance before addressing the room. Over the past few weeks, he explained, he had reached out to scattered descendants of the Vallois lineage—those who still held valid claims to their family's 28 paintings. To his relief, after sharing the story of the Alliance and the commitment to honor its mission, every one of them had granted their blessing to donate the Vallois collection outright to museums worldwide.

"They all agreed these works were never meant to be hidden away," Gabriel said softly. "They were meant to be cared for and seen by everyone." A respectful hush settled over the audience, the gravity of the gesture resonating deeply with everyone in the room.

One by one, more representatives stood, each offering their own pledge. The commitments seemed to ripple, drawing out emotions that had been simmering beneath the surface.

Amelia could hardly believe it was all coming together. It was an affirmation of everything she and Gabriel had worked for—a collective effort to protect these paintings and ensure they would never be hidden away again. It was a pledge to the past, but also a promise to the future.

Amelia glanced at Gabriel. His expression was serious, but she could see the hint of a smile tugging at the corners of his mouth. Relief and pride overwhelmed her and she was starting to finally let herself believe they had pulled this off.

Then, as if on cue, a figure moved out of the shadows at the back of the room. It was the man she had noticed earlier. He stepped forward slowly, his polished shoes echoing against the marble floor. The sharp lines of his dark, tailored suit caught the light, giving him an air of authority. His expression was calm, almost too calm, but his eyes glinted with a cold, calculating edge as they scanned the room, locking onto Amelia and Gabriel with a predatory focus.

Amelia felt her heart skip a beat, a chill running down her spine. She didn't know who he was, but everything about his demeanor set her on edge. There was a confidence in his posture that suggested he was here for more than just an idle objection. They had taken every precaution to ensure this was a controlled event, but it seemed not everything could be accounted for. The room, which had been filled with a sense of unity, suddenly felt tense as everyone watched the man walk to the front of the room.

"Excuse me," he said smoothly, his voice cutting through the murmur like a blade. "I have reason to believe this event is premature. There are outstanding claims that must be addressed before any of this can proceed."

Chapter 90

All eyes turned to the darkly dressed man. The steady hum of conversation vanished in the room, replaced by a tense silence as curators exchanged uncertain glances. The once-cohesive atmosphere seemed to fracture, splintering under the heaviness of his presence. Amelia felt a knot tighten in her stomach and her pulse quicken. She had anticipated the possibility of objections—but not like this. Not something so direct, so public.

She met the man's gaze, unflinching, but inside, she felt the first stirrings of panic. The room felt smaller. The walls were closing in.

"And who are you?" she asked, her voice steady despite the tension edging it like a blade.

The man's lips curled into a faint, almost mocking smile. "I represent the interests of several parties who have a legitimate claim to these pieces," he said smoothly, his eyes moving to the ledger, then back to Amelia. "Non-blood relatives, yes, but relatives nonetheless. If you continue this charade, I guarantee these paintings will be tied up in legal disputes for years. Are you really willing to risk that?"

The air in the room grew heavier, a ripple of unease spreading through the crowd like the shadow of an approaching storm. Curators shifted in their seats, whispering in low tones, their murmurs laced with doubt. The carefully constructed confidence Amelia and Gabriel had worked so hard to build seemed to teeter, fragile under the unspoken questions. Amelia felt it creeping in—the same doubt she saw reflected in the faces around her. She stole a glance at Gabriel, and for a moment, she saw it in his eyes too—a glimpse of uncertainty breaking through his usual confidence.

But he stepped forward, his voice strong. "These paintings were entrusted to the Alliance with specific intent," he said, echoing Amelia's earlier words. "That intent was clear: protect, not profit. The historical documentation, including this ledger, proves that. The Alliance's promise was to ensure these pieces would not be lost to time or greed."

The man's smirk deepened, his eyes narrowing. "Intent is one thing, but legal precedent is another. If there are heirs, they have rights—whether you like it or not." His voice was cool, confident, like he was laying out a simple, indisputable fact. "You may think you're safeguarding these pieces, but without resolving these claims, you're only inviting further complications. The paintings will remain in limbo, trapped in legal battles. Is that what you want?"

Amelia felt a wave of dread wash over her. The man's carefully chosen words hung in the air, their scheming insinuations threatening to take root. She could see how they might begin to plants seeds of doubt, and for a fleeting moment, it felt as though everything was slipping away. All their efforts—the careful planning, every precaution—seemed to teeter on the edge, one fragile thread away from unraveling entirely. But she could *not* let that happen.

Stepping up beside Gabriel, she forced herself to meet the man's gaze, her eyes hardening. "You're not here to honor anyone—you're here to profit," she said, her words sharp, cutting through the tension. "These paintings were hidden to keep them safe, not to be sold off to private collectors. That's why we're here tonight—ensuring these works go to places they can be seen, appreciated, and protected."

The man raised an eyebrow, his smirk never faltering. "You assume that everyone who has a claim wants to sell. But what if they don't? What if they want to honor *their* family's legacy by keeping the paintings themselves? Your plan undermines that possibility."

Amelia's jaw tightened, but she was ready for this. "If that were truly your intention, then you would have no issue standing with us," she said, her voice calm but resolute. "The families who entrusted these paintings to the Alliance did so because they wanted to ensure their art would be safe, even if they could no longer protect it themselves. The lines in this ledger are clear: they placed the paintings in the care of the Alliance to protect them—from *all* manner of threats. That is the legacy we are safeguarding."

She took a step forward, her eyes sweeping across the room to make sure everyone could hear. "Look around you. Every institution here has pledged to respect those terms. They have agreed to preserve the paintings and make them accessible to the public—not hidden away in private collections or tucked away behind closed doors. And if your 'so-called heirs' *truly* cared about any genuine legacy, they would celebrate this decision instead of seeking to disrupt it."

The room was silent, but Amelia could feel the tension shifting again, the murmur of agreement rippling through the crowd. She turned back to the man, her eyes sharp. "And let's not pretend that legal challenges will somehow preserve these works. The moment they are caught in litigation, their fate becomes uncertain. They could end up in vaults, locked away for years—lost to everyone, including your clients. That's the real risk here, and it's one we're not willing to take."

She gestured to the ledger on the podium, letting her hand rest on the glass over its worn cover. "The provenance we've established, the line of custody, is clear. The only way to challenge it would be to prove a direct, unbroken line of inheritance—a possibility we have *thoroughly* investigated for each painting here. And even then, the original agreement was not for these works to be scattered into the hands of individuals, but to be preserved as cultural treasures. The families wanted these paintings to be part of a legacy that transcends one person—one that would be shared, not hoarded. That's why we're here, to ensure that vision is respected."

The man hesitated, his confidence wavering. "You're making a lot of assumptions—"

"No," Amelia cut him off, her voice firm. "We're supporting documented facts. Everything is listed here," she said, gesturing toward the ledger. "And we're bound, both legally *and* ethically, to follow it as faithfully as possible. Your claims, on the other hand, twist the truth to benefit only those you represent. And unless you can provide undeniable proof to the contrary, your arguments won't hold up under scrutiny."

Amelia stared at him fiercely, her voice steady and resolute. "Everyone in this room is here for the paintings, for their preservation and rightful place in history. So, do what you must. But we all know how this will end—the courts will side with us. They already have," she said, lifting the cy-près declaration as a tangible reminder of their victory.

The curators and representatives in the room began nodding, a few even exchanging words of agreement. Someone from the MFA in Boston stood and addressed the man directly. "Enough of this," he said coldly, his gaze cutting through the tension. "Ms. Beckett has already proven her case. The courts agree, and so does everyone in this room. You're wasting your time—and ours."

A ripple of applause followed his words, with many murmuring their approval. The man's eyes darted around, realizing that his attempt to sow doubt had backfired. He had lost the room, and the support he might have hoped for had slipped away. His jaw tightened, frustration clear, but he said nothing more.

Amelia felt a brief wave of relief, but she knew the battle wasn't entirely over. She glanced at Gabriel, who met her eyes with a small, encouraging nod. They had come prepared for this moment, and now it was hers to see through.

She stepped forward, her voice clear and resolute as it carried across the room. "Now," she said, "let's place these works where they truly belong—in the care of those who will protect and share them with the world. That's the commitment we make tonight."

The man's smirk faltered, doubt creeping into his expression. He scanned the room again, searching for a lifeline, but found only harsh stares on the faces of the curators, historians, and experts—people who stood for everything he didn't. For a moment, it seemed as if he might challenge her again, but then he saw it clearly—he had lost. Without a word, he turned sharply, his shoulders rigid, and made his way to the exit, the echo of his footsteps the only sound in the otherwise silent room.

As the door clicked shut behind him, a palpable wave of relief washed over everyone present. Amelia exhaled deeply, only now realizing how tightly she had been holding herself together. Gabriel reached out, his hand brushing hers in a reassuring gesture. "You did it," he said softly, a smile tugging at the corner of his lips.

She smiled back. "*We* did it."

The rest of the evening felt like a blur. One by one, the curators stepped forward and confirmed their commitment to the pieces. Each steward reviewed and signed the necessary documents, ensuring the transfers of the paintings were airtight and indisputable. Once the paperwork was finalized, museum representatives carefully inspected the paintings, assessing their conditions before arranging for their secure transport.

With practiced precision, the teams packed each piece into protective crates. Layers of foam cushioned the delicate works, and custom-built frames kept them secure—a last safeguard for their journey home.

They already endured enough. Many of their families likely lost everything to the Nazis—their homes, their possessions, and even their lives—leaving no one behind to reclaim their heritage. Yet these fragile remnants remained, bearing witness to lives that had been erased. Now, through this dedication, their stories would endure. The art would not vanish into obscurity, but find new life in museums that would honor and share their legacies, ensuring that the cultural threads these families once wove would not be forgotten.

Amelia stood back, watching as the last of the 108 pieces were sealed away, her chest tight with a bittersweet mix of relief and hope. She silently wished these crates would be the last the paintings would ever know, on their way to a place where they could truly belong. The process was swift and efficient, and by the time the room emptied, a warmth settled over her—a sense of closure she hadn't expected but deeply needed.

As the last curator departed, Charlotte approached, her expression a mix of exhaustion and triumph. "We did it!" she exclaimed. "Transferring the paintings to these institutions has solidified their provenance. No one can challenge this now—at least not without going up against some of the world's most respected museums."

Amelia nodded, the finality of their achievement slowly settling over her. "So that's it, then?" she asked softly, still trying to grasp the reality of it.

Nearby, Gabriel had been quietly packing up, but stepped closer, resting his hand lightly on the small of her back. "Yeah," he said, his voice confident as a small smile curved his lips. "We really did it!"

The room settled into a stillness as the lights cast gentle shadows across the now-empty salon. Gabriel continued his packing while Amelia lingered near the podium. She picked up the cookbook, her fingers tracing its worn edges. It felt heavier than it should, not just as a relic, but as a symbol of everything they had fought to preserve. She let out a slow breath, her mind drifting over everything that had brought them to this moment. It wasn't just the paintings that had been transformed—it was her, too.

When she began this journey, Amelia had seen her role as a restorer in its simplest terms—preserving the integrity of the artwork and caring for a physical object so that its beauty could endure. She had always been meticulous, focused on detail, and proud of her work. But over the past year, she had come to understand that her work was never just about preserving the paint and canvas. It was about protecting the stories, the memories, and the lives entwined with each piece. The ledger had been her first clue—a reminder that behind every painting was a name, and behind every name, a life that had been forever changed.

Caring for these works meant caring for the legacy of those who had trusted the Alliance, acknowledging the sacrifices they made to protect a piece of themselves.

She glanced at the spot where Gabriel had stood beside her, reflecting on how his family's connection to the art deepened her understanding. For him, preserving a legacy was about reclaiming a part of his own story that had been lost to time and tragedy. She learned that true stewardship wasn't just about ensuring the art's survival but about keeping alive the stories they carried, connecting people across generations—not unlike the recipes in the cookbook.

Amelia traced her fingers over the cover one last time, feeling the leather's texture. This, she realized, was the heart of it—the understanding that had reshaped her view. Ownership wasn't about possessing something; it was about safeguarding it, nurturing it, and, when the time was right, letting it go so others could experience and learn from it. It was about passing down a legacy—not just preserved but enriched, fuller, and more deeply understood than before. And in that, she had found her purpose—not merely restoring canvases but reviving the stories embedded within them, ensuring they inspire and endure for generations to come.

Chapter 91

The call came in two days later. After everything became official at the dedication, Charlotte knew this was her final hurdle.

She sat at her desk, phone pressed to her ear, her pen poised over a legal pad. The name flashing on her screen had made her stomach tighten: *Hans Brecht, Legal Counsel for Keller Group AG.* She'd anticipated this moment since the announcement of the discovery, knowing full well the implications of what Amelia and Gabriel had done. The Keller Group's vast resources and corporate greed were infamous. This call was the last obstacle standing between celebration and controversy.

"Ms. Hawthorne," Brecht's clipped, precise voice greeted her after a long silence on the line. "I trust you're aware of the ramifications of what your clients have made public."

Charlotte adjusted her posture, her tone calm and professional. "Mr. Brecht, I can assure you that my clients acted in good faith to ensure the return of what was never theirs to keep. The Alliance's ledger was clear, and the art rightfully belonged to families and institutions that had placed it in their care."

There was a pause, and Charlotte braced herself.

"I'll be frank," Brecht continued. "The Keller Group has no interest in the public spectacle this could have turned into. We value our reputation and have no desire to be associated with the… moral ambiguities of hoarding priceless works of art."

Charlotte allowed herself a small exhale. He wasn't starting with aggression—a good sign. But she knew better than to let her guard down.

"We understand the Alliance's motives," Brecht added, his tone neutral. "The paintings were hidden to preserve them during a dark chapter of history. What these families and the Alliance did was noble, even if… unconventional."

"That's precisely why it was imperative they be returned," Charlotte replied smoothly. "My clients made every effort to ensure this process was transparent and respectful."

"However," Brecht interjected, his voice sharp now, "the Keller Group owns the mines where those paintings were found. By legal extension, one could argue that we have a claim to those assets—especially considering your clients trespassed onto private property and accessed restricted areas without authorization."

Charlotte's pen stopped moving. There it was—the angle she'd been waiting for. "I understand your perspective," she said carefully. "But those assets were never legally the Keller Group's. The artwork was placed in the mine by members of the Alliance, two of whom were Vallois family members—the previous owners of the mine. These paintings were not transferred as part of the mine's sale, as evidenced by the documents filed with the Canton's Land Registry, which contain no record of their inclusion. At the time, the paintings weren't disclosed, nor were they owned by the Vallois family themselves. Instead, they were safeguarded on behalf of the families listed in the ledger.

"As for the trespassing," Charlotte continued, her tone even but pointed, "while I acknowledge that my clients took unauthorized actions to access the mine, their intent was to recover items that never legally belonged to the Keller Group. If anything, their actions protected your company from unknowingly being associated with the withholding of historically and culturally significant works."

"Building on that, Swiss property laws are clear: undisclosed items, especially those proven not to be abandoned, don't automatically transfer ownership to the new property holder. The Keller Group's lack of knowledge at the time of purchase is irrelevant because the ledger and supporting documentation establish that the paintings were never abandoned, nor were they part of the mine's assets. Legally, they still belong to the families who entrusted the Alliance with their preservation. Outside of that, the cy-prés doctrine takes effect."

Brecht was silent for a beat, but she could hear the soft click of a pen on the other end of the line—a sign he was weighing her argument.

"Your points are… compelling," Brecht admitted, though his tone carried a note of reluctance. "It's clear the paintings were never part of the mine's assets, and the ledger provides a strong basis for the families' claims. That said, from the Keller Group's perspective, this situation still touches on our operations and, more importantly, our reputation. We're fully aware of the optics. After reviewing the documentation and observing the dedication's announcement, it's evident that the Alliance's motives and historical context have been firmly established. For us to pursue ownership now, given the public narrative, would not only appear opportunistic but outright distasteful. Such an approach would conflict with the Keller Group's carefully maintained image."

Charlotte suppressed a smile. She knew corporate PR mattered more than principle in cases like this. "I agree," she said. "The dedication honored the Alliance's work, and the Keller Group was not implicated in any wrongdoing. In fact, the discovery adds to the mine's historical significance—something that could greatly enhance Keller Group's branding. The restoration of these artworks and their safe return reflect positively on the integrity of the mine itself, as a place where such treasures were preserved, even if unknowingly."

There was a faint hum on the other end of the line. Brecht was considering her words. Finally, he spoke, his tone less rigid. "The board recognizes the potential goodwill this situation could bring to our image. The press coverage alone has positioned the Keller Group in a favorable light—so long as we don't oppose the return of the artwork."

Charlotte seized the opening. "Exactly. A cooperative stance reinforces the Keller Group's role as a steward of historical preservation. We're happy to emphasize that in future communications."

Another pause. Then Brecht sighed, his voice softening further. "We won't contest the return of the paintings or the dedication. Nor will we pursue charges of trespassing. However, the Keller Group will *expect* acknowledgment in all official materials moving forward. Let me be clear—we're not philanthropists, Ms. Hawthorne. But we have no interest in attracting bad press, either."

Charlotte smiled. "That's more than reasonable, Mr. Brecht. I'll ensure your contributions to maintaining the mines are appropriately highlighted."

"Very well," he said briskly. "Consider this matter resolved."

As the call ended, Charlotte leaned back in her chair, the tension finally draining from her shoulders. She had done it. No lawsuits, no drawn-out legal battles—just a cautious but agreeable resolution. By emphasizing Keller Group's opportunity to align with a greater legacy and reinforcing the importance of preservation, she'd guided them toward cooperation—much like the Alliance had once united in the spirit of safe-guarding a history meant to benefit humanity as a whole. And for the first time in weeks, she allowed herself a moment to breathe.

The paintings were safe, and so were Amelia and Gabriel's efforts.

In the end, the Keller Group had done exactly what she'd counted on: prioritized their reputation over resistance, proving that even in corporate boardrooms, the weight of history could tip the scales.

Chapter 92

Moscow makes Berlin feel like a retreat. Even St. Petersburg has an old world charm. But here, post-war, everywhere I go, suspicion clings to me like grime from a smoke-filled room. I hate this place now. A city forever marked by war's aftermath, it bears the scars openly, each corner haunted by the sacrifices it demanded. But I didn't come back to Russia for a vacation—or for safety. I came to honor the promise I made—to Sergei, to myself, to everything that was taken from us.

After my father died, after the war, my inheritance from the Vallois estate gave me the means. But even with every resource at my disposal, navigating Soviet bureaucracy is like stepping into a lion's den.

I've already been warned by Viktor, Sergei's associate who sent me the letter: *the Soviets might be watching me.* And if they are, they know why I'm here. But their surveillance, their eyes hidden in the corners of every room, no longer hold power over me. Fear is a luxury I left behind. All that's left now is a relentless drive—a need to complete what Sergei began. I need to protect his collection and his life's work from being reduced to mere instruments of propaganda by a regime that sees art as nothing more than a tool to wield or a commodity to control. They want to erase Sergei, the man who defied them, who built a collection that breathed that defiance. I will not let that happen.

As I step into the cold, lifeless walls of the USSR's Central State Archives of the October Revolution, a familiar dread grips my chest. And yes, that's really what it's called. Leave it to the fucking Communists to create a name so absurdly self-important, as if stringing together enough grandiose words could somehow compensate for the suffocating dullness of this place. It's not enough to just call it 'The Archives,' no—it has to be a shrine to their whole absurd narrative.

The room is dimly lit, oppressive, and reeks of stale paper and dust, like even the air has resigned itself to the weight of bureaucratic drudgery. The clerk behind the desk barely glances up at me. She is indifferent to my mission, to the determination etched into my face. I slide my forged documents across the desk with a silent prayer in my chest. The network my father built crafted these carefully, with a precision that could mean the difference between success and a prison cell—or worse. It's amazing the Kremlin even gave me permission to be here. But I am not here to worry about outcomes. The war has stripped that from me. What remains is a single, burning need: to finish what Sergei started.

The documents pass inspection with a disinterested nod, and I am let in. Room after room stretches before me, dusty shelves packed with records and ledgers, each containing fragments of countless lives—ruined, erased, stored as data to be forgotten. I work quickly, scanning each file with practiced eyes, searching for the barest traces of what I'm seeking. They would have hidden it, filed it under misleading entries, even altered ownership records to keep it hidden from view. But I've spent years with Arnaud and my father in the Alliance; I know how to spot deception in ink and paper. And as I delve deeper, bit by bit, I uncover faint threads —the telltale signs of bureaucratic deceit.

Finally, I find a record. And another. My pulse quickens with each discovery. Sergei's collection, his life's work, isn't gone. It's here, stored in forgotten basements of government buildings, hidden in the private stashes of Soviet officials, locked away under the state's suffocating grasp. These paintings are probably faded now, covered in dust, some perhaps stolen or damaged, but they still exist. The knowledge that they have survived fills me with a strange sense of hope—a tenuous thread, but one that urges me onward. Now I just have to find them.

Hours pass as I pour over every page, every folio, each entry carefully cataloged in my memory. But the longer I stay, the heavier the silence around me becomes, the dim light casting shadows that shift and watch. I feel the eyes on me, the whispers of the clerks, the sudden hush as officials pass by, their expressions unreadable yet ominous. I am not alone here. They *are* watching, and I know it's only a matter of time before they act.

I gather my papers quickly, trying not to draw attention as I slip the files back into place. My heartbeat quickens as I move toward the exit, each step echoing in the quiet, until I reach the dim lobby. But just as I'm about to leave, a figure steps into my path.

He stands in plainclothes, his eyes like ice, fixed on me. *Ministry of State Security?* My heart stops. His expression is cold, unreadable, but the intent is clear. We stare at each other, a long moment stretching between us, and I wonder briefly if I'll ever make it out of this building. I've come too far to turn back, and yet, in this silent standoff, I feel Sergei's legacy bearing down on me. It cannot end here. *I* cannot end here.

The man's lips curve into a faint, chilling smile as he finally speaks, his voice low and edged with menace in a thick Russian accent. "You shouldn't have come back."

And then he left.

As I step away from the encounter, his words echo in my mind, heavy and unshakable. Maybe I shouldn't have come back. But the fight for Sergei's paintings is far from over. In fact, it may have only just begun —and this time, the stakes are higher than ever. The Nazis were monsters, but at least their brutality was direct. The Soviets thrive on manipulation and psychological torment, grinding people down until hope crumbles like old paint. Then they get to work on you.

The regime knows I am here, and it seems they'll do whatever it takes to keep me from uncovering the truth. I came to Russia to reclaim Sergei's legacy, but as I stand here, heart still pounding from the confrontation, one question haunts me: will I survive long enough to see it through?

Chapter 93

Château Bourget, Modern Day

Amelia stepped out of the taxi and into the fragrant embrace of summer. The imposing gates of Château Bourget rose before her, and the scent of blooming flowers lingered as she walked through, gravel crunching softly beneath her shoes. The mid-afternoon sun bathed the estate in a warm, golden light, making the ivy draped along the walls shimmer in shades of green and blue. It was almost like the entire house was welcoming her back. It had been months since she'd last been here, and as she approached the door, a strange mix of nostalgia and anticipation stirred within. She was here to return the original Bourget Family Cookbook, lent for the dedication—the very artifact that had set her on a journey she never could have imagined.

The Moreaus greeted her warmly at the door, their smiles tinged with a hint of excitement that caught Amelia off guard. "Thank you for bringing this back," Christian said, his voice genuine as he took the well-worn book from her hands. "This cookbook has been in this house forever, but we never knew the role it played. A secret of the past hiding in plain sight, right under our noses!"

Amelia smiled as a touch of warmth filled her. "I'm just glad I could return it to you! This home is where it belongs. Thank you for letting us use it."

She began to turn, ready to leave, when Christian's wife, Isabelle, stepped forward, her eyes bright with eagerness. "Wait!" she said, carrying a hint of secrecy. "Before you go, there's something we'd like to show you." A coy smile played on her lips, and Amelia could sense the energy bubbling beneath the surface. "After you shared the full story—the toolbox, the cookbook, the mine—it inspired us to do a bit of digging ourselves. And, well… we found something."

Christian nodded, his enthusiasm unmistakable. "We've lived here for the last 30 years. We thought we knew every corner of this house. We were wrong!"

His expression softened as a calm pride came over him. "Would you like to see?" he asked, gesturing for Amelia to follow them inside.

Amelia's curiosity piqued, and she eagerly nodded. "Yes! What did you find?" she asked, her mind already racing through possibilities.

Isabelle's smile widened, a gleam of anticipation in her eyes. "Come with us, and we'll show you."

Amelia followed them through the grand halls of the estate, their footsteps echoing off the polished floors in an uneven rhythm, like an improvised jazz beat. They reached a narrow, spiral staircase and began their descent into the depths of the château, gripping the aging wrought-iron railing for support. She had never been in this part of the house before, only the old staff kitchen in a distant wing on the main level. But now, as the staircase wound deeper, a fleeting memory of Bex surfaced, bringing with it the same blend of excitement and nerves she had felt back then. The air grew cooler with each step and carried a faint mustiness that hinted at secrets long kept.

They stopped in front of a heavy iron door, where Christian pulled an old tarnished key from his pocket and slid it into the lock. A low, resonant click echoed softly around them as he turned it. The door creaked open, revealing a vault-like room lined with metal cabinets and drawers. The dim lighting cast long, shifting shadows across the walls, giving the space an almost mystical atmosphere.

"Over here," Isabelle said, leading Amelia toward a set of drawers at the back. "This is the old Bourget family vault. When we bought the estate, the room was empty. We did an initial search through these drawers and cabinets, but found nothing at the time. The space became a bit of a curiosity—a novelty to show guests, something with a touch of intrigue. We never thought much more of it... until you came into our lives. After hearing everything you uncovered—the toolbox, the patents in the Lodge—we decided to take a closer look. And this time, we found these, hidden away in the back of one of the drawers."

Amelia watched as Isabelle carefully pulled open one of the compartments, her hands gentle yet deliberate. Inside, nestled snugly, was a small bundle wrapped in an old, faded handkerchief. Amelia's breath caught, a wave of déjà vu washing over her. The way the fabric was folded, the way it rested neatly in the drawer—it was all too familiar. It reminded her of the toolbox she had found at the Marché—the toolbox that had set this entire journey in motion. She remembered finding a similar bundle inside, wrapped neatly in a handkerchief with the light blue initials 'EB' stitched delicately in the corner. That memory, vivid and sharp, surged in her mind as she watched the scene before her.

Slowly, Isabelle unfolded the cloth with deliberate care. As she lifted the final layer, tiny flashes of light burst forth, unconfined, the glimmers dancing in the dim vault. Nestled within was a beautiful diamond ring. The gem caught a beam from the overhead light, refracting tiny, shimmering prisms onto the walls. For a moment, it felt as though the entire room was illuminated by its brilliance.

Amelia gasped, caught between disbelief and wonder. At first glance, it appeared to be the same ring she'd found in the toolbox. *How did they get this?* But, leaning in, her pulse quickened as she noticed the defining difference. One by one, she counted the prongs—*One... two... three... four*. Her heart skipped a beat. Four prongs, just like the ring in the painting of Eloise! This was the original ring!

She reached out, letting her fingers graze the cool, smooth metal, tracing the delicate floral engraving along the band's sides. It felt solid, real—an object that had guarded a hidden truth for decades. "This is the original!" she whispered to herself.

Her mind flashed back to the moment with the jeweler, where they had carefully examined the fake—a glass paste stone meant to deceive, a clever ruse to mislead anyone who might uncover it. But this ring... this was no imitation. This was the real thing, holding a story of its own, the inspiration for a secret that had waited all this time to come to light.

She could almost see it now—Eloise, slipping the ring on her finger. It was more than just a piece of jewelry; it was a message, a symbol of what had been hidden and protected. Amelia closed her eyes, letting herself be drawn back in time, imagining the vibrant salon scene from the painting. She could almost feel the room come alive around her, bustling with warmth and laughter, the faint rustle of fabric and the soft hum of conversation filling the air. As she let the vision unfold, she glanced over to the chaise, where a woman in an emerald silk dress sat gracefully, smiling back at her. *Hello, Eloise*, she thought.

In that moment, the room in her mind was a picture of elegance and ease, the guests unaware of the trials that lay ahead. Little did they know they were preserving more than just this gathering, more than a fleeting moment of beauty. They were safeguarding a legacy, a memory that would become crucial in unraveling the mystery of the Alliance—a testament to resilience, to a defiance that refused to let history erase them.

When she opened her eyes, she found Isabelle watching her, a knowing smile on her lips that seemed to mirror the one Amelia felt on her own. "We thought you might appreciate it, my dear," Isabelle said. "But there's more."

She reached back into the drawer, her hand emerging with another small, dark object worn smooth by time. It had a short wooden handle attached to a block, and Amelia gently took it from Isabelle's outstretched hand. She turned it over carefully, examining what she had in front of her. Then, when she angled it under the light, her eyes widened. Staring back at her was a blackened woodcut of a symbol she knew all too well:

A single paintbrush merged with a key.

Amelia gasped. *The key and the brush will guide us,* she thought. It was the collection stamp used by the Bourget-Vallois Alliance!

The stamp was simple, unassuming, yet as she held it, she could feel the weight of its history. This was the tool that had marked each painting hidden in Bex—a small, deliberate act that signified the Alliance's protection, linking them all under a shared legacy. She imagined the moment the stamp touched each canvas, leaving behind its emblem, a promise that the art would survive, no matter what. Standing in the vault, surrounded by the dim, flickering light, she felt as though she were among those who had once wielded this very stamp—Nadejda, Arnaud, and the others who had dared to defy the forces that sought to erase culture and humanity itself.

"This must have been the original collection stamp," Christian said, his voice almost reverent. "We found it tucked away in one of the drawers with the ring. It must have been here all this time, waiting."

Amelia nodded and looked up at the Moreaus, gratitude swelling in her chest. "Thank you so much for showing me these," she said softly, her voice filled with emotion as tears welled in her eyes. "You have no idea how much this means. To see these pieces, to hold them… it feels like everything has come full circle."

Isabelle's smile widened. "Then let us gift them to you," she said. "You have done so much to bring this story back to life. It's only right that these pieces be with someone who truly understands what they mean."

Amelia's breath caught as a wave of unexpected emotion overcame her. She wiped her eyes quickly with her sleeve, a lump forming in her throat. Carefully, she wrapped the ring back in the handkerchief and tucked it into her bag, along with the stamp. When she looked up at the Moreaus, gratitude was written plainly on her face. "Thank you," she said softly, filled with sincerity. "I'll make sure they're taken care of."

The taxi ride back to Paris was peaceful, with the ring and stamp nestled safely in her bag. Though small, their presence felt significant, a reminder of everything they represented. Amelia thought about what she would do with them—how to best honor their history.

The ring, she decided, would be donated to the Jewish Museum in Paris, where it would find its rightful place alongside the portrait of Eloise. Together, they would stand as a symbol of both resilience and love —a testament to the story they carried. It was what Arnaud would have wanted, and honoring that felt like the right thing to do.

But the stamp... The stamp she couldn't part with. It was more than a relic; it was a personal connection to everything she had discovered and everything she had been through. It would stay with her as a small reminder of the journey she had taken, of the secrets she had uncovered, and of the lives that had intertwined with hers, stretching across decades and continents.

As she turned onto the familiar streets of Paris again, her thoughts drifted back to the moments that had led her here. She remembered sitting with her father as a child, playing guessing games and imagining the stories behind objects they found. He had taught her to see beyond the surface, to look for the layers, the untold stories—to see what was hidden in plain sight. That was what had driven her, what had allowed her to peel back the layers of history and find the truth.

She glanced at the bag on the seat beside her, feeling a sense of closure, but also determination. The journey had been long and winding, filled with unexpected twists, danger, and moments of doubt. But as the taxi turned onto Rue du Bac, a calmness settled over her—a clarity she hadn't felt in a long time. She wasn't just restoring art now; she was restoring stories, giving voice to those who had been silenced by history.

The taxi came to a gentle stop in front of her studio, and she looked out at the old oak door, its weathered wood bathed in the warm, golden light of the setting sun. It stood as it always had—sturdy, resilient, enduring. Splintered at the edges, weathered by time, yet unyielding in its strength. As she stepped out and approached the door, she felt that same strength within herself, and knew this was just the beginning.

The Alliance had returned. And so had she.

Chapter 94

Arnaud returned to Château Bourget after the war to find it a shadow of its former grandeur. Though the walls still stood, the bold beauty that once defined his family had been stripped away, leaving the halls shrouded in silence. This was no longer the grand estate he remembered, and his return was bittersweet. Two years earlier, Lucien's death had placed the château in his hands, a final inheritance that now weighed heavily on him. The Nazis had dismantled the family's merchant operations, leaving little to rebuild, and he felt neither the strength nor the desire to resurrect them.

Yet, despite the emptiness that filled the rooms, Arnaud felt a renewed sense of purpose. Another mission awaited him here, a last chapter. He had come back to protect what remained, to safeguard the last relics of the Bourget legacy and the cause that had defined his life. Eloise's cause.

Within the château's walls lay the Bourget vault, holding the last few tangible remnants of his family's past and of the Alliance. Inside, the collection stamp with its key and brush insignia—a symbol of his pledge to protect 486 paintings—rested as a testament to his vow. Alongside it lay the Bourget heirloom diamond ring—the one he had given to Eloise on their wedding day. But most significant of all was *The Portrait of Eloise*, draped in an emerald silk dress, reclining gracefully on a chaise. This painting was the one piece he could never bring himself to hide away in Bex.

For Arnaud, the portrait offered solace, a link to both a love and a life lost. Often, he would retreat to the vault simply to be near her, feeling her presence in the soft gaze preserved by the brush's careful strokes. Standing before Eloise's likeness, he felt a calm settle over him—a strength that served as a reminder of his purpose.

Among the other items in the house, however, one remained in plain sight: an unassuming leather-bound cookbook that helped catalog the secret efforts of the Alliance's hidden artwork, still resting on the kitchen shelf. The Nazis had looted Château Bourget twice, first in 1941 and again in 1944, yet they overlooked it both times, just as Arnaud had expected.

Before the raids, he had hidden the home's remaining valuables, including the three vault items, just outside the Artisan's Lodge. Inside the château, all that remained was the cookbook and 74 nearly perfect forgeries of the original pieces his family was known to own. The genuine collection—their 74 irreplaceable paintings—already lay safeguarded in the Bex Salt Mines in Switzerland. When the Nazis came, eager for something to confiscate, Arnaud gave them exactly what they wanted, hoping they'd be satisfied—and foolish enough not to return. He imagined, with a dark satisfaction, the shock Herman Göring might have felt if he discovered the prized Vermeer hanging above the fireplace in his Ritz Imperial Suite was nothing more than a convincing fake.

Once the château was left in peace, Arnaud returned the painting of Eloise and other items to the vault. Though it had suffered some water damage while hidden, the painting could not be sent away for restoration or concealed once more—she belonged here. Each day, he found solace in her painted gaze, a reminder of all he had fought to preserve—a reminder of her. Eloise's image breathed within Château Bourget, becoming his constant companion and silent confidante as he prepared to ensure the Alliance's mission would continue beyond his own lifetime.

As the world settled into an uneasy peace, Arnaud knew he had to plan for a time when he could no longer defend the Alliance's legacy on his own. Too many uncertainties still hovered after the war, making it unsafe to reveal what they had hidden. He and Nadejda were all that remained of the Alliance, but she had vanished, her absence echoing as a profound loss and a stark warning. Realizing that age was catching up with him—that time itself was now an adversary—he accepted he might never complete their mission. He couldn't trust the present, but he *could* prepare for the future. Arnaud's new mission was clear: the story of the Bourget-Vallois Alliance, its sacrifices, and its artwork, had to remain hidden until the world was ready to receive them. He couldn't predict how future generations would treat these treasures, but he knew now was not the time to unveil them. Instead, he resolved to pass the baton, ensuring that only someone capable of understanding the mission's true significance would eventually uncover it.

With his heart tethered to the painting of Eloise, Arnaud felt an intense pull to preserve it. Though the portrait belonged with him, he understood she deserved a sanctuary beyond the château, a place where her likeness would be safe—a place where *anyone* could see her. A place where she could become immortal. After coming to terms with his choice, he entrusted her likeness, anonymously, to the Jewish Museum in Paris, releasing her with hope. She would be safe there, shared with the world, her connection to the Bourget family and the Alliance concealed.

The painting bore the Alliance's mark, as they had originally planned to safeguard it in Bex—but Arnaud couldn't bring himself to part with her, and the mark remained. Its true importance lay hidden in plain sight, in a seemingly unremarkable piece with no provenance or traceable signature. Arnaud went to great lengths to ensure the artist's identity was unknown. *Eloise* was one of only five paintings he had ever created under his pseudonym, Henri Vallin, an identity he crafted during the artistic boom of Les Années Folles in Paris. In those years, creativity flourished, and under his assumed name, Arnaud could be recognized as a true artist—rather than simply as a Bourget.

Initially, Eloise had shied away from sitting for the portrait, fearing the opulence would misrepresent her simplicity and spirit. But Arnaud had reassured her, explaining that it wasn't about grandeur—it was about capturing her strength and elegance, the qualities that made her uniquely herself. Reluctantly, she agreed, and the result was a striking image: Eloise in an emerald silk dress, reclining with quiet confidence, her gaze steady and filled with life. To Arnaud, it was more than a portrait—it was a testament to her essence, immortalized in brushstrokes, and a reminder of the love and inspiration she had given him.

Despite Eloise's public presence in the museum, Arnaud kept the other items in the vault, leaving the heirloom ring and the Alliance stamp hidden within its locked confines. These items held no immediate significance to the casual observer, and Arnaud intended it to stay that way. The ring—the genuine ring, without the engraving—served as a decoy if anyone were to stumble upon it. To a stranger, the items might appear valuable but unremarkable, diverting attention from the true depth of his legacy.

As for Eloise's simple gold wedding band, it found its place close to his heart: after she died, he slipped it onto a gold chain and wore it as a testament to the love and history they had shared. The band's simplicity mirrored the pure, unwavering devotion he had always felt for her.

Arnaud's greatest act of preservation for the Alliance's work was the careful creation of a breadcrumb trail. Each clue was meticulously curated, each step leading closer to the legacy he had so carefully shielded. For him, it was like a game crafted for a worthy opponent—a test of insight and determination. Confident that one day the right person would pick up the trail, he ensured each hint, each breadcrumb, would be ready for those capable of understanding—and continuing—the Alliance's true mission.

Among the artifacts he chose for the trail were items steeped in significance. First, a glass paste ring, crafted by a jeweler friend to replicate the authentic Bourget piece with near-perfect likeness—except for the addition of an extra prong. Arnaud then meticulously engraved it with a simplified brush and key to start the trail. The ring's apparent insignificance was a deliberate ploy, challenging its finder to question why someone would go to such lengths to hide an imitation diamond—encouraging further investigation, and leading to the first clue. He wrapped it in a delicate handkerchief embroidered with "EB," and found a photograph of Eloise that matched her likeness in the portrait he'd donated to the museum.

The ledger entries, originally encoded in the final pages of the cookbook, had served as a critical link in the Alliance's mission as long as its members were alive. Yet, with his own mortality in mind, Arnaud knew this combination of secrets was too dangerous to leave intact. To further safeguard their survival, he removed these pages and recreated them in invisible iron sulfate ink on the back sides of an eight-page letter he had written to Eloise. Finally, he placed these carefully chosen artifacts within a false-bottomed toolbox—a curious object for a man of his status, yet one whose craftsmanship would endure, waiting for the curiosity of the right person to unearth its secrets.

With a modest buffer from his family's remaining fortune, Arnaud took the toolbox and lived out his days in the apartment he had rented on the Left Bank during his time with the Alliance—far from the memories that haunted him at the château. Here, he savored a simpler life, blending into the quiet rhythm of his surroundings. Mornings often began with leisurely walks along the Seine, where he would pause to browse the bookstalls and exchange a nod with familiar faces. Afternoons found him at nearby cafés, enjoying small pleasures—a glass of red wine, the crisp pages of Le Monde, or an afternoon spent observing the lively street painters and musicians. These modest indulgences allowed him to blend into the vibrant heart of Paris, relishing the calm and distance from the life he once knew.

He placed the toolbox in a corner of his main living area, letting it blend in with his modest furnishings. No one ever gave it a second glance —even when the Nazi's ransacked the apartment years earlier. Yet Arnaud found himself glancing at it often—a silent reminder of Eloise, of the Alliance, and of the hope he continued to hold for the future.

Following his passing, the toolbox's journey began in anonymity. Arnaud entrusted it to an old, unsuspecting estate worker, one who had worked the grounds of Château Bourget with dedication through the years of war. To this man, the box was nothing more than a thoughtful memento from a kind employer, a handsome object he used to store letters and small keepsakes from his own past. Arnaud knew, over time, the worker would pass it along to someone else, eventually finding its way into the world. The quality of its craftsmanship would ensure it was preserved, never discarded.

As generations turned, the worker's children, and later their children, inherited the box, all unaware of the secrets hidden within. When its story eventually fell silent, it was sold at an estate auction and found its way to the bustling stalls of the Marché aux Puces just north of Paris. There, it sat among other relics of other forgotten lives, waiting for the right person to revive its story and discover what it held all along.

Arnaud's plan was complete. Though he did not live to see the art returned, he had laid each piece in place, knowing that someday, his mission would find its heir. His legacy, the Alliance's mission, and the hidden treasures lay dormant, waiting patiently until someone worthy of the truth would be drawn to them. This future guardian, he hoped, would not only find the ledger but also grasp the true depth of what he, Nadejda, and the rest of the Alliance had fought to protect.

In his last days, Arnaud found peace knowing that he had done all he could. The mission was no longer his alone; it was entrusted to fate, to time, and to the enduring hope that someone would someday understand. Eloise's spirit remained his steady companion in those final years, her calm strength watching over him. And as he looked out over the dimming Parisian skyline, he felt the faintest trace of comfort, knowing that the Alliance's legacy lay hidden but not forgotten—a testament to defiance, resilience, and the belief in preserving culture and humanity against all odds.

Epilogue

The Grand Palais was alive with energy, the air humming with the thrill of discovery. Amelia wandered through the exhibition halls, the elegant glass-domed ceilings bathing the room in a warm, diffused light. It had been over a year since the dedication, and now many of the paintings once feared lost to war and injustice had returned. The gallery was filled with visitors, their eyes wide with wonder as they moved from piece to piece, each one a testament to the resilience of those who had risked everything to protect art—*to protect culture*—during one of history's darkest periods. Paintings long thought lost—some hidden deep in the Bex Salt Mines, others looted by the Nazis, and many seized by the Soviet regime—now hung side by side. Their colors were vivid, their stories were untold yet palpable, and they quietly resonated with the past they had survived.

Amelia felt a peaceful satisfaction as she moved through the exhibit, stopping to admire a recovered painting by Cézanne. She could see the interwoven legacies of the Bourget, Vallois, and Shchukin families in every brushstroke, each piece telling a silent story of survival and defiance. The exhibit was more than a showcase of art; it was a tribute to those who had fought to protect and reclaim it—Nadejda, Arnaud, Sergei, and countless others whose names might never be known.

Yet it was *The Portrait of Eloise Leclair* that drew Amelia in the most. Hanging prominently at the front of the room on loan from the Jewish Museum, it was the same painting she had restored years ago in graduate school. Back then, its cloudy provenance left its subject shrouded in mystery, labeled *Unknown* for decades. But now, with the truth uncovered, the painting stood fully recognized, its title honoring the very woman who posed for it. Amelia greeted her again, smirking at the all-knowing smile that now seemed more inviting than enigmatic. What had once hinted at an untold story now felt like an acknowledgment of everything she and Gabriel had brought to light. Her gaze fell once more to the glimmering diamond ring on Eloise's hand—an unmistakable sign that this resilient woman was, beyond any doubt, the very heart of the Alliance's story.

Over the last year, Amelia and Gabriel had petitioned the French government to officially recognize each member of the Alliance, including Eloise, as a *résistant*—a celebrated member of the French Resistance during World War II. Their efforts were driven by the desire to honor those who had risked their lives—and sometimes lost them—in secret to protect their culture and heritage from the Nazis. Now, their memory was finally being commemorated at the Museum of National Resistance, just outside Paris, a place dedicated to preserving the stories of those who had fought back against oppression.

But tonight was also a recognition of Amelia and Gabriel's efforts, their determination to unearth what had been lost and return it to the world. This was the culmination of everything they had worked for, a moment that brought light to what had been hidden, allowing the world to see the art as it was always meant to be seen.

As Amelia moved past one section, she noticed a small plaque noting several missing pieces from the Shchukin collection—works still unaccounted for, their locations unknown. The sight made her pause, a familiar feeling of unease stirring within her. The exhibition celebrated what had been found, but it was also a reminder of what was still missing. She thought of Sergei's vast collection, much of it lost somewhere in the sprawl of Soviet history, their fates unknown. Nadejda Vallois Shchukin had fought to protect what little she could, but much of Sergei's collection remained hidden, scattered across territories where no one dared to search. The plaque was a small, stark reminder that their story was not yet complete.

As she wandered deeper into the exhibit, she thought of Nadejda—of her strength, her defiance, and the sacrifices she had made. Nadejda had stood against not just one regime but two, preserving what she could of her family's legacy in the face of forces that sought to erase it. Amelia felt that history pressing down on her, a responsibility she hadn't expected. There were still secrets buried, stories yet to be told, and the thought made her heart ache. She knew that as much as they had recovered, the entire journey was far from over.

Just as she was about to leave, a voice called her name. She turned to see a museum curator approaching, a man she vaguely recognized from earlier conversations about the exhibition setup. He carried a small envelope in his hand, its edges worn and discolored, bearing the marks of time and travel. "Excuse me, Mademoiselle Beckett," he said, offering a cryptic smile. "This arrived this morning. It's addressed to you." He handed her the envelope and walked away, leaving Amelia to stare at the worn seal on the back. It was the Vallois family crest, faded but unmistakable.

Amelia's eyes widened and her heart raced as she carefully broke the seal, unfolding the aged paper inside. Her eyes scanned the words, and she felt her pulse quicken with each line.

Dear Ms. Beckett,

The ledger you hold has guided you far, but its story is incomplete. Not all of Sergei's paintings were recovered. Some remain hidden, in places even the Soviets could never reach.

I am Nadejda's daughter. I was born in a Soviet gulag, where my mother was imprisoned. She told me stories as a child, tales of my step-father and their lost collections, of her fight to protect what little remained. I was too young to understand, and much of what she said faded as I grew older. But when I was released after the collapse of the Soviet Union, I began to remember her words.

It wasn't until I read recent reports of the missing Vallois art that I realized the significance of what my mother had told me. She had tried to recover Sergei's art before her arrest. Her final clue, the key to what remains hidden, is etched in stone—on Sergei's grave in Montmartre Cemetery.

I cannot search for the art myself. My life has been one of survival, and the world beyond Russia is a place I fear I do not belong. I have lived in the shadows for so long, and I know this journey is one I cannot complete. But you, Ms. Beckett, have already uncovered much. You understand the weight of history, of legacy, and the power that lies in what has been lost.

If you are willing to continue, go to Montmartre Cemetery. There, you will find the next piece of the puzzle, a message my mother left behind in her final act of defiance.

Look for the engraving. It will lead you to the rest. My mother's legacy is now in your hands.

Sincerely,
A Daughter of the Shadows

Amelia's hands trembled as she read the letter, the words blurring slightly as she took in what they meant. Nadejda had a daughter, someone she had never known about, and that daughter was reaching out across decades, across continents, to finish what her mother had started. The ledger had been incomplete all along, and Nadejda had left the final clue in a place she knew would endure—on Sergei's tombstone, hidden in plain sight, just like everything else they tried to protect.

For a moment, Amelia was transported back in time, her mind's eye envisioning Nadejda standing before Sergei's grave, chisel in hand, her heart heavy with grief but burning with an unyielding drive. She could see the sharp, deliberate movements, the way Nadejda's hands would have steadied themselves as she carved the message into stone—a final act of defiance against those who sought to erase everything they had stood for.

Amelia's heart pounded as she reread the last lines of the letter. If Nadejda had left a message on Sergei's tombstone, it could be the key to unlocking the last of the hidden art. The thought of another discovery, of pieces still waiting to be found, filled her with a sense of urgency. She knew she couldn't walk away now, not when she was so close to completing the story they had all fought so hard to uncover.

The gallery seemed to fade around her as she folded the letter carefully, slipping it into her coat pocket. She turned and made her way out of the Grand Palais, her mind already spinning with possibilities, her pulse quickening with anticipation. There was still more to do, more to find. Nadejda's fight, Sergei's legacy, and the art that had been lost were all calling to her, pulling her forward.

As she stepped out into the Parisian night, the cool air brushed against her cheeks, and she felt a familiar thrill—a sense of adventure, of something just on the edge of discovery. The city was alive with light and movement, but Amelia's thoughts were already focused on what lay ahead. She hailed a taxi, and as the cab pulled up to the curb, she slipped inside, clutching the letter in her hand.

The driver glanced at her in the rearview mirror, his expression polite but curious. "Where to, mademoiselle?" he asked.

Amelia hesitated for only a moment, a flicker of excitement, intrigue, and a hint of fear crossing her face. She met his gaze in the mirror, her voice steady but brimming with determination.

"Montmartre Cemetery," she said.

And as the taxi merged into the flow of Parisian traffic, Amelia knew her journey was far from over. Sergei and Nadejda's legacy remained unfinished, and whatever secrets still lay buried with him in Montmartre were calling her to act. She would follow the trail—to the grave, and beyond.

Afterward

Between 1933 and 1945, Nazi Germany orchestrated one of the largest art thefts in history, looting nearly 20% of Europe's cultural treasures. Masterpieces by Rembrandt, Vermeer, Monet, and countless others were seized, hidden in vaults, or vanished into underground networks.

This theft wasn't just about monetary value—it was about power, cultural domination, and erasure. High-ranking Nazis plundered art for their own collections, using it as a symbol of prestige while dismantling the heritage of those they persecuted.

More than 650,000 works were seized or sold under duress, affecting not only museums and wealthy collectors but also ordinary families. Many lost irreplaceable heirlooms—portraits of ancestors, religious artifacts, or a single cherished painting passed down through generations. These were more than objects; they were pieces of identity, their loss immeasurable.

The war's end did not bring full restitution, either. To this day, an estimated 100,000 artworks still remain missing. Some are believed to be hidden in forgotten bunkers, concealed within private collections, or buried in locations yet to be rediscovered.

Author's Note

The inspiration for *The Portrait of Eloise Leclair* began with a serendipitous discovery I made during a 2009 visit to the Marché aux Puces in Paris. While wandering its endless stalls of forgotten treasures, I came across an unassuming old toolbox, expertly crafted and still bearing its original key. It was only after returning home that I found inside, wrapped in a handkerchief, two rings—a solitaire diamond ring and a simple wedding band—accompanied by a love letter and a photograph of a woman. This find sparked my imagination and became the seed from which this novel grew.

Sergei Shchukin, a pivotal name in the story, was indeed a real person. A prominent Russian art collector, Shchukin was an early champion of artists like Monet, Matisse, and Picasso. He is buried in Montmartre Cemetery in Paris, alongside his second wife, Nadejda. However, the surnames Vallois and Bourget, as well as their family histories, are entirely fictional products of my imagination.

While the *Doppelblitzfalle*, the Nazi boobytrap described in Postojna Cave, is a fictional creation for the book, the larger backdrop of Nazi brutality, art smuggling, and resistance efforts is rooted in reality. During World War II, resistance groups across Europe risked their lives to smuggle paintings, sculptures, and other priceless artifacts out of Nazi-occupied territories, saving them from looting, destruction, or private confiscation. These brave individuals played a vital role in preserving cultural heritage, ensuring that much of what could have been lost forever survived the horrors of war.

The use of salt mines as repositories for looted art is historically accurate. The Nazis systematically hid thousands of stolen masterpieces in mines throughout Austria and Germany, most famously at Altaussee in Austria. The natural climate control of these underground chambers—cool temperatures and consistent humidity—made them ideal for preserving delicate artworks. The recovery of these hidden collections by the

"Monuments Men" after the war represents one of the greatest art rescue operations in history.

Rose Valland, whose courage and dedication to preserving art inspired aspects of this novel, was a French art historian who secretly documented Nazi art thefts while working at the *Jeu de Paume* Museum in Paris. Rather than smuggling paintings, Valland maintained meticulous records of the origins and destinations of looted works at great personal risk. She then passed this critical intelligence to the Allied forces about where the Nazis were sending stolen art, enabling the "Monuments Men" to locate and recover thousands of masterpieces after the war. Her extraordinary bravery and commitment to cultural preservation shaped much of the novel's emotional core. Like my protagonists, Valland understood that art represents not just aesthetic value but also cultural identity and human memory worth fighting to protect.

Raoul Minot and his wife, Marthe, were real people whose extraordinary story remained hidden until investigative journalist Philippe Broussard at *Le Monde* recently unearthed it. The couple took illegal photographs documenting the Nazi occupation of Paris. Arrested for their actions, they were tragically sent to Buchenwald concentration camp, where they both perished. Their bravery, like that of so many others, is a testament to the unsung, often unrecorded resistance that took place during the war.

The science and mathematics in this novel, including the use of iron sulfate ink for writing and its revealing process, as well as the art restoration techniques and most code descriptions, are grounded in historical and scientific accuracy. These details were carefully researched to ensure authenticity in the story's depiction of methods used during wartime and in modern restoration practices. However, the specific code used in the ledger is a creative adaptation—a fictional modification of the Vigenère cipher that I developed to suit the narrative. While inspired by real cryptographic principles, this variation was created to blend seamlessly with the story's themes of art, history, and hidden messages.

While the museums, buildings, and locations depicted in this novel are largely drawn from reality, Château Bourget and the Vallois mansion exist only within the pages of this story. Despite these imaginative elements, the historical methods, descriptions, and ideas referenced throughout the story have been meticulously researched to ensure accuracy.

One conscious deviation I took from this historical authenticity involves the cover design. Though initially featuring a historically-accurate swastika flag, I ultimately chose the *Reichsadler* (eagle) emblem instead. This decision reflects my belief that displaying such a profound symbol of hatred on the book's cover would be culturally insensitive, even in a historical context.

Efforts to return Nazi-looted art have persisted for decades, yet the legacy of this dark chapter remains unresolved. The cy-près doctrine, featured prominently in the legal aspects of my story, continues to be an important principle in restitution cases today. It allows courts to fulfill the original intent of ownership when exact compliance becomes impossible —a crucial tool when dealing with art that has changed hands multiple times over decades or when original owners or their direct heirs cannot be located. Through this doctrine, landmark cases have resulted in works hanging in prestigious institutions being returned to descendants of Holocaust victims despite the passage of time, demonstrating that the pursuit of justice in art restitution acknowledges no statute of limitations when rectifying the cultural crimes of the past.

Despite these successes, of the hundreds of thousands of paintings stolen during the war, an estimated 100,000 are still unaccounted for. They may be hidden in private collections, stashed away in basements, or lost entirely to history. These missing pieces of culture represent not only extraordinary artistic value but also fragments of the lives and identities that were destroyed during the Holocaust.

In telling this story, I sought to explore the interplay between history, memory, and art. While many of the specific events of this novel are fictional, they reflect the very real shadows cast by war—shadows that still linger today. My hope is that this story serves as both an acknowledgment of the immense human cost of cultural erasure and a reminder of the enduring power of those who fought to preserve our shared heritage.

Thank you for joining me on this journey.

Acknowledgements

First and foremost, I want to thank my wife, Laura. You have been my editor, my muse, and the source of so many incredible revision ideas that have made this story stronger. Your unwavering enthusiasm and support throughout this lengthy journey of writing a novel have been nothing short of inspiring. Thank you for believing in me and in this project from start to finish.

To my advanced review readers, your thoughtful feedback and ideas have been invaluable. Each of you helped shape this novel in ways I couldn't have done alone, and I'm deeply grateful for the time and care you dedicated to improving this story.

I also want to thank my parents, Kathy and Earl, and my sister, Laura, for their steadfast encouragement throughout this process. You've always supported my creative endeavors, allowing my imagination to flourish and my ideas to take flight. Your faith in me and your love have been constants in my life, and for that, I am endlessly thankful.

Finally, to anyone who picks up this book and takes the time to read it: thank you. Stories are meant to be shared, and your interest in this one means the world to me.